MURDER IN CALEB'S LANDING

A THIRD-CULTURE KID MYSTERY

MURDER IN CALEB'S LANDING

D-L NELSON

FIVE STAR
A part of Gale, Cengage Learning

Detroit • New York • San Francisco • New Haven, Conn • Waterville, Maine • London

GALE
CENGAGE Learning™

LIBRARY OF CONGRESS CATALOGING-IN-PUBLICATION DATA

Nelson, D. L., 1942–
    Murder in Caleb's Landing : a third-culture kid mystery / D.L. Nelson. — 1st ed.
      p. cm.
    ISBN-13: 978-1-59414-897-2 (hardcover)
    ISBN-10: 1-59414-897-X (hardcover)
    1. Women authors—Fiction. 2. North Shore (Mass. : Coast)—Fiction. I. Title.
PS3614.E4455M87 2010
813'.6—dc22   2010019573

First Edition. First Printing: September 2010.
Published in 2010 in conjunction with Tekno Books and Ed Gorman.

To Llara: I know, one real murder and straight to the nursing home.

ACKNOWLEDGMENTS

If I did not receive support from many people (and at the risk of sounding like an Oscar winner thanking everyone they ever met including their gardener) I would never be able to write anything. There's Susan Jordan who once asked what was stopping me from writing with the uncomfortable answer hanging in the air that it was me. My daughter never complained when I spent hours at the computer, telling people I was working on her inheritance. The Geneva Writers Group, under the magical spell of Susan Tiberghien, gives a synergy to writers at all stages of their careers (www.genevawritersgroup.org). Sylvia Petter, my Australian writing mate, was and is a major part of my development as a writer. Words will never express my appreciation for all the shared times going over our work phrase by phrase. Of course I do not want to do without Julia of the twenty pages, who saves my editor Gordon Aalborg many growls by reducing typos and inconsistencies.

For this book Bill Jordan helped me revisit the Massachusetts North Shore. Although a regular childhood haunt years away required another look, and it was as beautiful as I remembered it. Caleb's Landing is not a real town, but I hope I have captured the feel of the many seacoast towns that make me proud of my New England Yankee roots.

Had it not been for Dr. Mary Blewett and Dr. Patricia Goler at Lowell University, I would never have developed my love of history and have read so much about the pre–Civil War period.

Acknowledgments

Two books in particular, *Incidents in the Life of a Slave Girl* by Harriet Jacobs and *Journal of a Residence on a Georgia Plantation in 1838–1839* by Frances Anne Kemble, helped me greatly in creating the feel of the world that Mathilde lives in. I recommend them highly to anyone interested in that period. Although I could not visit The Freedom Center in Cincinnati, Ohio, their website (www.freedomcenter.org) was a good place to double-check my reading on the subject over my adult life. Stone Mountain National Park in Georgia, which I visited a lifetime ago, stayed in my mind and its plantation—although not a prototype for the one in the book—again helped me create a feeling of place. I would also like to remind readers that slavery did not end with the American Civil War. At least 12 million people are enslaved today and human trafficking remains a real problem, as does domestic violence.

Lastly, to Jennifer McDermott for sharing her language-shock experience.

Chapter 1

Life be what it be. I used to thinks nothing can be changed. That be before the Massa Edward brought his wife to Two Pines. If he hadn't, I could never writes this. I never sees a pencil or paper before she comes. Without her I'd still be a garden niggah.

My Mama and Papa be born on Two Pines. Don't know why the plantation be called that. Weren't no pines. Cain't have no trees in fields. Maybe the pines be cut down long ago.

I never knowd my grandmamas. Nor my grandpapas. They be long dead before I saw my first sunset. Working in fields wears a body out.

My Papa ain't no field niggah. He be a blacksmith. The Massa rents my Papa out to other plantations around here. Horses loves my Papa. He makes their feets feel good.

Me? My name is Mathilde. I ain't sure how old I be now, but I starts my monthlies the same time the Mistress comes. I done works in the family garden from the time I can remember along with my Mama. That woman can coax a vegetable from a stone, she can. "Listens to them," my Mama says to me. "They tells you what they wants." As for me, I never heard vegetables say nothing.

Mama may listen to vegetables, but she don't wants to listen to me. I had all these words running around in my head, but whenever they falls out of my mouth, Mama says, "Hush girl." Papa too. No one talks all that much round here.

Before the Mistress comes, I never thinks about being a slave. There be slaves. There be white folks just like there be sky and dirt.

9

The white folks lives in the big house. Niggahs lives in slave quarters. Before the Mistress I never even steps in the big house. They, the white folk, gives orders. We takes them. Mama says God made things that way so there's no use in complaining. Life be what it be.

CHAPTER 2

Thursday, November 11

"Wake up, Annie. Welcome to Caleb's Landing." David Young shut off the car's engine and touched his daughter's shoulder. Despite her thirty-three years she looked like a little girl with her curly red hair tumbling over her freckled face. Her green down jacket, unzipped when the car's heating drove away the winter cold, revealed a navy blue turtleneck over jeans.

Annie stretched. "I must have fallen asleep."

"Kitten, we weren't out of Logan's parking lot, and you were dead to the world."

She took a scrunchie from her pocket and battled her hair into a braid. Stray ends formed corkscrews around her face.

"You haven't been home in nineteen years, and the first thing you do is conk out."

She rubbed her eyes and glanced at the house in front of which they'd parked. *"C'est très mignon."* It was sweet. She slipped into French, the language she spoke most of the time. The house was more a two-story cottage with weathered shingles. Two windows, symmetrically arranged around the door and three on the second floor, were much like a child's painting. Window boxes were planted with what Annie called purple cabbage flowers. Plants were not her thing. She loved looking at them but refused to risk their lives by tending them. "I'm still getting used to you inheriting this."

"So is your Mom. Auntie Helen hated her. When I heard

11

from the lawyer, your mother half expected the will to say I could keep this house only if I divorced her."

"*Pas de chance.*" No way. Annie's parents were one of the happiest couples she knew. Maybe it was all the moving around that had made them such a close family.

She'd spent her first eight years in Sudbury, Massachusetts. Her father worked for Digital Equipment Corporation. Her mother was a commercial artist, who tried to do her own art between clients' demands. Annie was an only child, not like most of her friends. They complained about brothers and sisters. She would have loved to have brothers and sisters to complain about, but her parents had said that since they'd been given the most wonderful child possible, why risk having another. Annie suspected her mother didn't have patience for two.

Everything was normal until one night, over the first corn of the season, her father announced they were moving to Nijmegen.

"Nijmegen?" her mother had asked.

"Holland," her father said.

In days Annie was on a plane, her dog stored with the luggage, and then in a school where people spoke in strange grunts. None wore the wooden shoes, long dresses or starched caps like her storybook about the boy who stuck his finger in the dike, although she did see lots of windmills.

Never had she felt so alone. Children spoke to her but soon lost interest when she couldn't respond. When she cried at night, her parents talked about switching her to the International School but decided the chance to learn another language was invaluable.

The television showed many American programs and movies in English with Dutch subtitles. Annie had been in Holland three months when her teacher said something that she understood almost like a click from turning on an appliance. Things that first had seemed strange, like restaurants with tiny carpets in place of cloth on the tables, soon became normal, and Annie no longer felt like a stranger.

Then her father came home and said, "Stuttgart."

Another language. Annie looked at the German and decided if she took out a vowel it was almost the same thing as Dutch. Learning time was shorter.

Then her father said, "Geneva."

She and her mother groaned.

As a teenager Annie found French the easiest to learn, once she learned to wrap her tongue around the sounds. In Geneva almost half of her classmates were from somewhere else. Their parents worked for the UN or for various diplomatic missions. They came and went with their parents' assignments. As soon as Annie developed a good friend, that friend would be off to their home country or another assignment. Promises were made about letters and visits. Two or three cards would be sent within a few weeks reporting new adventures. Then they tapered off until all contact disappeared.

Although she didn't dwell on it, Annie never felt like she really belonged anywhere. When it came time for university, she asked to be sent to the States.

"But it costs almost nothing here, and less in Germany," her father said. "It's not like we can't afford it, and with your languages . . ."

"I want to spend time in my own country."

When Annie enrolled at UMass in Amherst, instead of having a feel of coming home she felt more of a stranger than when she had first moved to Holland. Although the other freshmen were new too, they shared cultural experiences that she'd missed. She knew Elton John, Depeche Mode and most American and English singers, but no one else had heard of Johnny Halliday, Serge Gainsbourg or Claude François. Some of her classmates had never left Massachusetts. Some confused Switzerland with

Sweden and Swaziland, although those who had read *Heidi* immediately pictured Annie milking goats. After a year, she'd decided to finish her studies at the University of Geneva. She hadn't been "home" since.

Only last year she'd heard the term "Third Culture Kid," which described a person neither part of her birth culture or her host culture, but a mixture.

She'd finally set down roots in a small French seacoast village, which she fell in love with, and bought a studio in the attic of a 500-year-old building and turned it into her nest. To support herself and to use her four languages she took tech writing assignments around Europe. However, Annie refused to work full time. Because her expenses were well below her income she was free several months a year to indulge in her real passion—history. If she felt frustrated that she couldn't earn her living by working with what she loved best, she accepted that she had at least worked out a second best solution.

Susan Young burst through the cottage door. She looked far younger than her fifty-four years with her spiked blond hair and one silver hoop in her left ear. She wore a long, flowing skirt and a sweater patch-worked of several yarns and different stitches. Annie rushed into her arms. Mother and daughter danced in circles. When they stopped, Susan brushed a stray curl from Annie's face. "I'm thrilled you're here. How jet-lagged are you?"

"Very. I didn't sleep on the night train to Paris. The flight was too bumpy to sleep. I've been awake maybe twenty-three hours," she said as Susan swept her into the cottage.

Dave followed and dropped two suitcases on the braided rug. "Except for in the car."

"Let's put you to bed. We'll talk later," Susan said.

Annie nodded. The coziness of the cottage registered in her half-asleep brain. The walls were wood paneled and beige café curtains hung at the windows. The sofa was in a brown plaid and all the wood was Early American maple. A fireplace, big enough to walk into, dominated one wall. The second room on the ground floor, a kitchen papered in red polka dots with red painted cabinets, was visible through a door. All she wanted was a bed.

Her father's white hair was backlit from the doorway making him look like an angel. What he said was even more angelic. "I'll show you your room."

Annie followed him up wooden stairs. The second floor had two bedrooms and in between the rooms through a door she saw a claw-footed tub. The outside had been painted blue with white stenciled flowers matching the wallpaper. Annie suspected this was her mother's work.

"This will be your room." Dave led her to the smaller room with white wood paneling. Pine bunk beds shoved up against one wall had matching quilts.

She slipped off her boots and without taking off her jeans fell onto the bottom bunk.

"Get some sleep. I've big plans for you tomorrow," Dave said.

He pulled the covers up to her neck as he had when she was little and slipped downstairs.

Her mother's voice drifted up the stairs. "Are you going to work on the black hole from hell?"

CHAPTER 3

Friday, November 12

Coffee and bacon smells woke Annie. For a second she wasn't sure where she was. Outside the window, blue sky shone through pine branches grazing the pane. They clicked against the glass. Strange the wind hadn't woken her. She was used to different winds, the Geneva *Bise* and the Argelès *Tramontaine*. Did they have a Massachusetts wind? Did it have a name? Her dad had talked about old-fashioned Nor'easters, but that had to do with school closings and snow shoveling.

Her bladder told her to get out of bed fast. She showered and threw on clean jeans and a sweatshirt that said *Argelès-sur-mer*, a reminder of her nest, her boyfriend and his daughter.

Downstairs her parents sat at the maple kitchen table. They smiled as she entered.

"I wasn't much of a conversationalist last night." Annie sat down.

Her father dropped an egg in an electric fry pan. It sizzled. Within minutes he said, "*Voilà*, an American cholesterol breakfast: eggs, bacon, bagels."

"Wow, bagels. I loved them when I was at UMass."

"Yoo hoo!" The backdoor was thrown open and a six-foot woman filled the kitchen. Although she wasn't fat, she was substantial. Dark hair with a white streak over the forehead framed her face. "Darlink, you arrived. Your mother has *so* been looking forward to you. All I hear about from her is her smart, pretty daughter." She strode over to Annie and kissed her on both cheeks. "Like the French, no?"

Annie wasn't sure of the accent. However, the clothes, a combination of colors and lengths, swirled around the woman creating a moving rainbow.

"Your mother says you speak four languages. Me, I speak English, German, Hungarian, French, and a bit of Russian, but hate Russian. Do you want to practice any other language, no of course you don't." She pinched Annie cheeks. "She's more adorable than you said, Susan." The woman poured a cup of coffee without asking. "I'll have what she's eating."

"Annie, meet Magda," Dave said. He took bacon and two additional eggs from the fridge.

"Did your mother tell what we're doing?" Before Annie could answer, Magda plunged on, waving her hands as she talked. "A cooperative, Darlink. An artists' cooperative, all women. I design cloth, clothes, quilts—anything with textiles. Your mother has wonderful mirrors in art she's creating."

"We'll open next tourist season." Susan looked closely at her daughter.

"But aren't you're going back to Geneva as soon as you sell this place?" Annie said.

"Your mother thinks maybe we should divide our time between here and there," Dave said.

Granted, Annie didn't live with her parents except when she was on assignment in Geneva. But she often worked in other Swiss cities and shared weekends with them. Argelès, only an overnight train trip from Geneva, made visits a spur-of-the-moment possibility. Annie couldn't imagine not sharing a continent with them. "You guys said you'd never move again."

She remembered the trauma when Digital had given Dave a very golden handshake—changing the family's future plans. The Young family had just bought a house they loved in Geneva.

After the shock wore off, he started a consulting firm that now had six employees. It suited everyone. Never a workaholic, he let the younger men take over. Sometimes he went weeks with only e-mail and phone check-ins.

"Mom, I thought you said moving countries gave you hives?"

"I know you're thinking that aliens are occupying your parents' bodies." Dave dropped two more eggs into the hot bacon fat. "We're hoping you'll stay for a while. You've another assignment?"

"Not for a while, but Roger and Gaëlle. . . . Oh, my God."

"I love the sound of French names. Roh-jay. Roh-jay." Magda rolled the French pronunciation around her mouth. "So much nicer than Rodge-er." She gulped her steaming coffee then fanned her mouth.

"What?" Susan asked.

"I forgot to call to say I arrived."

Susan patted her daughter's hand. "I did. Told him you fell sound asleep and would call soon. He and Gaëlle send their love."

"Invite them for Christmas. It would do Gaëlle good to see the U.S.," Dave said.

"How much longer will Roger be on disability?" Susan asked.

Annie shuddered as she remembered Roger in the hospital while the doctors searched for the bullet in his leg. He wasn't even shot in his line of duty as Argelès' police chief but in an out-of-season hunting accident. They'd been hiking through the mountains when the bullet hit him. Annie had applied emergency first aid. Thank God she'd had her cell phone to call for help. "I'm not sure he won't stay on disability. He needs a cane to walk, hardly good for chasing crooks."

"No more on who did it?" Dave asked.

Annie shook her head. "They don't think the hunter knew he hit someone. Or if he did, he'll never show himself."

"Then there's nothing to stop them from coming," Susan said.

"Maybe when Gaëlle gets out for the Christmas holidays," Annie said. She wasn't sure she wanted to stay that long herself, but the idea of having everyone she really cared for together for the holiday was appealing.

Annie briefed her parents on how well the teenager was doing.

Dave slipped the bacon and eggs onto Magda's plate. She picked up her fork and waved it around. "Thank you, Darlink. I love your cooking."

"I want to show you our studio and gallery," Susan said.

"Darlink, you'll love it," Magda said with her mouth full. She reached for a napkin and nearly knocked the sugar bowl over.

"But first you are going to meet the boys," Dave said. "Get your coat."

"And cleaning the black hole?" Susan asked. "That, Annie, is the basement."

"Later," Dave said. "Want to help, Annie?"

"I traveled two days just because I knew there was a basement waiting to be cleaned. Of course."

CHAPTER 4

Friday, November 12

Annie walked next to her father, her head swiveling as he pointed out the architectural features of the houses on both sides of the street. They were pre–Civil War to Victorian, and were painted in avocados, slate blues, barn reds and golds. "I love the picket fences and small gardens in front. And look at the muted pastels of the flagstone walks."

"Yards. They call 'em yards here. Look at that widow's walk."

Her father's English had fallen back into the New England accent with the replacement of many *r*'s with *h*'s. His "yahds" and "heahs" had been diminished by years of living abroad.

"You'll love the history of this place." He proceeded to explain how from before the Revolutionary War to just after World War II Caleb's Landing had been a sleepy little fishing village. "Now in the summer it goes from 5,000 to 50,000 people, including artists." He pointed out the lobster pots pulled up along the dock. "And they refuse to join with other towns and insist on running their own school, police and fire departments and public works systems. Stubborn New England Yankees, still."

It felt good to be going back into their habit of exploring the history of every place they ever lived, poking into old buildings, checking out battlefields, churches, houses, museums, anywhere that held a key to the lives of those that had lived there before them. "This town was a fort during the 1812 War."

"Remember when we visited the little church in Leiden where the Pilgrims worshipped?" she asked. "And how much the pastor wanted to tell us, once he learned we were New Englanders?"

"And how he showed us documents with their plans for escaping to the New World?"

She followed her father as he turned on to the main road where the green-gray Atlantic peeked between a series of little multicolored shops, galleries and restaurants. Most were closed. "What time do they open?" she asked.

"Some later today. Some only on the weekends, at least until the Christmas season. See that box over there?" The box was decorated with candy canes. "That's where kids drop their letters to Santa. He'll arrive by boat the Saturday after Thanksgiving. I'm on the Christmas Festival Committee."

Annie stopped. Her father was not a joiner by nature, although he participated in Democrats Abroad helping ex-pats of either political persuasion to register for each election cycle. He continued on a couple of steps, turned and pointed to a red barn-like building with white things hanging from it that overlooked the little harbor. "That's a fisherman's shack, and it or one like it has been there since before I was born. They rebuilt it after the huge storm in 1978 took it out. Artists are always painting it, and they say it is one of the most painted buildings in the world. I can't imagine Caleb's Landing without it . . ." He shook his head.

Her father seemed so happy guiding her around the place that seemed so familiar to him, yet he had never mentioned it in all her growing-up years, before or after they left the U.S. She took a second look. Little boats, mostly fishing boats, bobbed in front of the fishing shack in the water. A fat seagull stared at them from a post as if daring them to move closer.

He guided his daughter past more galleries and told her to

21

take a left. Shops and galleries, all cottage-like with weathered shingles and large windows, faced directly onto the sidewalk with one or two granite steps at their entrances. One sold saltwater taffy and chocolate, another Norwegian sweaters and carvings. A sign, *The Coffee Bean,* hung over a red door. Three round tables filled the window. A woman, dressed in gray slacks and jersey with a string of pearls and her gray hair frizzed, occupied one as she read a newspaper and sipped something frothy.

Father and daughter entered. A bar set-up was empty of humans, but had cups and a blackboard listing offerings.

"Hi Dave. I see your daughter got in all right." The waitress appeared behind the counter as if by magic. She was probably Annie's age, but outweighed her by at least seventy-five pounds. She wore a T-shirt with *The Coffee Bean* emblazoned over ample breasts. "What'll it be?"

"Tea," Annie said.

"Herbal or natural?"

"Natural."

"English breakfast, Irish breakfast, Earl Gray, Lady Gray . . ." and went on to list choice after choice until Annie's head reeled.

Annie held up her hands. "English breakfast."

"Milk or lemon?"

"Milk."

"Cream, half-and-half, 1%, 2%, nondairy?"

"Normal." Annie glanced at her father who moved his hands in a pattern as if to say stay calm.

"We also have raisin, sesame, pumpkin, onion, and garlic bagels." She listed five types of muffins and a choice of toasts.

"Just the tea," Annie said.

The waitress disappeared.

"Was that a test?" Annie asked.

"Get used to it. Don't act indecisive," Dave said. "You'll

learn to like lots of choices."

Annie doubted it.

The waitress reappeared with a tray of clean cups. Steam rose off them. She handed Dave a cup of coffee without asking any questions.

Annie followed her father to the back room. Six round tables surrounded by soda fountain metal chairs faced a solid glass wall. The Atlantic lapped at cottage-sized boulders.

Three men about her father's age sat with their backs to the door. Dave walked over to them. When the men saw father and daughter they jumped up, flashing smiles.

"Annie, let me introduce you to my friends." Dave pointed to the tallest, who was the best dressed with pressed gray trousers and a gray and blue paisley scarf tucked into the neck of his blue shirt. He was thin with wavy strawberry blond hair. "Meet Len Haskell, local real estate agent and selectman."

"Your father has talked and talked about your coming."

The shortest of the group stood up. "I'm Paul Mangone, the only non-WASP."

"He does government, too." Charlie said. "He's chairman of the school board."

The fattest of the three stood. He reminded Annie of a smiley face on a Michelin tire body. "Charlie Tucker." He thrust out his hand. "I don't do government, I just pay taxes."

"He's Caleb's Landing's largest employer. Publishes scientific stuff I don't understand," Len said.

Annie let them rearrange the tables to make room for them all. "Well, you certainly made friends fast, Dad. And with the mighty of Caleb's Landing."

"I had a head start. These were my boyhood chums."

Annie looked confused. "You grew up in Sudbury?"

"He was a summer boy. We usually didn't associate with them," Len said. "But we discovered he was as nuts about history as we were so we let him into our club."

"After all, he had the best collection of Landmark books," Paul said.

Annie looked confused.

"It was a series put out by some publisher, I forget who, for kids. One was on the Battle of Britain, another on the Tudors. They got top writers like Quentin Reynolds," Paul said.

"Between us we had them all and shared," Len said.

"Teenage boys are usually more interested in girls than history," Annie said.

"Oh, we were interested in them, too," Charlie said. "Remember Debbie Heath?"

"What happened to her?" Paul asked. "She had the biggest . . ." he glanced at Annie.

"She certainly did. I lost track of her when she moved out west," Len said.

Annie figured if she sat there long enough there was no telling what secrets from her father's past would emerge.

"I spent the summers here with Auntie Helen," Dave said.

Auntie Helen was not someone Annie had ever heard of before her parents called her in Argelès to tell her that they were going home to claim an inheritance. Her parents never saw her during their summer Stateside holidays. Except for visiting the House of Seven Gables and the Witch Museum when she was twelve, Annie didn't remember being on the Massachusetts North Shore at all.

"What a hoot she was, at least until Vietnam," Charlie Tucker said. "Once she knew we were against it, none of us were welcome again."

"Except me," Dave said, "until I started dating Susan. My aunt couldn't stand the sight of her."

Annie's mother was one of the sweetest people Annie had ever met. When she was growing up, it annoyed her because she couldn't complain about her mother to her friends, who would have traded mothers in a second.

"Auntie Helen thought of her as a hippy artist. She was. Unfortunately for Auntie, she gave me a choice." Dave did a shoulder shrug.

Len tapped his coffee cup. "With a college kid in love there's only one choice. What a mixed bag your aunt was. She'd let us drink beer with her, but wouldn't let us drive. More than once she drove us home when she shouldn't have driven herself."

"She taught for years, high school history. She's why I fell in love with it. Even before I met these guys. She took me to the re-enactment of the first battle in the Revolutionary War in Concord, and I was hooked," Dave said. "I must have been seven."

"Which is where you come in," Charlie said to Annie.

All four men stared at her.

Annie felt uncomfortable. "What?"

Paul Mangone spoke first. "I'm a retired junior high history teacher. I serve on the school board." He moved in closer. "I'm shocked by what is passing as history lessons today. My grandkids bring home stuff that's either superficial or just plain wrong. Not just here, but all over."

"I know," Annie said. "I was on a train going to Geneva last summer. There were American college kids on the train. They asked me what there was to do in Geneva. I told them it was more a government town, but there was lots of history. I told them Calvin was big. They had never heard of Calvin or the Protestant Reformation."

"That doesn't surprise me," Paul said. "I used to teach history in the local middle school until the politics got to me."

"But then I said Pilgrims, and they hadn't heard about them either. At first I thought they were kidding, but one said he didn't know much about history. He was an engineering student." She shook her head. "I finally got some recognition with the word *Thanksgiving.*" She stopped, thinking that maybe she'd said too much.

Charlie spoke. "Your Dad told us that story: this is why we want you to write an exciting proactive history book, or maybe a CD-ROM game. You'd have creative freedom, just so long as it is accurate and educational."

All the men waited for her to speak. She didn't, letting silence become a personality in the conversation, a technique she used at work but certainly hadn't expected to use while meeting her father's buddies. In fact, she hadn't expected her father to *have* buddies. All she'd expected was a three-week visit with her parents, experience a Thanksgiving in her birth country then back to her real life in southern France, her boyfriend and her next assignment.

A few drops of sweat glistened on Charlie's brow. Although he was far from handsome, Annie found him appealing, a grandfatherly type. "See I own a publishing company, although we do mainly scientific stuff. Over the years, I've earned more money than I need."

"What do you publish?" Annie asked. Changing the subject was another of her favorite communication techniques.

Charlie touched her hand with the first two fingers of his right hand. "Right now we're working with Harvard on a study of weather before records were kept. There's thousands of ship logs that tell of winds, etc. and one of our guys and one of Harvard's are in London and Amsterdam . . ."

"We need to sell Annie on this idea, Charlie," Paul said.

Even if this is a set-up, I want to hear it, Annie thought. She flashed a look at Dave that she could see he read correctly as *I'll-settle-up-later.* She smiled at Charlie.

"The nice thing about being independent, I don't care if we make money or break even."

"We just want to get kids interested in history," Paul said.

"A democracy needs educated citizens," Len said.

Charlie leaned forward. "It's my giving back."

Giving back was one of her father and mother's phrases. They did X amount of things for whatever community they lived in—not necessarily by being on committees, but by helping an elderly neighbor shovel her walk, donating blood, whatever. That Annie was expected to do the same was as much a part of her training as learning to say please and thank you. Although not rich, her family never stopped telling her how much they did have, compared to the majority of people who were living or had ever lived on the planet.

Charlie sat so far forward on his seat that Annie worried he might tip his chair and fall onto the table. The men stared at her.

Giving back did not include volunteering for bankruptcy. "I need to find a new contract. I've a mortgage to pay." Granted the mortgage on her studio was miniscule, a deliberate decision to allow herself the freedom of not being tied down to a job. Even with Europe's obligatory minimum four weeks of holiday a year, it wasn't enough. Freelancing had been her salvation, allowing her an income to meet her needs and the freedom to pursue her real love: historical research. She could easily work through a three-month contract writing and translating boring technical stuff if she knew it would be followed by three months off even if there were nothing she could do with her findings.

Someday, maybe, she would go back and get her doctorate, but she'd missed her chance at an academic career.

"Think of it, Annie." Charlie tapped her hand again. "This is a chance to portray the founding of America the way it really was, the cold, the hunger, the bravery, the true story of the Indians. I can pay you, probably not as much as you earn over there, but give us a figure you need," Charlie said.

Now it was getting interesting. More and more she liked Charlie, although she liked anyone who didn't always think of profit. She wished she were in the same situation. There was a point that she did not want her bank account to dip below and next month she would reach it.

A moderately pregnant woman waddled into the room with a hot chocolate in one hand. The other hand rested on the stomach of the forest-green loose-fitting jumper she wore over a white turtleneck jersey. "Hey, you guys."

The men rearranged themselves to make room for her.

Len spoke. "Annie, this is my daughter-in-law, Melissa; and my new granddaughter or grandson."

"The new Madison Haskell," Melissa said. "Or Aiden."

"What happened to Mackenzie or Ethan?" Len asked.

"Jason and I changed our minds."

"This baby has at least seven names a week per sex," Dave said. He looked at Annie, "But she is producing a grandchild for Len."

Annie felt slapped. Her father had never said anything about her reproducing or marrying or anything like that. The move had changed more than she thought.

"Just kidding, Kitten," Dave added. His eyes said the apology was real.

"Your dad told me all about you. I can show you all the neat shopping places around. Although it has to be on my day off. I'm a secretary at Pop Len's real estate office. My husband works there too, and sometimes we don't get the same days off, so it'll be nice to have a new friend to keep me company." Melissa spoke with almost one breath.

Annie would rather go to the dentist than shop. "Well, maybe we can have lunch or something." If she were going to be here any time at all, she might as well put her integration skills to

28

work. At least this time she didn't have to learn another language.

"Hey Melissa, what's that bruise on your wrist?" Charlie asked.

The girl quickly pulled down the jersey sleeve to hide it. "I am so clumsy with this baby." She turned to Annie. "Pop Len has your phone number?"

Annie nodded.

"Let me show you the rest of the Landing," Dave said. "Then I need to get going on the basement or Susan will kill me."

"Be careful. People have gone down there and have never been heard of again," Len said.

"As kids we would go there and tell ghost stories until we were too scared to move," Len said.

As they got up to leave, Paul Mangone said to Len, "Good on you. This is the first time you haven't tried to convince Dave to sell you the cottage."

"Oh, I still want to buy it, but I thought I'd give him a rest because his daughter's here."

They barely made it to the door when Charlie came after them. "Len will bring a book over for you to look at. It might give you ideas."

"I'll think about it. Let me talk it over with my boyfriend." Annie didn't say that if she had been convinced she would have told Roger that she was doing it.

CHAPTER 5

Friday, November 12

"I said I'd ask Roger to come at Christmas, I didn't say I'd do the history project," Annie said. "And stop smiling." Dave and Annie sat at the Young kitchen table.

"I wasn't smiling." He smiled.

"I didn't say I would." She shivered. The sun had set and she felt the draft from the window. She reached up and pulled down the white paper shade.

"All you said was that if Roger was okay with it you would consider it. We both know when you want to do something, you tell him as a *fait accompli.*"

She looked at her watch. Eleven at night in Argelès and Roger would be laying in bed reading. Hannibal, the German shepherd, would be on the floor waiting for his master to fall asleep so he could sneak onto the bed. She went to the old-fashioned white princess phone hanging next to the fridge. Before she could dial they heard the front door open.

A male voice called, "It's me."

"Come on through. We're in the kitchen," Dave said.

Len Haskell walked in. After moving the newspaper and thumping a large grocery plastic bag on the table, he folded himself into a kitchen chair.

"Wine?"

"Coke. At least we got him out of the Frenchie way of calling it an *apéro.* Where's Susan?"

"At the studio. Once the light goes, she heads home so she should be here soon," Dave said.

Annie didn't like the use of the word *home*. Home was Geneva. Remember all the times your parents didn't like your choices and said nothing, she thought. They probably developed ridge marks in their tongues. What you can't control, accept.

"I brought you something to whet your appetite, Annie." Len pulled a big book with a black leather cover and gold lettering from the bag. It was the size of at least six encyclopedia volumes. He pushed it toward her.

She took it and opened it. The book contained the early writings of all the people who sailed on the *Mayflower* and who had set up the first Massachusetts colony.

"How's that for source material?" Len asked. "Only place I know of that all the information is between two covers. Limited edition, too. Done by someone descended from the original *Mayflower* passengers, so don't write on it."

Dave leaned over her shoulder as she flipped through the pages.

"If we take her to Plimouth Plantation, all she'll need is a bit of creativity," Len said.

Dave winked at his daughter. "Can you swear to me that you have no interest?"

She stuck her tongue out. Her father ignored her. She imagined herself as one of the one hundred and two people on the *Mayflower*.

The room faded and she tossed and turned aboard the small wooden ship. As she took care of her seasick child, she wasn't sure if her queasiness was from the churning sea or her new pregnancy. Why had she let her husband talk her into coming? He was more religious than she was. However, who was she to fight the community? They might brand her a heretic. Her mother disapproved of her leaving England. How she missed her, but she didn't miss the Church of

England. It strayed too close to popery with all its rituals and its music. She liked walking to the university chapel and listening to William Bradford speak. They should have stayed in Holland, not boarded this horrible vessel. She should pray harder to God to make her more obedient to her husband and to the pastor.

That thought made Annie's feminist heart leap back to the Caleb's Landing kitchen. What were Len and her father talking about—oh yes, the reproductions of the *Mayflower,* The Beaver and the Boston Tea Party ship anchored in various places around the Massachusetts shore. "How accurate are they?"

"I've heard plank for plank," Len said.

Susan entered, carrying a grocery bag, which she dumped on the counter. Several kinds of cheese, a loaf of bread and a butternut squash tumbled out. She wore paint-streaked blue denim coveralls. Pinks and yellows dominated, but all rainbow colors were represented. Her whole body radiated a contentment that seemed to reverse the aging process.

Dave walked over to his wife and rubbed a smudge of paint off her cheek. He said nothing about the blue paint in her hair.

"I see the propaganda team is hard at work," Susan said.

"You knew and didn't warn me?" Annie asked.

"I kinda hoped you would stay a while longer. Learn to love Caleb's Landing as much as we do," Susan said. "But only if you want."

Annie found all three looking at her.

Susan broke the staring circle. "Want to stay to dinner, Len? Or have you got a hot date?"

"At my age all dates are lukewarm," Len said.

"Don't ruin your image as the town's most eligible bachelor," Dave said. "We married guys need our fantasies."

Annie thumbed through the book, deciphering the older English, the thous and thees, while only half listening. If they did a story about a boy and a girl on the *Mayflower,* made it interactive, described life as it really was . . . no, kids were too accustomed to action heroes. They wouldn't really have that much interest in the slowness of 1620.

"Have you folks given any more thought of selling this place?" Len asked.

"You couldn't go a day without asking, could you?" Dave asked. "We're still trying to decide if we want to rent it summers and spend winters here."

"Or the reverse," Susan said. "I would like to see how the gallery goes this summer."

Annie's world tilted. "And Geneva?" Images of winter nights by the fireplace, her room kept ready for her at all times, the kitchen where they had discussed everything: her homework, Dave's work, lunch, a new bestseller. It was where her friends went after a day skiing in the French Alps just across the border and waited for her father to serve fondue or *raclette* and *vin chaud*.

Grow up, she told herself. I'm an adult with my own place. I've a career that lets me work in most European countries, a boyfriend who might become my fiancé if only I say yes, a future stepdaughter. I even have a future stepdog.

Susan rested her head on her daughter's head totem-style and dropped her arms around Annie's shoulders. "After following your father around the world, I'm finally where I can do what I want."

"It's your mother's turn," Dave said.

"But you might want a different place," Len said. "Even your aunt only used this as a summer home." He shivered. "It's drafty in the winter."

"Until she retired. Then she lived here all year," Dave said. "We're adding more insulation."

"But, she became such a hermit. Not like the woman that let us put up tents in the yard and cooked marshmallows over a candle flame during a power failure." Len turned to Annie. "And when she died it took her lawyer a couple of years to find your father, or maybe he already told you that."

"I'm the new kid on this block," Annie said. "Until my parents called me in July and said they'd inherited a house, I didn't even know I had a Great Auntie Helen."

"Why do you think she changed her mind about you?" Susan asked.

"I probably was the only one left to leave it to," Dave said. "She'd alienated everyone else."

"It was the alcohol. Once she retired she had nothing to limit her drinking," Len said. "Alcohol does a real job on people."

"She did like her beer," Dave said. "I remember her and my mother talking on the phone, and Mom warning her not to drink while I was here. Auntie Helen made mocking faces, holding a beer can as she agreed. She'd tilt the phone so I could hear what Mom was saying. The sisters were always at war and I was one of the skirmishes."

"Anyway," Len said, "If you want to rent it summers, my agency can handle it."

"We wouldn't give it to anyone else," Dave said.

"When was the last summer you were here?" Annie asked.

"My freshman year at UMass. I worked at the Blacksmith's."

"You shod horses?" Her parents might have been sixties hippies, but they were never part of the back-to-the-earth movement.

"It's a restaurant, kitten. I was a waiter. Then in my sophomore year I met your mother. Auntie Helen met her at Christmas and did everything she could to break us up."

"She came into Mass Art to offer to pay my tuition, if I gave him up," Susan said.

"Were you tempted?"

"Our hormones were on overload. Also Auntie Helen was a

died-in-the-wool Republican and gung-ho Vietnam," Susan said.

Annie knew her parents in their youth were just slightly to the right of The Weathermen, the most violent anti-Vietnam group ever, although they'd just turned twenty at the end of the Vietnam War. Had Dave been drafted they'd have gone to Canada. She knew her father would defend his country, but even then he knew enough, or so he claimed, that the United States wasn't in danger from the Vietnamese.

"What about the history book, Annie?" Len asked. "Charlie figured I was a better sales person than he is. He's more a scientist."

"Depends on Roger," she said. Annie looked at her watch. It was dinnertime here, after midnight there. She would call tomorrow.

Chapter 6

Saturday, November 13

"Snow, kitten."

The voice pulled Annie awake. Jet lag had hit her at two in the morning, and she'd twisted in the narrow bed until she decided to read herself back to sleep. The book that Len had brought over was not a book for reading in bed. Its heaviness meant that Annie had to stack the pillows behind her and sit up, resting the book against her raised knees. Any discomfort was forgotten as she let herself be drawn into an earlier time. When she'd glanced at the clock thirty-five documents later it was almost five. She had no recollection of turning over and falling asleep.

She rolled over to look out the window, knocking the book on the floor. It thumped loudly enough for her father to ask if she were all right.

"Fine. I dropped Len's book." When he said nothing more she looked at the pine tree grazing the window panes. They were frosted as if attacked by confectionery sugar. The little sky visible through the branches was gray. "If you don't like New England weather, wait a minute," Mark Twain was to have said, or at least he did according to her father.

Footsteps came up the stairs and approached her room. Dave poked his head through the door. "Mom's making breakfast. When will you call Roger?"

"This afternoon."

"Why not now?"

"You have the making of a first-class nag. I want to wait till Gaëlle is home from school and not out with her friends so I can talk to her, too.

"And since you're into nagging, let me nag for Mom. Basement?"

From downstairs she heard her mother holler, "Keep at him Annie."

Susan left to slog her way to the studio, leaving her daughter with the history book and her husband with the basement project. Mid-morning, Annie sat on the third stair from the bottom, a mug of tea cupped in her hands, watching her father move boxes. Although he had exempted her from helping to read the history book, she needed a break.

All that hell, fire and brimstone in the sermons depressed her. She imagined herself sitting in a pew, worrying whether she'd baked enough the night before so she wouldn't have to cook on the Sabbath. Her feet tingled, and she wiggled her toes. Back to modern times, she thought.

Although on one level she understood how fundamentalist the Pilgrims had been, their certainty of knowing what God wanted bothered her. And although the sermons were unusable for her project, she figured she needed to read them to have a full understanding of the time. She wasn't about to admit to her father that she was beginning to think of it as *her* project.

Annie gazed at the boxes and piles. "Didn't your aunt ever throw anything away?"

Dave lifted a box from the floor to a table. "When she bought the house, a lot of this junk was already here." His face was streaked with dirt and cobwebs were entwined in his hair. "Wanta see what's in this?"

"Sure."

He slit the box with the Swiss Army knife he kept in his back pocket. The box was chockablock full of lumps wrapped in yellowed *The Boston Post* newspapers.

"I never heard of *The Boston Post*," she said. Paper crackled as she unrolled one lump to reveal a goblet of cheap glass.

"It went out of business when I was a kid." He picked up the rumpled paper and read the headline. "Truman Recognizes Israel."

"That means this stuff was put down here sometime in the 1940s."

Dave touched the masthead gingerly. "May 14, 1948. Different boxes are from different eras."

Lump after lump became glasses, cups, saucers. Almost nothing matched.

Annie wondered who had packed this stuff away. And why? What were their lives like? Had they been happy as they ate off these plates? She gazed at news about the 1952 Oslo Olympics and the photos of brides-to-be, maybe now long dead. An editorial talked about corrupt politicians. Not all the stories could be read in full. Some said continued on page x; page x wasn't in the boxes.

"Your aunt was a reader," he said. He handed her copies of *Main Street, The Age of Innocence,* and *Mountain Interval.* The books smelled like the antique bookstore on rue du Mont Blanc in Geneva where Annie browsed many rainy afternoons. As Dave combed through more boxes, she thumbed through *Advise and Consent, Frankie and Zoey, A Nation of Sheep,* and *The Rise and Fall of the Third Reich.* "What will you do with this stuff?"

"The *we-sell-antiques-and-we-buy-junk* man said he would stop to cart stuff away. And there's Goodwill or the trash." He dove into another box stuffed with blankets that looked like Swiss cheese. "The moths must have thought they'd found a gourmet restaurant." He coughed as dust filtered up.

By late afternoon after the junk/antique guy left and the car was filled for a Goodwill run, they had lined up twenty large black trash bags like soldiers outside for the trash man. The books had been either packed for the library or added to the shelves upstairs.

"Good day's work." Dave leaned against a shoulder-high oak chest with wood swirls visible through the grime. "Let's push this over there. Heavy son-of-a-gun." He rocked it back and forth, and then stopped to wipe his face with his handkerchief, leaving a black swath on the material.

Annie put both hands against the chest. She loved antiques because they had a history. Maybe long ago a craftsman had cut the wood before stopping for a lunch his wife had prepared. With his stomach full he could have come back to fit the parts together without using nails.

Together she and her father struggled to push it to the middle of the room. She stood back to admire it. "It'll look great polished up." She wiped her hands on her jeans as she planned a hot bubble bath in the claw-footed tub upstairs. Maybe her mother had some candles to light and she could listen to soft music. She glanced where the chest had stood. "Dad, there's a door."

"But there's no place for a door to go." Dave joined her. The door was waist high. When they tried the ancient brass handle it was locked. There was no key, nor had they found one during the cleaning spree. "Get me a screwdriver, kitten." After she handed it to him, he fiddled with the lock. The tool made metal on metal scraping noises. It refused to budge.

"Take off the hinges," she said.

"I need more light, please."

The long black cord of the lamp trailed behind her like an undernourished snake. She held it over his shoulder as he twisted each screw. The hinge itself was plain black ironwork. It existed only to do the job, not to be decorative.

When he pulled the hinge, the wood splintered. He pried the rest of the hinge off and then tackled the second. The door gave.

The light illuminated a space six feet deep and high enough that after they crawled through the door, they could stand. The room must have been dug under the front yard. Dave's head grazed the ceiling. A bunch of blankets were piled to the left. The lamp cast light on a small table with a half-burned candle. A notebook with yellowed pages, a pen and inkwell were on the table. Annie picked it up and shook it. Paper flakes floated down, reminding her of a paperweight from her childhood only when she shook her paperweight white snowflakes fell on miniature children skating.

Annie bent to read the top paper. The letters were spindly, almost childlike. *"Life be what it be. I used to think that nothing can be changed. That be before the Massa Edward brought his wife . . ."*

"My God, Dad, look at this."

He thumbed through the pages. "This room must have been dug out under the yard and used as part of the Underground Railroad. You know, where runaway slaves hid on their way to Canada."

"Daa-a-ad." Annie made it a several syllable word as she had as a teenager when her father told her something so obvious. "Imagine hiding here. Imagine sleeping here." She went to the pile of blankets and picked up one corner and screamed.

Dave turned to see a skeleton dressed in long rags.

CHAPTER 7

Saturday, November 13

The Caleb's Landing police chief's weight prevented him from crawling through the narrow doorway to where the skeleton lay askew. He stuck his head in. "I can see that the femur has separated from the rest of the body." He struggled to stand up. "Brian, go look. You're skinny enough," he said to the younger cop, standing behind him and holding a lamp.

"Did you touch anything? I know you were cleaning and all," the chief asked.

"I've seen enough cop shows to not touch a crime scene, but before we found the skeleton we touched the table, the blanket and the diary we found," Dave said.

"I'm not sure this is a crime scene. I'm not sure what it is," the chief said. "And what diary?"

Annie ran upstairs where she'd taken the yellowed pages with the spindly, childlike writing. She wished she had read it, but the police arrived within minutes of being called. It wasn't as if the skeleton was going anywhere or the murderer was in the process of fleeing.

The chief thumbed through the diary. "Judging by the clothes and diary, this happened sometime before the Civil War. That makes, er, 150 years plus."

"You going to dust for fingerprints or anything?" Dave asked.

The chief's face reddened. "You trying to tell me how to do my job?"

41

Dave shook his head.

"Every Goddamn person says do this, do that. I'm fed up." He stormed up the cellar stairs still carrying the diary. "And Brian, call the medical examiner." The chief slammed the kitchen door.

"Sorry about that," Brian said as they went upstairs. He pulled his cell phone from his back pocket and briefed the medical examiner.

"I'm not crazy about having a skeleton in the house," Annie said.

The examiner did not arrive for another three hours. By that time Susan had cooked dinner for everyone, including the cop.

The examiner, a woman probably about Susan's age, stuck out her hand. "I'm Dr. Carpenter, Victoria Carpenter. Sorry to be late, but this is my third call today. And Saturday is my day off."

"Crime is up?" Dave asked.

"I'm covering in Boston. There's a lot of flu around and people are generous germ sharers. So staff is down." She took off her glasses to rub her eyes.

"The chief said that this death probably wasn't a murder?"

"People aren't dead until I certify them, but a skeleton . . ." the examiner smiled. "What do we have, Brian?"

He filled her in.

"Bizarre. Let's take a look." She took off her coat and snapped on a pair of rubber gloves. "Stay up here, folks. Brian, come with me."

Susan, Annie and Dave sat at the table. Once, Susan called downstairs asking if they wanted coffee or anything. A "No, thank you" floated back at them.

When the examiner emerged from the basement she looked more tired than she had when she went down. "Brian is bagging the remains. We've taken photos."

"What's next?" Annie asked.

"We'll do an examination when we get a chance. Looks like the skeleton has been there through a couple of centuries, so we'll handle it after more current cases."

After everyone had gone, Susan said, "You know those stories about haunted houses and people feeling ill at ease?"

Dave and Annie nodded.

"Well, this house never felt the least bit haunted."

CHAPTER 8

If I lives forever, I'll never forget the day I first sees Mistress Elizabeth. Massa Edwards be up north a long time. He left when the lettuce and spinach be peeking through the dirt. He comes back after the fall squash be picked.

When he be gone, his younger brother Richard be in charge. We had no overseer no more. Good thing. The last one stole and stole. The two brothers makes sure the work be done. During planting and harvest times they hires drivers to push us slaves. Nothing like a flashing whip to make hands fly. Two Pines slaves ain't beat too often or too much. Hurt slaves don't works well, the Massas always says. Yet sometimes we still needs lessons.

At Two Pines we grows tobacco, corn, some wheat but mostly rice. We be sixty slaves like me. I cain't count that high, but that's what the Massas says. Two Pines has two cows, sheeps and enough horses to pull plows and gets the family from here to there. And we has some mighty fine pigs and more chickens than insects. Well, that might depend on whether it be bug season or not.

I be weeding the carrots the day she arrives. She be the Mistress. Carrots be my favorite vegetable after beets. Most vegetables are green, but carrots are orange and beets purple, colors that feels good on the eyes. Also carrot leaves be like the lace I sees on white women's dresses. The Mistress has lace on the dress she wears as her wagon comes by. Her clothes be covered with dust. She looks tired.

I cain't imagine at the time, much less dream that someday I would travel away from Two Pines to places I never knowd existed.

44

I writes about Mistress Elizabeth now because I can. I just picks up my pencil and makes certain marks on the paper. I can visits them anytime I want. Or anyone else can reads them too.

Two Pines been without a woman running it since the old Mistress and Massa died before I be born. The two brothers, the Massa Edward and the Massa Richard, must have missed a woman's hand because they lets the new Mistress change things. The Massas don't do nothing they don't wants to. That be why they be Massas.

Two Pines be different from Running Mead. That's the plantation next to ours. Their slaves works all the time at anything. Ours, well they each has their own jobs and when we be done, we be done. This means in the planting and harvest seasons the field slaves be at work before the sun wakes and they don't quits until they need a light to walk home. But in between they only work during sunlight, less if there be no weeds to pull or dirt to turn over.

Slaves, like my Papa and Mama, works even less hard, although the Massa Richard hates to see Papa's fire go out. There always be metal to put around the barrels or a new tool to make if not for us, then for others.

There be a hospital on Two Pines, and that's where I first meets the Mistress face to face. The day after she arrives, I gets bit by a snake. Mama said I should have knowd better than to just put my hand down into a patch without looking first. She ties a cloth around my arm and carries me to the hospital. Chloe, she's the niggah who cares for the sick, cuts it with the knife she always carries and sucks and sucks, spitting my blood on the floor. Lord did it hurt.

When I whimpers, Chloe says shut up, a little pain be better than being a lot dead.

I wants to go home. Mama says she don't have no time to look after me what with having to finish picking the last squash of the season and all, so I can just stays with Chloe.

I hates the hospital. At home I has a place to sleep, not like a white folks bed, but a piece of wood above the floor with lots of moss. Here be only the floor to lie on, although Mama gots my blanket to keep splinters out of my legs and arms.

I not be the only one there. Priscilla sits in the corner rocking her new baby, who don't wants her nipple. Peter be there too, with his leg wrapped tight until it mends from being broke. Peter gets lots of broken bones. Massa Edward says he would sell him, but no one would buy him.

The snake bite makes me right sick. Chloe makes me drink some chicken broth, but it comes up faster than it went down. She says I going to be all right, but I needs to keep my strength up.

The third day I feels better. That be when the Mistress Elizabeth comes in with Massa Richard, her brother-in-law. I tries to imagine what she be thinking as she sees the three of us just laying on the wood floor. She needs a candle cause closed shutters hides the windows.

She asks Chloe lots of questions about how she bathes the patients. Simple. Chloe don't. She don't get no water here unless she carries it herself.

"What do you use for medicine?" the Mistress Elizabeth asks.

Chloe lists herbs she grows, dries and sometimes soaks in oils or alcohol.

To this list the Mistress nods. "Why no beds?"

"Never thought of them," Chloe says.

The Mistress goes to Priscilla and takes the baby, cradling it in her arms as if she be her very own baby. I seen lots of black women suckle white babies, but I never seen a white woman with a black baby. She tickles its lips with her little finger. The baby don't do nothing. The Mistress walks over to one window. With one free hand she opens the shutters and looks out for what seems like a bit more than forever. When she turns back, I seen her cheeks were tear-washed.

CHAPTER 9

The "boys" and Annie were at The Coffee Bean. *The Boston Globe* was spread out on the table. Paul, Charlie and Annie were seated, but Len and Dave stood reading over their shoulders.

"Listen to this," Charlie said. "A skeleton, probably from before the Civil War, was found in an old house near the dock in Caleb's Landing late Saturday."

Len took a long drink of his coffee. "So what happened next?"

Dave shrugged. "Not much I guess. They took the remains away. A forensic expert will look at it sooner or later."

"Poor thing. I've a funny feeling about the skeleton," Annie said.

"You're just spooked," Len said. His tone implied women are easily spooked.

"No, I'm not. Someone locked her in there, but she could have screamed."

"From the diary it sounds like she was a runaway slave," Len said. "Caleb's Landing was part of the Underground Railroad. Unitarians I guess ran it. Annie, did you know how many of the most important forefathers were Unitarians? Adams, Emerson, Alcott . . ."

"You're getting off the subject, Len. If she didn't want to get caught she wouldn't have screamed," Charlie said.

"Maybe she was sick and died of some disease," Paul said.

"But why didn't the owners of the house bury her?" Annie asked.

"Because that would have blown their part in the Underground Railroad," Paul said.

Charlie looked at Annie. "There are lots of loose ends, but we probably will never know."

CHAPTER 10

Susan Young unlocked the studio space she shared with four women artists. The front was an empty store. The walls still smelled of fresh white paint. Track lighting was directed to shine on the empty walls. Several waist-high pedestals stood to one side.

Annie followed her mother through an open archway into a room the size of half a car dealership showroom. One wall had been replaced with floor-to-ceiling pane glass that looked out at gray, angry waves rising and falling hypnotically. Cotton puffs fell from the sky.

"Isn't it wonderful?" Susan turned around and around, her arms outstretched. "The space is divided." She strode over to one section. "Heather sculpts over here."

Little terra cotta girls held dolls, two little boys played marbles, a third boy held a joy stick and stared off into space. The statues were twelve inches high.

"She wants to do big work, but small sells better," Susan said. "And over there are Patty's collages, and here Judith throws her pots. Her kiln warms this place, but since she's not here I'll fire up the stove."

Annie hadn't noticed the stove or the basket of logs, pine cones and rolled paper next to it. Susan laid the fire without effort. Within minutes flames were consuming the paper and pine cones. Susan held her hands over the cold metal. "Give it a

49

minute." She pointed to the front. "When customers come in, they can also watch real artists working. Good marketing?"

Annie nodded as her mother continued the tour of the studio.

"The glass windows give great light, but heat escapes faster than a convict slipping out of a jail if the doors are left open. If we'd had more money we'd have bought double-paned glass, but we put everything into the gallery."

"Did you guys fix it up yourselves?" Annie wondered how hard it was for five women to agree to buy and renovate a place, but since her mother didn't recount any problems, maybe not all that hard.

"We sure did." Susan smiled. "What do you think?"

Annie thought she wished the stove worked faster. She kept on her down jacket, glistening with melted snow, but as an act of faith unzipped it. She'd never seen her mother so eager for approval. Susan had always carved out work space for herself wherever they lived, which sometimes was a corner of a bedroom. Her Geneva atelier was their basement. Although the windows looked out on the lawn leading down to the lake, it was dark and cramped. "An artist's dream. Where's your area?"

Susan led her daughter to an easel next to a bookcase holding paints, brushes, a few books, assorted colored papers, scrap material, and bits and pieces of tile. Frames were piled in one section, mirrors in another.

"What are the mirrors for?"

"I'll show you." Under a cloth was a series of paintings, all which included real mirrors: a woman stared at herself. Susan had painted a different image in the mirror than the person looking. "I'm exploring how women see themselves, how others see them."

"Darlink, it's like your mother. She never saw herself as a housewife, but as an artist. Don't you think her exploration of self-image wonderful?" Both women spun around as Magda strode toward them. She grabbed Susan first and then hugged Annie, who braced for an affection attack.

"I brought lunch." Magda swung a brown woven picnic basket, just missing the statue of the boy with the joy stick. The basket landed on a paint-encrusted table in the middle of the room. "Not to worry, Darlinks. I'll create a magic moment." She pulled out a faded yellow linen cloth to hide the table's crudiness, followed by a gray clay casserole still hot to the touch, causing her to blow on her fingers. In a swirl, dishes, wine, glasses, napkins, a vase with a single yellow rose, forks, knives and spoons appeared.

With a flourish worthy of a chef in a five-star hotel, she swished off the casserole cover to reveal white gloop. Annie had eaten enough strange dishes to withhold judgment. She also knew not to take great amounts of unknown dishes. However, her serving revealed eggs, potato, and sausages layered in a white sauce. Two bites into the dish she said, "This is wonderful."

"My mother cooked this for me when I was little. No sausage unless we'd just visited my grandparents in the countryside outside Budapest. Then *nagyapa,* my grampy would load us down with sausage he'd made, eggs, dried beef if a cow had died and jams. *Nagi,* my granny, made the best jams." Magda sucked her cheeks in memory of tastes gone by. She waved her fork as she talked and took great gulps of wine. "You." She pointed the fork at Annie. "Staying? Doing the history thing?" A droplet of white sauce escaped her lips.

"You know?"

"Darlink, this is a small town."

Magda didn't have to say anything more. Annie wondered who had said, "Every man is surrounded by a neighborhood of voluntary spies." It was true in Argelès. When she and Roger first dated and walked down her street with houses only a car-width apart, most neighbors had a sudden urge to shake rugs or hang out clothes to dry, including clothes that were dry to start with. Why should Caleb's Landing be different?

"Paul Mangone. Now he's a love, Darlinks. Isn't he, Susan? Forced into retirement. Too outspoken. Expected the kidlings to work too hard. Great on the School Committee, though."

"I don't really know him," Susan said. "We've chatted a few times at The Coffee Bean."

"I call that place The Boy Clubhouse." Although no one had asked, Magda put a large second helping on all their plates. "Trust me, Darlinks. Paul is a love. Happily married in this day and age. Imagine?" Magda took another mouthful but continued talking. "But Len Haskell. He is what you call a snake in the weeds."

"Why?" Annie asked. "Has anyone been cheated by him?"

Magda pursed her mouth and frowned. "Intuition."

Then Magda asked about the skeleton.

Annie repeated the story yet again. When she'd called the police station to ask about the skeleton, the cop on the desk referred her to the chief—who'd hung up on her. Forget it, she told herself, but herself argued back that she shouldn't. The next time I'm born, I want to be born imaginationless, she thought. Then she changed her mind.

After lunch Magda's sewing machine chugged in the background as Annie washed the dishes in the bathroom sink. When she came out, both women were so engrossed in their work that they paid no attention to her as she zipped her jacket. She debated slipping away, hesitating to interrupt them, but decided politeness was more important. "I'm outta here." Time to convince Roger that he should come for Christmas and to explain why she hadn't called or e-mailed.

CHAPTER 11

Tuesday, November 16

"I thought maybe America didn't have telephones." Roger's voice was soft, but he always lowered his voice when angry. Annie imagined him limping around his house as he talked, the phone tucked under his chin. By the sounds she suspected he was in the kitchen running water into the kettle. "And I've never known you not to e-mail as long as there's a computer in easy reach," he said.

"You're right," she said.

The line was static free, creating an international silence followed by a sharp intake of breath. "Excuse me, did you just say I was right?"

"*Bien sûr.* Because you are." She thought this was a good strategy: give in when wrong and save energy for other battles. One thing she loved about Roger was how she could be honest, saving the wasted time of emotional games. They might fight well into the night, but even when he disagreed with her to the marrow of his bones, he didn't stop loving her. Not like other men she'd been with who insisted she fit into their image of her or they would stop caring. He loved her in spite of herself, which didn't mean that he didn't sometimes try to mould her into the woman he wanted rather than the woman she was. At least he gave up gracefully.

"*Merci.*"

"*De rien.*" No need to concentrate on being wrong. "I think aliens have occupied my parents' bodies." She recapped her parents' new life, her father's friends and the history project.

Silence. It seemed like a long time before he spoke. "Sounds right for you, if—notice the word *if*—it doesn't take too long."

"Well my parents have invited you and Gaëlle for Christmas."

"Which means I won't see you for several weeks." His voice grew softer. "And who knows where your next assignment will be."

The more objections Roger put up, the more she wanted to tackle the project. "We've been separated longer. Imagine! I'll finally get paid for what I usually do for free."

He sighed. "I give up. I have to get used to a now-you-see-her-now-you-don't lover. I'll come for Christmas, but I don't like . . ."

"You don't have to finish," she said. Her frequent disappearances for her work and private research would always be their major point of contention. "I'll need to earn some money, so don't worry. I'll come home."

"Home," he said, "is where I am. And you earning money means you're somewhere in Europe. We don't need to make it different continents."

"Hmm," she said. The *hmm* contained the doubts that she still had about being part of a couple . . . not just with Roger but in general. She'd set up her life as she wanted it, and she wasn't sure how much she could sacrifice. They discussed the minutiae of their lives until she said, "I love you." That she didn't doubt. She told him about the skeleton.

"Sounds like sloppy police work," he said.

"Even if it is a skeleton from the nineteenth century?"

"They won't know until they test it," he said. "How long do you think it was down there?"

"According to my dad, probably since before Auntie Helen

bought the place in the late forties."

"Still sloppy police work, but small-town America . . ."

"And you're in small-town France . . ."

"But I used to be a Paris *flic*. That's big-time police work."
He took a sip of something. The noise came over the telephone
line. "With all that's been going on, I can understand you not
calling."

"It's still my fault. When I thought of it, it was too late, and
believe it or not I haven't checked my e-mail since I arrived."

"Voice on the telephone, have you stolen my Annie?"

Annie laughed. "Okay, okay. Now put Gaëlle on, *s'il te plaît,
mon grand flic.*"

"C'est vrai?" Gaëlle asked. *"Nous allons Les Etats-Unis?"*

Annie assured her that it was true: they would be together in
the States for Christmas. They chatted about the unfairness of
Gaëlle's geometry teacher, the latest Patrick Fiori CD, what her
arch-enemy Amelie had said about her and Gaëlle's revenge
plan. Annie wanted to introduce Gaëlle to those adults who
complained that teenagers didn't communicate to adults.

Dave came into the kitchen from the basement as she hung
up the phone. Dirt streaked his face and cobwebs added gray to
his hair. He emptied a bucket of water the color of charcoal in
the sink.

"Roger and Gaëlle are coming," she said.

"It'll be good for them to see your roots."

Annie wasn't sure about how deep her roots were. How much
had her personality been shaped by her parents' New England
heritage, and how much came from the different places she'd
lived?

What she was sure of was Roger's and her parents' relationship. He was fifteen years older than Annie was and only fifteen
years younger than Dave and Susan were. Her parents liked the
widower. They felt sorry that his first wife had been murdered

as much as they admired the way he had made a new start as the Argelès police chief, choosing the village to give his daughter a more stable environment. The bond had grown so strong sometimes Annie worried that her parents might side with him against her.

Stupid, she told herself. I should be happy they approve of him. They hadn't liked her previous lover, a French business-man driven by his need to be successful. Come to think of it, Annie hadn't liked him much either. Her parents accepted him as they did all her friends male and female, but Annie read their views in their body language, which was louder than spoken words.

She nodded toward the basement door. "Why'd Aunt Helen hate it so?"

"Said it gave her the creeps. Each summer when I came, she said that was the summer we would clean it out together, but she always found better things to do."

"And you never forced her?"

"What kid does chores when they can be off with their bud-dies?" He rummaged in a drawer and pulled out a screwdriver. He thumped down the cellar stairs.

She followed, holding onto the banister as she placed her feet between the holes and loose boards. "Now I know why the word *rickety* was created."

Dave had jury-rigged the old lamp on the beam that ran the length of the house. The light threw shadows, giving credence to Auntie Helen's opinion of creepy. Without all the junk she could see half the floor was dirt, the other half lumpy and cracked cement. Two tiny windows on the front side of the house were no wider than Annie's two hands thumb to thumb with the fingers spread. Thick stems from unknown plants blocked whatever sunlight might make its way through them— assuming it was a sunny day, which this day definitely was not.

"What's your goal?" she asked.

"Clean it up, put down a cement floor, paint the walls, buy some new furniture."

"I meant for today."

"Wash the walls enough to paint them."

"What can I do to help?"

"Nothing for now. Go read the history book Len brought over." As Annie walked upstairs, her father asked, "Want to go to coffee with me and the guys in a couple of hours?"

"Why not?"

CHAPTER 12

Tuesday, November 16

Charlie and Paul stood as Annie and Dave Young walked into The Coffee Bean. The rest of the tables were empty. Clouds raced across the sky.

Dave looked nothing like the imitation coal miner of a half hour ago. His hair was freshly washed. He had changed into clean jeans and a sweatshirt that said *Caleb's Landing, MA* over a picture of the fishing shack.

"Annie, what did you think of the book?" Paul asked. "You did have a chance to look at it, despite all the excitement?"

"I did and it's incredible. Such an insight into the Pilgrims' minds."

"There's one place where a person talks about a young man doing it with animals," Dave said.

"However, we won't include that in a kid's history book," Annie said.

Charlie leaned forward. "Then you'll accept."

Annie held up her hands. "Not so fast. All I've done is to get my boyfriend to agree to come for Christmas."

Charlie took a pen from his pocket and picked up a napkin. The corner was stained with coffee. He wrote something and handed it to Annie. "Would this convince you to do it?"

She read the figure: $6,000. She frowned.

"Not enough?" he asked.

Annie's billing rate was usually $55–80 an hour. That allowed her to meet her expenses and take time for her own research. Although American history wasn't her specialty, she would be paid to do what she loved best—research. She would be paid for what she loved second best—write. Despite telling herself she wouldn't get involved, she had already mentally sketched out the script making the story interactive on a CD-ROM. She wanted to do more than give them a rough manuscript. She wanted to see the project completed.

She delved into her pocketbook and pulled out her fountain pen and wrote $9,000 on the napkin. The paper absorbed the ink, making the figure look fuzzy. "This is for delivery of a completed CD-ROM."

Charlie shook Annie's hand. She figured that they would negotiate and she would have been happy with the $6,000 but she had learned not to sell herself cheaply. Wow! A vacation where she made money on having fun.

Len walked in and sat down. "Not too late, am I? Annie, what did you think of the book?"

They recapped the discussion for him before launching into a discussion of his latest date.

Walking back to the house, Annie asked, "Len is quite a ladies' man, isn't he?" She needed to watch her footing on the icy dark brick sidewalks.

"He dates a lot. His first wife deserted him, and he had two live-in women that didn't work out."

The street lamps flicked on, only slightly improving the lighting.

"But he seems so charming."

Dave shrugged. "Maybe he makes lousy choices."

"Can Charlie afford $9,000?"

"Is that what you asked for?"

"Yup."

"You should have asked for more. He's a millionaire, but lives very modestly."

"Bit player philanthropist?" she asked.

"Yup."

They jumped as someone poked them in the back. They turned to see Susan. With her camel's hair coat buttoned to the neck and a scarf wrapped around her head she looked as if she would be more at home on the streets of Damascus than Caleb's Landing. "Hey guys, can I buy you dinner?"

"Sure. But after that I have to get back to work on the basement."

"And I need to tackle the book. Since Roger doesn't like the idea of my staying after Christmas, I must get it done before he comes."

Her mind played with ideas. She pictured herself as a little girl living in Plymouth.

The spring earth smelled muddy. A new baby, the first born to the Pilgrims since they landed, cried in the house. An Indian stood at the door. She stared at his skin. No one she knew showed so much skin. Even in hot weather, people were covered head to toe. Without thinking she reached for the cap covering her curls.

Before the Indian spoke, Annie brought herself back to the present and looked at her father. "Stop smirking, Dad."

"I was just thinking of how I'm going to work on the basement this evening."

"Right," Susan and Annie said together.

CHAPTER 13

Tuesday, November 23

"So what does the new police chief say?" Charlie Tucker asked. The regular group—Charlie, Len, Paul, Dave and the newest member, Annie—were not at The Coffee Bean but in a small conference room in Len's real estate offices.

"I was shocked when I heard that the old chief just walked away from his desk, packed up his car and took off," Charlie said. "Left an 'I quit' note on his desk."

"Gotta admit a couple of times when I was at DEC, I had the fantasy of doing it," Dave said, "but it passed."

"We lucked out in getting a temp in fast," Len said.

"Will he be made permanent?" Dave asked.

"Let's just say the situation is highly charged at the moment." Len leaned back in his chair. "He looks good, but some of the guys already on the force want the job." He smoothed his hair. "However, this guy looks really good on paper. Let's see what he does."

Annie knew after working in places all over Europe that office politics were a bug-a-bear. Another thing she loved about her lifestyle was that she never really got embroiled in them. Had she been stuck in an office she wouldn't be here at this minute looking around the room that was painted institutional white with prints of American Civil War uniforms on the walls. Each had a simple silver frame. Venetian blinds kept the sunlight from overpowering the room. They were seated around a light oak table with matching chairs.

"The new guy thinks it was a slave. A runaway," Dave said. "Didn't seem much more concerned than the old chief, considering it happened a long time ago."

"Probably more worried about the kids that have been vandalizing houses around here."

"The remnants of the dress are what a slave might have worn and the diary points in that direction," Annie said.

"Diary?" Len asked.

"We found a diary with her along with a pen and some matching empty paper, plus a dried-up ink bottle. Wish I'd had a chance to read it completely."

"Fancy that," Len said. As always he was what Susan Young would call sharp-looking. Today he wore beige corduroy pants and a dark brown pullover. A silk scarf, a paisley of browns and beige, was draped around his neck. "So what happened to it?"

"The old chief took it," Dave said. "Although I assume he didn't take it with him wherever he went to. The medical examiner never saw it, but like I told you, she didn't treat it like a crime scene because of the clothes and the length of time the skeleton had been there," Dave said.

"Imagine escaping from slavery only to die alone in a little room so far from anything she knew," Annie said.

The men were silent.

"Dad told me the chest had been in place since he was a boy. He was sure Auntie Helen didn't even know the secret room was there," Annie said.

"If she had she would probably have let us use it as some kind of clubhouse," Charlie said.

Len Haskell moved forward in his seat. "I would love to look at the diary. In fact, I think I'll ask the chief for a copy. Could be the source for another CD. What do you think, Annie?"

"I was able to glance at it, and yes it would be, but only if I can work on it from home." When the men smiled, she said, "Home for me is France."

"Still can't persuade her to live here, Dave?" Charlie Tucker asked.

"Well, Susan and I haven't decided ourselves." Dave glanced at his daughter.

"The way your wife has set up with those women artists, I'd say the husband is the last to know," Charlie said.

There was a knock at the door. Len's daughter-in-law entered bearing a tray with cups and saucers, a silver coffeepot and a plate of bakery cookies shaped as turkeys and frosted in chocolate and orange frosting to mimic miniature versions of the real thing.

"Anything else?" Melissa placed the tray on a side table that had a number of folders bearing the names of deals awaiting mortgage approval.

"Nothing, thanks, Melissa." Annie noticed that like in Europe, secretaries were often considered part of the furnishing, not worthy of hellos, thanks or good-byes. The girl looked pale, but then she was in the seventh month of pregnancy. She wore a loose green corduroy jumper over a white turtleneck sweater and boots. Her hair hung in a long brown braid down her back. Annie had turned down three requests to go shopping. "Melissa, if you haven't any lunch plans, want to grab something to eat with me?"

Melissa looked at her father-in-law.

"Your husband will be showing houses to the Bronners."

"I'd love to," Melissa said. "Oh, and Charlie, your office called to have me tell you that the costume place will deliver your Santa suit on Tuesday. They've scheduled a fitting before Thanksgiving."

Charlie swigged his coffee. "Ho, ho, ho." He opened the huge black book that was the major source of Annie's work to the

Defense of the Synod of Dort. "How do you decide what to include?"

"Certainly not the dry parts if we want to attract kids. I've the beginning of a CD-ROM prototype to show you." She ignored the men's grins as she plugged in her laptop and attached it to the projector. "And remember it is only a prototype."

Len turned the handle until the blinds were as tight as he could make them. Paul doused the lights.

A boy and girl dressed in somber gray appeared on the screen. "These aren't the final graphics. I got kids next door to do the initial poses in costume that one of Mom's arty-farty friends whipped up."

"Magda?" Len asked.

Annie nodded.

"The bitch finally did something useful," Len said.

Annie ignored his comment. Obviously their feelings for each other were identical. "Then I took out the shadows to make these flat characters. I'll be able to manipulate them. Also by changing hair color, we can have more boys and girls that viewers can choose to be. I need to do Indian children, too." She placed the youngsters against a background of a wooden house that could have been built in the 1620s. "I've talked to Plimouth Plantation and several historians. The museum was great in sending me photos. They're interested in the project. I've an appointment to talk to them after Roger and Gaëlle come so they can see it too. And the historians have filled in even more details to make sure I don't have the kids looking at television."

"Won't it be too late? I mean, when they come?" Charlie asked.

"Not really. They can verify if I've been accurate. Then I'll tweak where necessary, and I'm outta here." She flipped through several screens. "However, back to the concept. Kids can choose between scenarios. For example, Nathaniel's mother dies or his father is later killed by Indians, which means he has to apprentice to others. But if his mother dies, he gets a stepmom and has to do more chores around the farm. Edward's parents build a house and are quite successful, relatively speaking."

"Sounds complicated," Paul says. "But I never got into computers. My kids would know."

"Now look, they can also build a house step-by-step, or plant a field." She clicked the computer: trees fell, bark hacked off, and planks smoothed. In the field corn was planted three kernels to a mound of dirt and began their growth as a calendar elapsed. "Here's a section where they shoot a deer and skin it."

"A bit graphic," Paul said as the deer closed its eyes and bled into the ground.

"Most kids don't know where their food comes from other than a supermarket. You wanted it to be real," she said. "We'll have a section on King Phillip's War from the settler *and* Indian perspectives."

"I can't believe you did all this in a week," Charlie said.

"She's worked day and night," Dave said. "I can barely get to my computer to check e-mails."

"I work hard when I work," Annie said. "I talked to Kendra Jones at the grade school. She teaches fifth grade. When I'm further along, her kids will test the project, content, artwork, etc. The only thing I'm not that good in is computer graphics. You might want to consider a professional artist to improve it."

"I'm impressed with what I've seen so far," Charlie said. "I think this girl is underpaid."

"If you want to pay more, it is okay," Annie said.

"Ho, ho, ho," Charlie said. "Will I sound okay as I sail into the harbor on Saturday?"

"Great," they said.

CHAPTER 14

Tuesday, November 23

"Am I walking too fast?" Annie asked Melissa as they headed to the Lobster Shack.

"No, I just get winded easily." They opened the door to the restaurant, which was anything but a shack. The walls were wood paneled with natural pine and the tables were a baby blue washed pine. Each one was set up with blue scalloped paper placemats. Blue paper napkins were stuffed into water glasses and fanned to look like flowers.

The hostess greeted Melissa by name then turned to Annie. "You must be Dave Young's girl. How's the history project going?"

Annie was taken aback for a moment, but remembered that in Argelès if she sneezed, someone on the other side of town said *santé*.

"I'm Paul Mangone's daughter, that's how I know," the hostess said. "Ashley." She shook Annie's hand and then handed the women menus. "I'll give you a seat by the window."

The view was equal to The Coffee Bean's but had a small pebbly beach. A little boy in yellow boots and a snowsuit carried a red pail and squatted to add shells and stones to his collection. He held up one to a young woman, whom Annie guessed was his nanny or a very young mother. "What's good?"

Melissa smiled. "My favorite is the lobster roll, but if you're cold, there's clam or fish chowder."

Although Annie wore jeans, a heavy sweater and boots, the damp sea air had left her chilled. "Fish chowder. Mom makes it New England style. I can check to see how authentic a job she does."

"It must be glamorous to live in Europe," Melissa said after they ordered. "My husband doesn't like to travel. He says we have everything we want right here."

"It's pretty nice here," Annie said.

"And after the baby comes, he wants me to stay home. My world is getting smaller and smaller." She sighed. "But we need my salary."

Annie reached out and laid her hand on the girl's arm, but withdrew it equally quickly when Melissa flinched. Probably didn't like open shows of affection. The waitress brought them two glasses of tomato juice with a slice of lemon slashed and balanced on the rim of the glass.

During the meal both women tried to find an area of mutual interest. Annie had no interest in shopping or brand names. She refrained from giving Melissa her favorite lecture that wearing a brand name was like providing free advertising for a company. Melissa didn't read that much but watched TV. When she said she loved *Grey's Anatomy,* a common bond for the series and McDreamy was forged.

"We must go to the movies," Annie said after Melissa said her husband didn't like films.

"I'd love to, but he doesn't like me out of the house when I'm not working."

"How'd you meet him?" Annie asked.

"At UMass Amherst. He was a senior. I was a freshman. I was raised in Three Creeks, although a stream and two puddles would be a better name." When Annie looked confused, Melissa said, "It's not far from Springfield."

Annie learned in detail about Jason Haskell spotting Melissa at a dance, how after that she'd spent every spare second with him until they married the day after he graduated then moved to Caleb's Landing where he joined his father's real estate agency.

"Does your family miss you?"

"My parents died when I was little. Car crash. My aunt and uncle raised me. They belonged to a small church and thought I'd go to hell if I had sex even after marriage." The laugh was anything but joking. "Jason is the first person I remember loving me. And he wants me as close to him as possible." The girl looked out the window. "It's the first time anyone ever cared where I was or whom I was with."

Without saying anything aloud Annie compared Jason to Roger, who objected when she wanted to go to another country to work for extended periods of time, but when they were both in the village didn't care who she was out with or when. Now he was getting used to her going to Zurich, Paris or Frankfurt for a few weeks or months at a time. He had learned e-mail and instant messaging. Of course, Roger was in his forties when she had met him, a widower, not a kid fresh from school.

"Jason works so much that we haven't had time to develop any friends. I need someone to go baby clothes shopping with. Jason won't let me go alone."

Annie didn't know any women who were "let" do things by their husbands.

"I was hoping you'd be my friend," Melissa said. Her face flushed and she twiddled the stem of her water glass.

"I can always use another friend, but I won't be here that long. My life is in Europe."

"Europe," Melissa sighed. "Paris, London. I always imagined going to the top of the Eiffel Tower, and drinking coffee in a café like Hemingway. I saw it in a made-for-TV movie. The rest of the movie was boring. Jason wants me to watch TV with him, except he's usually so tired, he falls asleep."

Annie wondered what harm one shopping trip would do. It would be an act of kindness. *Only if she asks again.* She prayed Melissa wouldn't.

They paid the bill. As they passed the ladies room, Melissa stopped. "I'll leave you here."

"See you soon," Annie said. She was halfway out the door when she decided that Melissa had the right idea. Roger's nickname for her, Bitty Bladder, was based on reality.

When she shoved the ladies room door open, the first thing she saw were sinks and toilets from the forties. The large green and black square linoleum looked as old, but the liquid soap was modern, sending the aroma of almonds through the enclosed space.

Melissa stood at the sink washing her hands. The girl had rolled up the sleeves of her white sweater. Both forearms were black and blue, not slightly, but completely like someone who had tattooed all the skin. She quickly lowered her sleeves.

Annie had already seen that. She pulled them back up. "Who did this to you?"

"Annie, I am such a klutz. I keep bumping . . ."

Annie looked at the girl debating whether to let it go or not. "Melissa, if you need help, you can call on me anytime."

CHAPTER 15

I be standing in the garden. The sun be not quite overhead when Molly, the Two Pine cook, says "Mathilde" so loud I almost hits my head on the sky.

"Don't do that," I says crosser than good sense should tell me to be. Molly ain't someone to get angry if you wants to eat good. If she be happy with you, extra food from the kitchen sometimes walks into your house. But if she be unhappy with you, that food goes someplace else.

"The Mistress wants to see your skinny body. Now."

Me? I follows Molly through the kitchen that is bigger than our cabin. A lump of bread dough floats on a pile of flour in the middle of a table. A pot boils giving off smells that makes my stomach jump in joy until I realizes that it will never meets my stomach.

We goes through the dining room with a table and five and three chairs. Five be as high as I can count so when I gets there I starts in again. The Mistress be in the parlor. She looks up from the book when we walks in.

"Here she be," Molly says.

"Thank you, Molly. Sit down, Mathilde." Her words be hard to understand. It be like she cuts them off in the back of the mouth.

"I am going to need a maid. Are you interested?"

"I don't knowd nothing about how." I didn't just says it, I stammers it. Slaves don't get choices about whats they wants to do, although the Massas be apt to put them to work at things they be good at.

"Of course you don't, but you strike me as a smart girl, one who learns quickly."

I looks closely at her. Her eyes looks as if there were tears behind them. Later I learnt the tears were always there and that just having white skin don't makes happiness, but that day I didn't knowd that. All I could think of be I'd be a house niggah. No more working in the hot sun, rain or cold.

"You'll need to sleep in the house in case I need you during the night."

I never sleeps no place but by my family and in the hospital three nights when that snake done bite me. In the rain my bed be under a drip. "I'll try really hard, Mistress."

"Good, first thing, you will need to take a bath and get into some decent clothes. Maids don't look like ragamuffins."

Molly grumbles as we puts more and more water into the tub. Then she hands me the bucket. "You do it. I ain't breaking my back for the likes of you, I don't care what Mistress Elizabeth says."

That be the first time I'd ever been in a tub. I takes baths in the river watching for water moccasins. My mother says snakes loves black skin so I goes in and out so fast the water forgets to ripple.

When I be done, Molly brings me a dress like I never seen before on a slave, even on Molly, the only other house niggah.

When I be dressed, I goes to the Mistress.

"Now, let's teach you how to iron my clothes," she says. "And you have to be careful not to burn them, because it takes forever to get more from England. We'll start with my nightdress. At least new ones can be easily made."

"My Mama will wonder where I be."

"Well go tell her then, but hurry back."

I rushes out of the house. Mama be in the garden. She walks up to me and slaps me hard across my face. "Where you disappear to, girl? There be work to do." Then she steps back. "Where you get those clothes?"

71

When I tells her, she smiles. I kisses her on the cheek, something I never does. I rushes back to the house to learn how to iron.

CHAPTER 16

Tuesday, November 23

Annie entered her mother's studio on the way back to the house. She wanted to talk to her about Melissa. Sun poured into the room giving a warmth that contrasted to the chilliness that pervaded the walls last time. Damn. Magda was there.

Magda looked up from her sewing machine. Cloth patches were piled in helter-skelter piles around her work area. A quilt that resembled a half-finished Matisse painting was laid on the table. Before Annie could say how incredible the project was, Magda jumped up, knocking her chair over and sweeping Annie into her arms. "Hello, Darlink. Come to see your mother? Look, look at her beautiful work."

Susan put down her brush and ran her hand through her blond spiked hair, leaving a small dab of sea foam green. "What have you been up to?"

"I met with the guys. They like what I've done so far. Hopefully, I'll be through by the time Roger and Gaëlle get here."

"Be careful before they capture you in their plans to do all of American history. Roger will never get you back. Unless of course it means more to you than he does."

This was not the mother who fit her work around her family. Annie's friends staying over, Dave's business dinners and travels. This was the first time Annie ever knew her mother to make her own work a priority. Yet despite that, wherever they lived there had been an area dedicated as her mother's studio that was

73

sacrosanct. No one went in, but Susan always came out when called.

Until now Annie hadn't wondered what her mother missed. So many accompanying spouses weren't allowed to work by foreign permit systems. Some, like her mother, painted, others wrote. They volunteered in schools and for charities. Some drank. Others gave up and went home to find their own lives. Annie wanted to ask Susan what her sacrifice scale had been, if she'd been happy at all. Did she realize what she missed only when she came back and found her own place with like-minded women?

Magda set a copper tea kettle on the wood-burning stove. "Wimpy tea like your mother, Darlink, or do you want a really good Hungarian coffee, strong enough to put hair on your chest?"

"I'm a wimp like Mom."

Annie perched on a stool drinking her tea while Magda and Susan went back to work, stopping periodically to blow on their drinks. Susan and Annie's tea were in mugs that said *Caleb's Landing, MA* and had pictures of the fisherman's shack on it. When Magda poured her coffee into a demitasse the liquid looked thick enough to spoon up like pudding.

"I've invited Magda for Thanksgiving," Susan said. "I'm so excited. It's a real holiday this year."

"You made it a real holiday every year," Annie said. She inhaled the mint fumes wafting from her cup. "I remember the smells coming from the kitchen when I came home from school on Thanksgiving."

"Sometimes we postponed it until the weekend, especially if Dave was traveling. It's not the same thing as having the Macy's Thanksgiving Day Parade and football games on the television, and everyone popping in and out of the kitchen," Susan said.

Annie hopped off the perch to hug her mother. For the first

time she realized her mother had been trying to recapture something from her childhood with those faux Thanksgivings that Annie took as her real ones. Had they had this conversation five years ago, she would have felt unsettled by her mother's confusion. Now she took it as what it was. Her roots were not geographic nor were they national or even linguistic. Her roots were in the strength, love and memories her family had provided her over the years. However, the recognition wasn't going to stop her from wanting her parents to live within drop-in distance. Drop-in could be a loose term, defined as within eight hours—eight land hours, not eight airline hours.

"Your mother has been talking about pumpkin and apple pie." Magda smacked her lips.

"I'm glad you're coming, Magda. By the way, I had lunch with Melissa. She still needs someone to go shopping with. Speaking of that, can you do the food shopping?" Susan went to her denim shoulder bag. She took out a roll of toilet paper, a box of new pastels, a newspaper clipping, scissors, cough drops, a dish, a sewing kit, bandages, an *Evita* CD and *The Essential Bach,* an electrical cord and a legal pad of paper. She rummaged through several pages that Annie knew had random jottings, sketches and notes, tore out one and handed it to Annie. "Imagine just being able to get a whole turkey." She turned to Magda. "In Geneva they sold parts, but to get a whole one required a special order. And it couldn't be too big, because the ovens are small. I jumped for joy when I saw the size of the stove at Dave's aunt's."

Magda had swallowed her coffee in a single gulp. "Your mother and I talk much about food as we work. Food is art too. Sensual. We talk until we're famished."

Three more women walked in. They were dressed in jeans and splattered paint shirts. "Annie Darlink, meet the rest of our group, Heather, Judith and Patty," Magda said.

Annie decided to wait to talk to her mother about Melissa until they were alone.

CHAPTER 17

When Annie left, Magda went back to cutting a Matisse-shaped nude bather from a piece of purple silk. The deadline for her commission to do a Matisse quilt from a Boston designer was much too close. Stupid designers. Good art needs time. Quilt making was rapidly replacing her dress designing as her major source of business, the last having sold for $10,000. Life was a series of connections, one melding into another.

This studio was more than a connection. It was a whole map. Bringing all these talented women together and putting them under one roof, that was her miracle. Now if only their work could sell during the season. Her tiny scissors had gold-winged handles, not like regular cloth-cutting scissors, forcing her to work slowly. When she cut out anything as graceful as the nude figure, she wanted the color to penetrate her eyes, the smoothness of the silk to caress her skin.

Creating art was like making love. Lord knows she had had enough lovers in her day. Her mother, God rest her soul, had been a devout Catholic despite the Communists ruling Hungary. How she had pleaded with her daughter to keep her virginity. In a different time Magda was sure she would have sent her to a convent. Thank you, Communism. Saved from a convent.

Her scissors rounded the head, leaving space for seaming. She mentally ran through her list of lovers dividing them into

77

nationalities: Hungarian, Romanian, German, Yugoslavian, French, Italian, American. Fifty-three. One for every year in her life. Among the Görans, Olafs, Pietrs, Pierres, Matts and Brians there were a smattering of Annas and Joans. That was a separate but smaller list.

If she found a hundred women she might sleep with one but like ninety. If she found a hundred men she might sleep with five and like one. At least two she would hate for their violence. Shortly before she left Budapest, a lover slapped her. She had kicked his balls, and while he was down broke two of his ribs. Other women lacked her strength physically and mentally.

Snip, snip—the scissors cut around the leg. Magda knew that she could only live the way she wanted to, never kowtowing to others. She also knew she needed to make a difference in women's lives. To those whom much is given, much is expected, she thought. Not original but so heartfelt.

Her emergency cell phone rang *Amazing Grace*. If she were working she would ignore her other cell or her land line—never this one. A female voice said, "Magda, we need you now."

"The usual pickup place, Darlink?"

"Yes, take her to the safehouse in Maine."

"I'm on my way, Darlink." She looked across the studio to where Susan dabbed tiny brushstrokes on the face of the Goddess she was creating. In the past few months Magda had seen progress in her new partner's work. Heather, Patty and Judith were not as lost in their mediums. They let their families encroach on their work, but when they were all there working together, the air was as charged with creativity as if a lightning bolt had broken through the window.

"I'm going out and won't be back. Susan, see you for dinner Thursday, if not before."

CHAPTER 18

Tuesday, November 23

Annie should have been concentrating on her driving, but her consciousness had disappeared into an Indian girl's who wanted to hunt.

How frustrating to be told to tend the small tribal gardens. Her father and brothers had ignored her when she watched them make arrows. Now hers, made in secret, were better than theirs.

What next? Annie wasn't sure where to go from there. Maybe she was wrong to impose her 21st-century feminist values on a 17th-century Indian girl.

She pulled the family car into the driveway. The seat and floor were hidden by the paper grocery bags filled with the contents for Thanksgiving dinner.

Parked by the curb was an old Mustang with rust dominating the white paint. The driver behind the wheel stared at her parents' house.

All she wanted to do was to unpack the bags and call the Wampanoag historian who was acting as her consultant to verify the accuracy of her new scenario.

Definitely an up and down day: a good meeting on her CD-ROM was followed by a tasty lunch, although the sight of Melissa's bruises worried her. Her discomfort about the life of the young girl contrasted with a satisfaction about her own. Her stop at her mother's studio had left her with a warm feeling, substantiating that to be truly happy a woman had to have meaningful work, and each woman had to define meaningful for herself. The downside was she hadn't had a chance to speak with her mother alone.

The shopping trip had worn her out. Did anyone need so many choices? God, just trying to find plain oatmeal was enough to send a person screaming from the store. She regretted spreading the joke that a person knew they had lived in Switzerland too long when they thought it was normal to only have one brand of everything at the supermarket. Oh, to be back to just one brand!

Had she been a housewife in Plimouth in 1621 preparing the First Thanksgiving, she would have had to kill the turkey, pluck it, churn the butter then melt it to pour on bread she'd baked to stuff the bird while worrying about her family not becoming religious fanatics. That would be how she would have thought of her husband who insisted on coming to this desolate land with the rocky soil. It would be dark before she could settle with a book to read in the flickering light from the candle that she also had made. But what book? The Bible? Probably, or a series of John Edwards's dreadful sermons. She needed to double-check the timeline on Thanksgiving versus John Edwards preaching. No sermons on the CD. No need to bore the children to death, although she planned to have something on the long Sundays in church. Make them grateful for computer games and running free.

A car door slammed. Annie saw the man approach. He wore stiff jeans, a soft brown suede jacket and an Irish knit sweater. His leather boots had been shined to a point where they would pass any Army inspection. He put his money on his back, not in his transportation. That car was bordering on antique.

"Let me help you." He didn't look dangerous, but neither had Ted Bundy.

"I've no idea who you are," Annie said. She glanced toward

the street to see if anyone was around. No kids played in their yards. Come to think of it, she never saw kids playing outside like she had growing up. Kids did live here. She saw them getting in and out of cars mornings and evenings.

A truck with the words *Lappin Plumbing* pulled up behind the Mustang. The woman next door stormed out to meet him. "About time you got here. I took the first part of the afternoon off from work, and I had to call in and say I wouldn't be back." She stood with her hands on her hips.

The plumber hefted his tool box. "Sorry lady, sometimes the projects don't go as I want them."

"Let me show you a little invention." She pulled a cell phone from her pocket.

"She should learn you get more flies with honey than vinegar," the Mustang owner said.

"And the plumber should show up on time. Who are you?" she asked again.

The man reached into his inside breast pocket and pulled out a small silver card case. "Freelance Journalist Des O'Flaherty at your service." He swept into a bow without his blue eyes breaking contact with Annie's.

"And?"

"I'm following up on your skeleton."

"Not my personal skeleton, and it was a one-day news story," she said to his back. He was toting two bags to the house. "Hey, stop."

"I'm doing the sugar bit."

"Which means you think of me as the fly," Annie said.

"It means I want to talk to you, get some background on the house. The medical examiner hasn't done much with the skeleton except to guess she was strangled. There's a broken hyoid. It's a bone." Des put his hand to his throat and made a chocking sound.

"Charming."

"Right now the medical examiner is swamped. Seems an unusual number of nursing home deaths are happening. They've bodies stacked up so she kicked the skeleton over to the forensic anthropologist who is on holiday."

Annie decided not to tell him that was where the skeleton was assigned anyway.

"I certainly can't do anything about it."

"But it was this house."

"My father just inherited it. Before that it belonged to my great aunt. I've no idea before that."

"A Simon Howell owned it. And before that his father. That takes us back to about 1910. Miscellaneous families owned it before that. In the early 1800s when the Underground Railroad was active it belonged to a family called Thorndike."

"So the diary was genuine."

"Diary?"

"We found a diary with the skeleton. Seems to have been written by a slave with bad handwriting and worse grammar." Annie wished she'd read it from beginning to end. She liked to read almost anything that was original to a period. That poor girl must have arrived in the middle of the night and been ushered down those narrow stairs. Perhaps Mr. or maybe Mrs. Thorndike led the way, holding a candle. If she arrived in winter, it would have been cold, but if she arrived in summer the basement would have offered protection from the heat. The runaway would have walked by barrels of apples and potatoes, jars of canned goods and maybe dried fish hanging from the rafters. Mr. Thorndike could have been a fisherman or a merchant in the village.

Annie touched her throat. The girl must have felt claustrophobic as the door swung shut and she heard the chest being moved, locking her in. She might have imagined Thorndike going for the authorities. Maybe she'd been hungry. There were no dishes found, but the Thorndikes could have cleared those away. Material goods were too hard to come by to leave with a corpse.

Annie could see her dipping her pen in the inkwell and writing to pass the hours until she would be on the route to Canada, hoarding the candlelight, afraid to ask for another or even a little water. When the girl lay in bed did she hear mice or rats— no, because they would have eaten the apples and potatoes.

What did she think when the chest was pushed aside and the door opened? Annie pictured Mr. Thorndike in a nightshirt, swaying from too much rum. It could just as easily have been beer or hard cider. Trying to prove Thorndike raped the runaway slave would be impossible without tissue. The girl pushed him away. He fell back. Her refusal infuriated him. His hands closed around her neck, applying more and more pressure. She tugged at his hands, but he was too strong. As it became harder and harder to breath she knew she could no longer fight and her body went limp.

What had Thorndike felt? Was he shocked at his own behavior? At least he was safe, for no one knew about the room dug into the soil under the house.

"Did you get to read the diary, Ms., Ms. . . . ?"

Annie brought herself back to the 21st century. "Excuse me . . ."

"Did you read the diary, Ms. . . ."

"Young, Annie. No, but I would love to. I fancy myself a bit of an amateur historian."

"What happened to it?"

"I guess the police have it."

Dave Young walked up to them. "And who do we have here?"

Des O'Flaherty stuck out his hand. "I'm a freelance reporter and I've been explaining to Ms. Young here that I think there may be a story in your skeleton."

Dave straightened his shoulders. "We don't have any information, and I suggest if you want more, you talk to the police."

"Cheeky fellow," Dave said. He and his daughter were now inside. All the bags were piled on the kitchen table, chairs and counter. Annie handed the things to her father who tried to locate places for them in the already filled cabinets and refrigerator.

"Handsome."

"Black Irish. Roger wouldn't like you ogling another man."

"Ogling is okay. Acting on it is a no-no. Dad, you think we could get a copy of that diary?"

"Why?"

"It would make a great second CD-ROM." When she saw her father's look, Annie added, "Which I will do from home. My home."

CHAPTER 19

Saturday, November 27

The aroma of turkey soup simmering on the stove hit Annie as soon as she walked into the kitchen. Piles of carrots and celery waiting to be chopped were to one side.

"This will be so good." Susan held a piece of bread in her mouth as she chopped onions. She swore it stopped the fumes from making her cry.

"Aren't you going to see Santa arrive by boat?" Annie asked.

"Nope. I've been at the studio every day this week except for Thanksgiving, so I'm catching up on laundry and cleaning." She scooped the pile of onions into the large pot and gave it a stir. "It'll be a nice peaceful day. Your dad is already gone."

Annie had half been planning to continue working on the CD-ROM, have a nice long messaging session with Roger, but a look at her mother's face led to an instant decision to go see Santa. She always liked local events and festivals, be it carnivals, parades or the Geneva Escalade with its medieval costumes. Local events done by local people. "Maybe I will go," she said.

"Bundle up. There's a cold wind off the water." Susan attacked the celery with her knife.

CHAPTER 20

Saturday, November 27

"Come on, O'Flaherty. Give me a break. One Irishman to another. I'm new on the job." The acting Caleb's Landing Chief of Police sat forward in his chair and rested his hands on his desk, which had a stack of folders to his left. The name Tim Doherty was pasted over a metal nameplate.

Des O'Flaherty, notebook in hand, sat opposite him. Years of practice allowed him to read upside-down the handwriting on the desk blotter of the last police chief who had walked off the job last week. The words, "life is too short," were written over and over around sketches of trees, boats, fish and circles.

"Last chief couldn't take it?" O'Flaherty asked.

"Said the politics got to him. Took off and is heading to Florida to buy a fishing boat."

"So where did they get you so fast? You aren't local."

"Powers that be figured they needed someone from outside. A few phone calls were made, I was job hunting . . ." Doherty passed his hand around the room.

"Will you have trouble with the current force?"

"None of them seem thrilled with an outsider. Let's face it, there's not much chance for promotion on a small force like Caleb's Landing's."

"You want the job?" O'Flaherty asked.

Doherty shrugged. "Off the record? Not sure I do or don't. I'd be happy to be caught up."

O'Flaherty could have asked about the plague of cottage vandalism, which looked like the work of teenagers, maybe seniors from the local high school. Each year some senior prank drove the local police crazy, but he wanted the story about the skeleton. The Boston papers hadn't shown much interest, but if he could come up with something spectacular, they would buy it. He had a gut feeling, and his feelings were more often right than wrong.

Long ago he decided working for one paper was not for him. He detested the behind-the-desk battles and jockeying for assignments. He understood the former chief wanting to take off. Hats off to him, he thought. Most people don't have the guts to cut loose. Not fair, a little voice said to him. Most people have kids, mortgages. They aren't willing to pay the price that the rent will be late, and that their cars look like someone stole them from a junk yard.

"All I want is a copy of the diary," Des said.

"Negative."

"Chief, it isn't like it's a current investigation." The reporter leaned on the chief's desk.

The chief sat back in his chair. "You're a pain in the ass, you know that?"

O'Flaherty flashed a smile that had women falling at his feet, but didn't do much for police chiefs. "My mother used to say that, God rest her soul."

"Probably you drove her into an early grave. What do you want it for?"

"Not sure. It could make a great story. Plus there's this historian who's doing a project for Tucker who wants to look at it." He didn't say, I'd like her to look at me. It hadn't taken much leg work to find out about the redhead with the long curls who would be perfect step-dancing in any Michael Flatley production. He needed to move fast, because the word was she wanted to go back to Europe.

"I don't have it. The last thing the old chief did was to send it off to a Professor Manchurian, Mansorian . . . something like that, at Harvard. Hey, don't write that down."

O'Flaherty erased the pencil marks. Lots of university websites listed faculties along with their contact information, but he suspected Harvard wouldn't. It would be a start for this poor Dorchester boy. No way could he have gone to Harvard; had to make do with UMass Boston and working full time besides. He did it on his own with no help from his family.

His father, an Irish immigrant, hardly a novelty in Boston, had worked in the freezer for an ice cream plant in Framingham. If any of his five sons complained they didn't have the latest whatever, it earned a smack and the comment, "Ya got food, a roof over your head and clothes. If you're sick you goes to the doctor. If your teeth hurt you goes to the dentist. I've done my part."

His mother stayed at home making sure the house was clean and meals were on the table.

Des wouldn't have dared come home with a bad grade or a bad report from a teacher. He did come home with trophies, for both parents made it clear their boys would not only play sports, they would win. The desire to win carried over to every story he ever went after. "Any more info on the body?"

"The medical examiner is more concerned with recent stuff than some 150-year-old corpse. Now go. I've work to do," the chief said.

CHAPTER 21

The mistress give me two new dresses because I now be a house nig-gah. The gray fabric be softer than dandelion fluff. They has to be clean. Clean be God's commandment to my Mistress. I bathes more the first week I be in the house than all the rest of the spring.

Twasn't just me that be bathing. Mistress Elizabeth be down in the hospital insisting that Chloe bathes every patient every day. Mistress pulls some niggahs out of the fields to make sure we alls has enough water, and she sets two women into making more soap to be given to all us slaves. Niggahs don't talk a lot, but they sure talks about all this washing stuff.

The Massa Edward be none too happy about it. In fact, he yells at the Mistress to stay out of Two Pine business. She yells right back that clean slaves means healthy slaves and that be good business. Healthy slaves works harder. He slams the door.

She also fights him on Ruth and Matt. Ruth belongs to the last overseer that be at Two Pines, but when they dids away with an overseer, he done leaves Ruth behind. When Ruth first sees Matt and Matt first sees Ruth, well it was like the sun coming out after a big storm.

Ruth goes on working at Two Pines as the laundry slave. God may strike me dead, she had to be part white. Her hair weren't kinky, but wavy. Her skin be the color of too much milk in coffee.

Now Matt, he be born here, and he sure be easy to look at. I'd seen him lift a half-grown calf. Matt, he loves animals. Can talk a calf out of a cow's belly.

They done gets married, but Ruth, she worries a lot. Her owner be gone, she ain't free so who does she belong to? One day when she delivers the clean sheets to the kitchen, I hears her talking to Molly. Ruth says she be afraid 'cause she didn't know who she belongs to. She knowd her heart and soul belonged to Matt but if the overseer comes back for her he can sells her or takes her away.

Molly ain't the only one who hears. The Mistress be in the dining room with the door to the kitchen open. My Mistress asks Ruth about it. Poor Ruth. She almost disappears in a puddle of fear.

Ruth stammers and stutters. What scairt her most be that they will send her away from Matt. She be from a place called New Orleans, and she been raised different than us. At the end the Mistress said she will find out who was her owner and then she can stay at Two Pines.

It turns out the Massa Edward owns Ruth. Bought her from the overseer. For the first time in my life I hears Ruth singing when she does laundry.

But the next week Ruth be crying. The Massa goin' sell Matt. Molly tells Ruth to tell the Mistress. Ruth don't wants to, so Molly does.

That makes a fight worse than two tomcats fighting over a pussy wanting kittens. The Mistress threw the Massa's pillows out of their room. I don't knowd who said what to who, but the next night he and his pillows be back in the Mistress's bed, and Matt don't go no place.

My first lessons be on ironing. Boy that be hard to make sure the iron be just the right temperature so as not to burn the clothes but still gets the wrinkles out. The Mistress knowd better not to give me her fine dresses to work on. She gives me old scraps of cloth. Later she has me sew those patches together to make big pieces of cloth that she done gives to the field niggahs as blankets for their families.

I'd never really sleeps on a mattress before I comes to the big house. My old bed be made of moss. It takes me a long time to get used to not smelling dirt before I falls asleep at night. The Mistress' and Massa's mattress made of horse hair. Mine be straw, and that smells the best. Sometime it sticks me in the night.

I also learns to sew, not like the long stitches I do to make my own dresses, but little tiny stitches. I always had problems seeing the little, teeny hole in the needle, but the Mistress, she has this funny glass that you sees clear through that makes everything bigger. Sure helps. However, the Mistress and me, we agrees that I should never be a dressmaker. At least I gets good at mending what has holes.

CHAPTER 22

Saturday, November 27

Des drove to the North Road cottage next to The Neck where he lived as caretaker during the winter. The secret of freelancing was to keep overhead low enough that when assignments grew sparse he still made basic expenses—that and being totally immune to a consumer culture except in clothing, which he considered as a code that said success.

A disadvantage was that the cottage was drafty. Drafty—hell, he could see his breath as he entered. He clicked on the space heater, ignoring the article he had written on the danger of space heaters. He plugged in his laptop and brought up Amazon .com and typed in Manchurian. No history books came up. Then he tried Mansorian. Three books about slavery and six about pre–Civil War history came up all written by a Dr. Gregory Mansorian. By nature Des suspected information too easily found.

He then brought up Harvard's Web site and using the search typed in Dr. Gregory Mansorian. Several hits came up. Eureka! For all the times he had to dig and dig and dig to get the right contact, maybe this was celestial balance assuming that this Mansorian was the person to whom the old chief had given the diary. The good doctor had to be Armenian. If the man taught at Harvard he must live in Cambridge or maybe Watertown, which was almost an Armenian colony.

Des checked the online phone directory. Ten names came up:

two in Cambridge, one in Watertown and one in Springfield. He dialed the G. Mansorian in Cambridge on Brattle Street. Good chance the professor would want to walk to work.

"Hi. To all Grace's friends, leave a message. The rest of you go bother someone else," a young woman's voice said.

The second was located on Auburn Street. "Mansorian Properties: Please leave a message. We check our messages at noon and six P.M. on Saturday and Sundays. For emergencies, call 617-555-3288."

Des punched the first Watertown number. A pleasant voice of a middle-aged woman answered.

"I'm looking for a Professor Gregory Mansorian."

"I'm his wife." The tone was cautious or maybe it was years of practice defending her home from marauding students.

"I'm a writer. I want to talk to him about slavery." Des knew the best approach was the direct one. Build up a sense of trust to increase his access, but writer was more worthy sounding than journalist.

"My husband is running errands. May I take a message?"

Des recited his cell number. If the professor didn't call him back, he'd drive to Watertown and knock on his door. He turned on his computer, but there was nothing he felt like working on. He played half a game of spider solitaire. When he felt this itchy the only thing to do was to go for a walk. Unlike many people, Des walked for hours at a time, using it to think. There wasn't a stone, tree, house or bush along the coast that he didn't know.

Dock Square was full of rug rats clutching parents' hands. Shit. He'd forgotten Santa was due by boat any minute. For a moment he imagined himself as Godzilla stomping on snow-suited little bodies. Small hordes of children gave off a certain smell, not that unpleasant but nothing that was part of his life. Hell, it was three years since he'd been involved with a woman, although he had had a number of short affairs. To have kids you need a woman.

Up ahead he saw a mass of red curls. He zigged and zagged, causing one father to growl, "Be careful," before Des managed to get three steps ahead of the red curls. It was Annie Young.

"Here we are, two people without a kid," he said.

She looked confused.

"Des O'Flaherty. The guy at your house the other day."

Annie nodded.

"What are you doing here?"

"Dad is on the committee. My boss is Santa." She put her hand over her mouth. No child heard the words to make them wonder if Santa were a fraud. "Besides, I've seen Santa come on a fire engine, a car and a horse. I even was in Finland where they have a Santa village with Laplanders and reindeer, but I've never seen him come by boat."

The boat appeared with Santa on deck waving and yelling, "Ho, ho, ho," through a mike. The kids waved back as the boat angled into the dock. An elf who worked at the bookstore the rest of the year threw a rope to a waiting elf weighing at least 200 pounds. He grabbed it and tied it around a post.

"I wonder if there's a Weight Watchers at the North Pole," Des said. "Now you've seen Santa, want to get a hot chocolate, it's freezing."

"Sounds good."

"Not here. It's too crowded. Let's go to Gloucester."

They ploughed through the crowd going in the opposite direction. "I feel like a salmon going downstream in mating season," he said. When Annie giggled, he added, "I always use that line whenever I'm in this situation."

"So you're often in Santa Claus crowds?"

"No, going the wrong way." His parents said he went the wrong way when he gave up a fixed job. Des told them he lived on his own terms, causing his father, who was feeling no pain, as was often the case, to guffaw.

Jason Haskell and a young couple walked toward them. Probably clients. Des swallowed his distaste and told himself he wasn't jealous. It made him tired to dislike every smooth man about his age who had been born into a family that could set them up in a business. Jason probably made more in a month than Des earned in a year. Even with the downturn. Choices. He had made his, and once made they must be lived with. Besides, he would hate being in sales.

As they walked by, Jason smiled at Annie. "I'm showing Mr. and Mrs. Roberts how civic minded this community is."

The couple held hands. Mrs. Roberts's coat bulged at the waist. "It's like a movie set."

"This area is often the set for movies. Cher, George Clooney, Brad Pitt, among others, have all walked down these streets," Jason said.

"Good luck." When Des took Annie by the elbow, she pulled away and frowned.

"Sorry," he said. "The guy makes me want to wash."

"Any reason?"

"Instinct." He didn't say jealousy. Only a wuss was jealous. He was a freelance journalist in the spirit of Hemingway or Mailer.

The coffee shop was next to a small amateur theater. Matchstick wood covered the bottom half of the wall. The top half had yellow paint that peeled near the ceiling. In one spot a picture had been moved, leaving a cleaner square. Plastic-coated menus showed hamburgers, BLTs, chowders, hash and pancake breakfasts served all day. The round tables with red-checkered table cloths were empty.

Des blew on his thick white mug. "There's still a working ice company here?"

"People have refrigerators."

"But restaurants need ice. Chefs do sculptures. Did a story about it once."

"Do you like being a reporter?" Annie asked.

"I like digging up facts. What do you do?"

"Freelance tech-writer. Leaves me time to explore history. My specialty is Medieval European history, heresies, that sort of thing."

As a reporter Des had two interviewing techniques: to pepper people with questions and to let them talk. He picked scum off his hot chocolate and listened to Annie talk. She's becoming more and more interesting, he thought. She wasn't the prettiest woman he had ever seen. Most of her attractiveness was in her eyes and her expression. Plus she had a great figure.

"Isn't that hard living in foreign countries? The language problem?"

"I speak French, Dutch and German. And English."

"I speak English and ig-pay atin-lay."

Annie giggled, not a flirty giggle, but an appreciative one. "You didn't have to learn languages. I did. Only way I was going to get through school."

"Actually, I studied Latin, the real Latin not pig, for five years and French when I was in high school, but I've forgotten almost everything."

A middle-aged couple entered and stood at the counter waiting for service.

Des watched Annie watch them and then asked, "So how does it feel to be home?"

"This is a foreign country for me—not home." Holding her mug in both hands she sipped.

"And . . ." Des prompted.

"And you're probably going to use this in a story. I'll pay for your chocolate."

Des's cell phone rang. He pulled it out.

"Mr. O'Flaherty, this is Professor Mansorian. You called me?"

Des debated saying anything in front of Annie, but if he could intrigue her in the historical aspect, he might get more information out of her. And he could spend more time with her. "Thanks for calling back. I understand you were given a manuscript, a diary written by a slave." He made an okay circle with his thumb and first finger.

"Yes, but to whom am I speaking?" The professor had an orator's voice.

"I'm a writer doing a story on the manuscript. Is there a chance I could look at it—that is, if you think it's authentic?" Des wanted to stay away from anything that would refer to the police. Now he added his flattery approach, one that met with frequent success. "I know you're one of the major authorities on slavery and I've heard of your books." He threw in the titles. "I won't take more than a half hour of your time." A lie. Most interviews he set up for a limited time ran over, once the person got talking.

"I've a terribly busy week coming up, but this afternoon is free."

Des pulled his free arm down in a YES! salute.

Annie cocked her head.

Good, he thought. She's interested.

After getting directions, he hung up. "Want to come with me?"

"I'd kill for the chance."

Des smiled the smile that he used when he was in a dating bar. "Not a good encouragement."

CHAPTER 23

Saturday, November 27

"I've driven this route so many times, I feel I know each pine tree personally," Magda said to the woman in the passenger seat. This was her second trip this week.

Two children, a boy of five with his right arm in a cast and a girl of four, slept in the back seat of Magda's 1995 compact. Despite the car's age, there wasn't a rust spot on it. Magda, determined the car would outlast her—and she planned to live a long time—made sure each knock or ping was inspected.

The children had nodded off before they crossed the Massachusetts/New Hampshire border and had not woken for the tollbooth. When they had rumbled over the bridge into Maine, they stirred. Their faces were reddish with a few beads of sweat from the sun pouring in the window. After glancing in the rearview mirror, Magda cut the heater. "Tell me if you get too cold, Darlink," she said to her passenger who was biting what was left of her nails.

The children's mother was in her mid-twenties, who should be taking the responsibilities of adulthood, but had let life carry her along. Her right eye was swollen. Six stitches road-mapped her cheek. Without insurance the girl could have no hope for plastic surgery. Scarring was the least of her problems at the moment.

"Are you sure I can't call my mother?"

"Not unless you want to risk your kids, yourself and every

woman and child in the shelter." Magda's voice was harsh. "I told you I would drop a postcard from Ipswich saying you and the kids are safe, but you won't be if you go back."

"He didn't mean it." The girl almost pouted.

"He didn't mean it the last ten times either?" Magda was not into nondirective counseling. "This time he went after Adam." Women might remain passive when beaten, but the protective urge for their children was no less ferocious in the human species than it was in animals. "This isn't about you anymore. This is about saving your kids, Darlink."

Magda pulled onto the shoulder and looked at the girl. "I am serious about this, Darlink. You have a chance to live without being hit. You've a chance to find a job. You've a chance to raise your kids so Adam won't grow up to hit women and Caro won't be hit. It'll be hard. Other women have done it. Our group will give you more support than you probably have ever had in your life. Until we find you a job you won't worry about food or a place to sleep. But if you put any of us in danger by wimping out, I will personally make your life a living hell. Now what is it? Do we go on, or do I take you back to your miserable life where you and your kids will be in constant danger?"

The girl said nothing. The pine tree branches reflected on the windshield. Magda shifted in her seat. Her back hurt. These frequent runs didn't help. "Look, I've got other things I want to do." She mustn't let the tears running down the girl's cheeks soften her. Tough love was needed. It takes guts to live sometimes.

"Let's go," the girl said.

"North or south?"

"North."

Magda put the car in gear and looked in the rearview mirror until she could pull out onto the highway.

CHAPTER 24

Saturday, November 27

Des O'Flaherty pulled up in front of the large gold Victorian house with black shutters and trim. There was a turret on each side of the house. The top half of the windows had squares of glass alternating purples, greens and blues.

"Resident parking only." Annie pointed to the sign above the car.

"Shit."

"Go in the driveway."

Des angled in behind two Japanese hybrids, making an unmoving parade of cars.

The doorbell chimed an unknown melody. A woman, her dark hair cut in a pixie and in her early fifties, answered the door. Although she was dressed in maroon sweats with Harvard written over the chest in gray, there was something sensual about her, a person confident of her own being.

For a second Annie debated asking why that maroon color was called Harvard crimson when it wasn't crimson, but she didn't. It wasn't why they were here.

"You must be Mr. O'Flaherty. Greg said you were coming. He just ran to the store but will be back in a few minutes. I'm Margaret, his wife."

Des introduced Annie.

"Would you like tea, coffee?" Margaret Mansorian asked as she led them into a study.

"Coffee," they said.

When she left, Des said, "If I were making a film and needed a Harvard professor's study . . ."

". . . this would be it." Annie walked around reading titles. She flopped down on the rust love seat that invited a person to curl up with a book in front of the bay window. There were no curtains, just the half-colored stained glass on top.

An oak flat-pack computer desk was in one corner with a laptop, a small photocopier, a fax/phone/answering machine and a printer burdening it. The second desk, an antique oak rolltop, was open. Papers stuck out of various cubby holes. A matching oak three-drawer file cabinet was in one corner. A plant in a blue ceramic pot draped its branches to the floor. One branch bore only dead leaves. Annie imagined it in a horror movie, strangling anyone the professor told it to.

It was not Mrs. Mansorian who carried a tray with three espresso cups, three spoons and a silver sugar and creamer, but a man somewhere in his mid-fifties. He had a complete head of hair, graying at the temples. He wore a light gray sweater over dark gray flannel slacks. "I'm Greg Mansorian." With his chin he pointed to a set of oak TV tables that Annie hadn't noticed. She quickly set one up. Dr. Greg Mansorian centered the tray, which overlapped. Sticking out his hand, he said, "I'm sorry I'm late. Everything takes longer than we plan, right?"

Des and Annie nodded. They sat on the loveseat in the bay window. The professor settled in his computer chair, which he moved so he faced them.

"We're here about . . ." Des began.

"The slave diary. Found with an old skeleton in Civil War clothing. In what could have been part of the Underground Railroad. Very, very interesting. And you?" The professor looked at Annie.

"The diary and skeleton were found in my father's house. He

just inherited it from his aunt, but it has only been in the family since somewhere in the early 1950s," she said. "By the way, I read your book, *The Economics of Slavery.*"

The professor cocked his head. "Not light reading and recent. You a teacher?"

"Tech writer, but I love history. Majored in it first at UMass Amherst then at the University of Geneva. Medieval history interests me more, but after your review in *The Economist,* I ordered it from the Internet." Annie caught Des's surprised look while keeping eye contact with the professor.

"My students should be as dedicated." The professor slapped his knees and got up and downed his espresso. "What do you want to know?"

"Is it authentic?" Des asked.

"Yes."

"How do you know?" Annie asked.

"The paper. I had it tested. The ink. Handwriting analysis. The style of writing would be appropriate for the period and lack of formal education of the writer. I would have loved to have met her. She seems like an exceptional young woman who exceeded her circumstances." He got up and after searching through the rolltop picked up a binder. "I copied the original so as to not risk damage."

Annie and Des stood to look over his shoulder.

"See how the *m*'s and *n*'s are pointed? A handwriting analyst would say that showed the writer was quick to learn, intelligent. Now that bears out in the contents. But at the same time, according to the diary, the writer was in her teens before she was taught to write by her Mistress, something that would not go down well with their masters." The professor shook his head.

"Where was she from?"

"Hard to tell. Probably she didn't know except for the name of the plantation, which we can trace, but saying that there had to be more than one plantation by that name. Southerners weren't all that original in naming their places."

"Anything else . . ." Des started.

"Lots of things. The crops would point to Georgia. Maybe. Then we could check to see if slave sale records match the information we have. Of course, they aren't complete, but if we put everything together, we might be able to get the whole story. Then again, we might not."

"It would make a great article," Des said.

"There's one thing that makes me cringe from all the PC brainwashing. Every time she calls herself a niggah," Mansorian said.

"But it is time appropriate," Annie said.

Mansorian shook his head, not to negate Annie's statement but his thought process. "I know, I know. If she called herself an African American, the manuscript would have screamed fake. As much as the ringing clock in Shakespeare's *Julius Caesar.*"

"You're right on brainwashing. Annie, were you here during the OJ trial?" Des asked.

"Missed it."

"Lucky you. A media feeding frenzy. Took people's minds off anything important for weeks, but part of the frenzy was the police using the N-word."

Mansorian settled back in his seat. "Hell, it would still make a great book. Sorta like Ladurie's *Montaillou* about a medieval French village."

"Never heard of it," Des said.

"I've visited it. On a Pyrenees mountaintop," Annie said.

The professor turned to look at Annie. "You are *not* an ordinary tech writer, young lady."

"Can we have a copy—of the diary, not *Montaillou?*" Des asked.

"I wish I could, but I can't at the request of the police. I'm sending them my report and the original Monday. Maybe he'll let you look at it."

Des stood up. "Come on, Annie. Thank you, professor."

Annie put her hands up. "On the other hand, I'm working on a history project here for a company to make interesting historical CD-ROMs for young kids. This would make a great base. If I could show you what I've done about the Pilgrims, would you let me do one on the life of a slave, assuming of course my publisher is interested?"

"Same thing. The diary and its copies don't leave my hands, except to the police chief."

"There's a new police chief, the other one walked off the job," Des said.

"I gave my word, even if I don't agree."

"But it was found in my house," Annie said.

Mansorian paused. "Let me check with the new chief whomever he is."

"I understand," Annie said. "However, this is for kids not academia."

"It would have to be here, and then I would prefer you only look at the copy. The original is too delicate. And I only would want you to use it for what you said. I would hate to read about it in a newspaper." He looked straight at Des.

"And I won't bother you unless my publisher is interested," she said.

At the door they shook hands.

"One more thing," the professor said. "The writer of the diary went another route. There's nothing about her being in Massachusetts but New York. But that doesn't mean that whomever the skeleton was didn't have another slave's diary with her."

"I'll get back to you after I talk to my publisher," Annie liked the way "my publisher" sounded.

After getting behind the wheel of his car, Des started to turn the ignition key then paused. He turned to Annie. "That was really good thinking. If you get to work on the diary, you can make a copy on his photocopier and give it to me."

"No, I can't."

"Why not?"

"Because it isn't ethical."

"Shit. Don't you ever do anything unethical?"

"Not if I can help it or only under special circumstances. Your story, Des, isn't special enough."

CHAPTER 25

I never works so hard in my life, but not like garden work. That be back work. This be finger work, brain work. My fingers be bloody from trying to sew tiny. My Mistress never acts mad. "Tear it out and start over." I be good at cutting cloth. I don't need a pattern I just sees how the scissors should go.

Now the brain work be something different. Mistress Elizabeth loves to stare at books all day long when she not be busy in the hospital or out visiting. She don't much like visiting people. She calls the neighbors ignoramuses, something that got the Massa Edward real mad and they fights real bad.

They be fighting so much I be real surprised when she starts throwing up mornings and sleeping all day long. I knowd she was going to pop a youngun long before she did.

"It ain't the grippe," I tells her, but she says of course it be. I be right. After that the Massa Edward and she don't fight no more. He treats her like those glasses that be so thin a mere look breaks them. He insists she rests, but she still goes to the hospital to make sure everyone be fine down there.

I'll never forget the day she tells me one of my chores be to learn to read and write. Slaves don't read. Slaves don't write. She be sitting up in bed. I brings her a tray with toast and tea. Her hair be brushed back. Lord it was hot that day. We could fills a river with our sweat.

"Get the sampler off the wall," she says.

Now I has no idea what a sampler be until she points. I takes it down and she pats the bed for me to sit down. Niggahs don't sits on

106

white ladies beds, I says, but she says they do when they be told to.

She holds the sampler so we both sees it. There be an apple and a letter. She traces the A with her finger. Then she told me it was an A and the word apple started with the letter A and it had the sound ah.

"Ah, A," I repeats.

"Except sometimes it sounds like its name. That's because it's a vowel."

"I thoughts you said it be a letter."

"We have twenty-six letters and five are called vowels, twenty-one are consonants. The vowels let us tie consonants together."

"Like rope?"

Oh did she laugh, but she not be making fun at me. More like we'd done shares a good story.

"From now on every day, we're going to spend at least two hours teaching you to read and write. We're going to prove that slaves aren't stupid" she says.

To me it sounds like real bad trouble.

CHAPTER 26

Tuesday, November 30

"*Je t'aime.*" Annie, with the phone tucked under her chin, hung up her coat in the hall closet. Roger had caught her as she walked in the door after meeting with the men whom she now called her Historical Committee and sometimes her Hysterical Committee.

Three thousand miles away or so in a small southern French village the words were received and returned. "Soon I'll be there," he said.

Annie pictured him in the kitchen, espresso cups piled up in the sink with Hannibal, his German shepherd, watching him talk. "We can text later, but I really am happy to hear your voice," she said.

Susan walked through the room and mouthed, "Give him my love." She went back into the kitchen to pull out the last batch of chocolate chip cookies. The smell of baking and chocolate permeated the kitchen. This might be a good time to talk to Annie, she thought as she heard her daughter say, "My parents send their love." A few seconds later Annie came into the kitchen and seated herself at the table.

"You miss him," Susan said as she put the tea kettle on, an automatic gesture from thousands of readings of her daughter's moods. "Are you getting serious?" Susan reached for the tea leaves and ran hot tap water into the violet-decorated pot while watching her daughter. Give her lots of room as always. Annie was like one of her paintings that came from experimentation. There'd been false strokes and right ones. Now this young woman was launched into the gallery of life. As Dave said, she was often over the top with her emotions, an artistic personality, but that was okay. He had enough common sense for both.

"I really would hate not to have him in my life."

The kettle whistled. Susan shut off the heat and emptied the tea pot and filled it with leaves, then poured the hot water. Her daughter put two mugs, a small strainer and milk and sugar on the table. Her daughter: a woman, a woman who was still part rebel, a *non-producing-grandchild* woman. She would never chide Annie over her lack of reproduction, but she felt sorry if Annie never experienced the joy that she herself had had in raising Annie. If she couldn't give Roger a greater endorsement than that she would hate not having him in her life, maybe he wasn't the man for her. On the other hand, Roger was good for her and to her. If only Annie wasn't perfectly content to have him as an eternal boyfriend. Sometimes she wanted to shake her daughter and yell, "Don't mess this up. Don't let this good one get away."

She never would. Susan and Dave waited for Annie to come to them. Although sometimes Dave couldn't contain his advice, he always cloaked it in questions: "Have you considered this or that?"

The doorbell rang.

"Pour the tea, I'll get it," Annie said.

Susan heard a strange male voice, soft with a bit of drawl. No one she recognized. She looked through the doorway.

Acting Police Chief Tim Doherty stood at the door, his bulk filling the frame. None of his body was fat, just muscle and big bones. He held his hat in his hand. "Ms. Young?"

"Yes?" Annie's voice rose.

"I'm sorry to bother you, but we have to talk."

Susan stepped into the living room, where she could see the entry. Her hand flew to her throat and she stepped toward the door. Dave was late coming home. "Is it my husband?"

He shook his head. "I didn't mean to frighten you, ma'am."

"But you frightened my mother. I'm Annie Young. And you are . . . ?"

"Tim Doherty, Chief of Police. Acting."

Susan let out the breath she'd been holding. "Come sit down." He sat on the edge of one of the overstuffed fading-brown chairs of no style and turned his hat in an never-ending circle. "We are going to open an investigation about the body you found in your basement."

Annie was now in the living room. "The skeleton? I thought everyone decided . . ."

"The forensic anthropologist finished her holiday, ma'am. She figured out right off that slaves never had the kind of dentistry this corpse had. It's more likely she died closer to twenty years ago."

CHAPTER 27

I cain't say I ever likes my lessons. At first those letters don't make no sense. But the Mistress says that she be going to teach me to read and write if it kills her. To makes me want to learn she reads stories to me, but she always stops just when things gets extra good. If I complains she done says, "If you knew how to read, you wouldn't have to wait for me to read."

We has our lessons in secret when the Massas be far, far away. One day Molly catches us. "That not smart," she says. Molly never be a slave that knowd how to hold her tongue. It got worse after the Mistress taught her how to cook fancy, 'cause Molly knew the Mistress didn't want to have to teach another niggah. But Mistress Elizabeth puts Molly in her place when Molly gets too sassy. "I can always get a real cook from up north that is a lot better than you are." That shuts Molly up for a while.

This time Mistress Elizabeth says, "I can teach you too, Molly, if you want."

"No Ma'am, not me," Molly says. "God don't want us niggahs to read."

Well I don't believes that at all. I realizes why reading be real important. Not doing it makes us blacks less than whites. From then on I works real hard until I can reads and writes, which is why these letters now be on paper. And I even learnt that you put funny marks around when you want to writes something someone really said.

I promises the Mistress that I will never reads in front of anyone, not the Massa, not his brother, not any slave. No one. If they sees me with a book I is to turn it around and around and cock my head like I didn't know which way was up. Or I is to shake it, dust it, anything. Most times when I reads I be in bed.

I don't knowd if it be Molly that blabbed about the reading lessons, but the Massa Edward finds out anyway and there be one huge fight.

"I don't care if you are carrying my baby, you've no right to interfere."

"She's my maid. I want her to be able to read if she is going to take care of my child."

"It's against the law, damn it."

"The law is wrong."

"It's still the law."

I think the Massa be afraid of a reading niggah.

At the same time Mistress Elizabeth teached me to read she also works on my speech. Verbs she calls them, and she sure don't like the way I uses mine. And she laughs when I says verb tenses make me real tense.

The Mistress also insists I learnt to write. At first it be, no was, harder than sewing, but then it gets easier. I wishes I'd been able to write when it happened instead of going back in time. But I thinks I remembers really good and gets most of the details down. Maybe not everything be in order, but it is as close as I be able to make it. The pencil moves lots easier than the needle. A letter can be any size. A stitch has to be tiny, tiny, tiny or at least a finished stitch do. A basting stitch don't. Letters could be any size, but after a while I learnt that if I made them smaller more fits on a piece of paper.

Mistress Elizabeth lets me have all the paper I wants.

Writing done gave me a place to spill my words. All those words that Mama and Papa didn't want to hear I puts on paper. And unlike spoken words that got lost the second after they fell out of my mouth, the words on the paper lasts forever or at least as long as the paper lasts. I use half my paper to show her how my writing be/is get-

ting better, but the other half is my secret writing.

One time I wrote horrible things about the niggahs being the bosses at Two Pines and the two Massas doing all the plowing, planting, weeding and picking. I writes how they done sweat and how their arms and legs hurts and how they be always hungry and their moss beds never rid of pebbles and twigs that itched them. I write/wrote it all one night in the summer when the light lasts long. Although no one ever comes to my little room, I never be so scairt that someone might comes and reads them.

The next morning I hides the pages under my dress. In the kitchen when I makes up the tray for the Mistress and Molly's back is turned, I throws them in the stove and lets them burn. It hurts me to see my words turn to little bitty ashes, but it will hurts me a whole lot more if someone reads them.

After that I writes about things like the color of the sky, the weather, what I eats. The Mistress corrects how I speaks too so I starts sounding like a white woman. I never talks white with my family. They say being a house niggah makes me too big in my head. I talks black with them. I likes talking black better. That be who I am. I writes black too, because that's how I thinks. But when I writes what white people say, I writes white with correct verbs.

Mistress Elizabeth never says she don't believe in slavery, but once I learnt to read, I reads her diary. The Mistress writes in it every day, and I knowd I shouldn't read it. I only did because she was unhappy with me, and I was scairt she'd send me back to the garden. Turns out I be wrong. She be unhappy all right, but not with me, but with Two Pines, with the Massa, and she don't like slavery not one bit. I never thinks about there being a choice on slavery before I reads that.

She talks about the plantation being primitive in comparison to London where she comes from. I learnt London be across wide water. The Mistress says she dreamed of getting on a boat and never seeing this place no more. I don't know what primitive means. I cain't ask because she'd knowd I read her diary.

Things went from worse to worser between her and the Massa Edward. I heard him tell his brother that pregnant woman oughta be locked away.

When Mistress Elizabeth has a stomach so big she needs to carry it in a wheelbarrow, we hears hoof beats. I helps her out of the chair but she makes it to the window all by herself. Her window looks out over the porch and the road to Two Pines.

"Aaron!" She squeals his name better than a stuck pig. I worries she might fall as she runs down the stairs out the door, and down the path. He jumps off his horse and they hug and hug. The Mistress tells me Mr. Aaron is her friend from London. He talks as funny as she do, cutting of parts off his letters.

I wonders as I listen to them talk if I can writes down all the words they say when I goes to my room. Some words that falls out of people's mouths stay sounds and last only as long as it takes to hear. Then they are gone forever, like a dried up rain drop.

I loves my tiny room. It be about as long as me and with one window. I keeps my blankets and extra dress under the bed. Every week I be given a candle. The first night I sleeps there be the first time I ever sleeps alone. Sleeps the wrong word. I barely closes an eye. It be too quiet. I miss Papa's snoring and my mama's soft breathing.

This morning the Mistress takes her breakfast with Mr. Aaron, her husband and his brother. When the Massa Richard and Massa Edward leaves the table Mr. Aaron talks-talks to the Mistress. "Elizabeth, how can you stand it here? It took me weeks to get to you and there's nothing. Nothing. Nothing around." Mr. Aaron says lots of things more than once.

"I love my husband," Mistress Elizabeth says.

Mr. Aaron raises one eyebrow. He does that a lot. "But what do you do in this wilderness? No theater? No restaurants? And God, how do you stand, stand those beasts?"

"Now that is more of a problem. This system . . ."

"*How long are you going to continue with this farce?*"

The Mistress touches her stomach. I sees tears start.

I don't know what happens next, because the Mistress told me to make sure there be a fresh pitcher of water in Mr. Aaron's bedroom to replace the one he washed with this morning.

CHAPTER 28

Tuesday, November 30

Acting Police Chief Tim Doherty found a spot at the Young kitchen table with Annie, Susan and Dave, who hung his jacket on a chair back. The chairs scraped as the chief and Annie settled down.

"I know none of you had anything to do with the murder, because it happened probably a good twenty years ago, and you weren't here. But I'd like to ask you some questions about the house. Dave, what can you tell me about your aunt?"

"My mother's sister was a junior high school teacher, English and History. In Sudbury."

"How far away is that?" Tim asked.

Like the chief, Annie wasn't sure how far the two towns were apart. She didn't say, I'm a stranger in these parts myself, partner, although the phrase jumped into her mind.

"Over an hour," Susan said.

"But she didn't commute?" Tim asked.

"No," Dave said. "This was her summer home and a weekend retreat. During the week she lived in a two-family in Sudbury. I'm not sure when she bought this. I do know I was eight the first time I spent the summer. That would be 1961. After she retired she lived here full time."

"Did she know about the room in the basement?"

Susan nodded. "The place was crammed with everything under the sun when we arrived. We've hauled a ton of news-

116

papers, books, papers, dishes out of here when we arrived so we could just walk around. The basement was the last thing we tackled."

Dave glanced at his wife.

"You tackled, sweetheart." Susan turned to the chief. "I'm too involved in my work."

Annie watched the conversation ping-pong back and forth. There was a knock on the door. "I'll get it." Des O'Flaherty, in his pressed jeans, leather jacket and shiny boots, smiling. She wondered if he ever wore anything else.

"I saw the police car. Everything okay?"

"The chief is here."

Des came in without being asked. He smiled at Dave and Susan "Hey Tim, what's happening?"

Tim sat up straight and frowned. "Nothing I want to release to the press."

"So this is a social call?"

The chief shifted in his seat. Every muscle in his body was rigid.

"I came by to ask Annie out to dinner, tonight." Des, unlike the chief, looked relaxed.

"Better than trying to dig into police business," Tim said.

"I've no problem with either, but, if you do have any information on the skeleton . . ."

"Not a chance." Tim scowled at Des.

Des turned to look at Annie.

Annie admired his willingness to be rejected in front of a group, or maybe he thought she would be too considerate to say no under the circumstances. That Des chose to live as she did, outside normal employment and having a passion for what he did, made him attractive. The fact that he was drop-dead handsome didn't hurt. Oh why not, at least he was interesting. "Okay, as long as you realize it's just friendly. My boyfriend is due in a couple of weeks."

Des smiled. "Six thirty okay?"

"Dressy or casual?"

"With my budget? Casual. It'll be better than a hamburger joint." He turned to the chief. "I met with the professor you sent the diary to. He said he was sending it back with a report. You got it yet?"

"He sent it out this morning by courier."

"I would love to look at it."

"Me, too," said Annie.

The chief didn't say anything but glared at Des.

"I'm heading out," Des said. Annie walked him to the door.

"I'm going to ask you not to discuss this case with him," Tim said. "Of course, I can't force you."

Dave nodded. "We'll cooperate. It's weird enough to think that a body was here since we arrived, but weirder still to think of it as a modern murder." He paused. "I assume it was a murder, although we can't tell for sure."

"Most people don't dress themselves in a 100-plus-year-old dress, put themselves in a hidden room and magically hide the entrance with a chest before committing suicide."

"You can't have much to go on," Susan said.

"Aunt Helen could be the killer for all we know," Dave said. "She may have been eccentric, although I never thought her violent."

"What about missing persons?" Annie asked.

"No unsolved cases. I checked for the last fifty years. Of course, this isn't my first priority. We've got the usual problems: drunk drivers, teenage vandals, domestic abuse. Problem is, I'm still learning about the community. It's way over the first forty-eight-hour rule."

"What's that?" Susan asked.

"If you don't get a lock on the crime within the first forty-eight hours it probably won't get solved," Doherty said.

"Chief, I've an idea about your learning about the community," Susan said. "We're having a Christmas tree decorating party the Sunday before Christmas with some of our new friends. Why don't you and your wife come?"

"Marsha and I would love to."

CHAPTER 29

Zeb disappeared. This be the first time in anyone's memory that a slave disappeared.

"He runs away," Ruth says.

"Snakes goin' to eat him," Shadrack says.

"He goin' get lost in the swamp," Moses says.

"He no idea where to go. He goin' starve," Jenny says.

My Mama says he just be gone in the morning. He been beat the night before, not a lot, three lashes. Too much beating puts a slave in the hospital. Lash marks fill with pus. A gentle beating reminds us what we oughta be doing.

"Maybe he be kilt. Maybe the Massa kilt him," Moses says.

No one believes that. Zeb be too valuable to kill.

The Massa be furious. Then Moses comes running and hollers a canoe be gone.

"He musta rowed outta here," Moses says.

"Dogs cain't follow him in the water," Shadrack says

"Shut up," Massa Richard says. "When we find him, he's going to be one sorry niggah." He looks at me. "Your Mistress is looking for you."

I finds my Mistress sitting in the parlor. Mr. Aaron be with her. Her new baby be in the same cradle that the Massa and his brother used. She be a good baby, crying only when she be hungry or wet.

I no longer sleeps in my tiny room. I sleeps in a room next to the nursery in another real bed with sheets, pillows and blankets. Only, I never uses pillows. It feels wrong to have my head high. The Mistress does a lot with the baby herself. Nancy nurses her. White women ain't got a lot of spare milk, and Nancy's baby be dead so she has too much. Nancy sleeps in my old tiny room in case the baby be hungry at night. I takes the baby to her if she cries.

"You wants me to takes her to the nursery?" I asks.

The Mistress looks into the cradle and touches that sweet face with her finger. The baby moves her lips as if suckling. "Leave her. However, I suggest you change the sheets on her cot."

I slips out of the room but listens at the door. When I scooches down I can see him through the key hole, but I cain't see her.

"You have to come back with me Elizabeth," Mr. Aaron says. "How can I leave you in this God-forsaken place? How he could have brought you here is beyond me."

"It's home for him. I just had no idea when we met in London or again in New York, how end of the earth this was. He seemed so . . . so . . . worldly."

"But as soon as he came home he reverted to the country bumpkin," Mr. Aaron says.

I wishes I can see the Mistress's face through the keyhole.

"He did graduate from the University of Georgia."

"I would be more impressed if it were Harvard."

That's when she did it. She flaps her skirt. I hears it. She does it when she's upset.

Mr. Aaron put his hand ups in the air. "Whoa." Then he moves so I cain't see him, but I can hears him. "There's not a decent store within five hundred miles. We won't even discuss this slavery thing, and no, don't tell me you approve. I see it in your face. I know you better than you know yourself."

I hears footsteps and gets away before anyone sees me.

CHAPTER 30

Tuesday, November 30

As soon as Des left the Youngs' house, he headed for the police station. The entrance was deserted except for one very young rookie behind the desk. Midafternoon wasn't a busy time. Workers were back from lunch, and housewives or babysitters were picking up the kids at school. The patrolman was talking on the phone and waved his hand, which Des took to mean he'd be with him when he could.

Des mouthed, "I'll wait for the chief in his office."

The patrolman pressed the buzzer to open the door that led to the offices and cells. Stupid to leave a rookie alone on the desk, but Des couldn't ignore an advantage. He heard the rookie say. "Your neighbor does have the right to cut down a tree on his own property."

The new chief, unlike the old one, believed in a clean desk, well almost clean. There was a fax with the medical examiner's logo on the top. Advantage number two, this was his lucky day. The chief had a copier next to his desk, advantage number three. Des copied the report, folded it and put it in his pocket. Under some papers was the diary. "Yes!" He copied that too.

"My supervisor's name is Chief Doherty, but he's out. If you want to call him later, he's on duty until this evening," he heard.

Then silence from the other room. The copier hummed.

"The shift ends about four, but the chief usually stays later."

Again, silence from the other room. The copier spit out a few more pages.

Des was back in his chair, his foot resting on his leg in the four position. The copy of the report was safe in his pocket, and the copy of the diary under his shirt when the patrolman walked in.

"Maybe it's a bad idea that you wait in here." The patrolman had the skin of a youth that lost the acne battle a few years ago. He couldn't have been more than the minimum age for a cop.

Des dropped his crossed leg to the floor and used his arms to lift himself from the chair.

"You're probably right." He glanced at his watch. "I'm already late for my next appointment." He strolled to the door, letting his hand rest on the knob. "If you think I might have gotten you in trouble, I won't mention that you let me in."

By the twitch in the young cop's mouth Des saw the fight between self-protection and total honesty. Des prided himself on reading body language. If he ever won a Pulitzer, it would be because he had watched a finger move that would lead him to the question that would break the story. Okay, most freelancers never win Pulitzers. Still he dreamed. Among the papers that he had sold stories to, he had earned a reputation for reliability to a point that they all had offered him jobs. He always said no, but call when you need extra word power.

The baby patrolman was back in his seat, and Des was at the door when two other patrolmen walked in and greeted him. "What are you doing, Des?" the older one asked.

"Just checking if there's any news. You should teach the new guy how to speak. He's monosyllabic." His eyes met the young patrolman. Good, the man was in his debt.

Des took out his keys as the police chief's car pulled up. Tim Doherty got out. "Twice in one day. Can't say which one of us is luckier."

"Me, hands down. Got any news on the skeleton? Something

that you didn't want to say in front of the Youngs?" He deliberately did not raise his voice to make it a question. He let the silence hang. Silence was good. Silence made people uncomfortable. Silence made them rush to fill the void.

Doherty massaged the silence.

The two men stood looking at each other for a while, the professional reporter, the professional cop—both well trained in questioning techniques. Their eyes became an ocular arm-wrestling match. Together they broke out in laughter.

"You're good O'Flaherty."

"You too, Doherty." He reached out his hand, which O'Flaherty shook firmly.

CHAPTER 31

"Hello, my name is Jeremy. I'm your waiter tonight." The young man with the blond hair and blue eyes resembled a Christmas card angel except for the stud in his left ear and the ring through his eyebrow. The former held a tiny diamond.

"Hello, Jeremy," Des and Annie said together. Annie felt as if she were in some AA meeting.

Jeremy reeled off the specials. I'm not in a Harvard Square restaurant, I'm at a cooking school, she thought as the waiter listed herbs used in the veal and the amount of simmering time.

"We have three salads, but I counsel you to choose the house. The chef has a special dressing that includes soy sauce and toasted sesame seeds. He adds them hot to walnut oil to release their flavor."

"Flavor release is good," Des said.

"Would you like the dressing on the side, or gently tossed to not bruise the greens?"

"I've always been against cruelty to vegetables," Des said. "How long does it take to memorize everything?"

"I've a photographic memory," Jeremy said. "We've tap water, which I advise against because the chlorination leaves an aftertaste, diminishing the pleasure in your meal. We have Evian if you would like French still water and a Pellegrino if you prefer sparkling. And there's the local Poland Spring."

"Pellegrino," Annie said.

"Tap." Des's look dared Jeremy to contradict him. "I love chlorine."

The waiter's expression said *stupid man.* "And wine?"

"Do you have a nice Gamay? And I'll have the mushroom soufflé," Annie said.

"The filet mignon. The one cooked five minutes on each side, with Indian chutney added then flambéed in cognac," Des said.

As the waiter left, Annie said, "I had to stop him before he mentioned each grape in the bottles."

"You'll never guess what I . . ." Des stopped when Jeremy placed a filled salad bowl on the extension of their table and divided it on two plates He also left a basket with mixed rolls.

"I'll never guess what?" she asked.

"I just happen to have a copy of the medical report on your skeleton. *And* the diary."

"How in the hell did you get that?"

Jeremy arrived with a pepper mill, a slightly miniaturized version of the Eiffel Tower. "Fresh pepper. It is from the island of Ponape and is the best in the world. Most people spell it p-o-n-a-p-e but it is now called Pohnpei, spelled p-o-h-n-p-e-i."

"When did they change it?" Annie regretted asking the second she spoke.

"I don't know, but I do have a showing map where the Micronesian Islands are, along with photos of the pepper growing. I can get it if you wish."

Annie shot Des a don't-you-dare look.

When Jeremy disappeared Annie said, "Let me see them, please."

Des put the papers out of her reach. "I suppose if I said you would have to sleep with me . . ."

"I would tell you to go to hell."

"Then say please."

Jeremy appeared at their table as if he rose from a hole in the floor like those of theater stages. "How is your salad?"

"Fine. Thank you."

"Your dinners will be ready in about ten minutes. We do not have a Gamay, however, I *do* have a solution. Here's our wine list." He flourished it to Des who handed it to Annie.

"Annie you do it, since you live in France."

"You live in France. *Je voudrais parler avec vous en français.*" Jeremy explained how he spent three weeks there in an extensive language course. He had never heard of Argelès-sur-mer, but that did not bother Annie, since most Americans hadn't. Many Americans knew Paris and maybe the Riviera where she wished she could send the waiter. Now!

Annie selected wine based on the look of the label. The prettier it was, the more apt she was to buy it. Then if it were good, she would buy the same label and year another time. What was important was taste and how well it married to the meal.

She and Des had not finished even ten percent of their meal when Jeremy appeared again. "I notice your oatmeal rolls are gone. Would you care for more?"

Annie felt Des's foot tapping under the table as he said, "Thank you for your concern, but I want to try the sweet roll. Annie, have you reached a sweet roll decision yet?"

"I was pondering it," Annie said. "But I believe it is worth the investment. However, could we have more oatmeal rolls in case the sweet roll solution doesn't work out?"

"You know you've a bitchy side," Des said after Jeremy undertook his oatmeal roll mission.

"Is that guy for real?"

"I know the proprietor, and he had been worried that his wait staff didn't have the right customer service skills, so he insisted they go for training."

"To be food psychologists?"

Des shrugged.

"May I see the report?" She held out her hand.

Des pretended to hold it back, but then relinquished it. Annie scanned the pages. A woman probably in her late twenties, early thirties—healed cracked ribs, healed broken arm, healed broken fingers on right hand, no signs of osteoporosis. "Wow! She had a hard life."

"She could have been in a bad accident," Des said.

"Or a victim of abuse."

"Cause of death probably strangulation based on the broken hyoid bone, but impossible to tell. Her two front teeth were missing, her nose was broken and there's a skull fracture that wasn't healed," Des said. "Could have been beaten to death. Or strangled. The broken neck."

"By the way, how did you know about the hyoid bone before you saw this report?"

"I used to date one of the technicians in the Medical Examiner's Office."

"And she still speaks to you?"

"When I broke up with her, I introduced her to a friend whom she married. They were suited; we weren't. However, she's not grateful enough to give me copies of stuff. I have to be satisfied with a few casual leads thrown my way."

"May I clear your salad plates?" Jeremy asked. Both Annie and Des jumped.

Annie ate her last round carrot with a small leaf of coriander attached before relinquishing her plate. "We could invite him to eat with us," she said. "It might keep him from interrupting."

"I'd rather *counsel* him to a long walk off a very short pier. Except there are no piers in Harvard Square." He leaned forward. "I'd like to find out who the skeleton was. Want to help me?"

Annie loved the idea. She would be a real-life Jessica, Kinsey or Stephanie. "Does Caleb's Landing have a small-town paper that would have reported missing people?"

Des scratched his chin. "Not sure. I do remember something about a *Coastal Times* that went bust. Maybe there are old copies in the library. What are you doing tomorrow?"

"Except for a meeting at 10 A.M. with my Historical Committee, nothing. I'll bring up the diary. I can tantalize them with a few hints."

Although Roger had accepted that her being away for a tech-writing assignment made sense, she wasn't sure if she could sell him that anything historical, even a paid one, was a good enough excuse to put the Atlantic between them. Anywhere in Europe she just had to catch a train or a cheapy flight for a weekend together. However, there were only indirect routes between Argelès and Boston via Paris or Barcelona. She felt both confined by the relationship and glad it existed. Things should be better once he went back to work, if he were able to go back.

When the meal came, they ate in silence, savoring each bite. They accepted counseling on dessert, selecting the Black Russian cake made with a special black chocolate and Kaluha and dribbled with a hot, black chocolate sauce. Much to their surprise, the waiter did not give them a history of where the cocoa beans used in the sauce came from.

Des drained his coffee. "I've got to work on a travel guide for a client."

"I thought you were a reporter."

"That's my love, but if the money doesn't come in fast enough I take any type of writing assignment I can get. Anyway, meet me at the library at two?"

"Sure," Annie said.

A man in a white hat, black checkered pants and a white chef's jacket with side buttons stepped out of the kitchen and stopped at each table for a few minutes. When he reached theirs he let out a whoop.

Des introduced him as André, but the man leaned down and whispered, "My real name is Andrew. Des and I went to high school together. He went to college, but I went to Johnson & Wales for chef's training instead." He turned to Des. "I suppose this is on the house?"

"After all the press releases and stuff I wrote for you, you bet your life. And André, we need to talk about your customer service. I'll call you tomorrow."

No matter how André/Andrew tried to pump Des, Des said no more. "Look, I'm out with this new girl I want to impress. Bug off." The tone was friendly; both men smiled.

"Tomorrow, first thing," André/Andrew said as he moved on to the next table.

"He's done well, but I enjoy harassing him. Now that I know I don't have to pay for this meal, I can afford to go to Passim's."

Annie knew about Passim's. Her parents said they'd heard Joan Baez play there before she was Joan Baez. Over the years Annie had heard a lot about Harvard Square where her parents had hung out while dating. They had talked about carrying a roll of quarters to pay street musicians. Her mother admitted making love once in the bushes along the Charles River, claiming that her bum on twigs and stones was more romantic in concept than reality.

This was one of her missing roots and Roger or no Roger, Annie was going to enjoy it.

CHAPTER 32

Zeb be back. He be one sorry-looking niggah. Massa Richard beats him within an inch of his life. Everyone watches. We ain't got no choice, but I stares at the ground. They can makes my body show up, but I controls my eyes. The sound of the whip stabs my ears. I waits to hear him scream or even moan, but there is nothing. Nothing.

Then he not be allowed to go to the hospital until the Mistress cries. The Massa Edward does anything for the Mistress when she cries. Except this time crying ain't near enough. He ignores her when she says she's going to go back to England and take little Missy Annabelle with her. It be only when she says if Zeb dies the Massa loses a $1,000 slave and a man who does the work of two. Then the Massa sends for his brother to go tell Chloe to fix Zeb up.

I seen him once when the Mistress tells me to take clean linen to the hospital. She insists Chloe use only clean sheets. The sick now sleeps in real beds. The Massa and the Mistress fights about those beds, too. He says niggahs will never want to leave the hospital if they be too comfortable. She says the hospital can make them more sick the way it was. She be right. Simple cuts don't get all puss-filled no more. Chloe be none too sure at first, but she sees the results. Mistress Elizabeth be smart. She tells Chloe what a good nurse she be and never once done she says, "I was right, and you was wrong."

When I goes in with the basket of clean towels and sheets, Chloe be nowhere around. We be alone. I couldn't help but stare at him. He be on his side with the sheet pull up to his armpits. The whip lines on his shoulders be deep, raw. He goin' to have some mean scars.

131

"*What you looking at, girl? You never sees a whip mark before? Let me show you.*" *He turns onto his stomach and pulls down the sheet so I seed his bare ass. His back looked like a skinned deer.*

I gasps. "*I don't know how you done dare run away.*"

He gives a low rumble that is not a laugh, snort or a groan but all of them in one sound that comes from Zeb's soul. "*A man must prove he belongs to himself.*"

I don't know what to say. Niggahs don't talk about being men.

"*I almost made it.*"

"*The other niggahs says you was going to get eaten up by the snakes in the swamp.*"

"*The swamp doesn't go on forever. Come here girl.*"

I goes closer.

"*Sit.*"

I sat. He be the handsomest niggah I has ever seen. His skin be so black that if he be outside on a night with no moon you coulds walk by him and never knowd he be there. You can cut wood on his cheekbones. He never shuffles like most niggahs but struts to the fields, his shoulders back, his head high. Because he does the work of two niggahs, the Massa and his brother never faults him, but more than once I'd seen them stare at him. He always looks them in the eye when he talks to them. Although he always be polite enough so they couldn't do nothing to him, its like he says he be one of them, not one of us.

"*You ever been off Two Pines?*" *Zeb asks me.*

"*I be born here.*"

"*There's a whole world out there you cain't even dream of. And there be white people who don't believe we should be slaves. They wants to help us.*"

"*Didn't help you do nothing but get whipped.*"

"*I won't get caught next time. Will make it beyond Atlanta. Will make it all the way to Canada.*"

I cain't believe he will try again. "*Talk like that some nasty nig-*

gah will tell the Massa."

"I ain't gonna talk about it again. I just gonna do it."

I hadn't heard Chloe come in until she speaks in my ear. "You stay away from Zeb. He trouble for all of us."

I jumped. "You scairt me."

"I do more than scairt you if you spends more time with this stupid man."

Chloe picks up the basket and carries it to the closet. Her back be to Zeb who gives me a smile enough to makes me itch between my legs.

I helps her empty the basket and walks back to the house. I wants to talk more to Zeb, not just because he be the most beautiful man in the world, but because I wants to know what he seen. I wants to know what be beyond Two Pines. 'Til now I thought the Mistress be the only white person in the world that don't like slavery.

CHAPTER 33

Wednesday, December 1

"Test day," Charlie Tucker ushered Annie into his office. His company occupied a square, flat, two-story industrialized building with no charm at all. Ten people worked in the office. She had no idea how many worked in his printing plant.

Lemon walls were hidden by maps and sailing charts. A clipper ship model in a glass case sat under the bay window. Charlie had spent nothing on furniture. Desks, chairs and filing cabinets were mismatched from various eras. The computers, however, were the newest models. Cords were nonexistent.

"Yup. We might love the CD-ROM, but unless kids take to it, we'll never accomplish our objectives. Are Paul and Len here?" Annie asked.

Charlie closed his office door, cutting them off from the click of computer keys in the main room.

"Paul has the flu, and I haven't heard from . . ." The phone interrupted Charlie. He picked it up. "Hello . . . we were just talking about you. . . . Oh, I'm sorry . . . no, I understand. . . . We'll brief you later." He turned to Annie. "That was Len. He has two salesmen down with flu, and Melissa is out sick. He and Jason are holding down the fort."

"Too bad, I wanted to propose a second CD-ROM based on the diary we found in the basement."

"You got it back from the police?"

"Let's say I have access to a copy of it. It's fascinating."

"We don't know if it is authentic."

"We do."

Charlie leaned back in his chair. He twirled a pencil through his fingers like a baton. His smiley face was so full of intelligence and energy that Annie understood why people were drawn in by his enthusiasm. "I feel like a little boy before Christmas. Think about it, Annie. I've always believed in this country, but I've become so worried about the watered-down education our kids are getting, yet I had no idea what to do about it. Sure, I sent my kids to private school, but not every one has that option."

"And now you're doing something about it."

He stretched back. "Exactly. If this first CD-ROM works, I'd be interested in doing a whole series. And we'll set up a Web site. As I said before, we don't have to make money."

"Your choice if you want to charge for it or not."

"Sadly, nothing will reach poor kids without a computer." Charlie leaned back in his chair.

"And in the schools?"

"Poor schools don't have computers. And for that matter the stuff we're saying might never get approved. Remember some places in this country forbid teaching Darwinism."

"Not Caleb's Landing?"

"Definitely not here, but we do have lots of political problems that are hampering our schools, more than many of the communities around. Annie, if this works, I'd be interested in making you a full-time employee doing only this. What's the good of money if you can't buy a dream or two?"

"True."

"And coming to work for me?"

"We'll talk about it," Annie said. Getting paid for having the fun she'd had in trying to re-create the thoughts and feelings of two Pilgrim and two Indian children was tempting. Reading through all the documents had been an education in itself. Pleasure came from talking on the phone with the American Indian Council. No cowboy movie wigwams for her. She learned about an oval-shaped structure made from bent tree poles and spent a day trying to find out how animal skins were arranged over the structure in winter to keep drafts out. She had scheduled an appointment with the chief of the Wampanoag to make sure her portrayal was accurate.

What a holiday this had become. Yes, she would love to do this, but the idea of spending her time in this office, working 9-to-5 with only two weeks vacation a year? No, that she didn't want.

"I offer great health insurance," Charlie said.

"France has universal health insurance. The World Health Organization calls it the best health care system in the world."

"What would it take for me to get you on staff?"

"It's premature."

"Not that premature. I wish I could go with you this afternoon," Charlie said.

"Having too many people watching the kids won't be any good."

Charlie nodded. "I've got a friend in advertising who said he'd arrange for a real focus group room."

"Let's take it step by step. See what the kids react to." She got up to leave.

"Tell your mother both the wife and I'll be at her Christmas tree decorating Saturday night."

"Then you can meet Roger and his daughter."

"How old is she?"

"Twelve."

"Would you like me to bring my grandsons so she'll have someone her own age?"

"Great."

Annie had her hand on the doorknob when Charlie called her name.

"Phone me as soon as you get out of the classroom."

CHAPTER 34

Wednesday, December 1

The car engine had cooled while Annie had been meeting with Charlie. As it warmed, her imagination visited 1623 Berkshire, England.

She was a married Puritan woman with four children and expecting another. This baby had made her ill throughout the pregnancy. Her husband, a minister, was in London, leaving her alone to cope with the children. What had made her mother decide to risk a voyage to the other side of the world? The letters from the Massachusetts colony were sparse. Talks of stony soil, bad crops, Indians, and illness sent her to her knees praying for her mother's health. Although it was ungodly, she wished that the situation in the new land would become so bad that her parents would come home.

Annie put the car in gear. She needed to kill some time before she went to the elementary school. Her mother was at the studio. Her father was redoing the upstairs hall, and the last thing Annie wanted was to go home to smell paint.

As she drove down Route 127 toward The Dock, she realized she was near Melissa's. If the girl were ill, maybe she should pop in to see if she needed something. Annie slowed to try and remember which house her father had pointed out. What a pretty stretch of road this was, lined with old houses, some with widow's walks, some with picket fences entwined with dead roses, making them both plaintiff and hopeful at the same time. She hummed a few bars of "The Rose," although no one would

138

have recognized it.

There it was—a Cape Cod smaller than the houses on either side and painted white with black shutters. A white picket gate hung by a single hinge but the fence had three new pickets waiting for paint. The front garden each side of the flagstone walk was well kept. White muslin curtains hid the inside. The front door bell had a buzz resembling the sound of a swarm of angry bees.

She waited. No one came. After she buzzed a second time, she took five steps back to see if a light were on inside. Melissa might have gone to the doctor. No, her car was in the attached garage unless Jason had taken her. Not possible: Charlie had said that Jason and Len were both in the office.

A curtain moved so quickly that Annie wasn't sure she had seen it. She went back to the house and rang a third time. This time she heard footsteps. "Who is it?"

"It's me. Annie. I wanted to see if you were okay. If you need anything . . ."

"That's sweet, but I'm fine."

"Melissa, please open the door."

"I'm not dressed."

"I'll wait. Please, Melissa."

The door opened. Melissa stood in its shadow with only half her face showing. "I'm fine, Annie, really I am. Just a touch of flu."

Annie debated for a nanosecond about saying fine and leaving. Although she had little in common with Melissa she found her likeable in a puppyish way. She grabbed Melissa's arm and pulled.

Melissa's hand flew to hide her face.

Annie pulled it away. The girl was dressed in jeans and an oversized dark beige Irish sweater. The area around her left eye was purplish.

"My God!" Annie said.

"I banged it against the kitchen closet, and I look so horrible I didn't want anyone to see."

"It looks more like you ran into a fist," Annie said.

"Who would beat up a pregnant lady?" Melissa laughed. "Well as long as you've seen my ugly face and haven't run away screaming, come on in. Coffee? I can give you a tour of the house."

An antique grandfather clock chimed eleven as Melissa led Annie through the living room furnished with a sofa and lots of throw pillows. A TV stand held a giant-screen TV. "I made the slipcovers, but the couch is Goodwill," Melissa said.

"You did a good job," Annie said.

"Jason loves his TV. He's a real sports fan."

Annie noticed that the dining nook was empty of furniture.

"This is our starter house. Jason wants us to have a big house one day, but I think we're so lucky to have a house at all. Most couples our age rent for years and years and then all they can afford is a condo, but Jason works so hard. And with the financial problems these days . . . and he thinks it is important not to live beyond our means. We don't have any credit card debt at all. Isn't that amazing? But he feels bad we don't have all the things we want. Of course the things for the baby can't wait until we have the money. I go to garage sales. The clock is Ethan Allen and I got it for about ten percent of the original price. The rug was only five dollars, but isn't it a great match?"

The barrage of words did not convince Annie of anything other than this was a woman in trouble.

The kitchen was a sunny yellow with a yellow checked tablecloth matching a café curtain at the window. The cabinets were painted white with yellow trim. The appliances looked like an advertisement from a 1950s magazine that Annie had found in her parents' basement during the clean-out.

"We want to remodel, but it has to wait. I did what I could in painting, but I can't paint anymore . . . the fumes . . . the baby. But I think the yellow makes it cheery, don't you?"

Annie barely had time to nod.

"I made the curtains myself. I think it is so important to create a good home ambience. Women get too wound up in careers these days and don't spend the time creating a family." All the time Melissa talked she was picking up the coffeepot, pouring water, taking out cups, filling the sugar bowl. She had to keep rolling up the sleeves of the sweater that came well over her hands, a clown's costume.

"I love oversized clothes for bumming around the house. They are so comfortable, except when I wash dishes. . . . It is so important to keep everything clean . . ."

"Melissa?"

"I go to the library for all the magazines to read about how to be a good wife . . ." She placed two spoons on the table.

"Melissa?"

"That way I don't spend money on buying them . . . but you can't cut coupons from a library maga . . ." She swirled to the fridge and brought out the milk and sniffed it.

"Melissa! Stop talking!" Annie took the milk from the girl and holding her two hands looked into her eyes. "Which cabinet did you run into?"

Melissa's unhurt eye darted around the room. All the cabinets were too high or too low to inflict such an injury.

"Who hit you?"

Melissa shook her head. "No one. I hit my eye on the bathroom sink."

"You said the kitchen. Melissa, if Jason hurt you . . ."

"Jason loves me."

The front door opened. "Melissa honey, you here?"

"I'm in the kitchen."

141

Jason carried yellow and white rose buds wrapped in cellophane and tied with thin yellow and white ribbons. He wore a well-pressed blue suit and a maroon turtleneck. His hair was so well honed that not a strand could fall out of place even if it wanted to.

He looked at his wife before seeing Annie. A flicker of an indescribable emotion flashed over his face and then disappeared. "Annie, how come you're here?"

"I was at Charlie Tucker's and your father called and said Melissa was sick. I know how busy you are, so I thought I'd be a good neighbor and stop to see if she needed anything."

"And you saw how my clumsy love hurt herself. It must be the new weight she's carrying." He patted his wife's stomach.

Annie watched Melissa flinch.

"What beautiful flowers," Annie said. "You're a lucky girl to have such a romantic husband." And unlucky that he's also a bastard. Melissa was not the only battered wife she knew. One of her university pals married a businessman who considered her a punching bag. The girl had left him, but the husband had stalked her until the girl left Switzerland to work in England. Until now, the husband had never found out where his wife had escaped to, but during holidays he drove past his former in-laws' house, despite having remarried twice. Both new wives had divorced him.

"They'll look wonderful on the table." Melissa took the flowers. "Get a vase, sweetheart."

Jason opened a cabinet and took down a square crystal vase.

"Won't the flowers look incredible in here?" Melissa stared at Annie. Or maybe prayed at her.

"Well, I should be going along, as long as I know you're all right," Annie said. "By the way, I hope you are both coming to my parents' Christmas decorating party."

"We don't go out much," Jason said.

"Your father is coming. And who knows, you might get a listing," Annie said. "But I don't want to pressure you."

The grandfather clock struck noon.

"My God, I'll be late for my next appointment."

Once in her car Annie sat back in her seat. Her hands shook. She breathed in and out several times. Helplessness was not something she liked to feel, but it was overwhelming. That poor, poor girl.

CHAPTER 35

Wednesday, December 1

The corridor outside the fifth-grade classroom was like millions of other schools all over the world with polished floors and doors with the top half glass. A bulletin board to the left of the door featured colored drawings of Santa Claus, decorated trees and Christmas stockings.

Annie was surprised until she realized that the drawings represented the commercial Christmas. No crèche, no shepherds, no star. The board had notices for band practice, the Holiday Fair and Parents' Night. The smell of damp wool coats hanging on pegs combined with that of heating fuel.

The teacher, seeing Annie peek in the window, poked her head out. "I'm Kendra Jones, super fifth-grade teacher about to submit my class to your history experiment."

When Annie had spoken to the teacher on the phone, she'd pictured her as her mother's age. The young woman looked more like a high school student with her long blond hair held back by a band.

They looked at each other and laughed because both wore khaki pants and navy blue pullovers. "Annie Young. Obviously we're in uniform."

Kendra slipped into the corridor and stood leaving the door partially open. She poked her head back in. "I can hear everything you do, so keep working."

"I brought everything. I was hoping we could project it on a screen."

"There's a pull-down behind my desk. Need help carrying stuff in?"

As Annie set up the laptop, Kendra spoke to the class. "This is Annie Young and she's written a computer program for kids your age and you are going to be the guinea pigs. Can you tell us what it is about, Miss Young?"

"Thank you. We just had Thanksgiving. What did you learn about that?"

Different voices spoke out so fast that Annie couldn't find the corresponding mouths.

"The Pilgrims cooked a big meal and invited Indians."

"We always color Pilgrims every year."

"It's not much fun to use so much black."

"And turkeys. We color them in brown, red and yellow."

"And make Indian headdresses. With lots of feathers."

"One at a time and raise your hands," Kendra said.

"Do you know why the Pilgrims left their homes to come here?" Annie asked.

Silence.

"Can you name any of them?"

Silence.

"The name of the boat they came on?"

"The *Mayflower*. My family visited it when we went to the Cape for vacation," the girl in the skirt said.

"That's a model of the original, but it is supposed to be identical, plank for plank," Annie said. "Miss Jones, may all the boys sit on the left side of the room and the girls on the right?"

Kendra clapped her hands. "Do it."

None of the kids were very big, but they made much noise between squeaking desks and thumping feet. One boy started to push another, but Kendra had anticipated it in advance and put herself between them.

"Don't you dare look in my desk, Jared," someone called out.

"Sit." Kendra would have made a good dog trainer. "Put your paws on the desk."

"We have hands," a voice said.

"If you behave like animals we'll call them paws. Now quiet."

"How many of you play computer games?" Annie asked.

Almost all their hands went up. "Well, this is a computer game in one way, and like a book in another. Girls, I want you to close your eyes and pretend you are a Pilgrim girl. Your name is Priscilla. Boys, shut your eyes and pretend you're a Pilgrim boy. Your name is Edward."

"We all have the same name?" asked a kid who wore a Celtics sweatshirt.

"Yes," Annie said.

"My name really is Priscilla," the smallest girl said.

"Then you won't have to pretend as hard," Kendra said. "Tommy, shut your eyes."

Annie looked at the faces. One little girl peeked and Annie winked at her. The girl winked back and shut her eyes. Cute kids. Please let them like this. What did she know about kids except for Gaëlle?

While their eyes were shut she had started the program, which showed a bunk with a blanket providing some privacy from the other Pilgrims inside the *Mayflower*. "Open your eyes." For the next ten minutes the kids were imagining themselves on the boat. Annie had them sway back and forth. "Just pretend you're seasick. No throwing up."

"Bleck," a boy said.

She had them select between storms and calm weather. She had them catching fish and munching dried biscuits to avoid the dry heaves in heavy waves.

"I wish he wasn't watching," one of the kids said as he virtually scaled a fish that gave a final shudder before dying.

They ran through the desolation of the landing, the building of the first houses, the planting of crops, the long Sunday sermons.

"Kids really worked hard," one girl said. She had just been assigned candlemaking and her choice had burnt her hand virtually.

"Their clothes were boring."

"Too bad they didn't have a shopping mall."

"When do we get to shoot some Indians?"

Annie brought up the second part. Her problem had been to reduce the atrocities to something that would not have parents suing for destroying their kids' mental health yet keeping to the facts. Indian children witnessing the death of their loved ones hurt just as much as Pilgrim children.

To keep a proper timeline she had the war as a separate section. At first the children got into their roles as an Indian girl and boy that went from babies to old Indians when they lost their families in King Phillip's War. When the children made their last choice, forcing them inland to seek new land away from the white settlers, they were almost crying. The time period covered for the Indians was much longer than for the Pilgrims.

Annie shut off the laptop. She looked at the somber children's faces. Kendra Jones was rigid. "Okay, let's talk about it." For the next half hour they talked about freedom of religion, as well as what happened when it was only freedom for you, but not for others. They talked about genocide and hardships.

"This is not alleged reality TV. This was reality for the people of the time," Annie concluded.

"Okay kids, take out your math books. Page 58, do problems one through ten," Kendra said. She walked Annie to the door and shut it behind them. "It will be a miracle if I don't get fired for this. I expect at least some parents to come looking for my skin."

"Do you really think that? It was all true." Annie thought Kendra was overreacting.

"On the other hand, it was the most meaningful lesson I've presented in my two-year career. Just think of it. Pilgrims who weren't absolutely perfect people. However, the violence against the . . ."

"Sorta like a television program," Annie said. "I can back up all my material, if you need me to go to the school board or whatever they have here."

"Still . . . this wasn't an approved text. And by the way, I loved it. I'd love to talk more about what you're doing."

"You free Saturday night?"

"Yes."

"Good. My folks are having an open house on Saturday. A Christmas tree decoration extravaganza. My mother goes nuts at the holidays. Would you like to come?"

"Yes again. I better get back in before they act up." She opened the door. "Probably nothing will go wrong."

CHAPTER 36

Zeb, Zeb, Zeb. No matter what I do his face be everywhere: in the bowl where I pours water in the morning to wash my face, on the dishes where I puts the toast before taking it to the Mistress, on the white walls. I wants to spend all my minutes talking with him. I wants to touch his chest. I wants to look into those eyes and feel his breath on my cheek.

However, with Mistress Elizabeth busy with Mr. Aaron she needs me to spend more time with Missy Annabelle, who has a right bad cold. Poor little thing. That baby be up all the night. Her nose, which be almost too tiny to breath through, crusts over. I wipes so careful because it hurts her. If Missy Annabelle ain't be so sick, Mistress Elizabeth might have sent me back to the hospital to see how Zeb be.

"That poor niggah. He must be in agony," she says to Mr. Aaron lots of times.

"Well, he probably won't run away again."

"There's something in his eyes. Some of them are so stupid, but not this one."

"Are you talking about Zeb?" Massa Edward done enters the room.

The Mistress jumps up to kiss him.

"Is he getting better?" She leads him to a chair and pulls off his boots that be all mud covered.

"I should have known better than to buy a niggah off the boat, no matter how strong he is. Takes at least a generation to domesticate them."

149

The Mistress and Mr. Aaron exchange glances, but the Mistress changes the subject. They talk-talk-talk about the old days in London and New York. Those places sound like one of the fairy tales the Mistress gives me to read. They names stores. I only ever seen one store and that carries a bit of this and a bit of that and that was just last week. I goes to town one day with the Mistress who needs new cloth. She kept sighing that there be no choice, but I sees piles and piles as high as my thigh. Enough to make a new shirt for every nig-gah at Two Pines.

She talks about how much she misses the theater and the opera. And restaurants. The Massa finally says, "We must get you to New York, Elizabeth."

"But it is such a long trip," she says.

"And such primitive conditions," Mr. Aaron said. "Lord, it made a trip between London and Glasgow look like a Sunday drive."

"You didn't have to visit," Massa Edwards says, but before anyone thinks him unfriendly he adds, "Although it would have broken my wife's heart."

I bets to myself the Massa wishes Mr. Aaron will leave for New York or London soon. He's been here for months and months.

"Maybe spending next winter in New York would do you a world of good," Massa Edwards says.

The Mistress clasps her hands together. "And would you come? Please say you will. It would be like another honeymoon."

"Who'll look after Two Pines?"

"I will, of course." The Massa's brother walks in. Now no one ever told me, but I thinks that the two brothers don't like each other. Oh yes, they always talks sweet-sweet to each other, but under all those sacks of sugar knives be hid. Maybe the younger one wants Two Pines for himself, even though he lives here just like it be his. "You don't trust me, big brother?"

"Of course, I do."

When all this be going on, I stands by the table in case they needs me to add food to their plates. They be too helpless to do it themselves.

Another funny thing—although the Mistress be really helpful to us slaves, who fights the Massa against what she says be injustice, she also thinks we be animals pretending to be human. More than once she says we be filthy and stupid. I never asks how we can wash when we has only enough water to cook our food. Sometimes we be too tired to pump enough to wash the dishes, and we just eats on the plates left from the last meal.

Course since I becomes a house niggah, I eats in the kitchen with Molly. We use wooden plates, not the Mistress's shiny plates. Hers be always twinkly like the stars when you hold them to the light. Mistress be Queen Clean the First. That's what the Massa calls her. I didn't know what a queen be until I asks her, and I gets a long talk about governments and countries. I never knowd those things exist, but as I keeps reading more and more I realizes how much I don't know.

About the same time I find Zeb living in my head and heart, I looks in the Mistress' mirror. I knowd my breasts grew until they begs for a baby to suckle. Lord, Zeb and me would make beautiful little black babies, for now that I has enough to eat I has become one pretty niggah. Chloe says that if we women chews cotton seeds we won't grow bellies. Massa Richard grows rice, corn and tobacco so cotton seeds be hard to come by. But if Zeb wants to put his thing in me, I'll lay down as fast as a leaf falls off a tree in a big wind, cotton seeds or no.

The first time I thinks of myself as pretty I be serving sweet potatoes to the Massa Richard. I feels his eyes piercing my clothes. He says, "Elizabeth, look at this slave of yours. She is one spectacular woman." Later as I clears the table, and everyone else done gone into the parlor he comes in looking for something and he put his hands on my breasts. "Nice." I don't knowd what to say, I just picks up the dishes and heads to the kitchen.

Two things hit me. One that I was pretty and the second was— whose slave was I?

I wants to ask the Mistress who be my owner, her, Massa Richard or Massa Edward? I knowd she got upset when us slaves asks her things she cain't answer without asking the Massa.

Before she asks him she practices what she is to say. She works out how to hold her head and move her hands. It don't matter none how much she prepares. The Massa yells. She yells back. Sometimes she cries. Most times the Massa gives up before she cries and almost always after.

We be in the nursery. The Mistress baths the baby, who loves water. She hits it and laughs when it splashes her face. I loves the way the Missy Annabelle smells after her bath, sweet like the rose petals the Mistress puts in the water. In a few minutes she might stink and we needs to change her pants, but right from her bath while she is on the towel, I buries my nose in her stomach. She giggles. So I does it again.

"You're a wonderful nanny," the Mistress says holding a pretty pink dress. I loves that little baby, but part of me hates her too. If I has a baby she will never have a pretty pink dress. I'll never own no tub to bathe her in.

For a long time I believes in God, but I don't think a god would hate black people enough to make us live like we lives. Not any god I wants as mine.

I finally works up my nerve to ask her. I be helping her take off her dress so she can take a nap. "I've a question." My eyes looks at the floor. "Do you own me? Or the Massa?"

"My husband. Why?"

"The other night the Massa's brother says I was your slave and . . ."

"Richard? I think he just meant you work mostly for me. That's all."

Massa Richard. I never thinks of the Massa's brother by name without Massa before it. I never thinks of most white folk by name. But then there's Mr. Aaron.

"Has Richard . . ." *She looks at me funny. "You're becoming quite lovely a woman."*

Lovely. Who ever calls a niggah lovely?

She takes out the ring of keys that opened and locked all the doors in the house and took off one. "This is the key to your room. I suggest you start locking it at night."

CHAPTER 37

Wednesday, December 1

Annie sat in her father's Ford Escort in the school parking lot and punched in Charlie Tucker's number on her father's cell. The secretary patched her through.

"How'd it go?" Charlie asked without a hello.

Annie took no offense. She told him about the places where the kids did and didn't respond as expected, the issues raised in the discussion. "Kendra is a bit worried that she'll get into trouble."

"We used to be able to hit kids in school," Charlie said. "Now we can't do anything to upset the little dears." He laughed. "If she's worried then I think we're on the right track."

"I'm still not totally satisfied with the graphics, but I can't do any better."

"You're being a perfectionist. How about starting on the website?"

She hesitated. As much Annie liked the project she was being paid for, she long ago learned how easy it was for a client to go beyond the contract. *No* was a very effective word.

"I'm talking more money. Besides, this has been so much your baby you wouldn't want to let someone else do this, would you?"

"Okay, we'll talk about it, but we also have to talk about me working from Argelès. I need to go home." Annie wondered if she should put the sentence about going home on a tape and just press the button whenever she needed to say it.

Annie was beginning to think there was a novel in the diary, although she didn't consider herself a novelist. Many tech writers believed they had one or more novels hiding in their hearts or heads. There was no novel inside any of her organs. If she were to write anything it would be a history text.

The body in the cellar had not been the slave who wrote the diary. When Annie imagined herself living in other times, she always thought of herself as gentry, but this time she imagined herself as the slave girl learning to read. The letters made no sense, the voice of the Mistress drumming in her head. A-A or ah, B-bee, C-cee, D-dee. Just like Annie when she had moved to Holland listening to strange sounds that meant nothing until she suddenly understood, the sounds and letters matched. Ah-pull. Bay-bee, Cat, Dog.

There was no parking place near her mother's studio. Annie had not owned a car in her adult life, preferring public transportation and walking. However, Caleb's Landing offered no alternative. A bus doesn't get lost, she grumbled. A bus doesn't need parking. She took the car home and walked to her mother's studio.

Judith, the pot thrower, was just leaving.

"We must talk about Judith." Magda waved at Annie then walked over to the pots and started counting. "At the rate she's going there won't be enough when we open to justify her part of the shop."

"Maybe she's planning to work harder after the first of the year," Susan said as Annie perched on the stool next to the easel. She'd been so wrapped up in the history project that she had a frisson of guilt that she hadn't paid enough attention to her mother's studio problems. She vowed to listen more.

Susan's coveralls were more color splattered than usual with

155

yellows and whites dominating the denim, but the rest of the rainbow had satisfactory representation. Susan Young never claimed to be a neat artist. "How did it go?"

Annie told her.

Magda stopped sewing. There were pins, their multicolored heads sticking into her red cardigan with the worn sleeves. "Fantastic, Darlink. I'll put on the kettle. No. I've an idea better." She rummaged in the studio's mini refrigerator and brought out a split of champagne. "We try to find excuses to have champagne. Sometimes it's because it's Monday, but this is a real reason."

Susan dropped her paintbrush into a glass of gray water and went to a closet and pulled down three crystal flutes.

Magda twisted the cork until they heard a palate-satisfying pop and poured the champagne into the glasses without spilling a drop. She raised her glass. "To your success, Darlink."

Susan's and Annie's eyes met as required by Swiss manners and habit, but Magda had already taken her first sip and was heading back to her sewing machine. The hum of the needle provided a bit of privacy to their conversation.

"Tell me all about it." Susan said the same words whenever Annie came back from school, a riding lesson, a play rehearsal or anything else she did.

"What a day you've had. It seems as if you're either locked away by yourself for days at a time or you're drowned with people," Susan said. She put her flute down among tubes of paint.

"How true," Annie said. She debated not saying anything about Melissa, but her concern for the girl was such that she wanted her mother's guidance. Offloading some of the responsibility would feel good. "Something else happened." She lowered her voice and told about the bruises, Melissa's various stories of how it happened, Jason's flowers. "I don't think it is a one-time

156

occurrence. When we ate lunch together, her arms were black and blue."

"That poor, sweet child," Susan said. "I really would like to tear Jason's balls off."

Annie took a moment to digest what her mother said: Susan, the one who drifted in an unreal world of beauty she created herself, who didn't watch the news because it upset her, who picked up stray kittens, had just threatened to cut off a man's balls. "I guess maybe I wasn't overreacting."

Magda was next to them. Neither Annie nor Susan had noticed that the sewing machine had stopped. "Is Melissa being beaten, Darlinks?" They looked at her. "Seriously, Darlink, it is not gossip that I want to hear. If she's in trouble, we must help before she is killed." Only Magda pronounced killed in two syllables as kill-ed. "Darlinks, this is not overfeeling on my part. Do you have any idea how many women are kill-ed each year by their husbands or lovers?"

Annie and Susan shook their heads.

"Too many. One is too many. And what about the baby?"

"Melissa loves her husband. She talks about him as if he were her god."

"Making men gods," spat Magda, "is no good. Let me tell you about one god. My sister made her husband her god. He was a talented artist, but she was a genius."

Annie had almost grown used to Magda's intensity, but as she told the story it increased. The woman seemed incapable of normal movement. If walking was called for, she strode. If whispering made sense, she would speak in a normal voice and if a normal voice was needed, her voice would be louder than any other. Her arms flailed. Imagining her at rest was impossible. Even thinking of her on a couch turning the pages of a book was beyond Annie's ken. "I didn't know you had a sister."

"Not just a sister, my twin. We were like one. He beat her. I told her to topple her god. God. Beast. She made excuses: he had too much to drink, she hadn't stopped her own work soon enough to prepare his dinner, the meat was overcooked. Asshole!"

"Did she escape?" Susan asked.

Magda slammed her fist onto the table where Susan had arranged her paints. The blow upset the flute, but it didn't break. Magda didn't notice.

Susan dropped a rag on the puddle, but didn't wipe the spill.

"She won an award from the Budapest government. We had all entered, but she was better than we were. I knew that from the beginning. He did too. I accepted it. He couldn't. He'd been drinking almost non-stop for a week and making big brags to friends how he would win. His father was a friend of the judges, but my sister still won. That beast came home, broke a bottle and slit her throat. He then slit his own wrists and died."

Magda shook as if she had just heard the news. She sat on a stool and rocked back and forth. Tears ran down her cheeks. She reached for a paint rag and honked into it. A streak of orange paint marked her nose. "Excuse me, Darlinks. I should forget my anger, but I cannot. I am angry because I couldn't destroy him myself. I am mad at me. If only I had done something to stop it."

Susan, although smaller than Magda by at least six inches, scooped the Hungarian into her arms and rocked her back and forth. She didn't contradict anything the woman said, but Annie didn't expect her to. That was her mother's style: not to deny other people's beliefs.

What a day, Annie thought. "But if Melissa doesn't want help . . ."

"Leave it to me," Magda said. "I'll make her see."

CHAPTER 38

Zeb's body got well. His head didn't. I sees him when I can. "I won't die a slave," he says each time.

"Nothin' you can do about it," I says back at him.

"Girl, I plan. I wait."

One night when I comes back to the big house after visiting Mama and Papa, I passes him. Although I carries a small lantern, it be dark except for the little path of light in front of me. He sits dead still on a stump near the path. "Hey, girl," he calls out.

I jumps. "Don't do that. You near scairt the life out of me."

He takes my lantern to holds near my face. "You don't look near dead to me. You looks good."

One good thing about black skin in the dark, it don't turn red when someone says something we don't know what to do with. If it did, I be the color of a cardinal when he says that.

"When I be free, I will asks you to be my wife." And with that he disappears into the night.

I walks home. Lord I wants to lay down with him. I ain't never done it, but Mama and Papa does it. When I be little I thinks he be hurting her, but then she laughs, and my Mama don't laugh much.

I knowd the Massa and the Mistress does it because they have the little Missy. They ain't doing it much these days. Most nights he goes to his room and she goes to hers.

Mr. Aaron asks her right out, "You still have a marriage?"

The Mistress did the cardinal skin thing. "Of course," she says.

Then Mr. Aaron takes her hand, not like a lover, but like a brother or an uncle and says, "You never smile anymore. When I first met you all you did was smile." Then he talks about pride and admitting mistakes and showing courage and all that until the Mistress runs from the room crying.

I cain't spend a lot of time thinking about Zeb or the Mistress. I gots my own problems.

Massa Richard.

Sometimes I calls him Mr. Whip. He uses that whip more and more—not like before. I cain't think of one field niggah who the whip done missed. Only good thing is he limits the number of hits.

Whenever he catches me alone, and I tries real hard never to be where he might find me alone, but sometimes I done fails. "Call me Richard," he says to me.

"I cain't," I says. "Won't be proper."

"Proper?" he laughs. "I see my virtuous sister-in-law has done a fine job with you." And he walks away still laughing. I don't laugh.

I be asleep one night. Even if housework is a lot easier than garden work, there be still a lot to do and a lot to do right. The Mistress likes her tray with a cloth under her dishes and that needs to be clean and ironed. The dishes needs to be what she calls pretty. And she likes a flower in a vase.

And there be my lessons. They goes on many times a week with Mr. Aaron watching. Sometimes he gives me a lesson, but not in reading and writing. He talks about math. Before I counts to five: one, two, three, four, five, lots. He gives me the next few numbers: six, seven, eight, all the way to twenty.

He takes peaches from the fruit bowl on the dining room table. "How many?" he asks.

"One, two, three."

He adds two more. "Now how many."

"One, two, three, four, five."

He takes the slate that I uses for my lessons and writes: 1, 2, 3, 4, 5, 6, 7, 8, 9, 10 and 2 + 3 = 5.

"This is the symbol for two and this is the symbol for three and when you add them, that is the cross symbol, you get the symbol for five. If you go 5 − 5 you get zero.

"But then I don't have any peaches to eat," I says.

He laughs, but it ain't a mean laugh or a make-fun-of-me laugh like Massa Richard.

For a minute I be confused then it be like starting a fire. I understand.

The rest of the lesson we moves peaches all around. We even takes some away with a little line. After a while I has all fifteen peaches on the table. "What happens if I gets six more?"

"We make peach cobbler," he says.

The Mistress been watching. "Don't make fun of her."

"I'm not," he says. "She's really bright."

"I told you," the Mistress says.

I feels real proud, but I likes working with words more than numbers unless I can eat the peaches.

I trys to read a book she done gives me. The problem I has was although I can say the words, I don't always understand what they means.

"Ask me," says the Mistress so I writes a list. My writing has gotten smaller and better. The first word on the list was dignity.

"Dignity," she says. "That's when a person has a sense of him- or herself that is positive. Even under bad conditions. They walk with their heads held high. They have poise, self-respect."

Dignity. I says the word over and over. I likes the sound of it. I tried to find people with dignity. The Mistress has it. Mr. Aaron has it. Zeb has it even though he be black. Massa Richard, he walks with a swagger, but the Mistress says that ain't dignity. Swagger be outside. Dignity be inside.

Sometimes words be like the hidden branches and animals in the forest. They can be dangerous but they can also be beautiful. It depends.

I sometimes writes in a direct line, but sometimes another idea enters my head and it is pages later before I get back to what I meant to say in the first place. Sometimes I never get back to it, but what I is going to write next be too important to forget it.

Going to sleep never be a problem for me. I hears white people say they falls asleep the minute their heads hits the pillow. Me? I got trouble staying awake until I gets into bed. I sleeps like I be dead. So it takes quite a bit of knocking to wake me up.

"Who be there?"

"Mr. Richard. Let me in."

I wakes up real quick. There be more than one slave baby at Two Pines with white blood. The mothers never said who the father be, but women be always extra careful to be ugly when Massa's brother be around. "The Mistress wants me?"

"I want you."

"For what?" Stupid question. I knowd for what. As I talks to him through the door I cut myself and wipes blood on my thighs. I put on the monthly cloth and smears a little blood on the sheets. I had to work fast and quietly, but then I opens the door. "I'm not sure you wants me tonight," I says. I talks white with him. If I went back into black talk it might help me now, but then again maybe not. However, when I write, I want to write black. Cause that is who I am. It be a matter of dignity.

"Open the door."

I did. He carries a candle in his hand. He stank of bourbon and sweat. After putting the candle down on the floor, he grabs me and kisses me hard. I don't fight back but I don't kiss back none.

"You're not going to fight me, but you aren't going to give me anything."

"I got monthly pains. I'm bleeding," I says.

"Damn." He releases me. "I'll wait until your bath night. I want my women fresh." He sways and staggers out. Before I can lock the door he comes back for his candle. As soon as his footsteps disappears

I locks the door, but I knowd he'll be back, and I has no idea what I can do to stop him.

CHAPTER 39

Wednesday, December 1

Magda, wrapped in her fleece-lined red plaid poncho, rang the Haskells' bell. She felt as if she were living the myth of Sisyphus, only she wasn't the Greek rolling the rock up the hill every day for eternity. She was the rock doomed to fall down. It made her feel leaden, but like the rock, she had no choice but to be pushed up the mountain daily.

When there was no answer she walked around the back. A light in the kitchen shone above the café curtains. "Let me in," she called.

Few people said no to Magda. Her size and force commanded, obey me. Melissa, young enough to consider people over thirty as authority figures, unlocked the door.

Magda didn't wait to be invited in. She took the girl by the hand and walked to where the light highlighted the purple and blue bruises. "Have you seen a doctor, Darlink?"

"For running into a cabinet?"

"That was no cabinet. Your husband ran into you." Sometimes Magda wished she could just kidnap the abused women and make them realize there were alternatives. If she were going to be rolled up and down a mountain she would roll over every snake on route. She set the huge cloth sack she used as a pocketbook on the kitchen table. She pulled out a Polaroid. Before she could snap the photo, the girl covered her face.

Magda sighed. "You think Jason loves you. You think if you

try harder, it'll get better. You're wrong. Wrong! It'll get worse. One day he'll kill you. And maybe your baby." She knew she was harsh. Gentle didn't work. She'd have made a terrible psychiatrist, waiting for patients to discover their own truths. More likely she would say to the person on the couch, "Look Darlink, you had a rotten mother. She didn't toilet-train you right. That's past. So what are you doing about it today?" Anything else would be pussyfooting, and Magda was no pussyfooter. She pried Melissa's hands away from her face.

"What will you do with the photo?"

"I'm taking one for you and one for me to prove you were hurt."

"But not by Jason."

"Was this the first time, Melissa? Or the first time he went for your face?"

"I hit a cabinet."

"Darlink, do I look stupid?"

Melissa shook her head.

"Then tell me the truth."

"It would be disloyal."

"Beating you is disloyal. And don't give me any of the for-better-or-worse shit, Darlink."

Magda opened cabinets until she found the coffee. "Want any?"

"I can't have caffeine."

Magda raised one eyebrow. As she poured water into the pot and spooned four times the normal amount of coffee into the filter, she knew the girl must be wondering how to get rid of her, but she wasn't going anywhere. "Caffeine isn't good for your baby, but violence is, I suppose. And what will happen to your child when she or he witnesses scenes like this one?"

"Once the baby is here . . ."

"It'll be worse." Magda switched on the coffeemaker. "If it's a boy he'll think it is okay to beat women. If it is a girl she'll think it is okay to be hit. Did your father hit your mother?"

"My uncle hit my aunt sometimes. He said the man was the head of the house." The words were whispered. Magda strained to hear them. God, how many times would she have to go through this before women learned? She knew the answer—as many times as it took.

"Then it's time to break the pattern. It's beyond the time."

"I can't leave."

"Why not?" Magda knew the reasons that Melissa was about to offer.

"I'd never make enough to pay for the baby. And I wouldn't even have a job. I work for my father-in-law. He believes in marriage."

Melissa said exactly what Magda expected. The main reason was unspoken. Melissa didn't want to let go of the fairy tale. There would be no happily ever after. Magda must push the decision. Start with the bastard Len. "So much he cannot keep a woman. They all wise up and leave."

"Jason's mother just took off. Never contacted him. That's why my husband is so unsure of me. I need to prove . . ."

"Bullshit!" The word was projected with such force that if it were a cartoon Melissa would have been pinned to the wall.

"Bullshit! Bullshit! You need to prove nothing." Melissa's tears left Magda unmoved. "Have you any idea how many women have said that? Have any idea how many women end up dead? Dead, Melissa. Your life is in danger." Her coworkers in the movement often said she was too forceful, but she also had the highest save rate, not that it was a contest. Magda counted the women she lost, not the ones she won.

In a whimper Melissa said, "Jason would never . . ."

"Kill you? Didn't you think once he would never hurt you?"

Reality therapy was what this girl needed. Magda again delved

into her bag and brought out her notebook with page after page
of statistics of spousal abuse in all walks of life—doctors' wives,
lawyers' wives, businessmen's wives, and women who were doctors and lawyers and businesswomen themselves. "Do you really
think you can beat these odds?"

"There's nothing I can do."

"Sure there is. Go to the police and file a complaint. Get a
restraining order and don't let him back in until he gets counseling. Get a lawyer."

"I don't know any lawyers. I have no money."

Magda sat in front of the girl and took both her hands in
both of hers. "Darlink, there's women lawyers who help women
like you *pro bono*." When Melissa frowned, Magda said, "They
don't charge you, Darlink. They only want to help."

"Jason would be so angry. My father-in-law would be
ashamed of me."

"He should be ashamed of his son."

"A man should be the head of his house."

Magda imagined herself shaking sense into the girl.

"And how could I put Jason out of his own home?"

"Is your name on the deed?"

"I don't know."

Magda threw up her hands. When would women learn to
care for themselves? Probably never. She would like nothing
better than to be out of the movement, because that would
mean there was no more abuse. She was tired of broken bones
and broken spirits, but she couldn't quit.

"No judge in the world throws a pregnant woman out of her
house. No judge allows a man to beat his pregnant wife." Magda
wasn't sure how bad a case Jason was. She suspected his
lightning temper was like his father's. Patterns.

"There's another way." She couldn't reveal the depth of the
Woman's Underground Railroad that took women in jeopardy

to other states and set them up in halfway houses and with temporary jobs. In the worse cases they created false identities, but since 9/11 it was harder and harder. "We can get you out of here, if things get bad."

"I can't leave."

Magda had heard that too many times. Once a month she visited three graves and instead of prayers said apologies even if the victims bore part of the responsibility. She believed there were no victims, but volunteers, people who put themselves in bad situations and refused to get out. But there was also hope for women who forsook victimhood, women who took control of their own lives realizing whatever awaited them wasn't as bad as what they were undergoing.

"Melissa, this is my mobile number, my home number and a hotline. Call any of these numbers and someone will come to help you. ASAP, Darlink. And here's the police number."

She picked up the camera. This time Melissa let her take two photos. They both signed the back and dated them.

As Magda put things back in her sack, Melissa said, "Please don't do anything with your copy."

"Not yet, but I'm watching."

CHAPTER 40

Friday, December 17

Annie waited outside International Arrivals at Logan. The airport had expanded since she'd visited Boston as a kid. Or maybe she mixed it up with all the other airports she went through regularly: Orly, Charles de Gaulle, Heathrow, Luton, Zurich, Geneva, Gatwick, Skiphol, Frankfurt, Stuttgart, Munich. Usually she was the one coming in—with no one to meet her as she began a new assignment.

The flight board reported Roger and Gaëlle's Air France flight had landed at the same time as Lufthansa and Iberia. Annie stood behind the barrier as men and women trickled by behind carts loaded with baggage. A three-year-old girl staggered out rubbing her eyes. A boy about the same age bounced through the door delighted to be freed from being strapped in a seat too many hours. People waiting called out names. Those named rushed into hugs. On the outside of the waiting crowd, men stood with signs that said Perez, Chang, Schmidt, Harris, Joubert, Merkel. Annie was sure it wasn't *that* Merkel.

She hadn't seen Roger for six weeks, which seemed to go faster than the last minutes waiting for him to walk through the doors. Then he was there. His full head of black hair with the forelock streaked gray and falling over his left eyebrow was the same. The black sweater and pants accented his slimness; the months of forced inactivity had added no weight. He leaned on one crutch on the left side. It was the type where the top part circled his bicep. Real progress from the walker he'd been using when she'd left.

Gaëlle pushed their cart. Her brown hair was crew cut short in some places and pink sprouts sticking up at all angles. How that haircut had come about Annie wasn't sure, but she was sure it represented a real battle. When they were alone Gaëlle would give her the details.

Roger gathered Annie in his arms, the crutch in his hand. *"Tu m'as manqué, beaucoup."*

"I missed you too," she said.

"English. Papa told my school this trip would help my English, so no more French."

"This is the girl who fought tooth and nail to not speak a foreign language," Annie said.

"How can you fight tooth and nail? Do you shoot them out of guns?" Gaëlle asked.

"I suppose it means biting and scratching, although I never thought about it. You'll get used to all the expressions never taught in language courses." Annie broke loose from Roger to hug the teenager.

"All the swear words, too?" Gaëlle asked.

"No," Roger and Annie said together.

They drove out of the airport and up Route 1.

"Regardes. Les voitures sont très grandes." Gaëlle's head hadn't stopped swiveling.

Annie signaled to change lanes.

"No, English," Roger said. "The new priest is really strict, and church attendance is tapering off. Mamie Couges sends her love. Marie-France wishes you a great holiday and says come back fast. The *charcuterie* went bankrupt. He kept calling the women 'my little hussy.' They might have forgiven him his rudeness, if the quality of his meat hadn't gone down and prices up."

170

"I never went in. He always looked slimy to me."

"Now tell me your news. Any repercussions from your demo? I keep asking on e-mail, but . . ."

Annie smiled. Roger had resisted learning the computer, but with her frequent absences he had developed a love of e-mail and messaging not just to her, but to old friends in Paris. During his recovery from the shooting, he had reached a point that he was bored but not well enough to do anything. He discovered Web surfing. Declaring himself a news junkie, he read the French, Swiss, Belgian, American and English papers online daily. He found mystery sites, shopping, music and God knows what.

As they drove along the coast, Gaëlle said, "The houses, they're wood."

"These are the old houses. I'll show you the new ones later."

"Are they wood too?"

"Most. Sometimes you get brick, but mostly wood."

"Look at the gardens," Gaëlle said. She turned to the sea, which was gray and angry and crashing to the shore. "And the waves."

Annie parked the car. "We're here."

Dave and Susan, who were peeking out the window, ran to greet what they hoped was their future son-in-law and granddaughter-in-law and gathered them into the warmth of the house.

Although Roger and Gaëlle had eaten well on the plane, they were unable to pass up tea and slivers of apple pie. Both had been fully inducted into the best of American cooking by Susan on many visits back and forth between Argelès and Geneva.

"It's best to stay up as late as possible," Dave said. "Makes getting over jet lag easier. Tomorrow is a big day. We're going to get the Christmas tree and Sunday night we're having an open house and a tree-decorating party."

"Cool," Gaëlle said.

"Charlie Tucker is bringing his grandsons and his grand-daughter. That way Gaëlle won't be the only kid here," Susan said.

"Are the boys *beaux?*"

"Not if they look like Charlie. He has a face like a balloon, or maybe like a flesh-colored smiley face," Dave said. "But they'll help get you to meet other kids."

Susan answered the ringing telephone and after the normal politeness, handed it to Annie and mouthed that it was Melissa.

"How could you talk about my private business?"

"I don't understand."

"Magda came to see me. She was upset."

As you should have been, Annie thought.

"Thank God Jason wasn't here."

"I told my mother, Melissa. Magda must have overheard. I never told her to go see you."

"And who else have you told?"

"No one."

"Don't."

The phone went dead.

CHAPTER 41

Friday, December 17

Magda answered her phone about the same time Annie and Melissa hung up. The Hungarian artist was in her A-frame cottage on the other side of The Dock. She had rebuilt it from the foundation up after the blizzard of '78 swept the old structure out to sea, doing most of the work herself, learning about plumbing and carpentry as she went. The only thing she refused to do was the electricity. "A stopped toilet won't kill you, Darlink. An evil wire will."

The first floor had a living room, dining area and kitchen without separating walls. Her back wall was solid glass to the ceiling. Her bedroom and bath were in the loft. Rather than regular drapes she had bamboo roll-downs. The top half she left open, although she had a screen to fold in front of her bedroom window. She seldom used it, saying that if a sailor wanted to look at an aging woman, who was she to spoil his fun.

"Our cover has been broken," a woman's voice said. "Gretchen called her husband."

Magda sank into her aged chair. "What happened?"

"Gretchen's husband. He drove to Maine, found the house and stood outside screaming. She ran out, saying she would be safe now because he promised to get help."

Magda snorted. "Stupid bitch."

"Pamela, Karen and Diana are shook. They are afraid he'll tell others. We're moving them to Burlington, Vermont. Tomorrow. I already have this place up for rent."

"Good, Darlink." Burlington was a longer drive, but if it were necessary, so be it. "And Katie?" Magda had rescued Katie and her daughter Megan six months before. Her husband had been downsized a year before and could find no work that paid anything like his old job. Katie had been a bank teller. Another case that was so stereotypical that Magda could have written it and left the names blank and substituted any woman's name, any man's name, any child's name.

Potential outcomes were limited to four. She ticked them off with the names of the women that she could put faces with.

One, the woman would escape and rebuild her life, check.

Two, the woman would go back to her husband. The man would continue to beat up his wife, check.

Three, the man would kill the woman, check.

Four, the woman would go back to her husband, he would get help and they would live ever after. Not happily but normally: a quarter check. It almost never happened, but it wasn't impossible.

Magda matched too many faces with the first three. She felt so tired her bones ached.

"Katie has a job at the local bank. Megan is doing well in child care. She didn't want to leave, but we've found a one-bedroom for her two towns over. It'll be tight going. Are you there?" the voice asked.

"I'm here." I'll always be here. As long as there's a woman in need. "I'm working on another woman right here in town. Can you start working on identity papers?" She gave the voice Melissa's description and age. She had gotten really good in guessing height and weight, although she had no idea what Melissa might weigh once the baby was born.

"Are you sure? We don't want to waste the effort if you don't make a rescue."

False papers had been harder since 9/11. Thank goodness for larcenous people, Magda thought. At first it had cost them a fortune, but they had found a woman who had been a victim of domestic violence before serving time in jail for counterfeiting. She produced drivers' licenses, fake Social Security cards. The only thing she would not do was passports and she didn't charge, which meant the result of fundraising could go into apartment rentals, food and other necessities.

Magda sighed. "I don't know for sure. Maybe you better wait." Experience told her that she couldn't really short-circuit the process as much as she wanted to. Why couldn't life be like television? The answer arrived in an hour with twenty minutes of commercial breaks.

"There's a young girl coming up from Virginia tomorrow?"

"Is anyone else free?"

"Maybe, I can check."

"Please try. However, if you can't find . . ."

". . . anyone, I know you'll bring her. But this time to Burlington."

"Will there be anyone to meet her?"

"By the time she gets here, we'll be there."

"I'll keep my mobile on." Magda hung up.

She sat in the old chair molded to her body from years of sitting and reading. Books were stacked to one side. She loved biographies. How other people lived their lives became a roadmap. If she were angry at George Sand for not having a smoother relationship with Chopin, or at Collette for not seeing through Willy sooner, than she could make sure she didn't make the same mistake.

Two years was too long between lovers. "I'm a woman for lovers, not husbands," she told everyone. Men were for pleasuring her in bed, but there had never been one she wanted to wake up next to every morning. First they would say, no don't go to the studio today, stay with me, and then they would want their laundry done. She wanted a man to take his socks with him, not leave them for her to wash. More than once she wondered if she found a man who would wash *her* socks, what would she do?

At one point she was afraid she would forget one of her lovers, a shame really. If you shared your bed and body, then you owed that person the courtesy of remembering his name. Her one-night stands were few. Most had stuck around for a week, one for three years, and one brave soul for ten.

He'd been an artist and prized his alone time more than she did hers. Neither volunteered for extra sock washing, but they soaked each other's brushes. Pietr was the better artist, but it wasn't jealousy that tore them apart. Her dead sister came between them. Magda could no longer stand to be in any café, on any street or anywhere in Budapest. Pietr did not want to emigrate. At times she wanted to find out what had happened to him, but those moments ran away. Better to let sleeping dogs scratch their own fleas.

At least with menopause her hormones had settled down but on days like today she wished there was a body in her bed to engulf her in hairy, muscular arms. Probably all of the men in her age group couldn't do it these days, unless they used drugs. The commercial for a performance-enhancing drug that warned if an erection lasted more than four days see your doctor made her laugh. A pair of hairy arms was one thing, but trying to satisfy a four-day erection took too much time.

A good night's sleep would cure her blues. Or an old *ER* DVD. Looking at George Clooney was better than any antidepressant. She'd seen him on the street when a movie crew made a movie and he'd smiled at her. She didn't intrude on his privacy by asking for his autograph. Besides, she would just throw it away. An autograph on a check was one thing, but the signature on a piece of paper was one more piece of clutter. Now if he'd come home with her—from there on fantasy was better than reality. Fantasy and masturbation.

She heaved herself out of her chair and began to make dinner. The smells of searing meat and frying onions changed her mood to hunger and anticipation of a good meal, a good video and a night where she would concentrate on the good things she had rather than the things she didn't.

CHAPTER 42

Saturday, December 18

Des O'Flaherty crossed Copley Square to the Boston Public Library, entering the now not-so-new section designed by Mario Pei. Ever since he had been a high school student he'd loved the BPL. His favorite place was the holy of holies—the Periodical Room. Boxes and boxes of old magazines were filed in blue cases in monthly and yearly order. The first time he went there he had read *Time* and *Newsweek* for the week he was born. Neil Armstrong had walked on the moon on his birthday. For him it was a lucky sign better than Cancer being in the house of Aquarius or any astrological crap. But more important, he could check out the past and read about it like it was today. As he read, he felt like a seer. He knew as he thumbed through an October 1960 issue of *Time* that Kennedy would defeat Nixon. Although he hadn't been alive in spring 1951 he could prove that MacArthur was wrong: old soldiers both fade away and die despite what the General told Congress.

Luck had let him pass the admission test to Boston Latin. He had had no plans to take the entrance exam, but Mr. O'Brien, his sixth-grade teacher, gave him no choice. At orientation three weeks before classes started, he hated how the faculty hammered into the students how lucky they were to be at the oldest public school in America, how Harvard had been founded for their graduates, how many Nobel Prize winners, how many presidents, how many philosophers had gone before them, blah,

blah, blah. Now he could admit that when, as a scrawny seventh grader, he had sat in the auditorium and saw the names on the walls—Adams, Santayana, Kennedy, Bernstein—he felt that Des O'Flaherty from a poor Irish family didn't belong there. Someone would discover he was a fraud and he would have to go to Boston English across the street.

His teachers told him he did belong: he was intelligent or he wouldn't be there. They piled on homework: Latin, French, chemistry, English, algebra, history—hours and hours of homework. His studies caught his imagination as they hadn't in grade school. However, at home his father kept yelling, his mother kept crying, and his brothers and sisters made too much noise with their fights for him to concentrate on conjugations and formulas. When his grades slipped he found himself in the Head Master's office.

"Why?" the Head Master asked. The students suspected the man could spot a speck of dust two floors away and could read their thoughts through closed doors. Rumors of his powers were as much a legend as Benjamin Franklin being a dropout from the school. How else would the Head Master have known that the juniors had rented a hotel room for the prom and was waiting outside the door when they had arrived armed with grass, beer and condoms? Or how could he tell they were planning to sabotage the English High bus before their annual Thanksgiving football game?

Des refused to talk about his siblings mocking his studies, his angry father or anything else. "I can't study at home," was enough to reveal. Let the principal use his famous ESP.

"Come with me," the Head Master said. They took the short T's Greenline ride from Mass College of Art to Copley Square. The Head Master gave him a tour of the library including hidey holes where he could disappear into his books.

But that was then and this was now, he thought. Still, he

loved each time he entered this building. The contrast of the cold air in Copley Square to the warmth inside the library was a shock. Des took the stairs to the second floor two at a time and entered the Periodical Room.

Discipline was part of being a good journalist, but the balance between going off on a tangent and following the preselected path was a constant battle. More often than not he let the magic of the universe lead him where he needed to be led.

So far the magic had eluded him with Annie. He had forgiven her for missing their first library search. She had shown up the next day and told him that she didn't do guilt trips. "Damn," he'd said and they had both giggled. Together they had gone through Caleb's Landing library's microfiche until almost blind trying to find news of a woman's disappearance. Nothing. It earned him a dinner that almost became something more, but she'd slipped from his grasp.

The BPL librarian gave him the microfiche for *The Boston Globe* and he sat down and started to scan. He got caught up in Irangate, the death of Christa McAuliffe and Dukakis's defeat to Bush 41.

Discipline, he told himself, and limited himself to North Shore news. There were murders and robberies, stories about corruption in all areas of government. Had there not been a date on each issue it could have been that day's news.

His theory was that someone knew about the secret room. They had a female body to dispose of. Maybe the pre–Civil War dress and the diary were already there. Maybe the person had the dress and diary, but neither of those items were what the average man or woman just happened to have in a closet. That might be another way to attack this: find a Civil War buff.

He put in another tape and ran through the next series of articles. His eyes were almost crossing, and his back was sore from being locked in position. This wasn't a needle in a haystack. This was looking for a certain straw in a haystack. A needle would be easier. Stretching, he decided to abandon this tact and head home to get ready for the Youngs' party.

Outside the library he crossed Boylston Street to buy some flowers for Mrs. Young. He wasn't sure what they were, flowers not being one of his things, but they were red with holly and pretty. If he couldn't impress the daughter, maybe the mother would put in a good word for him.

CHAPTER 43

Saturday, December 18

"Gaëlle, want to check out the The Dock shops?" Dave asked as the girl bounced into the kitchen. She was still in her bathrobe. Her hair stuck up in spikes under tons of gel.

"Or do you want to stay here and make cookie decorations for tomorrow night?" Susan asked. "Dave is apt to show you off to his friends."

"Decisions, decisions," the girl said. "Do I investigate the area and meet some of the local wrinklies or do I indulge in a baking orgy?"

"If you're smart you'll be able to con my parents so you can do both," Annie said.

"Only if you help clean and set up the rest of the house before I start baking," Susan said.

Roger limped in wearing his pajamas. Annie had given Gaëlle her bed upstairs, while she and Roger had slept on the sofa bed in the living room. Slept may have been the wrong word. Not comfortable enough to make love with no door to close, they'd cuddled. Usually when they got back together after an absence it took a couple of days for Annie to get used to sharing a bed. This past night had not been good. At three Roger was fully awake. "Read," she told him, pulling the pillow over her eyes.

He looked around the room. "Plans for the day?"

"Assigning jobs," Susan said. "You and Annie can choose: shopping or setting up."

"I'm getting out of here until the good stuff starts," Gaëlle said.

"Good," Dave said. "We'll get breakfast at The Coffee Bean."

After Gaëlle left, Roger said, "He's the grandfather she wished she had."

Annie never understood why the girl's maternal grandparents never wanted anything to do with Gaëlle after her mother's death. She would have thought they would have held onto the living reminder of their only child. Even Roger's explanation that they were distant, cold people made little sense to her. His wife had not seen her parents after they were married. Their loss, Annie thought. Whatever happened between her and Roger, she knew she would never deny Gaëlle access to any of the Youngs.

Roger and Annie rushed around the Star Market throwing things in the cart and checking them off Susan's list.

"Tonight can you size up everyone there?" she asked.

"Do you think the person who left the skeleton will be there?" he asked.

"I just trust your opinion as a *flic*." She wanted him to like Charlie Tucker, because she wanted to continue working for him. She wondered if Melissa would show up, but she doubted it. What would he think of Des? He might pick up Des's interest in her, but Roger wasn't a jealous kind of Frenchman who loved the drama of protecting his woman against predators real or imagined.

They arrived back at the house at the same time Dave and Gaëlle did. The girl was smiling.

"Dave's friends thought I had a sexy accent and that I do English well. Monsieur Haskell wanted to speak French with me." She lowered her voice. "His accent was awful, and he used wrong verb tenses." She held her nose to mock the American accent. Annie didn't want to tell her that Americans will do the same to mock a French accent.

CHAPTER 44

Sunday, December 19

Melissa dabbed a layer of makeup on her face. When it dried, she added another. The bottle, although at least two years old, was almost full. The liquid was thicker than when new. Although she'd read makeup should be thrown away every three months because it grew bacteria-causing infections, she had no other. She peered into the glass. The swelling was gone, but a bluish green tint still showed through the makeup. The skin was tender when she touched the bruised area.

Jason hated her wearing makeup; tarting herself up, he called it. Even if she didn't wear it, she knew how to use it. In her senior year of high school she'd done the makeup for the drama club. The coach had been an actress with a real Equity Card.

Melissa had dreamed of playing Joan of Arc but had never tried out. Better to stay behind the scenes and learn how to turn young faces into grizzled warriors, English judges and women of a town that had disappeared into history. High school was several lifetimes ago when she'd also dreamed of escaping her aunt and uncle's ugly house with its daily prayers. Her knees ached just thinking about the hours spent against the rough floorboards.

When Melissa watched *Friends,* a program she loved even in reruns, she didn't see the antics of Monica, Phoebe or Rachel. She saw Courtney, Lisa and Jennifer who risked rejection to do what they wanted to do. But she also knew there were thousands of women who tried and failed like herself. Not in everything did she fail. In escaping her family, she'd created a home on its way to being magazine-pretty.

Turning her head left and right she was satisfied that her face looked almost natural. If she let her hair fall loose over the cheeks the bruise would look like a shadow. Then she could go to the Young party and for an evening pretend everything was all right.

She liked the Youngs. Dave, when he came into the office, always spoke to her before going to see Len. Most people treated receptionists like furniture. She didn't know Susan that well, although she seemed nice when they were looking to buy their studio.

As for Annie, how did she wander the world alone? How did she know where to go when she arrived in a strange city? How did she find a place to live? How did she find all those jobs? And she spoke so many languages. Melissa knew a little French. Her lowest grade had been an A–. Her marks had been high enough to get her into the National Honor Society. But brains and courage were different. Even the lion and the straw man knew that. She hummed "Over the Rainbow."

Time to make dinner. Jason was late. He had called to say he was showing the old Yates' house, a fixer-upper with the smallest commission in their other listings. Melissa tried to tell her husband that several small commissions were as good as one big one. She knew that clients would be happier if Jason searched for the house that they wanted rather than the one he wanted to sell. When she had suggested it, he'd yelled that if he wanted advice he would ask for it.

A can of chicken and noodle and another of tomato soup stood like lone soldiers in the cupboard. Jason didn't shop, didn't do household chores. Those were her jobs, and she had needed to go shopping before their last fight. Of course, she hadn't gone afterward.

Jason loved tomato soup if she added a dash of Worcestershire sauce. She opened the chicken and noodle. There were some frozen cinnamon rolls in the fridge. She sniffed the almost empty carton of milk. It hadn't turned.

While the rolls baked and the soup heated she saw that the tablecloth had a small stain. She whisked it off and threw it in the washer, replacing it with a clean one. When her aunt and uncle sat down to the table it was set with odd dishes with a discussion of sin in place of dessert.

Jason talked of the meals his mother made. If she served him eggs, she cut them in long quarters and made a little sail from a toothpick and construction paper. Gelatin would be molded into shapes. His father never prepared meals. They'd lived on whatever they could scrounge or went to restaurants. When Jason told her all this, she knew she would spend her life trying to make up for all he had lost.

"I will be a good wife and mother." Melissa jumped at the sound and force of her voice. I need to try harder. All marriages have problems. She bet even the Youngs fought now and then, although it was impossible to imagine Dave hitting . . .

"Honey, I'm home."

"I'm in the kitchen," she called.

Jason kissed her gently on the lips, making sure his face didn't press against the bruise. Life was best for Melissa after one of their big battles when a contrite Jason tried to make it up to her. Sometimes months went by with no problems. The last time had only been a few days apart, but that was an aberration in their pattern. The last battle was her fault. She should have been more supportive when he went so long between sales instead of worrying aloud about money.

He took her by the hand and danced her around the room as he hummed a song that was unrecognizable. Jason loved to sing except he couldn't carry a tune. "I sold the house."

"Fantastic."

"I haven't told Dad yet." He pulled his cell from his pocket.

"Will he be at the party tonight?"

Jason frowned.

"The Youngs. Remember?"

"I'd forgotten."

"Think, you can mention it and then you'll look good in front of a lot of people."

Jason peered at her face. "Are you up to it?"

Melissa pulled her hair back. "Yes. Let's eat fast." Tonight might be all right.

CHAPTER 45

Sunday, December 19

The Young house was chock full of people, friends, neighbors, friends of friends and friends of neighbors. Gene Autry sang about the tribulations of a reindeer with a red nose.

Dave passed a tray bearing his wife's creation, an ice bowl trimmed with green-colored ice chips. A dip was in the center: shrimp were draped over the edge. Dave knew he was the eternal optimist, finding a pony in the barn of horse shit. His glass was not only half full but filled with chocolate milk. How good it felt being home after all these years. Susan was settling in. Maybe it was time to stop wandering. There was something special about being surrounded by everyone speaking your mother tongue. Having lost almost three decades of cultural references despite CNN, MSNBC and American television series shown on Swiss and French television stations, he often felt like a stranger in his own country.

Their Christmas tree touched the ceiling and took up a good part of the living room. He watched the arm candy whom Len Haskell brought. The woman flicked her blond hair as she took a frosted green cookie decoration and hung it on the tree. Dave went up to his old friend. "What are you drinking, pal?"

"Coke," Len said.

"Red wine?" the woman asked.

She was younger than his Annie. Dave bet her breasts were larger than her I.Q. Maybe he was sexist jumping to the conclu-

sion that the woman was more interested in Len's money than
Len. Without realizing he was doing it Dave scanned the room
for his wife. When he spied her talking to an artist whose name
he'd forgotten, he said a quick prayer of gratitude that she was
in his life. Not that he thought a lot about his marriage, but
when he did, it was with satisfaction. Susan looked good in her
floor-length red plaid skirt and the red thingy top. He had long
ago learned to avoid naming clothes. Tights, leg warmers, stockings and other subtle differences were only important to his
womenfolk. He watched his wife point to the candles on the
Christmas tree.

"It shocked me too when I first saw real candles on a tree,
but I got used to it," Susan said to Tim and Betty-Anne
Doherty. The Police Chief's wife wore navy blue pants and a
matching sweater. The couple held hands. Her accent was
definitely not of New England. "Well, I would just be scared to
death." Her *I* came out as *ah* and her *death* was *dee-a-th.*

"You don't light those?" Tim asked.

Dave came over and put his hand on his wife's shoulder. "We
do, but my wife insists on having at least one pail of water
under the tree among the presents."

"How are you enjoying it here?" Susan asked Betty-Anne.

"I like it, although it is terribly cold in comparison to Georgia,
but Yankees are friendlier than I was told y'all would be."

The chief held up his hand.

"I'm not going to say anything against Northerners, honey."
She looked up at him. "He's been so busy. It's amazing how
much work the police can do even in a small town."

"I love small towns," Susan said. She took Dave's tray from
him and went into the kitchen to replenish the shrimp. She
heard footsteps coming up the stairs onto the back porch.

Magda took a deep breath, tucked the last wisp of hair into
her chignon before she opened the kitchen door. Her first sight

was her new business partner and friend. She thanked the goddess of moving people from one place to another for bringing the Youngs to Caleb's Landing. "Hello Darlink, I brought some treats. Now scoot off to your guests. I'll take over."

Magda nuked her tiny meatballs in the microwave before spearing each of them with a toothpick topped with green fizzy paper. Carrying a tray allowed her to make an entrance. People thought she adored parties because she was outgoing, but she preferred small gatherings where she sat at a table and talked about art, politics, movies and books.

Tonight she had a mission that was greater than her headache or aching bones. She had too much to do to fall victim to the flu that hovered over her. She must meet the new police chief and see how he felt about domestic abuse. Would he help her group or consider them mavericks?

Using her foot and hip to maneuver the door, she walked into the fray. "Hello Darlinks. The party can begin. Magda is here."

Annie turned when Magda's voice boomed over the party babble. She went up to the woman to take the meatballs but was waved away with a toss of Magda's head.

"I want to see faces when they taste them."

Annie continued to work the room. Charlie Tucker and his wife Barbara wrapped the tree in popcorn and cranberry strings.

"Here's my own private historian," he said when Annie approached.

"I've heard so much about you," Barbara said. The woman had long silver hair held back with a band. Her skin was taut but not face-lift taut, just good-genes taut. She and Charlie both had expressions that said they didn't sweat the small stuff.

Annie refused to do the traditional good-I-hope response. "The project is beyond fun. And thank you for bringing your grandson and his friend."

"They weren't sure until I said there was a pretty young French girl," Barbara said. "She's lovely. Where are they, by the way?"

"I'll check."

Kids ducking out to not deal with adults didn't surprise Annie. Maybe they were upstairs.

The living room was crowded to the point that multiple excuse me's were mandatory to make any progress. This wouldn't be an open house where people would come in, have a drink, nibble an hors d'oeuvre, hang an ornament and leave as the Youngs thought. People, many of whom Annie had not met, were holed up in corners deep in conversations with no thoughts of departing.

Upstairs a coat pile was all that was visible of her parents' bed. The door to Gaëlle's room was closed. Annie knocked.

"In a minute." A youthful male voice was followed by scuffling then the key turned. The two boys sat on the floor. Gaëlle had the look that any adult knew screamed guilt. It wasn't the look: it was the smell and the wide-open window.

"Hand it over," Annie said.

"What?"

"The grass. Or I'll call your father," she looked at the young Tucker boy, "and your grandfather."

The younger boy stood, although the bigger boy tried to stop him. He held up a plastic bag.

"How stupid can you be with the police chief downstairs? And Gaëlle, we won't even mention your father is a *flic* too."

"*Le diras-tu à Papa?*"

"I won't tell him, you will."

"*Mais non.*"

"*Mais oui,* but tomorrow. Tonight I'll enjoy watching you sweat."

★ ★ ★ ★ ★

Des O'Flaherty decided to walk to the Youngs'. The air was so cold he could taste his breath. The Dock was dark. Except for the lapping of the sea, which he had to strain to hear through earmuffs, everything was still. People must be home doing Christmas things. Lights shone out from the houses as he approached his destination.

Even as a little boy Des loved looking into windows. He wanted to see families eating together, watching television, washing dishes. One of his strongest memories was of a horrible family fight on Thanksgiving. He'd slipped out. His father, who was drunk, threw leftover turkey at his mother. Des had run out, then walked up and down the sidewalk to keep warm because he hadn't stopped for his coat. He passed the Malleys' where his best buddy Bobby lived. Bobby, his mother, father and big sister Annabelle sat around a table playing Monopoly. Everyone was laughing. Bobby had been killed in the Gulf War.

As he approached the Young house he heard the babble of people. He slipped through the open front door and wished he hadn't come until he felt an arm thrust though his.

"Des, so glad you could make it." Susan Young's smile, like Annie's, made you feel important. "My daughter told me about your research on our skeleton. I do feel as if she is ours, poor thing."

Des felt a finger in his back. He turned and Annie flashed one of those smiles that made him want to kiss her.

"Hi there, I want you to meet Roger."

Although Des didn't want to meet him, Annie dragged him through the crowd to a much-too-attractive man sitting on a hassock next to the fireplace. A crutch rested beside him. Annie had said he had been shot. Damn. Good looking, a hero— everything French lovers were supposed to be. Roger stood up. Why would this clever woman, who'd been everywhere he hadn't and done things he'd only dreamed about doing, give up a handsome Frenchman for a freelance reporter without a pot to pee in?

"Annie's told me about your investigations," Roger said after the introductions.

And he speaks excellent English with a sexy accent. Shit. His competition was too strong. Who was he kidding? Annie wasn't interested in him. The same optimism that sent him after impossible stories surged: "I'm not giving up."

"Excuse me," Roger asked.

Des hadn't realized he'd spoken aloud.

"Nothing."

"I've an idea," Annie said. "Let's see if there are any dentists who practiced at that time and are still alive but retired."

"Back to the library on Monday?" Des asked. Talk about a wild goose chase. Dentists usually had the name of a corpse to match the records to, rather than search for a name to match to the corpse. However, it would give him another day with Annie without lover boy.

"You don't mind?" Annie asked Roger.

"Of course not, but don't forget we want to take Gaëlle sightseeing."

Cozy family stuff, stuff that Des didn't have, and to be honest wasn't sure he wanted. Looking for an escape he glanced across the room to see Jason Haskell talking animatedly with his father, who patted him on his back.

Melissa watched her husband, too. He looks happy, she thought, basking in the praise for his sale. Her father-in-law was a hard task master. He rode his sales people hard, insisting that the office maintain its status as the best realty on Cape Ann. Although Melissa wasn't part of the sales team, Len expected much from her too, but when she messed up he didn't yell in front of others. He didn't go over every action to see where she'd gone wrong. She was looking forward to her maternity leave so she could concentrate on the baby and making her house a haven for Jason away from office tension.

She felt a sense of calm despite the party clamor. Maybe some day she and Jason would have everything the Youngs did. She didn't mean just money, because she didn't know how rich they were, but anyone who lives in Switzerland couldn't be poor. She meant how they looked at each other. They all seemed to like each other so much.

A man, tall, dark, good looking for an older man, kissed Annie. That must be the French boyfriend. He had a crutch. Annie called him *Rowshay* or something like that. She guessed he was in his forties. Well, Annie wasn't that young except for her name. Melissa smiled at her own pun.

Her stomach knotted as she saw Jason take what must be his fourth drink unless she'd missed one. She was about to go over to him when a man sat down beside her.

"Hi, I'm Des O'Flaherty, and you look lonely."

"I'm not. I don't mean you're not welcome to talk to me." Good thing she had so much makeup covering not only her bruise but also her blush. "It's just that I love watching people."

Des laughed. "I'm a professional people watcher. I'm a reporter."

"That must be glamorous."

"Not really, but I don't want to do anything else. Look over there. Paul Mangone and Charlie Tucker are engaged in something that isn't that pleasant. You can tell by their faces."

"I didn't say I agreed with the parents, but good God, Charlie . . ." Paul Mangone was the same height as his boyhood buddy. "You can't show something like that to school kids."

Charlie's round face was growing hot. He wasn't sure if it

was his blood pressure or the heat of the room or both. "You mean you can't show them the truth."

"Truth is relative."

"You should know, you were a teacher, and I used to listen to you bitch about how watered down the stuff was. That was what this project was all about. To offer more depth."

"But as a product. A give-away. Maybe a website."

Tucker threw his hands in the air. "It was a test."

"And one kid went home and told her parents that the Pilgrims were mass murderers and that parent called other parents. I wish I'd seen the later version."

"Not my fault you didn't come when I called. Anyway, from the Indian point of view the Pilgrims *were* mass murderers. Looking at both sides of an issue teaches kids critical thinking."

"They are too young. Too much violence."

"If you ever watched Saturday morning cartoons then you—"

Before Charlie could finish Susan moved in. "Charlie, can I ask you to help me to open another champagne bottle in the kitchen. I just can't get the cork off."

Melissa didn't know how long she had been talking to Des O'Flaherty. She hadn't laughed that much since probably never. They'd moved to the couch and sat facing each other.

"Time to go home." Jason stood over her.

He had that look, the look that told her she knew to avoid saying anything that might upset him more. Because the couch was soft-cushioned she couldn't propel her body out of it. Jason yanked her up and as he did, he pinched her arm. I won't cry in front of people, she thought.

Des's face went from a grin to a frown. "No need to be rough."

Jason flashed him a smile. "Hard to maneuver pregnant women around."

"Have a good evening." Des left the two of them.

Melissa half wanted to say come back but didn't dare. Jason's hand on her arm hurt.

"Walk to the door and stay there. I'll get our coats."

She did. If she passed people, she said, "Time to go home. I get so tired these days."

Susan must have an antenna in her head, Melissa thought, because as Jason came down with their coats, she was at the door. "So glad you could come, both of you."

"It was a great party," Jason said. As soon as the door closed, he growled, "What in the hell do you think you were doing in there?"

"Talking."

"Talking? You were flirting. Disgusting. What interest do you think a man would have in an ugly, pregnant cow?"

"None, I'm sure he was just pretending to be nice to me."

They got into the car. Before Jason started the ignition, he reached across to the glove compartment and took out a flask. He sat there a few minutes taking several swallows. After he put it back he brought his fist down hard on Melissa's leg above the knee.

Her hands flew to protect her stomach. This could turn out to be a very long night.

CHAPTER 46

Two pages are smudged beyond readability. By the crinkles it looks as if they had been dipped in water then dried, but I have no idea when the damage occurred and no reliable way to find out. (Note from Dr. Gregorian clipped to the page and xeroxed onto Annie's copy.)

The Mistress and Massa barely open their mouths to each other. When they do, angry words falls out. She wants them to go to New York for the summer. He says he cain't leave.

We ain't got no more company. No, what I should write is we haven't got any more company. The Mistress keeps correcting me. I still talks two ways. One when I be with my people. One when I am in the house. If I talk fancy with my people they will say my head won't be able to go through no more doors. The Mistress would say "not through any more doors."

White folks make such problems for themselves. They should try living our lives and then they might give thanks to God that their problems be only in their imaginations.

Imagination has been big around here since the little Missy starts talking. She be three now. She and her mother plays make believe all the time. "We have to encourage her imagination," the Mistress says. I ain't sure that we shouldn't do the opposite. The other day we be playing princess and trolls. She wants me to be the ugly old troll. I never heard of trolls, but the Mistress draws a picture of one like she says she seen when she be/was in Norway. I asks if that be part of England where she comes from, but she gets out the map. I has no idea of distance but she talks to me about the months it takes her to come down here from New York traveling every day and the time it takes for her to ride the boat from England to Boston. I is learning a lot about this old world of ours.

I gives up on writing like the Mistress wants me to speak. I just writes like I think. This be my diary, nobody else's so I do as I pleases.

The Mistress teases me about Zeb. We be married now, all proper in the church. She says to her husband how Zeb ran away but with a wife he ain't likely to take off again.

Zeb acts real humble around anyone white, but he ain't. He wants us to escape. I'm afraid. He says he won't leave without me, although I be afraid he will. Zeb tells me about his family in Africa. He misses his Mama, his six sisters and two brothers. His Papa be dead. Zeb be the oldest and now that he be trapped and brought here his brother be head of the family. Zeb also has a wife, who costs five goats. She be pregnant when he got himself trapped. He never knowd if the baby be a boy or a girl. He says his brother will marry her and take care of her. That's the way with his people. We sees white men not wanting to have nothing to do with another man's child. He says with his people the children belongs to everyone. And white folks don't thinks we be civilized. They could learn a thing or two from Zeb.

He wants me to teach him everything the Mistress teaches me. That man learns fast. I just tells him or shows him something once and he's got it.

I wants to have a baby, but he refuses to have any babies for the Massa. He makes me chew cotton seeds. He never does it like we should. He pulls out right before he lets go and lays shuddering on me. My stomach be wet with our babies unborn. "Someday, someday we will be free," he says every time.

I never thinks about being free before Zeb. Sometimes I dream about it now. I listen to the Mistress talk about cities and shops and things, but as a niggah I never be allowed in. Someone might say,

"There be a slave girl. We gotta find where she done come from."

Zeb says if we be free we have to learn to talk free white.

Sometimes he talks the talk of Africa to himself. There be no other slaves from his tribe. He be a Lobi. He says if he don't talk it, he'll forget it. I asks him if he wants to go back, and he says he doesn't see how. If we takes a boat, they make us slaves again. That means he would take me. I don't want to know his first wife.

He talks about a place call Canada. That be where he was going when he done run away. People who hides him, done tells him about it.

A letter comes today from the Mistress's parents. It comes all the way from England. She always be happy when she hears from them. I sneaks a look at it.

Dear Elizabeth,

The play has opened. You would have been proud of your old parents. We took six curtain calls, <u>six</u> mind you. We are trying to book a trip to take the play to New York.

We know you are still living in the backwater and from your letters, I do not understand how you do it. You, who had London at your feet when you played Cordelia. You, who were received by the Queen.

It must be so hard for you to not discuss your past because Richard wants you to put it behind you, not that we are criticizing him. He has no idea what a treasure he has.

We do so want to meet Annabelle. Imagine having a granddaughter who is already three and I have never laid eyes on her.

After you described your trip to that horrible place, I know we can't do it. I am dreading the sea voyage as it is, but at least that will allow me to share the same continent where my daughter and granddaughter are. Please come to New York to see us.

Other friends of ours have done quite well for themselves in that city, something about the mystique of the British theatre. Your father and I are convinced we will too. He is a good actor, but a great businessman. Most actors are so impractical. Not him.

He has just read this letter and wants to make sure that I add that as much as he wants to see you and your darling, darling Annabelle (how could any child of yours be anything but?) that I am interfering too much. I do want your happiness, and I must keep telling myself that my idea of happiness and yours must be different.

Saying that, I think we would all be happy to be together even for short while, although if we travel long over the ocean and you travel long over land it would make sense to do more than have a cup of tea but to spend several weeks or better months together.

Much love,

Mother

The Mistress reads that letter lots of times before she tucks it away under the place she keeps her cloths for her monthlies.

Meanwhile the crops comes in real good and during the winter we all do less work. At least the field niggahs has less. My job be the same all year round. Although Zeb starts out as a field niggah, the Massa discovers he be one good builder. He puts a new barn together better than anyone white or black. He gots a knack of how to cut a board just right. The Massa showed him a dining room chair and asks if he can copy it.

Zeb circles the chair several times. Then he sits for a long time. "I needs wood," he says.

"Wood costs money."

"Cain't make a chair from air."

The Massa finds that funny. "I'll get you the wood and tools."

Zeb makes his chair, but slowly, whittling each stick in the back and smoothing them. When it be done it be a perfect match except for one thing. "Don't know how to make it shiny," he tells the Massa.

"You need to learn about varnish," the Massa says. A couple of days later he sends Zeb away with a thick chain on his ankle in case he be tempted to run away. He goes to a carpenter to learn how to make all kinds of things. I misses that man while he be gone in more ways than one.

The Mistress lets Zeb sleep in my room with me after we be married. That done took care of the Massa Richard problem, but when Zeb goes away to learn how to carpenter the problem comes back.

The first night Massa Richard knocks on my door, I tells him to go away. He keeps telling me how beautiful I be as if I might believe that a white man finds a niggah beautiful. They may find their bodies a nice place to put their toys, but that be it. Finally he gives up.

The next day the little Missy has a bad cold. She be right crabby. Nothing pleases her during the day, and when she falls asleep that night her poor little nose be crusty and red. I tells the Mistress I sleeps in her room in case she wakes up in the night. And during lunch when Massas be at the table, the Mistress says how good care I takes of the baby.

That works until the little Missy be better. I never offers to go back, but the Mistress asks me if I don't want to sleep in my own place. "I feel better with the Little Missy, I says."

She looked at me strange like. That woman ain't no fool.

"I think," she says, "It'll be a better if you sleep with Annabelle until Zeb comes back."

Massa Richard don't give up. I be walking home from Mama's house one night. He jumps out from behind a tree and grabs me and kisses me and put his toy in and out of me so fast that if I weren't so sticky on my legs, I might have imagined it. I smells the liquor on his breath. If I has white skin, it'd be purple where he pushes me against the bark of that tree.

I eats cotton seeds like crazy, jumps up and down to shake out any baby that might be there and prays every minute I can until I gets my monthlies. Zeb might kill him or me if I brings forth a little mixed baby. And he won't want me no more, if he knows my hole be filled up by another man. He be too proud in my being his when we lays down together. I be his only possession.

CHAPTER 47

Sunday, December 19

During the party Magda observed Melissa and Jason. He'd started out congenial, but like Melissa she counted the amount of alcohol he poured down his throat, well aware that he drank to get effect, not the taste. Melissa, on the other hand, drank nothing as American pregnant women did. Not like back in Hungary, when women drank beer or wine with their meals until birth. Hungary was long ago.

For a moment she saw that Melissa looked pretty and relaxed as she chatted with that reporter fellow. He even had her laughing until she looked back at her husband.

Magda knew that Jason saw. His mood clouded. She watched him propel his wife out the door.

"I must go, Darlinks," she said to Dave and Susan.

To Magda cars were necessary evils, a device created by the devil to get her from A to B. What they cost kept money away from other things, yet without one she couldn't save her girls.

Rather than head home she followed Jason and Melissa, pulling up across the street. Although the heater had not had a chance to erase the cold, she shut off her engine. On the back seat was a quilt that she wrapped around herself as she watched their windows.

In the living room she saw Jason hovering over Melissa until he pulled down the shade. The living room light went out, the hall light went on then off and then the bedroom light went on.

Magda got out of her car and tiptoed to the front door. She could hear Jason hollering, "Whore. You made a fool of me."

There was a crash of glass, and Melissa screamed, "Leave me alone. Think of the baby."

Magda dialed 911 on her cell. The police car must have been around the corner. Magda had just clicked her car door shut when it pulled up. Two cops got out. She knew both: Brian and Phillip.

Phillip was the taller and the older, although old was relative. He was a good twenty years younger than Magda. Nice buns, she thought as he walked under the street light and hated herself for thinking that way when Melissa was in danger. She rolled down the window so she could hear but ducked down on the seat so they wouldn't see her.

"I hate these calls, especially when I went to school with the man," Brian said. He rang the bell.

The light came on in the hall. Jason stood at the door. "What's up, guys?"

"We had a complaint that there was a fight going on."

Jason looked to the right. "Must have been that old bitch next door. I'm sorry. My wife and I were having a little argument."

"Can we see your wife, Jason?" Phillip asked.

Magda peeked out her car window so she could see Brian standing behind Phillip.

"She's in bed. She's pregnant, you know."

"I know. We need to make sure she's okay. We can go up if she doesn't want to come down."

"It's all right." Melissa appeared behind them, her face tear-streaked.

"Where'd you get that bruise, Melissa?" Phillip asked.

"I ran into a cabinet."

"More original than a door," Phillip said. "Do you want us to take Jason with us for the night? Looks like he's had a lot to drink."

"I'm not drunk." Jason swayed slightly.

"You aren't sober either. Jason, come with me outside. Brian, you sit with Mrs. Haskell."

Magda ducked down in her seat again before the cops turned.

Phillip put his arm around the young man and walked toward the cruiser.

"You can't arrest me, I haven't done anything."

"Jesus, Mary and Joseph, why do people think when I want to talk with them it means they're being arrested?" Phillip asked.

Magda peeked to see Jason's body relax a little.

Phillip sat on the hood of the cruiser. The lights were off. They had never been on. "Pregnant women are really emotional, and they can drive a man nuts."

"You've got that right," Jason said.

"But we gotta protect them too. Soon you'll have a wonderful son or daughter and in a few months, Melissa will be back to normal."

Jason said nothing.

"Try and keep your temper under control, son."

"I didn't hit her."

"I didn't say you did."

They walked back to the house. When the door closed on the two cops, Phillip said, "He hit her. I bet it wasn't the first time."

"He's a good guy. We played football together," Brian said.

"Good guy for guys maybe." Phillip slammed the driver's door followed by the slam of Brian's.

When the police car disappeared, Magda sat up. Lights were off in the house. Once again she tiptoed to the door. Only silence greeted her. Check. She returned to her car and thought for a moment before turning the key in the ignition. Jason was on record as a potential abuser. Check.

As she drove home she didn't feel triumphant. What she wanted to do was to take a dive under her duvet and sleep and sleep and sleep. She could forget that without Melissa filing a restraining order to remove Jason from the house, he would continue to beat her. Even if there was a restraining order, that might not be enough. Magda had a bad feeling about this one. She cursed herself that she was right more than wrong in most of the cases.

CHAPTER 48

Monday, December 20

"The shit has hit the fan," Charlie Tucker said over the phone to Annie who paced around the Young living room. "Mangone called. He got a phone call this morning from Diane Ash who whipped up a bunch of parents with a petition to make sure this never happens again. I'd heard rumors something was coming down, but I hoped it would go away."

Annie let out a deep sigh. The shit had hit the fan here too. Her life was definitely brown today. Gaëlle was in her room crying. Roger had stormed out of the house after yelling at Annie that she should have told him that she had caught Gaëlle smoking pot. At least he stormed as fast as a man with a crutch could storm. He refused to listen to any explanations about the psychology of making Gaëlle responsible for her own actions by admitting her sins. This too will pass, she thought.

"Did I get Kendra in trouble?"

"Kendra?"

"The teacher."

"Probably. Definitely."

Shit! "What's next?"

"It'll come up at a board meeting. First of the year. They aren't meeting until after New Year's. Of course you'll come."

Double shit, Annie thought. Roger wanted Annie to fly home with them New Year's Eve. "How soon after New Year's?"

"Wednesday, January 5. Want some good news?"

"Yes."

"I definitely think we should go ahead with the second CD-ROM. And web page." Charlie gave a long sigh. "If everyone is so upset, we're definitely onto something. Annie, I want you to work for me full time. I know we've discussed the this-and-that of it, but I'm waiting for you to name what you want."

"Not to be in an office every day with only two weeks vacation a year."

"Okay, so only take a week. But I really don't like the idea of an employee in France."

Annie laughed. "Charlie, I like my freedom. I don't want to be based here."

"Is that a no?"

"It's a we-need-to-do-some-heavy-negotiating."

"Well, think about it. Caleb's Landing is a great place."

"So is Argelès. You think about it too. I can come here periodically."

"Usually employees argue about money, you argue about countries."

"Money is another issue. Let's wait until after the holidays and the meeting."

Charlie laughed. "I like you, Annie Young. Do you want some good news?" He didn't wait for her to answer. "Mangone is on our side."

"He should be. This was partially his idea."

After Annie hung up, she felt tired. The living room still contained last night's party remnants. She carried the last of the rented glasses into the kitchen and loaded the dishwasher. The trash can was filled with red and green Christmas paper plates.

Upstairs the toilet flushed. A few minutes later Gaëlle appeared downstairs plunking herself on the couch. "I've blown it."

"Yes, but your English slang is getting good."

209

The compliment did nothing to erase the unhappy look from Gaëlle's face. "Papa wants to go back to France. Tomorrow!" She started to cry.

Annie brushed Gaëlle's tears away with the back of her hand. She looks like a little girl, Annie thought. "I doubt your father will take you home early. It would disappoint my parents too much, and he won't want to do that."

"He said he would." More tears.

"We all say things when we're angry."

Annie knew that Gaëlle seldom messed up. Her mother's death had made the father–daughter relationship a nonadversarial one, but rebellion was normal for children. Roger needed to get used to that. Gaëlle needed to break away from him. More than once the girl said she was glad Annie was there to take over some of the care and feeding of her father, not that Roger turned Gaëlle into a house slave.

"A lot of kids at school do drugs," Gaëlle said. "I never tried grass before, and I thought if I did it here . . ." There were a few hiccups.

"That no one at home would know?"

"And the boys thought me sophisticated because I'm French, I couldn't admit I wasn't."

Annie suspected she needed several T-shirts to wear with Gaëlle depending on the role: friend, mother stand-in, confidant, disciplinarian, listener. Roger, although a good father, was as incapable of thinking like a teenage girl as if they'd asked him to become a prima ballerina. Before Annie could say anything else, Gaëlle started crying again and ran into her bedroom, slamming the door.

Annie decided to let her be for the moment and picked up the Sunday funnies that no one had the time to look at yesterday because of party preparations. In one a man and wife were disagreeing about the kids. She wondered if they both wished they were single again. She almost wished *she* were single again. She started upstairs. On the third step the doorbell rang.

Des O'Flaherty stood there. "Lovely party last night. I wanted to thank your mom. Also, are you ready to go dentist crawling?"

The fight had pushed the skeleton from her mind. "Give me five minutes. Go in the kitchen and pour yourself some coffee."

When Gaëlle didn't respond to her knock, Annie said, "I'm coming in."

Annie sat on the bed letting the silence work. Oh hell, Des is waiting. I can't take all day with this. "I'm the best chance you have at the moment."

"I'm going to be grounded for the rest of my life."

"I'm sure he'll let you out for your wedding."

Gaëlle's posture relaxed a little. "I'll never get married if I'm grounded."

"Maybe an arranged marriage, like in India."

"Why did you make me tell him?" Her lower lip stuck out.

"Because when you do something wrong and get caught you take responsibility. That's part of being grown up."

"I'm not grown up."

"You're on the road to it. Your father is disappointed with you because you broke the rules. He trusted you. Once trust is gone it takes a long time to rebuild it."

"*Merde.*"

"And now your father is angry at me because he thought I should have tattled."

Gaëlle rolled over and looked at Annie. "Does that mean you'll never marry my father?"

"If your father and I don't get married it will be about issues between the two of us."

"I don't count." She mumbled it so Annie had to ask her to repeat it. "I don't count."

At that Annie laughed. Gaëlle sat up and looked at her. "*Quoi?*

211

What?" She made both words into several syllables.

"I ain't going there, Honey Child. You and I play straight with each other. That's manipulation and not very good manipulation at that. Now I've some suggestions. Wanta hear?"

Gaëlle nodded.

"You know your father can't stay mad."

She nodded.

"Get showered and dressed. When he comes back tell him you were wrong. You're sorry. It won't happen again. You gave in to pressure. You wanted to be the cool French girl with the handsome American boys. Say you're ready to accept whatever punishment he wants to give, but you hope it can be postponed until you get home."

The telephone rang. Annie went into her parents' room where the phone was. It was one of the boys. "Gaëlle is unable to come to the phone. You guys got her into a lot of trouble."

"Are you going to tell my grandfather?"

"I'm thinking about it." Let them sweat, Annie thought. Charlie probably had smoked a lot of pot in the sixties. He ran his own business, but refused to let it grow beyond a certain point. A lot of the sixties had stayed in that man.

"I'm really sorry we got her in trouble."

"Maybe you should have thought of that first." Kids mess up. Let them deal with it. "Listen, I appreciate your calling, but we have things to do." She hung up and returned to Gaëlle's doorway.

"Gaëlle, I need to go out. If you want to start rebuilding trust, I suggest you go downstairs and clean up the kitchen while waiting for your father to come home."

"Where are you going?"

"To talk to dentists."

She looked confused. "To see if we can figure out who the skeleton was. While I'm gone, do you want to read the slave's diary? It might be hard going, but it's fascinating."

Gaëlle shrugged.

"Suit yourself."

Annie wrestled her curls into an elastic. As usual they didn't want to go, but she was determined to win. When God gave her kinky hair, he was joking. For a moment she debated wearing something nice. The decision was made for her because her good slacks and skirt needed ironing. She threw on jeans and a green sweater that matched the green in a blue and green scarf she draped around her neck.

Des was just finishing his coffee when she entered the kitchen.

"Dr. Dinan is the oldest dentist in town. We might start with him," he said.

The dentist was within walking distance of the Young house. One woman sat in the waiting room reading *People* magazine with Brad and Angelina on the cover. The way the receptionist clicked her computer mouse and stared at the screen Annie suspected it was a computer game, not work. They stood there several minutes. There was a final click, a sigh and a "May I help you?"

"We would like to see Dr. Dinan."

"Do either of you have an appointment?"

"No."

She did several things with her mouse. "He's booked up today. In fact, he's booked until January. If you give me your telephone, I can call when there's a cancellation."

Des smiled at the woman. Annie half expected a ray of light to bounce off his teeth and the sound *bing* to magically echo through the waiting room. "It's personal, not professional. Maybe we could just sneak in for two or three minutes before his next appointment.

"I can sacrifice my appointment," the reader offered.

"Nice try, Cathy. We finally got you here. You aren't getting out," the receptionist said.

Dr. Dinan appeared at the door. "Who's trying to escape now? Good thing I have a strong ego. Cathy, go on in." He looked at Des. "Aren't you that reporter fellow?"

"I interviewed you last year for an article on single-practice dentists, Dr. Dinan."

"Doing a follow-up?"

"No, investigating a murder. I'd like just a few minutes of your time." He introduced Annie and told him that it was her great Aunt Helen Tucker's house where the body had been found.

The dentist rubbed his chin. "I'll sick the hygienist on Cathy." He led the way into the office with its necessary framed diplomas and certificates on a baby-blue wall. They were surrounded by five cartoons all with a caricature of Dr. Dinan playing sports: golf, bowling, fishing, tennis and football. When he saw where their eyes were, he said, "Don't do much football these days. I'm pretty much down to golf and fishing. And about ready to retire to do more of those while I still can. Now talk to me."

They told him.

"I heard the skeleton was from the Civil War. Some slave diary was found with it. So that was all wrong?" Dr. Dinan said.

"We think the murderer wanted people to think that in case the body was found. The police are guessing it was put there about twenty years ago, although the room might have been part of the Underground Railroad," Des said.

Dr. Dinan looked at Annie. "I remember your Aunt Helen. She was still alive and healthy twenty odd years ago. Bet the murderer knew her and knew she would never sell the house."

"You knew my great aunt?" Annie asked.

"Took care of her teeth. Even off season she would come down to me. Said I gave the best Novocain in the world." He winked. "It's all in the wrist. Like golf.

"Your aunt never married. Some talk that she might be a lesbian. Never thought so myself. I just thought she was too . . . too . . . too much a complete character. But you would know that."

"I never met her. In fact I didn't know I even had an aunt until she left the house to my dad."

"Your dad?" Dr. Dinan tapped a pencil on his desk. "That wouldn't be the young Master David would it?" When Annie nodded, he said, "The sun rose and sat on that young man, according to your aunt. He was the smartest, handsomest, funniest boy to ever walk these streets. She loved it when he and his friends camped out at her place."

A thought flashed through Annie's mind. Maybe her aunt was the murderer. Maybe the skeleton was a previous girlfriend of her father's. No, her father had said that Susan was his first serious girl. The rest were practice. If she murdered anyone it would have been her mother. It had been hard to move the armoire from the door. "How strong was she?"

"Just a slip of a thing. Probably never hit 100 pounds. Lots of energy, but she was never into this exercise craze. She would drive next door rather than walk."

"We think someone broke into her house and hid the body off season," Des said.

We do? Annie wondered, although it made good sense.

"So what can I do?" Dr. Dinan asked.

"The medical examiner knew it wasn't a slave because the dentistry was modern," Annie said. "That means maybe dental records still exist. If she were local . . ."

"She'd have had a local dentist," Dr. Dinan said. "That works well in detective shows, but we're talking at least twenty years. I'm the only dentist that was practicing twenty years ago still around. I don't keep records any longer than ten years."

Des and Annie looked at each other.

Dr. Dinan repeated what Des had said earlier. "And usually it is the other way around. The police give us a name, and we check the records, not look through records in case we find a match."

"We know," Des said. "But we have no other ideas."

Dr. Dinan looked at his watch. "Why aren't the police pursuing this?"

Des leaned forward in his chair. "They are working on a string of robberies and some dope thing. Recent stuff, although the new chief said he was keeping it on the back burner."

Annie hadn't known that. "Can you think of any patient that might have disappeared?"

"Patients come and go. They move, they find new dentists. I can't remember anyone disappearing from town. Not to mention the summer crowd, regulars and day trippers."

Annie thought she had discovered a new depth for a wild goose chase. "The other dentists that were practicing at the time?"

"Matt Ganley. He died around that time, I think. Ray Butcher is in a nursing home. No use talking to him. Couldn't tell you his own name much less a patient's. Gene Rowan's still alive in Florida. Always hated snow. Sold out young. Think he opened a practice down there. We exchange Christmas cards, but I gotta admit that I only send cards out when I get one. Use the address on the envelope."

A new woman appeared at the door. "I've finished with Cathy," she said.

"We won't keep you any longer." Annie wrote her family's phone number on the back of one of her business cards. "This is my local number."

The dentist looked at it. "You're a long way from home, young lady."

216

"According to my parents, I have one root here in New England," she said. But do I have any roots at all? she asked herself.

Des and Annie visited two more dentists, both younger than Dr. Dinan, and with far less luck. They walked to The Dock, scarves fastened over their mouths and tied behind their heads to keep the frigid air from attacking their faces. A few brave shoppers hustled in and out of stores. Bells tinkled as the doors opened and closed. There was white frost on the Christmas greens decorated with maroon and gold bows wrapped around doors and posts.

Des didn't say a word but tilted his head as they came to The Coffee Bean. Annie nodded and walked up the two gray stone steps. They took their coffee and hot chocolate to the back where they looked at the gray water blending into gray rocks blending into gray sky as they unwound themselves from their outer garments.

"That was wasted time," Des said.

"Let's review what we have," Annie said.

"One skeleton," Des said.

"Check," Annie said.

"Dressed in the remains of pre–Civil War clothes."

"Check."

"A woman thought to be between twenty and forty."

"Check."

"Strangled. That *h* whatever, the bone in her neck, was fractured."

"Check."

"Dental work that would have been done around twenty years ago."

"Check."

"A genuine slave diary."

"Check."

"What else?" Des asked.

"She had more than normal healed broken bones."

"My turn to say check. What else?"

Annie shifted in her chair. "No missing persons from the time. Which means she might not be from Caleb's Landing. She could have been a summer tourist. Or . . . or maybe she was someone people thought moved away from here, but instead was killed the day she was leaving or something like that."

"Which will make the truth next to impossible to find. Maybe we should just pack it in," he said.

"Well, we can't do anymore until after Christmas. By the way, what are you doing?"

"Pretending it doesn't exist."

"Well, come on over to our place for dinner."

"I couldn't."

"My mother will kill me if she knew you were alone and I knew it," Annie said.

CHAPTER 49

Saturday, December 25

The Young house was full at Christmas. Susan prided herself on adopting strays for the holidays.

Magda, surrounded by Kleenex and cough drops, let Susan ply her with hot lemon tea until she had reached a limit. "Enough, Darlink. I want room for turkey and cranberry sauce. Even if I can't taste anything, I'll feel it. Leave the green beans crunchy."

Gaëlle and Roger had hammered out a reasonable punishment. She would be grounded for the month of January once they were back in France.

Likewise Roger, when he had calmed down, realized that Annie was in the middle between him and his daughter. Their peace was jarred by Annie saying she had invited Des to dinner. "He's after your—what's the American expression—your bones."

It took Annie by surprise since going off with Des the other day, which hadn't seemed to bother Roger at the time. "We are both after whom the bones belong to," Annie said. "If you're trying to clip my wings, you know what I become like when you do that."

"One mad bird." Roger kissed her nose. "I suppose if you were going to cheat . . ."

"I thought you were different than other jealous Frenchmen."

"I am a jealous Frenchman. I just don't usually let it show."

Heather, the sculptor, had been invited. According to her divorce agreement this was the Christmas her three children were with her ex. The contrast between Susan's arty long dress, one earring and funky hairstyle to Heather's upscale skirt and blouse and chignon amused Annie, who knew her mother thought of the woman as a housewife playing at being an artist. Her generous alimony and child support allowed her not to worry about money.

Len Haskell had been invited, but Melissa was cooking his Christmas dinner. Susan had invited them all thinking a dinner might be too much for Melissa, but Jason insisted that he wanted to celebrate their first Christmas in their new house.

Finally they settled down to dinner. The kitchen table had been moved into the living room and card tables put on each end. Folding chairs gave everyone a seat. "Good thing Auntie Helen was a fanatic bridge player, so she had enough chairs for two tables," Susan said as she covered one table with a Christmas tree design paper tablecloth. The paper dishes were decorated with a drawing of Santa clogging a chimney.

"A far cry from Geneva," Annie said. There her mother's table had thick linen cloths, matching napkins and a special set of Christmas dishes, hand painted by one of her artist friends. Wine came from their cellar, stocked by careful selection as her parents drove through both the Swiss and French countrysides. They loved dropping into local caves, taste-testing before buying.

"Smells the same," Dave said.

"The idea is to share a wonderful meal." Susan turned to her guests. "A complete turkey was next to impossible to find there. We settled for a Bourg-en-Bresse chicken."

"With *foie gras* and smoked salmon."

"Same as us, except we have a duck," Gaëlle said.

Magda sneezed her way to the table. "Put me at the end, Darlinks. I will propel my germs away from everyone."

"Appreciated," Heather said. "I guess the first Christmas is the hardest." She patted Des, who sat next to her.

"Heather has her claws out for him," Roger whispered to Annie as they both went into the kitchen to carry out more food. "Are you jealous?"

"No," she said.

He kissed the top of her head. "What's the story on Heather?"

Susan had told Annie that Heather had not wanted the divorce. Her husband, a lawyer in his early fifties, had come home one day to say he didn't want to be married. The kids were driving him crazy. About a week later he moved in with a fellow attorney, arm candy with a brain.

"At least Heather didn't go through getting a restraining order and worrying one night he would break the door down," Magda had said.

"Not all divorces are violent," Susan had said.

"Enough are, Darlink."

"We are keeping one French tradition." Susan carried a cake shaped and decorated as a fallen log into the living room after all the other food had been cleared away. A miniature ceramic squirrel, two robins and a fox perched on the frosting. *"Voilà, la bûche de Noël."*

A wave of being at home swamped Annie. Her parents were here, her lover and his daughter were here along with a couple of new friends. They had shared good food and kind thoughts. Christmas music subliminally had provided a backdrop. Life was good.

Her musings were interrupted by Magda. "Susan has prepared a wonderful meal, but she should enjoy the day. We'll clean the kitchen, Darlinks." No sheepdog could have herded the women into the kitchen any better.

"Are you feeling up to this?" Annie asked.

"I, Darlink, shall supervise. Gaëlle, you clear the silverware. Annie, run lots of hot soapy water for the silverware, which you, Heather, will gather. Des? Des?"

Des poked his head in.

"Under the sink, Darlink. Garbage bags. Gather up all the paper." Magda settled in the seat behind the kitchen table that was laden with the dregs of the final preparation of the meal and honked into her handkerchief. The sounds of water running and pans scraping dominated the room.

"It was a good Christmas," Annie said. "I wonder how Melissa is doing."

Magda let out a snort. "With that no-goodnick of a husband? But then he is the son of a bastard. Bastard DNA. Just like eye color. Goes from generation to generation."

"You really don't like Len," Heather said. "Really Annie, if Magda passes him on the street before coming in, she rages and raves about before she settles down for work." She did a passable imitation of Magda raging and raving as she made coffee.

"I've good reason, Darlinks."

"Wanta share?" Gaëlle asked.

Annie did a double-take at how American the girl sounded. "Wanta share?" Annie asked.

"I heard it on *Grey's Anatomy*. Izzy said it to George, you guys."

"You guys?" Annie asked.

Gaëlle shrugged. "I'm here to learn to speak English better. Well, American anyway. My teacher at school tells me English-English and American-English are two different subjects. Anyway, why don't you like Mr. Haskell, Magda? He seemed nice for a wrinkly."

Magda took her cigarettes from her purse and looked at them.

She coughed and put them back. "Damned cold. This was a meal that calls out for an after-dinner puff, I can tell you."

The work stopped. Heather, her hands in yellow rubber gloves, turned and faced Magda. Gaëlle sat down. Annie put down the dish towel she was using to dry pans.

"When I first came from Hungary, I had nothing. There was an artist on the corner of the Dock. Sold mainly blue paintings, but he was no Picasso, although he thought he was. I worked for him. Saved up for a sewing machine so I could make clothes to sell. I used to see Linda Haskell a lot. Jason was four, maybe five. Cute little thing. They would walk by almost every day. I knew by the way she walked this was an unhappy woman. Drank too much, though. But she adored her son. A blind cat could see that."

She took out her cigarettes again, only this time lit one. After two puffs she looked around for an ashtray. Annie handed her a saucer.

"Worse thing about a cold. I can't smoke. One day she has a broken arm. That heals and she doesn't walk by for a while. I see her in Star Market. She walks like she is in pain. Broken rib, she tells me, Darlinks. She was an abused wife."

No one had seen Des come in, but when Annie looked up, he caught her eye.

"That doesn't mean Len hit her," Heather said. "She could have fallen down the stairs."

Magda let out a snort and shoved the saucer with the two-puff smoked cigarette at Gaëlle. "Here, Darlink. Empty this please. Susan will have a fit if she smells ashes. I didn't blame Linda for taking off. However, she shouldn't have left Jason with that monster."

"How long ago was that?" Des asked.

Heather spoke before anyone answered. "Len was a good father. He was always there with Phil and me at my son's basketball games. My oldest son is two years younger than Jason."

"I thought you had young children," Des said.

"There were ten years between my first and second. Then I had one every two years. Now the bastard took them today to show his mother, the old bitch, that he's a devoted father."

"Did anyone ever hear from her again?" Des asked.

"Heather's mother-in-law?" Magda cocked her head at Des.

Damn, she's flirting, Annie thought.

Des laughed. "No. Linda Haskell."

"No, I assumed she didn't want to be found."

"When was it?" Annie asked.

"Right about the time the Baby Jessica fell down a well. I remember because Len said that maybe Linda did too."

"Bad taste," Heather said. "I think several of her friends got Christmas cards saying she was happy. We weren't that close so I didn't."

CHAPTER 50

I cain't really believe it. We be going north. Not just the Mistress and the little Missy but me and Zeb. Such fighting to work it all out. The Massa sure didn't want Zeb going anywhere. Massa Richard be against it too.

Ever since Zeb done come back from learning to carpenter, Massa Richard don't bother me at night no more, but when he passes me in the house and no one else is around, he thinks my breasts be doorknobs ready to turn. I knowd my breasts are big and full. Cain't understand why men get so excited about breasts. Maybe they remembers when they sucks milk from their mama's.

I debates telling Zeb, but I be afeared. Zeb calls me his woman, the one thing he can own. I ain't all that sure it be good being owned by a husband any more than being owned by white folk, but it sure be good being loved. I watch Zeb watch me and his eyes go all soft like. Zeb's eyes shows his soul. If white folks looks into his eyes they can see what that man be thinking. Anyway between Zeb's pride and temper, I ain't sure what he do if he learnt that Massa Richard touches my breasts. Now that it's certain I ain't going have any mixed baby, I sure ain't going to tell Zeb that Massa Richard rutted me.

I wants to ask the Mistress how she done persuade the Massa to let both of us go with her. I knows she tells him the little Missy needs her nanny. It ain't my place to ask, and I be afraid that she would tell me I cain't go for being too nosy.

One day as I be packing some of the clothes she says to me, "I

know you're curious why my husband said Zeb could go with us."
She sits on the edge of her bed and hands me her hairbrush. I stops
packing and starts brushing her hair. It's the color of shiny bark and
comes down to her waist. I knowd there no such thing, but if bark
were shiny, that would be the Mistress' hair.

"I am," I says.

She pats the place next to her and whispers in my ear, just like we
be friends. "I arranged for Zeb to take lessons from a master carpenter
in New York. My husband believes that Zeb will be able to make fine
furniture to sell if we come back."

That night almost as I falls asleep after Zeb pleasures me with his
tongue, and I left him weak from my mouth I realizes she said "if"
not when.

CHAPTER 51

Sunday, December 26

Although Christmas Day had been almost balmy, at night while revelers slept stuffed with food and overstimulated with presents, temperatures plummeted.

When Annie woke on the couch made up to a double bed, she opened her eyes. Light streamed in through a lace-patterned frosted window. She snuggled into Roger, who although still mostly asleep, gathered her in.

"It's cold out there," she whispered.

"Hmmm."

They fell back asleep until Susan bustled through the room followed by sounds of water running, pans clicking, the smell of coffee and bacon.

Roger rolled over and kissed Annie's ear. "Think your mother would come back to Argelès with us as our cook?"

"Fat chance," Susan called from the kitchen. She entered the living room and sat on the bottom of the sofa bed. "I'm taking Gaëlle into Boston today to show her the after-Christmas-shopping frenzies."

"Which will be a total change from last Christmas in Geneva when in between Christmas and New Year's lots of stores and restaurants close for a good part of the week," Annie said.

"Don't let her buy much. I don't want to turn her into a mad consumer," Roger said. "And no brand names written on anything unless the company promises to pay her for being a living billboard."

Susan patted him. "Agreed. But I will treat her to something. Trust me. I'm a mother. I even have a T-shirt saying that."

"What are we planning today?" Roger asked.

"Maybe a trip to the witch museum in Salem?" Annie said.

"Going to visit your sisters?" Roger asked.

Annie picked up a pillow, but before she could bat him, the telephone rang.

"Charlie Tucker here."

"Morning, Charlie. My dad's out or do you want me?"

"You. Do you think you and your boyfriend could drop by the office tomorrow morning?"

Annie covered the receiver with her hand to check it out with Roger.

"About 11:30. I can take you both to lunch, if you're still speaking to me."

CHAPTER 52

Sunday, December 26

Magda poured boiling water into her hot water bottle and wrapped it in a towel with much of the nub worn off. Once it might have been white or beige, but she neither remembered or cared.

She swallowed two aspirins before crawling back into bed. Her bones hurt. She clicked the television remote to C-SPAN to watch some senator sputter. There were great issues and little issues. Let the leaders lie their way through the biggies. She would deal with little issues—the things that made a difference in one person's life.

If the phone rang, let it. No, she couldn't do that. Some girl might need help. The Save Women team had identified four wives to monitor, not counting Melissa. Two had restraining orders that seemed to be holding. One was about to be spirited away with her children. The fourth looked as if she were going back to her husband.

The group was always debating about the returnees. Magda's co-founder said once they went back, forget them—no second chances. Concentrate on those that want to be helped. Magda had the opposite point of view. Those that went back, especially without counseling, were in even more danger.

What still amazed Magda was that so many women were in trouble. Violence was not limited by class or education. She had decided long ago that she could run the world far better than anyone she had ever met.

First, she would have people do their jobs. Second, she would design a hell for all the cops, lawyers and social workers who mealy-mouthed around. Even when the system worked, there was the toll on families torn asunder. Often the asunderers were the husbands themselves.

It had taken almost a year to set up her network, with the false IDs and false lives. The new anti-terrorism laws made it harder, but they still could do it. They had people providing false identities, false resumes, false job recommendations for jobs, although there the law helped. People could only verify employment.

When they failed it was because the women themselves found it hard to stay away indefinitely. Sometimes it was necessary to move not just them and their children but elderly parents. And there were some that didn't deserve to be saved. Not many but some, like the doctor's wife who'd looked at the cracked sink in the bathroom and the faded linoleum and said, "You don't expect me to stay here, do you?" Magda had wanted to strangle her herself.

"Look," she said. "Some women work two jobs to help pay for these shelters. None of us have much more than this to help you."

The bitch went back to her comforts and casts. She had outlived him. He'd gotten stoned on his own prescriptions and fallen down stairs and broken his neck. Magda suspected he had been pushed. The woman had inherited his house and bank account, so maybe she had been saved.

Magda's eyes closed. How she hated being sick. Too much time to think about things she didn't want to think about. She could see all the things she needed to do when she had the time to do them. Being sick gave her time, but robbed her of energy.

She needed to identify more hideaways, smaller towns near

jobs, where the women could build new lives. Perhaps she should visit the Middle West. She wished she knew more about the Internet. Maybe Annie would show her how to use it, but that meant buying a computer, something she had resisted forever. So much to do, and she felt so lousy.

CHAPTER 53

Monday, December 27

Melissa washed the last of the breakfast dishes. What a wonderful Christmas. Her meal had turned out perfect even by gourmet standards. Len and Jason hadn't fought about Jason's low sales. The bright kitchen cheered her. Now it was time to get to the office, although Len had said to cut back her hours because of the baby.

Madison. She had given in and asked her GYN after her last sonogram but hadn't told Jason or Len, although she kept referring to the baby as she.

Jason didn't want to discuss the possibility of a girl, but Melissa couldn't resist stopping to look at little dresses while ignoring boys' clothes. His chromosomes determined the sex of the child anyway; he couldn't blame her.

Had it been a boy she wanted the name Aiden after one of the *Sex and the City* characters. That was the type of son she wanted, someone sensitive who loved nature. Maybe her next child would be a boy and then she could name him Aiden. Since Jason refused to watch the program, he wouldn't know where the name came from. He called the program *Sex and the Bitches.* She only watched the reruns when he wasn't home.

She placed the last dish in the drainer and took out the cut-up beef to put into the Pokey Pot with onions and a can of tomatoes. To return at night and smell food cooking made her feel like she really was home.

Home—what she'd wanted all her life, a place with love and
safety: a place to escape from the outside world. She had made
this place a welcoming one for Jason and herself. Even with her
limited budget, a little paint and some colorful cloth, she felt
she had done as much as possible.

Jason needed a home too. Probably more than she did,
because she could make one for herself. He couldn't. His
mother's desertion, then a series of stepmothers, had left him
damaged; she would use her love to heal him. Once he felt safe
in her love the beatings would stop and life would be good
again. Or good for the first time.

Magda's worried look flashed through her mind. She knew
that the strange woman wasn't the interfering weirdo Jason
called her. She only wanted to help. Melissa liked Magda, had
seen the beautiful clothes and lovely quilts she had made.
Because Melissa loved beauty, she felt nothing but respect for
Magda's talent.

Jason disliked Annie and Susan Young. Said they were strange,
probably because they spent so many years in a foreign country.
"Why would any American desert their country?" he asked
Melissa. She didn't have an answer. Annie was amazing. Imagine
speaking so many languages and going to strange countries all
by herself without being a scaredy-cat.

After the baby is born, she thought she might try going into
Boston alone. Not very far. Just take the train as far as North
Station. See where the Celtics played.

So if she went into Boston maybe she could try a ride on the
T. Where would she go? Government Center? Boston Common? She wondered if it looked like it did in *The Parent Trap*,
one of her favorite movies when she was little. That and *Over
the Rainbow*. No wizard would give her courage.

CHAPTER 54

Monday, December 27

Charlie, Roger and Annie sat around the table in Charlie's office. Steam rose from the two full coffee cups and one tea cup. The smell of cold rose from Annie's and Roger's coats thrown over a fourth chair.

"I'll get right to the point," Charlie said. "Like I said before, all hell has broken lose."

"And that is?" Annie asked.

"Diane Ash. She has demanded a School Committee meeting. I've a copy here." He handed a manila folder to Annie. "It's worse than we thought earlier."

Roger moved his chair closer so he could read over her shoulder.

"Of course, I shouldn't have this, but Mangone slipped it to me yesterday," Charlie said.

Annie scanned the complaint that by allowing the showing of her CD-ROM in the classroom the teacher had undermined the patriotism of the class, threatened their sense of well-being with the violence, and showed the early settlers to be immoral people. "At least it is well written," she said. "Too bad they want to fire Kendra Jones."

"We already knew there would be a School Committee meeting on the topic. Have you talked to Roger about staying a few extra days to present your, our side?" He turned to Roger. "I know you were planning to fly back New Year's Day."

Roger glared at Annie for a second then laughed. "Why am I surprised? I do need to fly back, but I am so used to Annie disappearing for work for weeks at a time, a few more days without her will be . . . almost normal."

She reached for his hand. "You really don't mind?"

"Of course I mind. I just think you need to finish what you started."

"On the other hand, Charlie, this is the best thing that could have happened to our project."

Charlie blew on his coffee. "How do you mean?"

"It calls attention to the problems of a watered-down curriculum. The kids are learning pap and that isn't good for a democracy."

"Too bad these people don't think that way." Charlie pointed to the folder.

"What we need is lots and lots of publicity for this," Annie said. "May I use your phone?" When Charlie agreed she went to his desk to dial Des O'Flaherty's cell phone. She missed her own, but hers wasn't a tri-band. She had never thought she would need a tri-band because she had never expected to spend this much time in the States. She found it annoying that besides different standards for cell phones the U.S. had different-sized standard paper, television, DVDs, VCRs and God knows what else from the rest of the world. Nor did she like going out to buy duplicate technology even if she were a techie herself.

Des's recorded voice said, "I can't pick up, but please leave a message."

She'd expected something more original. "This is Annie. It's 11:30. I'm at Charlie Tucker's office. We need your help with something. Call me here or at home as soon as you get this message. Also, I've an idea on Gene Rowan." She turned to Roger and Charlie, "That should get him."

Before she could seat herself, Charlie's secretary popped her head around the door. "There's a Mr. O'Flaherty to see you."

"How did you get here so quickly?" Roger asked.

"I was around the corner when I picked up the message."

When Des had been briefed, Annie asked, "Can you help us get press coverage?"

"I'll talk to some of my friends. It's a news story when some school board comes out in favor of creationism. Ignoring history from original sources in favor of legend . . ."

"Well, I did make up the characters," Annie said.

"But you used all original sources. Can you prove everything?" Charlie asked.

"Absolutely."

At that Charlie clapped his hands. "You're right, Annie. I panicked. Thinking about it, I can see how this will launch the product. Especially since we're offering it free."

"Free is news. Almost unheard of today," Des said. "In fact, I've a couple of buddies outside the area: one works for the *New York Times* and the other for the *Washington Post.*"

Annie paced. She did her best thinking when pacing. Whenever she had a contract and worked in a room with lots of desks and there was nowhere to walk, she felt trapped.

"I'll double-check with Plimouth Plantation. They've really been helpful," Annie said.

Des had his reporter pad out and was sketching.

"I didn't know you could draw," Annie said.

"I can't, but look." He handed over the pad. The few lines resembled the building where the school board met, and Pilgrims were standing outside. "If we want to make this a media event, let's have people in appropriate costumes of the time appear outside. They are speaking up for the truth of their lives. It should make all the papers."

"Brilliant," Annie said. "So you'll call them?"

Des put the pad on the table. "Yup."

"I don't know," said Charlie. "I still have to live in this town."

Annie said nothing. It depended on his personal courage. His income wasn't in danger, but could he take being ostracized socially if that were to be the outcome?

"The CD-ROM will get all the attention you want. And the idea of free in a commercial world, seeker of truth, purity, etc., etc., etc.," Des said.

The only sound in the room was the ticking of the ship's clock on the table behind Charlie's desk.

"Okay, what can we lose?" Charlie said.

"Good." The other three spoke as one.

"Len will happily be a Pilgrim," Charlie said. "After I twist his arm."

"As will my mother and father. I bet Magda . . ."

"If it is outrageous, Magda will," Charlie said. "She might actually look like a real woman instead of an apparition."

"Maybe the other artists and some of their children." When Charlie looked confused, Annie said, "From my Mom's studio. Maybe they would even play the part of the Pilgrim children from the script. Too bad we couldn't find a real Indian child or a real Indian. I wouldn't want to conscript a white person to play an Indian."

Everyone was nodding.

"Maybe someone from Plimouth, a real Wampanoag, might be willing to do something. The Indians I spoke to during my research loved the idea their history would be properly represented."

Charlie stood. "We've a lot to do." He turned to Roger. "Is she always this fast?"

"Her mind goes a thousand miles an hour. I find it fascinating." He reached out and put his hand on Annie's knee, "Albeit it's very tiring."

Des opened his mouth to speak, but stopped. Annie looked

at him. He shook his head.

They put on sweaters, coats, scarves, mittens, hats to face the cold. "Annie, you look like the Michelin man, only in color." Roger pulled on her scarf ends.

The scarf covered her mouth. "Mmm."

"What?" Roger asked.

Annie pulled the scarf from her mouth. "I was going to ask Des to come back to the house. My thousand-mile-an-hour mind wants to play with the Internet on our other problem."

"My place is a little closer," Des said.

"Yours," Annie said.

"What about the lunch I promised you?" Charlie asked.

"Can I have a rain check?" Annie asked.

"Of course. Roger?"

"Love to," Roger said and kissed Annie on the cheek. "And Des, remember she belongs to me."

CHAPTER 55

Monday, December 27

The living room in Des's cottage couldn't have been 50 degrees. Annie kept her jacket over her shoulders. He dragged his portable space heater next to the computer. "When it's windy like today, the oil heater can't fight the drafts. At least we can't see our breath."

Annie surveyed the cottage. One main room divided the kitchen, living and dining areas. If she had chosen to run her fingers across any piece of wood, they would emerge clean. The many magazines were stacked without hanging edges. She could see into the bedroom where the bed was made. An Army sergeant could march in and bounce a coin off the blanket. No clothes were draped over chairs. The dishes that he must have used for his breakfast were in the dish drainer. She'd expected a bachelor pigsty.

Annie tried to ignore the chill. The heater glowed red, but since it wasn't much bigger than four shoe boxes, its chance of success was minimal. "Why don't you buy something bigger?" she asked.

"Haven't gotten around to it." He turned the computer on.

The computer screen lit up, but didn't ask for a password. She typed in *www.whowhere.com* and filled in the white page form asking for all Gene Rowans in Florida. There were six. "Let's start calling."

The first call rang four times. Then the voice mail said, "Yo,

239

you know what to do."

"Doesn't sound like an old man," Des said. "I'll try the next."

There was no answer.

"And I thought every person in Florida was old," she said after she'd talked to their sixth youth.

"We're assuming that the dentist is still alive and well in Florida. That's a lot of assuming," Des said. "I kinda hate eliminating this last one."

"I'll do it."

She was just about to hang up when a cracked voice said, "Hello."

"My name is Annie Young. I'm calling from Caleb's Landing, Massachusetts."

"You calling to tell me someone else is dead? That's about the only calls I get from back home these days. My daughter used to call, but she retired down here too."

After Rowan confirmed he was indeed the dentist they were looking for, Annie explained, "We were hoping you still had your dental records."

There was coughing on the line. "Excuse me, I've a terrible cold. How's the weather up there?"

"About two below. You don't want to think of the wind chill," Annie said.

"Makes me glad I'm here. Hate to disappoint you, Miss Young, but I put those records in storage. Company may be bankrupt 'cause they haven't billed me for I don't know how many years."

"What was the name of the company?" Annie asked. Maybe it still existed and his lack of billing was a fluke.

"Let me think," there was silence on the line. "Store it . . . Space-Saver . . . something like that."

Annie noticed Des rummaging in a drawer and bringing out

a piece of paper and pencil. He wrote, "Ask him about Len's wife."

"Was Linda Haskell a patient of yours?"

"Married to Len."

"Do you remember her?"

"Sure do. Memory's not that bad. Pretty thing. Think it was a bad marriage because she up and left. One time she came in with two front teeth broken."

"Did you ever see her after she left?"

"Can't say I did. Len was frantic looking for her, so I guess she didn't want to be found."

"Was she a local girl?"

Another pause. "Yup. Grew up with my kids. Maiden name was Chess. Worked summers at different restaurants, but that's normal. Kinda wild though. Was a heavy drinker. Slowed down a while after she had the kid, can't think of his name."

"Jason."

"Jason. Heard she was a real good mother except when she was drinking."

"Anything else you can tell us?"

Des gave Annie a thumbs-up.

"Had her real estate license. Was a better salesperson than him, and he was good."

Des wrote something on the notepad and tapped his pencil.

"Thanks for your time and . . ." she looked at the note that said give him your number. "Let me give you my number in case you think of anything. Call collect."

She hung up. "What was that all about? What made you think of Linda Haskell?"

"A hunch. She moved away about twenty years ago. It's the only one we know of."

"But Len heard from her."

"And who else? And he knew your aunt's house. He's a history nut."

Annie thought of Jason's violence, which would be in keeping with an alcoholic mother, but Len didn't seem the least bit violent to her. But then again some of her friends' husbands who seemed like nice guys turned out to be violent . . . not many, but usually the ones that seemed the least likely. She shivered and pulled her jacket tightly around her shoulders. "How do you live like this?"

"It's usually not this cold. What now?"

"Let's check real estate licenses to see if she's still active, but if she ran away she probably didn't stay in Massachusetts. I've no idea how to check realtors in other states. In fact, I don't know how to check here," Annie said.

"I can do it, but that's assuming she didn't remarry or go back to her maiden name."

"And that's assuming that the skeleton is hers. It could have been any summer tourist."

Annie was thumbing through the yellow pages. "Two storage places are listed in Gloucester. Wanta check them out?"

"Why not? It's warmer in the car."

The late-afternoon sky was darkening before Annie got back to the Young house. Gaëlle was in the living room showing her father her new pants and top by doing a catwalk, each leg crossing over the other and turning. Her midriff was bare.

"I like it if you don't freeze," Roger said.

"It's warm in here, but Boston was awful. We had to keep stopping for hot chocolate and mint. And there's lots of places selling croissant sandwiches."

The door opened. Dave came in with his coat dusted with white that caught the light then melted into nothingness. "It's warmed up enough to snow."

Gaëlle ran to the window. The flakes fluttered under the street lights. "Let's go outside."

"How about waiting until after dinner. There'll be more, and we can make snow angels," Dave said. "I did it with Annie when she was little."

"What's a snow angel?"

Annie laid down on the floor and moved her arms and legs. "You do it like this and leave your angel mark in the snow."

"Sounds cold. Maybe I'm a little too old for snow angels. We could do a snowman?"

"Wrong kind of snow," Dave said. "Not sticky enough."

"How 'bout I heat up some maple syrup and we gather a pan of snow and pour syrup on it. It hardens into candy, Gaëlle," Susan said.

"Fantastic," Gaëlle said.

"Dinner first." Susan produced turkey sandwiches with stuffing and cranberry sauce. She poured four glasses of apple cider. "You'll be so over New Englanded by the time you get on the plane."

"If it helps me understand Annie better . . ." Roger started to say.

"But these are my parents' childhood memories. Mine are all mixed up from four other countries," Annie said.

"You're lucky. I've only lived two places. Paris and Argelès. And they're both French," Gaëlle said. "Maybe I'll work for Air France when I grow up so I can see the world."

Dave reached for a celery stick and crunched loudly. "What did you guys do today?"

After Susan and Gaëlle finished talking about the shopping trip, Annie filled them in on the school board. "I love the idea of dressing up as a Pilgrim," Susan said.

"Me, too," Gaëlle said.

"You'll be back in Argelès. School," Roger said.

"Why not stay here and enroll me in an American school for the next few months?"

"You'll miss the *lycée,* then you won't pass your *Bac* and without your *Bac* . . ." Roger began.

". . . you'll never be hired by Air France and see the world," Annie finished.

Gaëlle threw herself back into her seat. "I could work for an American airline."

"No green card," Roger said.

"But if you marry Annie, she can adopt me, and . . ."

Roger gave Gaëlle his enough-is-enough look.

Annie launched into the Dr. Rowan phone call and her newly formed theory that maybe Len had knocked his wife's teeth out.

Dave sighed. "Annie, your imagination is going crazy. I've known Len for years. He's not a wife-beater. He's not a murderer."

"His son is a wife-beater."

"You can't be sure."

"I've seen Melissa's bruises, Dad."

"Maybe we should talk about something else," Roger said. "Can we take the car to Plimouth Plantation tomorrow?"

"Let's all go," Susan said. "I haven't been since a class trip in grade school."

CHAPTER 56

Tuesday, December 28

"I work in computers," Annie said to the Pilgrim woman sweeping the wooden plank floor of her cottage, a replica of one built in 1627. Bread was rising in a wooden bowl on the table. The smell of yeast mixed with that of wood burning in the fireplace. Walking through Plimouth Plantation was like entering a time machine. They were the only visitors on this cold day, and therefore the only ones in modern clothing. The people working at the Plantation wore period clothes.

The woman handed Gaëlle the broom made of a tree branch with straw tied at its base. "The devil does not like idle hands. Get thee to work, child." Turning to Annie, she said, "I have pewter, too. See this plate. I brought it from England. My husband said we should not bring things like this to the new world. Sweep child, sweep."

Gaëlle swept. When she was done she handed the broom back to the woman. "Cool."

"Yes it is cool, today. Thee is from where, child for thy speaketh with a strange accent?"

"I am from France."

"A place where they worship false idols, but thee was smart enough to leave and come to this Godly place. And what ship did thee come on?"

"I flew."

The woman whispered, "If thee took flight, then thy surely

must be in league with the devil. I think thee plays with me, for surely thee has the face of an angel, and a soul to match."

"She never broke character for a second," Dave said after they left and walked by the thatched wooden houses along the path. The gardens were snow covered, but there was less snow than in Caleb's Landing.

Annie, glad they hadn't let last night's storm postpone their trip, looked at her watch. "It's almost time for my appointment. Meet you at the dining room."

As she hurried up the frozen path she heard a bleat and looked into the slit eyes of a very pregnant sheep. "Hello," she said. The sheep walked toward her. "I don't have any food, but I won't say you are potential food. I'll tell you that your wool might someday be a blanket."

She entered the administration center. A man in overalls was putting up a new name plaque that said Dr. G. Andrew Yates. Annie opened the door to see a man in his mid-fifties talking to his secretary as she entered the office. He held out his hand. "You must be Annie Young. Please call me Andy."

"Better than Gay," the secretary, a woman who had a raspy smoker voice and a face that hid an age between fifty and sixty said. "The first sign had his name Gaylord Andrew Yates. I was afraid between his initials and first name everyone would call him Gay."

"When my mother named me she couldn't have guessed the connotation gay would come to have. Come in. Make yourself comfortable." With a flourish he swept his arm toward his office.

His room was functional, but a number of boxes were half-filled with books and papers. "I'm still getting settled. The last director had a heart attack and took early retirement."

"But I just talked to him a few days ago."

"He was still coming in part time until I arrived."

Annie wondered why the director hadn't said anything.

Andy ushered Annie to a seat. "I got a chance to see your CD-ROM. It's really good. I couldn't find one inaccuracy, although you did use your imagination in creating the children."

"When I was in school, I had two kinds of history teachers. With most I had to drink tons of coffee to stay awake. A few left me waiting to hear the next story." He pointed to the diplomas: B.A. History, Boston University; M.A. History, University of Michigan; and Ph.D. History, Harvard University. "I stuck out the bad."

"History has always been my passion. I grew up in Europe and my father had me exploring just about everything from Roman ruins to pacing off World War II battlefields."

"Was he a historian?"

"A businessman."

"You didn't want to be a historian?"

"There aren't many jobs for historians outside of academia. Teaching wasn't for me."

"I understand. Now tell me about the problem you mentioned when you set up this appointment."

After Annie briefed him on what had happened with the school board, Yates snorted. "I get so tired of fighting ignorance. And politics."

Annie had an idea, which he might reject, but she'd learned a long time ago to ask the questions that might be answered "no." If she didn't ask, it was an automatic no. "Do you think you could testify to the accuracy of the CD?"

"My board would probably hate me doing that. Maybe they'll never hear about it."

Shit. Ethics suck, Annie thought, as she debated not telling him their plans. "We want maximum publicity."

Andy sat back in his chair and tapped a pencil against his hand. "Hmmm."

"Is that a I-don't-want-to-do-it-now hmmm, or a the-risk-is-worth-it hmmm?"

"You do net things out, don't you?" Andy asked.

"It's a fault of mine . . . *or* a virtue depending," Annie said.

Andy laughed. "What's the worst that can happen? They fire me for advancing the cause of historical knowledge."

He stood up and ushered her out of the office.

Not wanting to be outmaneuvered, Annie asked, "So I can count on you?"

"Tell my secretary what time, where, and how to get there." He reached into his pocket and took out a card, a personal card. "Here's my home e-mail and telephone number."

After thanking him she walked to the door.

"Ms. Young? A guy's gotta do what a guy's gotta do." He took out, twirled, shot and blew on an imaginary pistol before returning it to an imaginary holster.

CHAPTER 57

Tuesday, December 28

Len and Melissa were alone in the real estate office. She had two window-sized boards propped up on her desk in front of her. They were covered with photos and property descriptions. Her father-in-law had lifted them from the windows for her to redo. Photos of newly listed properties were scattered on the desk. Three "solds" were printed in black ink on a bright green background. Because the windows were not blocked by the boards more light than usual streamed into the office, heightened by the reflection of the sun on the snow banks, which needed to be carted away and dumped into the sea. She thought, if this winter was any indication, the world was suffering from global cooling, not global warming. When she said it, Len laughed.

She'd taken over the window arrangements a year ago when Len gave her a digital camera. Now all listings had the photo of the building at the top and two smaller interior shots at the bottom with information about rooms and extras. Len told her she'd an eye for finding the right detail to photograph. Within a month several other real estate agencies in town had copied the format. Still, the agency was fighting the economic downturn.

The Haskell Agency had a triple window. In the middle section Melissa had put a Victorian dollhouse complete with tiny window boxes. Len had been dubious at first, claiming that the purchase of the dollhouse and its furnishings cost more than a real house would, but then every woman and child stopped to look.

"They're looking at the dollhouse not the listings," Jason had complained. Len stood on the street and watched people's eyes and they went over to the listings.

Two single women who bought properties said it was the dollhouse that had attracted them. "Would have bought anyway," Jason said.

When Melissa finished with the board she covered the dollhouse and the area in front of the house with white cotton. She placed a little shovel in the man doll's hand after gluing cotton to the shovel. Behind him she created a little snow pile and to one side, she had the two doll children half building a snowman from Styrofoam balls.

Len came up and behind her. She jumped.

"Sorry, didn't mean to startle you."

"It's okay. Let's go look," Melissa said.

Len took her arm as she walked over an icy patch. "If I'm not careful, you'll leave me to become a window dresser."

Melissa couldn't imagine anyone hiring her. She would never be able to produce enough ideas on demand. She was able to use her imagination on this window because she had lots of time to think.

As she cleaned up the bits of paper, cotton and glue she felt Len staring at her. "How are you?"

She felt her face grow hot. The blush, which left her even more embarrassed, was clashing with her pink turtleneck. "Fine."

"I was worried about you when you were sick."

"I'm fine now."

He patted her stomach. "We need to take care of my grandbaby."

Funny, she thought, how people felt they could touch a

pregnant woman's tummy, but would never dream of it when she wasn't pregnant.

"I'm going out to lunch. Hold the fort, Melissa."

She loved being alone in the office, although Jason thought it meant business was bad. For Melissa it meant that the three other agents were out either getting listings or showing houses. Today only Jason and Len were working. The other two agents were taking advantage of the lull between Christmas and New Year's to take their holiday.

Jason was putting circulars in people's mailboxes asking them that if they planned to sell, to list the house with him. Melissa had made up the flyer with a photo of the dollhouse, but Jason wanted it taken off. Len had sided with her, saying the dollhouse was brand recognition.

Melissa heated water for herb tea. When the baby was born the first thing she planned was to guzzle coffee and even more Coca-Cola. She put her hand on her stomach and felt the baby move. Madison. Jason would learn to love a daughter, she was sure of it, despite his insistence on a son.

As the kettle shut off, the bell over the front door tinkled. Two women in their early thirties walked in, laughing. Their cheeks were rosy from the cold. They were dressed in jeans and wore red ski jackets. One had a green ski cap, but the other had Jennifer Aniston hair. "Hi, I'm Jennifer and this is my friend Kristin," the Aniston look-alike said.

Melissa introduced herself.

"We saw the listing for the red house with the widow's walk. Can we see it?"

"All the agents are out," Melissa said.

The one with the ski cap looked at her watch. "We really can't wait or come back. Can't you show us?" Her tone wasn't demanding at all.

Melissa looked around the office. "I'm Melissa, but I'm here alone."

"The thing is, we're moving to the area, but we've a plane to catch this afternoon," Kristin said.

"Let me dial one of the sales people." Neither Jason nor Len answered. What to do? What to do? Although she wasn't a licensed agent, the agency needed every sale it could get. "Which house is it?"

"I'll show you."

They led her outside and pointed to the old Prior house. As she turned to go back in she skidded on a patch of ice and both women grabbed her before she fell.

"I'm a little off balance these days."

"When are you due?" Jennifer asked.

"Another month. Let me try the sales people again." No answer. "Let me get the file." The file contained photos of the inside as well as all the information on type of heating, taxes and easements. Not written was the fact that the Priors were divorced and both parties were anxious to be rid of the house. The note was that people could come in anytime. "What time is your flight?"

"Four, but we really should be at the airport by two. Damned security," Kristin said.

"Just remember, Logan is the airport of choice for hijackers so stop complaining," Jennifer said.

Melissa thought it must be wonderful to be able to joke. Without thinking words fell out of her mouth. "I'll show you, if you can drive. I can't fit behind the wheel." She plucked the key off the key board and turned the door sign to *Closed, Be Back at* . . . , setting the hand of the red plastic clock to 1:00.

During the ride to the house located off Maple Avenue, Melissa dialed Lexie Prior, who was staying in the house until it was sold. No answer: Melissa knew Lexie worked in Boston.

Let the house be neat, she prayed. And let it be set up for Christmas. That will make it look so homey.

Snow made the house look like it belonged on a Christmas card. The trellis was interspersed with dead roses, but the snow frosting gave them a delicate beauty. However, when they entered, back issues of *Time, Human Resource Management, Financial Times, The Economist* and *Wall Street Journal* were scattered everywhere. An old oak rolltop desk was piled with papers. A computer stand to the left of the desk held a printer, laptop and cords snaking across the desk.

No Christmas tree decorations were up. As they walked through the house, the kitchen had cold coffee in the coffeemaker and dirty plates and cups in the sink.

I should never have brought them here without checking, Melissa thought as she waddled up the stairs. She'd heard other agents talk about having fresh-cut flowers and baking bread to make a house appear desirable. "Where do you work?" she asked. She could see the master bedroom with the bed unmade. A pile of dirty laundry was under the window.

"I'm being transferred by my company, which you won't have heard of. They make very specialized software for hospitals. They need a local rep." Jennifer flipped her hair.

"I'm a web page designer and work from home," Kristin said.

"Well look at this," Melissa opened the door to each of the other three bedrooms. "An office and a bedroom for each of you." At least the children's bedrooms were pristine. She wondered if the two women might share the bedroom, not that it made any difference.

Kristin went into one of the rooms. The football wallpaper, the baseball bat and hockey stick in the corner left no doubt as to the gender of the occupant. "I could put the computer there, and also an easy chair over there. I'll want to change the wallpaper."

"Can we see the basement?" Jennifer asked.

The stairs going to the basement were steep.

"Better you don't come down." Kristin clattered down the stairs. "Hey, a modern heater."

"It's two years old," Melissa called.

Melissa also waited while the two women investigated the attic. They flicked lights on and off, tested each tap and finally settled themselves on the couch. "Can we talk a moment?"

"I'll go in the kitchen and write Mrs. Prior a note that we were here so she doesn't freak out about a burglar or something," Melissa said.

Before she finished, Jennifer stood in the doorway. "We want to make an offer."

Len was in the office when she got back. "I was worried."

Melissa introduced him and he took over. The women wrote out a good-faith check and rushed out the door for the airport.

"Good going, girl." He high-fived her.

Jason walked in. "What's up?"

"Your wife just sold her first house. Or at least she got an offer. We should think about having her get a license after the baby is born."

Melissa wanted to ask if she would get a commission, but held her words.

"You'll get the commission, even if Jason's name is on the contract. After all, a couple is a team." Len looked at his son. "What have you got to say to your talented wife, Jason?"

"Congratulations." His eyes said anything but.

Jason didn't speak a word in the car on the way home. Although Melissa wanted to stop at the supermarket to pick up lamb chops, she didn't ask, knowing enough to be quiet. She could make spaghetti. Jason didn't like her to use canned goods, but if she added oregano it might taste homemade.

He got out of the car and slammed the door. She inched her way up the icy walk and opened it. *Maybe he just wanted to save on heat.* He had thrown his coat on the floor. She hung hers up and used an old cane to pick up his rather than try and stoop over.

Jason's footsteps could be heard upstairs in their bedroom. *That man must be part elephant.* She went into the kitchen, but could hear the shower running. *Maybe the shower will improve his mood. Please, dear God, don't let him drink.* She poured the bottled sauce into the saucepan.

"Melissa, have we any Scotch left?" Jason called from the living room.

"Not that I know of." *Scotch costs a lot of money. More than we can afford.* None of the words that should be said would be. *This could be a long, painful night.*

"I'm going out for a drink."

"But I started supper."

"Tough shit."

Melissa wanted to mention they still had the hospital bills to save for. Jason had let their health insurance lapse when he went four months without a sale. Melissa's fixed salary covered the mortgage and food, but not much more.

"Where's my car keys?" He'd changed into jeans and a blue UMass sweatshirt.

"Did you look on top of the dresser?" He usually put them in his pockets and then emptied his pockets on top of the dresser. "Would you like me to come with you?" Maybe she could control his drinking. Maybe something would go right. She turned off the sauce that had begun to boil.

"You, little viper, are about the last person I want with me."

"What did I do?"

"You showed me up." He picked up the spaghetti sauce and threw it at her. Most of it went on her clothes, but some of it burned her exposed arm.

After the door slammed, Melissa threw her stained maternity top into the washer along with the towels she wiped up the sauce with. Her hands shook. *Jason would come home drunk. Unless he was ready to pass out, he would hit her.* Her hand went to her stomach. *Until now I thought the baby might make things better, but now I'm not sure. What if he hits my belly? How much protection does my amniotic fluid give Madison?*

I should eat something, feed Madison. Her legs sent a message to her brain that they would rather not support her. She sat at the table, the chair pushed out to make way for her stomach. As certainly as the tide washed over the beach, despair covered Melissa.

Still in the kitchen chair, Melissa started awake, her back aching and her bladder full. As she waddled to the bathroom she passed the clock. 10:37. *Jason is still out. He has probably been drinking all this time and will be in a horrible mood. I must get upstairs, pretend I'm asleep. I should have been an actress. I could audition for any role where the performer is asleep on stage or before a camera.* The first lesson was to relax her body. A tense body was a give-away. The second was to keep the eyelids still but move the forehead slightly if a light went on, turn away from a light. The third was breathing, deep breathing, maybe with a little putt-putt without or a tiny moan.

As she undressed she imagined a punching bag in a gym waking up each morning knowing it would be pummeled before the day was out. *A punching bag is made for that. A wife wasn't, but as his wife I've promised to love, honor and obey. I put obey in our marriage ceremony. A man should be the head of the house.*

She climbed the stairs. They still couldn't afford carpet, but they'd varnished the wood and painted the rails so they looked fresh.

If I'm to change Jason . . . change Jason? Up until now I thought I had to change myself to be what he needed. Was that impossible? Change someone who didn't see the need to change?

Her mind wandered to a conversation at Susan and Dave Young's party. That drop-dead handsome Frenchman had been talking with her and Des O'Flaherty. They'd launched into American versus French politics. Both acted as if the presidents of both countries consulted with them daily.

"Politicians are stupid. They make the same mistake everywhere," Roger had said.

"Anyone knows if you do the same thing and expect a different result, you'll be disappointed," Des had said.

If I keep doing the same thing, I'll be disappointed. But if I do something different will the result be worse? Her flannel nightdress hung on the bathroom door. *Silly that a nightdress could bring comfort, but this one did. I love the violets, the high neck and long sleeves ruffled at the edge. Jason claims it makes me look like an old woman and he loses all desire for me when I wear it.*

Melissa dropped her dirty underwear in the hamper and pulled the nightdress over her head. The fabric stretched tight. She might not be able to wear it much longer. What she wore to bed didn't matter. Once her stomach bulged, Jason hadn't touched her. Before he made love to her twice daily. He said pregnancy made her repulsive.

At first she thought he'd been thrilled to be a father and was showing her with his body. Then she asked him why he had stopped after being so ardent and he'd said, "I didn't have to worry about you getting pregnant."

The room was cold. The sheets were cold. To save money they deliberately kept the house at 60 degrees around the clock. Jason said raising and lowering heat burned more oil. The house needed more insulation, but that was out of the question. Melissa dug in her drawer for socks. The sheets felt less cold through her clothing. Soon her body heat would warm her, but nothing could warm the cold spot growing inside her soul. She shut off the light, but she'd slept just enough downstairs to keep more sleep away.

Had she tried everything to help Jason control his temper? What else can I do to be a good wife? I cook, clean, wash and work. I accept our financial restraints. Sure, I look at decorating magazines dreaming of my ideal house, but it isn't a criticism of our financial status. Thinking of the fight when Jason found her looking at the magazine and blew up, she rubbed her leg where Jason had thumped her with his fist.

Madison tap-danced on Melissa's bladder. Melissa heaved the two of them out of bed and went to the toilet. As she sat on the seat she prayed that Jason wouldn't come home before she was in bed.

A seed of anger planted itself in the cold part of her soul. Totally out of character, she reached for the telephone and dialed Magda's number. It rang twice, but she hung up. It was too late to call. Too late at night, too late to get help. The cold settled over the seed, but not before a tiny root sprouted.

CHAPTER 58

Tuesday, December 28

Magda reached for the telephone. All her bones ached. "Hello."

No answer. After hanging up, she rolled over in bed, where she'd spent the day. The faded flannel sheets smelled sweaty. She alternated sweating and freezing, shedding and adding clothes. At the moment she wore socks, leggings, a turtle neck under a long nightdress and a sweatshirt and still couldn't get warm. The two duvets didn't help.

I'm never sick, she thought, this is ridiculous. Without meaning to, she fell asleep.

When Magda awoke the next morning she saw new snow on the rocks leading to the sea and on the brown leaves of the oak tree. Living near the water usually meant rain when even a half a mile inland there would be snow.

Her mind rejected the idea of food, but she wished that a cup of coffee so strong that she could chew it would miraculously appear on her night table to give her strength to get through the day. All this time at home without energy to do one stinking thing but sleep and shiver, shiver and burn was a waste of her time.

To hell with it, I won't be sick anymore, she thought. However, the second she stood, the room swayed and she followed the wall to the toilet where she vomited bile.

Back in bed she slept, exhausted from her trip across the hall.

The phone woke her.

"Magda, where've you been?" Susan asked.

"Flu."

"Have you seen a doctor?"

"Do you think I'm rich enough to pay a doctor, Darlink?" Magda's voice croaked. Health insurance and doctors were not for artists. She wondered if in the new Hungary they still had health insurance for everyone. She should have gone to another country years ago, but she had made her decision for the American dream. Who could have foreseen the future? Besides, who moves countries for health insurance? You pays your money, and you takes your chances. Someone had given her a T-shirt with those words written on it. Until then she had never worn T-shirts, preferring to dress in her own creations. But if she were to be an American artist, she needed to try T-shirts and jeans. Regrets were a waste of time. Here she had a mission.

"What are you eating?"

"Nothing," Magda said.

"I'm coming over," Susan said.

An hour later Susan spooned chicken soup into Magda's mouth. "You're playing earth mother, Darlink," Magda mumbled between mouthfuls.

"If I were an earth mother this would be homemade, not canned," Susan said.

When Magda had finished eating, Susan bundled her up and made her sit in a chair as she changed the sheets. "You need to see the doctor."

"Doctors, what do they know? He'll say take aspirins. Stay in bed. Or he'll sell me some expensive drug that does the same thing and say to stay in bed. Or . . ." A fit of coughing interrupted. "You'll get sick if you get too close."

"If I didn't have a full house, I'd take you home, but I'll be back later to make sure you're okay. Now sleep," Susan said.

Magda knew how sick she was when she didn't want to argue. The clean bed felt wonderful. Ordinarily she loved living alone, but every now and then, she realized that she needed others. God, she hated needing, although she liked to be needed by the girls she worked with. No, she wouldn't change her life, as much as she wished the world were perfect.

CHAPTER 59

Friday, December 31

"If I forget something, Annie'll bring it back," Annie heard Gaëlle say to her father. Roger filled the doorway of the bedroom where Gaëlle had slept. His back was to her. Sometimes she thought men's backs were the sexiest part of them, especially in suit jackets or sweaters. He wore the Nordic sweater she had brought back from a month-long assignment in Oslo. His gray-streaked black hair grazed his collar, shooting a sliver of desire through her.

Annie sat at the desk in the corner of her parents' room that they had turned into an office with a laptop, printer, small fax and copier. The hand-embroidered screen that her mother had found at the dump, cleaned and used to hide the office stuff when no one was working, was folded and rested against the closet door that held no more than five of her mother's dresses and two of her father's suits. People didn't have a lot clothes when these houses were built, she thought.

She turned to look out the window. The sunshine made its last appearance of the year, painting the sky blue and banishing clouds into next year. Roger and Gaëlle should have a good flight. Although she regretted that they weren't spending New Year's Eve together, the upcoming school board meeting had preference over an airborne New Year's Eve spent sleeping.

Gaëlle said something and her father laughed. Unlike many adults, Annie was guilty of liking teenagers. She loved watching

Gaëlle and her friends take their first tentative steps into adulthood and responsibility. Just last night Gaëlle had talked about her latest career plans: medicine. This had been in and out of her mind since Annie had first met her four years before. In between the girl had talked about being an actress, a rock star (a goal ruined by her tin ear), a teacher, a flight attendant and a journalist. But she always came back to medicine. Annie had pointed that out.

Annie's decision to stay single and childless long ago was a result of her witnessing the early marriages, and sometimes remarriages, of her friends disintegrate. Her parents had talked about biological time clocks without asking Annie to pass on their DNA. Her clock must be running late because she had no desire to clasp other peoples' babies to her breast claiming them as her own. A couple of times she and Roger had been careless, and when her period had come she was surprised to find herself neither disappointed nor happy. Well, she still had five or six years if a surge of maternal urgings suddenly flowed through her veins.

Her Hotmail came up. Among the ads for Viagra, credit cards and titillation there was a note from Christianne, one of the agents that regularly provided her with assignments. She liked the tall German-American woman. Unlike many of the agents, Christianne was always honest and always willing to sort out any problems. She opened the e-mail first. It was a chance for a two-month assignment at a Zurich bank with the possibility of a minimum of 80 Swiss Francs an hour. Christianne had added that the bank had asked for Annie specifically.

Annie calculated: $80 \times 8 = 640$ a day. That was 3,200 CHF a week or approximately 25,600 Swiss Francs for about two months' work. The dollar was almost one-to-one at the moment. Annie had set up her place in Argelès so she could live on less than $10,000 a year. With Charlie's $9,000 she was almost there and the year had not even begun, but extra would never hurt.

Roger would be less than thrilled to have her away again so soon. Their major problem was her disappearing for months. Yes, they often had weekends together with her going to Argelès from wherever she was working. Even if he went on permanent disability it wouldn't change because he couldn't leave Gaëlle. And then there was Charlie's offer still floating. Better not to mention Zurich, adding another stress to his leaving. His tolerance for *what ifs* was surprisingly low considering that being a good detective involved a lot of *what if* thinking.

As if he knew she was thinking about him, he walked up behind her and put his arms around her. "I need a cuddle."

"I need to give you one."

Roger lifted his and Gaëlle's suitcases into the Youngs' trunk. Dave and Susan stood in the doorway. Annie held the car keys in her hand waiting for Gaëlle to climb into the backseat.

During the ride to Logan Airport Gaëlle was silent, not exactly sulking, but not her chatty self.

"Usually it's me who is leaving," Annie said. "I prefer being the leaver rather than the leavee."

"In most cases, including this one, it's your choice," Roger said.

"Don't confuse me with facts," she said.

He reached over to pat her head. She had forced her mass of curls into a French braid.

"I wish I could stay here and go to school." That was the first word Gaëlle had spoken since they left the Youngs. They had just passed the Hilltop Steak House in Saugus.

"What would you do about the *Bac?*" Annie said.

"I'd graduate here and go to university here," the girl said.

"Well, why don't you go onto the Net and look up the

universities that interest you when you get back," Annie said. She glanced over at Roger who opened his eyes wide. Later she would e-mail him, that once Gaëlle saw the price of tuition in comparison to the almost nothing it cost in France, she would change her mind. "Which ones were you thinking about?"

"Harvard was cool."

"They have a good medical school on the other side of the Charles," she said. Gaëlle did not see her grab Roger's knee. "They probably accept students with a *Bac* too."

The last part of the trip passed in seconds as they talked about Gaëlle's American education. The trip passed so fast from then on that Annie was surprised to find how soon she was parking the car as near to Terminal E as she could.

After check-in, when Gaëlle had disappeared into the duty free, Roger pulled Annie into his arms. "What were you doing with Gaëlle?"

"We had a choice. We could have told her the idea was stupid, which I think it is, or we could let her dream. Who knows, she might make it work. If it doesn't work, it will be because she couldn't pull it off, and she won't be able to blame us." She wanted to say more, but he gave her a long kiss.

"I had to do that while I still could. You aren't planning to bolt and stay here yourself, are you?"

"Your uncertainty is showing."

"Annie, lots of Argelès women want to stay put. Sadly, none of them are as interesting as you. They don't ring my chimes."

"Where did you hear that phrase?"

"A movie on television. Some hippie said it."

When Gaëlle and Roger went through passport control, Annie felt an overwhelming sense of pain and wanted to run after them. Instead, she turned and went back to the parking lot.

CHAPTER 60

Friday, December 31

Melissa sat at her desk. Although the street swarmed with people who must have left their work earlier than normal, no one came into the office. She assumed they were preparing for New Year's Eve and uninterested in buying a house before ringing the old year out.

The papers for her sale were ready to FedEx to the buyers. A small battle had been fought about who would sign them. When Jason had refused to, Len frowned and said, "Do it." Jason picked up a pen, signed and slammed out of the office.

After the bell on the door stopped tinkling, Len sat on Melissa's desk, one leg on the floor and one dangling over the edge. "Honey, is everything all right?"

"What do you mean?" She didn't look up at him, but shuffled papers.

"You and Jason seem uptight."

That's because he's been abusing me. This was the first time the words had formed in her consciousness. Yes, she had known it, but she had thought of each incident as the last time. But saying it gave it a new reality. "Nothing is wrong, Dad, really."

Len sat there for what seemed like hours, but it was probably not more than a few seconds. Melissa had shoved some papers in the wrong folder, realized it and rearranged them. Len stood up. Before going back to his own desk, he patted her back.

Tears dammed up behind her eyes. She went to the toilet and

locked the door. The sales people joked that she would get more work done if they moved her computer into the bathroom. Taking several deep breaths, she wondered what to do next.

Maybe the only way to be a happy family was to be a TV series. Being born to parents who died too young and being raised by rabid fundamentalists who thought smiling a sin wasn't her fault, but she'd sworn that she would marry well and make a wonderful home for her herself, her husband and her children. In her childish daydreams she lived in a Cape Cod house. She'd done it.

She would have a washer and dryer. She had both.

She would have a yellow kitchen. That she had painted her kitchen yellow herself.

Her house would always be neat and clean. Almost.

As she got older she added other things.

She would never refuse to make love when her husband wanted to. That had been easy until Jason started drinking so much.

She would cook great meals. Yes. Most of the time.

She wouldn't complain. Complaining to yourself didn't count.

She had read all the books about keeping your man happy. Some had dialogues written out, but Jason never said the part as the expert said he would.

So what now? Walk away? No, she would never, ever get divorced and admit failure. Besides, she wouldn't just lose Jason, she would lose her father-in-law and her job. How could she support Madison?

A series of gentle raps rang off the door. "You okay in there 'Lissa?"

"Fine, Dad."

She went back to her desk.

Jason said nothing to Melissa during their ride home. He left her to make her way up their walk. When she entered the house she heard him moving around upstairs. With her coat still on she stood at the foot of the staircase and called, "What do you want to eat tonight?"

"We'll eat at the party."

"What party?"

"Rob and Mike's."

"You didn't say anything."

"You weren't listening."

Melissa knew she would have remembered a party. They almost never went to parties and now two in two weeks. She'd heard Jason's boyhood chum Rob was home on Army leave. Mike was out of work, so they had all bunked down at Mike's parents who'd gone to Florida.

"I said we'd bring something. You'd better hurry."

Melissa really wanted to take a hot shower and crawl into bed. Her eyelids wanted nothing more than to shut, but that would mean disobeying her husband. The shower was hot and wonderful, but instead of a nightdress, she put on her one party dress.

"Everyone will be in jeans," Jason said.

Melissa changed and then went downstairs. She didn't have much in the house, but she toasted bread, cut them into squares and spread them with pizza sauce and a piece of mozzarella. Surely there was a broiler at Mike's.

The other wives were both pregnant, but neither as far along as she was, but while the boys sat in the living room drinking beer, the three women exchanged morning sickness stories in the kitchen.

Janie-Lou, the Army wife, had brought along lots of sandwiches that she had seen made on a TV cooking show. Melissa's bite-size pizzas disappeared. Ashley, Mike's wife, reminded Melissa of Tinkerbell the way she flitted around—Tinkerbell with a big stomach, that is.

The men stayed in the living room with beer and a DVD of the best of the Rose Bowl. Cheers and jeers came from the room, causing the women to jump.

"We're out of beer," Jason said.

"That's 'cause you guzzled two for every one we drank," Mike said.

"Let's try and find a liquor store open," Jason said.

"I'm not sure you guys should drive; we'll go," Ashley-Tinkerbell said.

They found a liquor store open and bought a case.

Mike and Rob half carried Jason to the car and put him in the passenger seat.

"Sure you don't want me to drive you?" Rob asked.

Melissa was sure. Mike and Rob were in no better condition to drive. She squeezed behind the wheel hoping she wasn't hurting Madison as it pressed into her stomach. When she moved the seat back far enough to accommodate her stomach, it left her barely able to reach either the gas pedal or brake.

"I can drive," Jason slurred.

"Sure you can, buddy," Mike said, but Jason had passed out. "Want us to come with you to help him into the house?"

"I'll be fine." Melissa just wanted to get out of there. At least Jason was too drunk to hit her.

When she pulled into the driveway, she wondered how she would get Jason out of the car as she stood by the passenger side with the door open. Her husband's head lolled backward and his snores could have brought neighbors to the windows. A cold breeze stirred the trees and nibbled her cheeks. Tentatively she touched his shoulder. "Jason, Jason."

He flicked her hand away as he would a fly.

"Jason, you need to go in the house. You'll freeze to death out here."

He moaned and shifted.

Melissa walked toward the house, stopped and returned to the car. What was she going to do? Even if she covered him with a blanket he would be too cold. If he woke up and was still drunk, he would be furious and take it out on her. God, she was sick of all this. For a moment she pictured herself throwing a bucket of ice water on him and smiled. She unlocked her front door and switched on the hall light before going back to the car.

"Jason." Her mouth was inches from his ear and she hollered as loud as she could.

He opened his eyes.

"You need to go to bed."

He swiveled his legs and sat on the edge of the seat.

"Lean on me."

"I don't lean on any woman, you bitch." At least that was what she thought he said, but his speech was so slurred, she wasn't sure.

Together they stumbled to the house. Where she got the strength, she wasn't sure, but they made it to the hallway, where he slumped on the floor at the bottom of the stairs.

Melissa went to the bedroom, got a pillow and a blanket and went downstairs to make him as comfortable as she possibly could. Although she tried to get his coat off, she found it impossible. By contrast his sneakers slipped off. After covering him, she went upstairs to bed and cried herself to sleep.

CHAPTER 61

Trunks for the Little Missy and one for the Mistress be open in the hallway. I irons all their clothes. It don't make sense to me to iron something then fold it away, but niggahs don't argue with mistresses even one as nice as mine.

I holds Amanda, Missy's doll. The Mistress made the doll and painted a sweet face with blue eyes. The doll has yellow yarn hair in two braids. The little Missy now wears her yellow hair like the doll's or maybe the doll's be like the little Missy. That doll gots more dresses than the little Missy and she gots a lot. They be all sewed by the Mistress who says, "Don't pack the doll."

This one time I dassn't listen. Little Missy would throw a tantrum without her doll.

I cain't believe that in two days I'll no longer be here. We will be somewhere heading to a place called New York for a long visit. Me and Zeb. The Mistress won the battle. She says to the Massa that Zeb will give us good protection on the trip. She says that he will learn even better wood skills. She says a lot of stuff, but between me and me, I don't thinks we is ever coming back.

I done seen letters she has written to Mister Aaron. He looks for an apartment for her and the little Missy. She doesn't say anything about Zeb and I? Is she going to sell us?

I am so scairt of the trip. I am so scairt of the future.

The first few days of our trip we drives by plantations like Two Pines. Some grows cotton, some tobacco and others rice. The niggahs look up from their work as we pass. I wonder if they wonder what

*two niggahs are doing with a white woman and child. They keep
their faces blank, but every now and then a child waves to us. We all
waves back. The Little Missy laughs.*

*The first night we stops at Ocean Breeze, a plantation where the
Massa knows someone. Zeb and me sleeps in the slave quarters.*

*"Do you know we could kill her and take the wagon. We would be
free," Zeb whispers in my ears. I puts my head on his chest. It's hard
as the wood he uses for things he builds.*

*"They kills niggahs that kills whites. I don't want to kill the
Mistress. She been good to me."*

"You a fool, woman."

I don't answer Zeb no more.

*The next morning the lady of the house hands us a towel with
chicken, bacon, cold beans, hard-boiled eggs, cherry jelly, cleaned carrots, and rolls wrapped inside. The food be enough to feed us for at
least two days.*

*It be cold in the early morning air, and the little Missy complains.
"It will be a lot colder in New York. You'll be able to see snow and
build a snowman," the Mistress says.*

"What's snow?" the little Missy asks.

*"It's white frozen rain that piles up sometimes up to your knees.
And you can hold your tongue out and catch a flake on your tongue,"
the Mistress tells her.*

*Me? I finds it hard to believe in white frozen rain that piles up
high, but I never thought I would leave Two Pines, so what does I
know?*

*The trees makes us a roof. We passes through so many pools of black
water I thought I be in Hell. Even the few sunbeams that makes their
way through the branches they gives up and dies. The Mistress hates
it too. She says things like "How could humans make anything of
this." Humans don't make nothing of this. We ain't seen a human for
almost two days. I think of all the snakes hiding in the water and this*

human has no interest in touching anything but the floor of our wagon. This ain't land to plant. This be land to get through. I worry it be like this all the way to New York. The Mistress says the trip will take a long time. A long time to be scairt. A long time of not knowing. Each day brings new fears as I sees new things that I don't want to see. I imagines me back in my own bed. Even Massa Richard knocking at the door would be better than this unknown racing ahead of me. I curses the day that I gives up the garden.

As I looks at the water on each side of the wagon and all the trees cursing us with their boughs, I prays as I never prays before. The wagon rattles along the path, and I wonders if we will ever escape this Hell. The Mistress says it's a terrible place, but it won't last forever.

The farther we go the less people we knows until we don't knows no one so we have to keep going. Zeb asks the Mistress where we will stay. There's no real safe place on the path, and if we goes off it we will be in the water. Snakes can get us. He looks at me. I prays he ain't still thinking of killing her.

We could hides the body under the water. No one would know. But we ain't got any pass papers. Any white who sees us knows in seconds we just runaways. They just don't know where we be running from.

I don't want the Mistress dead. I wouldn't wants the Mistress dead even if I knew the way to New York and has the paper that said I was a free black.

Zeb drives the wagon. The horses don't likes the path anymore then we does. They are skittish, but Zeb, he can control them. The little Missy and the Mistress hold on as we bounce around. My teeth hurts. My rear end hurts where it bangs up and down on the hard board.

Zeb's knuckles be white from gripping the reins.

"Everything all right, Zeb?" the Mistress asks.

"Yes, Ma'am." I don't believe his polite speech for one second.

The sun be almost down, and I be scairt we might have to all sleep in the wagon again no matter what the Mistress says. Any animal could get us if we did, so I thanks God when we come to a village called Sheldonville. It ain't much of a town: a general store, a warehouse to store crops and a wood hotel. It still amazes me now I can read the word hotel. I like the sound HO-TELL, but I cain't let on. That would put the Mistress in danger and me too. Zeb stops the wagon in front of the hotel.

"I told you Zeb. I stayed here when I moved down South," the Mistress says as she climbs out of the wagon, "At least it is a hotel such as it is." As we enters, she holds the little Missy's hand. Her other hand holds her skirts so they don't touch the floor or anything. We be dirty from driving, but it looks like all the dirt from the path came to the hotel to greet us.

The hotel owner wears long underwear instead of a shirt. "You can stay, but your slaves has to sleep in the barn. We will lock them in so they don't run away."

The Mistress gives me her I'm sorry look. Ain't nothing she can do. At least she insists that we get something to eat, but it ain't much. Some rice and maggots. We threw the maggots away, but our bellies be full. The straw in the barn pokes my skin as I falls asleep.

I wakes to the turn of a key. The Mistress walks in holding her skirts high to avoid the horse shit. "You ready?"

There be no more swamp land. Now we rides past farms. The sun melts the cold, and I sees sweat on the slaves picking tobacco.

We rides along a river and passes by an orchard of apple trees. The trees be almost red from all the fruit. Barely can see the leaves for the fruit. An apple would taste wonderful, but slaves don't ask for food. We waits.

My Mistress sells the wagon and the horses. Zeb and I be lucky. She don't sells us. Then life becomes real scary. We goes to what she calls the station. The trunks be already there and we sits and waits and waits and waits. The little Missy gets fussy. I tries to interest her in *her doll, but she tells me she can't change the doll's clothes outside where anyone can see. The Mistress smiles and says I was right to bring the doll.*

Then this huge black snake comes whistling and roaring in. Two people gets out of it. I ain't seen nothing like that before. The Mistress expects us to get into that thing.

"You so scairt you almost turned white," Zeb tells me.

I expect he be as scairt as me, but by making fun at me it makes him look more brave.

"There's nothing to worry about. I've ridden in trains almost all my life." The Mistress has never lied to me, but there's been so many nevers in the last week. She puts her hand on my arm and looks into my eyes through to my soul. "Trust me, Mathilde."

Mathilde. She called me Mathilde as if I be a person not a slave. Lots of white folks use niggahs' names, but not with that look and not with that voice.

Insides there be benches. At first I be afraid to look out the window. Farms and woods run by, but then I cain't look away. A black man comes into view. He stands by his hoe. He waves and disappears.

The door to our metal shell opens. A man talks to each person. He takes a piece of paper from them and cuts holes in them. "Your slaves can't sit with you," he says to the Mistress.

"I need their help. My little girl is really bored, and my slave is about the only one that can keep her amused."

He looks at me, and he looks at the little Missy. "And the man?"

The Mistress doesn't say anything.

Zeb gets up and asks, "Where do I go?"

As he walks away, I worries that I won't see him again.

The Mistress looks at me. "I can only do so much, Mathilde, but I will always do as much as I can."

I ain't sure what she means.

CHAPTER 62

Monday, January 3

Magda soaked in bubbles up to her neck. The water's heat seeped into her bones. It was her first bath since she fell sick, although she had passed under the shower. The sick stink soaked away. Three fat red candles threw a soft hue around the bathroom. Enya's voice drifted from the CD player. Magda sank back and closed her eyes.

"You okay in there?" Susan asked through the closed door.

"I'm in paradise, Darlink." After drying off, she put on a clean sweatshirt and tights and fully understood the phrase feeling like a new woman, although her bath had left her as tired as a full day's work followed by a long drive would have.

Susan stood at her bedroom door, dirty sheets in her arms. Magda sank into a freshly made bed. The dirty linen and Susan had disappeared. Magda heard the chug of her washing machine coming from downstairs. Susan had lit a scented candle and spice scent floated in the air.

Magda shut her eyes and fell asleep until Susan returned with a bowl of chicken rice soup. As Magda ate, she said, "I can't thank you enough."

"It's what friends do," Susan said.

After Susan left, Magda couldn't fall back asleep. She had only slept for days and days. Tomorrow she would get out of bed. For the first time in a week she clicked on the television. She was never a news junky, but she always checked daily to know the big stories: earthquakes, terrorist attacks, plane crashes, fires, etc.

CNN's headlines blathered the usual bad news followed by Larry King. "Tonight, three abused women will talk about the problem. Then we will have a panel discussion with a family lawyer, a shelter director, a policeman and a judge."

Magda reached for the telephone and her list of women whom she was working with and who had not yet decided being pounded was worse than being on their own. One by one she called them.

CHAPTER 63

Monday, January 3

Thank God Jason was out, because Melissa would have hated to explain why Magda phoned. He called her That Foreign Dyke. That she'd bought the studio building from a competitor after looking at several properties with him only increased his hostility. He'd tried to convince the artist that a certain property was the best, but Magda found a storefront with a larger window, something she'd claimed was important from the first. Melissa had tried to tell him the window was as important as the studio space, but Jason had ignored both women.

Melissa clicked the remote. Three women sat in front of the familiar blue and red dotted backdrop facing Larry. One was a lawyer, one had been married to a doctor and had been a nurse until their first child was born. The third was a secretary. Each told their story. Melissa felt as if they all shared the same hopes for their marriages; they all felt alone but guilty that they weren't better wives. Together they'd written a book. At the end Larry asked each one to talk to any woman being abused.

"Get out. It won't get better," the lawyer said.

"It is never normal to be hit," the former nurse said.

"Don't believe promises," the secretary said.

Madison must have picked up on Melissa's nerves, because she squirmed, aiming her feet against Melissa's bladder. By the time Melissa came back from the toilet, the experts were talking again.

"You're a lawyer," Larry said to the woman lawyer. "Were you surprised to see someone in your profession as a victim?"

The lawyer leaned forward. "Domestic violence has no class or professional distinctions. The roots are psychological both for the abuser and the victim."

"I once heard said there are no victims, just volunteers," Larry said.

Larry introduced a psychologist in another studio. The background was a skyscraper, but Melissa didn't know where the skyscraper was. The man, with a full head of gray hair and a beard, looked like a university lecturer. "For those who've never been in the position it is easy to say, 'I would never let anyone beat me up,' but real life isn't that simple."

A shelter worker joined the group next. "In some cases it's economic. A woman isn't sure if she can support herself and her children. It's true that she almost never can at the same level as before."

"Abused women are robbed of their self-confidence, because physical abuse often goes with psychological abuse," the psychologist said. "Or family influences. Some women, when they try to move home, are told it's their fault, and they should go back and work harder at their marriage."

"Yeah, that got to me, too," the lawyer said. "For a long time I thought it was me."

"We'll take your calls," Larry said.

Melissa had always wondered how the mechanics of the calls worked. The voices seemed to come from nowhere.

"Hi Larry, love your show. Can the law protect a woman totally?"

"That depends," the lawyer said. "Some husbands accept that their wife has left, but others become stalkers."

Melissa went to the telephone to call. She wanted to ask if any abusers were cured. As she dialed she listened to Larry field the same question to the woman who ran the shelter, who said, "Some women need to hide, but that is rarer."

As the key turned in the front door, she changed the station to a movie and pretended she'd fallen asleep.

CHAPTER 64

Tuesday, January 4

Magda sat at her kitchen counter separating the kitchen from the living room. The shades were drawn against night drafts seeping through the glass as the wind blew off the water.

Her skin bore the pallor of someone recovering from a bad bout of flu. Her hair was still damp from her shower.

Susan and Annie Young bustled about. The kitchen was so clean when Susan finished tackling it that a germ walking by outside might drop dead in fear. Tomato soup bubbled on the stove. Magda had threatened the next person who gave her chicken soup would wear it.

Annie grilled cheese sandwiches. "I am not sure they won't be too heavy for your tummy."

Visions of a steak, rare, with a good béarnaise sauce danced in Magda's head, giving new meaning to the phrase, I could eat a cow. However, she knew her nurses wouldn't hear of it, but she kept pushing to return to normal. "Coffee, I need strong coffee," Magda said.

"You won't sleep tonight," Susan said.

"I have slept for a week, Darlink. Enough is enough. I need to live again."

"She's better," Annie said. "She's giving us lip."

"Sounds dirty," Magda said. "Now what do you hear from the handsome man of yours?"

"They got back, no trouble," Annie said.

"You should not spend too much time away from him. Someone will sweep him into their dustpan."

"Then he would be dirt," Annie said.

"Have you told him yet about Zurich?" Susan asked.

"Cheese sandwiches are almost done." Annie used a spatula to turn them.

"That means no," Susan said.

Annie hadn't signed any contracts. The agent was asking UBS if Annie could do some work from Argelès and some in Zurich. They were thinking it over.

"I'll be with you tomorrow night in front of the School Committee," Magda said.

"Good, you can go as an almost-dead Pilgrim," Susan said.

"Can you say relapse?" Annie put the sandwiches on the plate.

"Relapse. Tomorrow night at the meeting, Darlink, I will say it in that funny way they talked. Thou will not haveth a relapse. Noreth will I."

The three women jumped when a rapid knocking at Magda's door startled them.

Annie peeked behind the shade. "My God." She turned the lock but it stuck. As she forced it she kept saying, "My God, my God."

"What is it?" Magda asked as Annie opened the door.

Melissa almost fell in dressed in her bathrobe but no coat. Her slippers were snow-covered. Her eye was swollen. She grasped her stomach. "Help me." Then she threw up.

Susan and Annie gathered her in. Magda grabbed a chair and led the girl to it.

Annie noticed blood on the back of Melissa's bathrobe. "You're bleeding. Mom, call an ambulance." She took a dish towel and ran it under the water, but before she could touch Melissa's face Magda grabbed it.

"First we take photos." The woman disappeared and came back with a digital camera.

When Melissa put her hands in front of her face, Magda said, "We must take photos."

"I look terrible."

"Exactly, Darlink. We need proof."

Melissa nodded.

Magda took the first shot. Then she brushed Melissa's hair from her forehead where it risked being dried into the blood.

The gentleness of Magda's huge hand made Annie want to cry. Instead, she swallowed several times. Wimping out would only make things worse for the poor child. However, Melissa wasn't a child. She was a wife and an almost mother, but the helplessness and pain made Annie want to protect her.

"Susan, call the police. Tell them to meet us at the hospital," Magda said, clicking the camera.

"No police," Melissa said. "That will make it worse."

"Worse? How? That Jason kills you?" Magda kept circling Melissa and snapping photos.

"I didn't say who did this."

Magda put the camera on the table and pushed her face close to Melissa's. "You don't have to."

Melissa sobbed. "Th-this was the worse. He k-kicked me in the stomach. He could have kill . . . killed Madison. I want to curl up in my own b-bed and die."

Jesus H. Christ, Annie thought. How can anyone let themselves get into a situation like this? Then she remembered all the articles against blaming the victim. Just because she would cut off the balls of any man that raised a hand to her didn't mean that all women had the same strength. She needed to say something, but what? Then it came to her. "You can't die without hurting Madison. You have to think of Madison," Annie said.

Magda flashed a nod of approval.

"You're bleeding and that's why you have to go to the hospital."

"I d-don't have any labor p-pains," Melissa said.

Susan appeared in the kitchen carrying a blanket. No one had seen her leave, but she covered Melissa. "Honey, how did you get here?"

"I w-walked."

The three women exchanged looks. A good three miles separated their two houses and it was 10 degrees. The siren whining in the distance grew louder and stopped in front of the house. Within seconds there was a knock at the front door.

Two men, one in his forties and one in his mid-twenties, entered the kitchen. They were the same cops that had answered Magda's call the night of Susan's tree-decorating party. The younger carried a stretcher, the older a blanket. "You have another one, Magda?" the older one asked. His eyes rested on the girl and he formed the name Melissa Haskell without making any sound.

"This isn't the first time," Magda said.

The younger cop reached toward Melissa to tilt her head into a better light.

Annie watched Melissa duck. At first she thought the girl was afraid, but then realized that she knew them and the situation was so out of control that she didn't know what to do next.

Annie knelt down and took Melissa's hands and stared into her eyes. "There's nothing to be ashamed of," she said. "You need help. These men will help."

"Melissa has been beaten and kicked in the stomach. She's bleeding, and I'm afraid for the baby. How fast can you get her to the hospital?" Magda asked.

"It was an accident," Melissa said.

"Stop it," Magda said. "You can't afford any more lies."

"You can't afford it for Madison," Susan said.

"Who's your doctor?" the older cop asked.

"M-Mark Guerra," she said.

"That's North Shore. How often are you having contractions?" he asked. The younger one shifted his feet and looked everywhere but at the women.

"I-I'm not."

"She's just bleeding, but I wouldn't waste any time," Annie said.

"Get your coat," the older cop said. He sounded like a father telling his kid to get dressed.

"It's at h-home."

"I'll get one of mine," Magda said. She frowned at the cops. "And if either of you tell Jason Haskell where you took her, I'll kill you personally."

"Don't worry about me," the older one said. "Nor Brian."

Brian looked confused. "But . . ."

"I'm serious, Brian. This girl could be in serious danger. Trust me on this. And if you don't, you won't ever get beyond rookie," Magda said.

When Annie looked at Melissa's face she thought of the last dog she had whenever he realized they were going to the vet. Terror and betrayal. A mixture. "I'll go with you."

Melissa clasped Annie's hand so hard that it hurt.

CHAPTER 65

Tuesday, January 4

Annie walked into the hospital waiting room where Susan and Magda sat staring at the door. The women jumped up. "How is she?" they asked as one.

"Sleeping. She isn't in labor. The baby has a strong heartbeat."

"Thank God," both women said at once.

"Annie, you probably got further with her than Magda could," Susan said.

"I am not a person to help, Darlink? There is something wrong with me?"

Susan blushed. Her blond hair was more disarrayed then usual as she ran her hand through it. "It's, it's just that I thought that she is so young and . . ."

Magda's eyes opened wider. "And you are saying I am over the mountain?"

"What Mom means is that Melissa is so young for her age, and you've nothing in common."

"We've lots in common. We're women in a difficult world." Magda lowered her voice. "I help women. That's all."

The police chief walked in, wearing jeans, an Irish knit sweater and a brown leather jacket that would have fit in at any pub in Dublin. "Let's go someplace to talk," Tim said after exchanging greetings.

They found a small room, probably where doctors gave family members bad news.

"My men told me you were here with Melissa. Because of Len, I thought I'd handle some of this. Has anyone called him or his son?"

Magda gave the police chief a look that would have caused him to go poof and disappear if this were a cartoon. "The son kicked his pregnant wife in the stomach. He doesn't need to be called. He needs to be jailed."

"You seem well informed. If this is a one-off case . . ." Tim was interrupted by Magda's snort. "Okay, so we have an ongoing . . ."

Another snort.

"Magda, I've taken all the domestic abuse courses there are to take. I know the problem. I want to work with Melissa, but hell, Len is Selectman Len Haskell."

"And you want to be more than the temporary chief."

Tim blushed. "Not if it will cost Melissa her or her baby's life. How bad is it?"

Annie told him of the bruises she had seen on Melissa at Thanksgiving.

"I hate these cases. She should go for a 209A," Tim let out a long sigh.

Magda snorted. "Filling out forms don't stop the abuse."

"It's a necessary first step."

"She needs more protection than the law will give her. I feel it," Magda said. She looked at Annie. "I've a sixth sense on these cases."

Tim put his head back and looked at the ceiling as if there were an answer on the acoustical tiles. "A judge doesn't respond to sixth senses."

"And more women would be alive if they did," Magda said.

"I'm not sure if Melissa is ready to go the legal route," Annie said.

"Then God help her," Magda said.

CHAPTER 66

New York. I ain't written since we arrived a month ago. Nothing prepared me for this place. Each building has more people than I ever seen in my whole life. The streets be chock-a-packed with more people and horses and carriages. I never knowd there were so many people in this whole world.

We stays in an apartment with the Mistress's mother and father. They talks as funny as she does. I understands them better than many New Yorkers who comes to see the Mistress. Everything runs together like one big word.

Mr. Aaron comes almost every day. The little Missy runs to him and he picks her up and throws her in the air and she cries again, again. He be thieving the Massa's family.

The Mistress be working. Imagine a white woman working. I never could before now, but I just adds it to my growing list of nevers. She has a part in a play. I usually goes to the theater with her and stands behind the curtain and listens to the words. It is about a banker who steals money. Every time I watches it is a bit different. When this play finishes she be doing another, but I gots no idea of the subject.

The Mistress sings to herself a lot now. She bustles around meeting old friends. It be like another soul steals my Mistress's body. This be a happy soul. When Zeb and I lie in bed, and we gots the biggest bed any black person ever slept in, we talks about her.

She works with abolitionists, people who wants to stop slavery. They comes to the apartment every Sunday morning. The Mistress asks Zeb and I to talk about what our lives be like at Two Pines.

At first Zeb doesn't wants to do that, but the Mistress argues with him. She says she wasn't going to make him, but God helps those who help themselves and the Mistress don't talk about God much.

There be five ladies and six men there when Zeb talks. He tells about being a chief's second son, but his older brother died and about his wife and two children with one on the way and how one day he be on a walk and gets hit from behind. He wakes up in a cage. The next day he be on a boat.

I cries as he tells about being chained to a man that died. Boiled in his own blood, Zeb calls it. He be chained to that man for three nights before they unlocks the body and throws it overboard. The rotting flesh stink overpowers the sweat stink, Zeb says.

Zeb looks at one of the women. "Imagine having to stand with other women as buyers looks at your teeth, feels your bellies, tests your muscles. They strips you naked to make sure what they buys. Like you buys a hat or worse a piece of meat." He stares at Miss Pamela. She tears up.

Another woman, I never can remember her name exact, something like Anna, Anita, she don't come all the time to these meetings, but she be there that night and she pats Miss Pamela.

Zeb tells them about escaping. He takes off his shirt and turns so they sees the scars on his back. The reaction be just what he wanted. A group in-breath.

Zeb has one beautiful body. I don't like those woman looking.

While I takes care of the little Missy and the Mistress, Zeb works with a Massa carpenter. He comes back talking about woods and tools and what you dos with them. Our bed be a white person's bed with sheets that I slide on and then blankets to keep us warm, although Lord knows sleeping with Zeb be like sleeping with fire. Sometimes I gots to push the covers back to breathe. But I ain't complaining. That man can pleasure a woman like an angel if angels do IT.

I be writing about his wood talk. One day he talks about something called teak from far away. The Mistress hears us talking and says he must learn all he can. Although she sleeps late mornings because she be at the theatre late nights, she takes Sundays to make sure he knows mathematics. She insists both of us work on our reading, numbers and writing for after . . .

When we asks after what, she says nothing.

Zeb and I talks about it in bed that night. "She'll sell us. She has no right. No one should sell another person." Zeb hits his fist against the bed with each statement.

"I don't thinks so, Zeb."

He don't believe me. "Don't call me Zeb. That be my white folks name."

"Then what shoulds I call you?" When he be in one of these moods, he gots to be handled carefuller than a rattlesnake. "Your African name? I don't even know it."

"And I ain't telling you."

"Never?"

"When we be free. We'll be free. We can run away. Get lost in this city."

That scairt me. Zeb felt me shake.

I wondered if we did runs away, would the Mistress look for us. If the Massa comes up North, he sure won't let a day pass without hunting us down.

The next day—it were a Monday—the Mistress told me on Sunday we would have a guest for dinner, a Rev. Hiram Mason from Syracuse. "He is a Methodist minister."

"Where is Syracuse?"

Once again she brings out a map book. She flips the pages. She shows me the difference between New York and Two Pines and New York and Syracuse. "Make sure Zeb brings his tools with him, Friday." I be getting good at reading maps.

"She gonna sell us to that minister," Zeb said. *"We gotta run away first."*

CHAPTER 67

Wednesday, January 5

Annie was curled up on the sofa watching *Good Morning America* and drinking a giant cup of tea before taking her shower when the phone rang. Her energy level after last night at the hospital was nil. Her to-do list was to talk to Zurich about the contract, put the final touches on her presentation for the school board meeting, go see Melissa and make a plane reservation. She reached behind her to answer.

"Annie?" the voice was raspy and breathless.

"Yes." Her answer was tentative as she tried to decide who it was.

"Magda here." The words were followed by a fit of coughing.

"My God! What's wrong?"

"I'm really sick."

Annie resisted saying, "I warned you." Instead, she said, "I'll call Mom and we'll be over."

Susan Young opened the door to the small wooden shed behind Magda's house. Hoes, pots, rakes and fertilizer filled the small space. Under the third pot to the right was the door key.

Inside the house the women heard only quiet. "Magda?" They called several times but there was no answer. After exchanging looks, they went upstairs.

The door to Magda's room was closed. Annie knocked.

"Come in." Magda lay on soaking wet sheets, shivering. Her

breath came in rasps.

Susan put her hand on her friend's head. "She's burning up. Thermometer?"

"Don't have one."

"I'm calling a doctor," Susan said.

"Can't pay for it." The statement was followed by a coughing fit.

"I don't understand the health system here," Susan said. "Len, maybe he can help."

Magda shot straight up. "Don't call that bastard." She fell back down.

"He's probably dealing with Melissa's disappearance this morning," Annie said.

"Ask him. He'll know what to do," Susan said. She dialed Len and explained the problem.

When she motioned for something to write on, Annie scoured for paper and pencil, which she found on Magda's bureau. It was a sketch pad and charcoal. Magda's eyes were closed.

"He knows a doctor in Ipswich we can talk to." Susan punched in the number.

The doctor answered himself and promised to come by.

"Doctors don't make house calls. Must be a quack," Magda said.

"Doctors make house calls in France, but it costs $45 instead of $28 for the office," Annie said.

Magda rolled over in bed, ignoring both of them. Annie shrugged at Susan who shrugged back. When the doctor arrived they understood that he must have escaped through a time machine. A few strands of white hair were combed over his otherwise bald head. His face had more lines than a road map. His cane tapped, tapped across the wood floor. Eighty if he's a day, Annie thought.

When he spoke, his voice was stronger and surer than his

movements. He almost yelled, making Annie wonder if he were deaf. "Don't practice much these days, but I keep my license. I can see in your faces that you wonder if this old geezer still has it. Well I do."

Annie and Susan blushed.

"No need to blush, ladies. My patients have no insurance. My way of fighting the system. Wish I could find a young man to come in with me, though. Can't die yet. Let too many people down."

Annie helped him up the stairs. He sat down on the bed and twisted his body around to open his little black bag. Each time he asked Magda to repeat the answers to his questions with an "Ai, what was that again?" Then he took out a stethoscope. Annie hoped he wasn't too deaf to hear. However, he shut his eyes. The only sound in the room was Magda's heavy breathing and a clock that ticked.

The doctor sat up straight and put his brown-spotted, veined hand on top of Magda's. "Pneumonia. Not sure if it's viral or not. Viral, can't do a damn thing. Open your mouth." He attacked her throat with a cotton swab that he dropped into what looked like a test tube to Annie. "Don't like to prescribe antibiotics unless necessary so want to wait for the results. However, we do need to get some oxygen in here to help her breath. She shouldn't be left alone."

When he left, Magda whispered, "Quack."

"Not really," Susan said. "Annie, you stay with her. I'll get the oxygen from the pharmacy."

"Melissa," Magda whispered.

"When Mom is back, I'll go see her," Annie said. She wondered if she would be ready for tonight's meeting.

"Here's what you have to tell her." Magda insisted that Annie write it all down.

The phone rang, and Annie picked it up.

"Magda, we've another girl to transport," the voice said.

"This isn't Magda," Annie said. "Hold on."

"You'll have to find someone else," Magda hacked into the phone. When she hung up she turned to Annie. "I suppose you want to know what that is about."

"Only if you want to tell me."

"You have to swear to keep it a secret, Darlink."

Annie swore.

CHAPTER 68

Wednesday, January 5

"I'm the only unbirthed," Melissa told Annie as she looked around the maternity ward, which she shared with three new moms.

Probably not the best place for her, Annie thought. One woman chatted about her newborn with her husband. Two were packing to go home. Annie pulled the curtain around the bed and pulled up a chair. She whispered to reduce the chances that someone might overhear.

"Magda wanted to come, but she's got pneumonia."

"We shouldn't have let her come with us last night."

"You don't stop someone that stubborn," Annie said. "How are you today?"

"I'm still spotting."

"Have you heard from Jason?"

Melissa turned her head.

"You know you can't go back there. Magda says you must get a restraining order. She'll get another woman from her group to come over and walk you through the process."

CHAPTER 69

Wednesday, January 5

"Len sounded normal when I talked to him. Not like a man with a missing daughter-in-law," Susan said. The sun had just set and Dave had joined his wife and daughter at Magda's. They were in her kitchen while she slept upstairs.

Dave was picking up his women for the School Committee meeting. Their Pilgrim costumes were draped over his arm. The first thing he said was, "I saw Len today. He invited me in for coffee as I walked by. I asked about Melissa and Jason, who was there, said she stayed home because she was tired."

"Bastard," Annie said.

"He sounded so sincere and so unworried I felt I was in a bad mystery movie," Dave said. "What's going to happen next? Melissa can't go back there. Can she get a restraining order?"

Annie wondered if she should tell them about Magda's Underground Railroad. If she did it wouldn't be a secret anymore, but she hated lying to her parents. As a compromise she decided to tell them as little as possible. "Magda wants to take Melissa and the baby out of state as soon as she can travel. She doesn't think a restraining order will work. She mumbles about her instincts on these things."

Susan said. "Annie, what about tonight? Can you get along without me? I don't like leaving Magda alone any more than necessary."

"We'll have to."

"I'll call Heather and see if she knows of someone to wear my costume."

CHAPTER 70

Wednesday, January 5

Except for Paul Mangone, the five school board members were women. The superintendent was new since September. They sat at a long table at the front of the room. Cameras from Channels 4, 5 and 7 were set up in the back.

Ten rows of ten seats each divided in five with an aisle down the middle filled rapidly.

When the committee took off their winter coats, their clothing was casual, slacks or skirts and sweaters for the women and sweaters and slacks for the men. The one exception was a woman in a blue power suit.

Annie's group kept their overcoats on over their costumes until Dave signaled them. Everyone took off his or her outer garments at the same time. Father and daughter were in their best Pilgrim outfits, along with Heather, Heather's children, Des and many of Charlie's employees. All together there were thirty-five founding fathers, founding mothers or founding children. Only the historian Dr. G. Andrew Yates was dressed in a regular business suit, but the three real Wampanoag Indians he had brought with him wore skins. Unlike the stereotype, no one wore feathered headdresses.

Not all those costumed were inside. Another thirty people outside carried signs reading "Truth in History" and "Teach Critical Thinking." Although they all had deplored the lack of sexiness in the signs, none of them could come up with something catchier. Annie wondered where Charlie was.

Diane Ash, the woman who had collected the names on the petition, stood in front of the committee. The mutter of the crowd drowned out what she was saying. Paul Mangone banged his gavel. Ash took a seat in the front row and periodically shot angry glares at the costumed audience.

Kendra Jones, the teacher in danger of being censured, whispered to Annie, "I really appreciate you coming to my rescue."

"It's my fault. I got you into this."

"Nevertheless . . ."

Paul called the meeting to order. The first part involved routine items: approval of minutes, a discussion over buying new chairs for the first grade, the cost of a new boiler.

The cameramen looked at their watches. One of the reporters tilted his head to the door. When Paul saw, he said, "Alright the next issue is a petition to censure one of our teachers from departing from the regular curriculum and teaching subversive information. I move we go into closed door session."

Kendra stood up. Annie could see that her hands were shaking as she shoved them into her pockets, but her voice was strong. "I would prefer we discuss this in an open meeting. My lawyer says I have that right." She pointed to the woman in the power suit and briefcase.

The School Committee exchanged looks. "Since the matter is to protect your privacy, Kendra, and you waive your rights, I don't have a problem with an open session. And my fellow committee members?" Paul asked.

Deidre White, a woman in her forties, asked for the floor. "I think, Kendra, it would be better for you to do this privately. I'm none too happy about the journalists in the back of the room."

The lawyer stood. "Are you saying you are none too happy

about following the law?"

"I'm saying that private matters should stay private," White said.

"The education of our children is public," the lawyer said.

"I wasn't asking for a vote on whether we want to break the law, merely being polite," Paul said. "The chair recognizes Diane Ash."

When Ash stood Annie remembered her mother saying when she made a face that if she weren't careful her face would freeze in that position. The woman had scowling developed to an art form. Despite that, she was quite attractive, in a tweedy, expensive way.

"You people," she said with a sweep of her hand toward the Pilgrims and Indians, "are making a mockery of our education system. We must educate our children to be good, patriotic, God-fearing Americans." Her voice was well modulated.

"Gives PC new meaning," Des leaned forward to whisper into Annie's ear.

She looked at him.

"PC—Patriotically Correct." This time his voice carried across the room.

Paul Mangone banged his gavel much as a judge would, but he couldn't quite control the smile playing around his lips. He grabbed the water glass near his right hand and swallowed.

"Our children need to know the values that this country was founded on, not some propaganda, and I have a list of over thirty names that agree with me besides those you already have." Ash placed the list before the School Committee Chairman who handed it to the superintendent.

"The petition censures Kendra for using non-approved materials and recommends that she be suspended for a week without pay as an example to the other teachers," Paul said.

"Three of the names are the same that don't want us teaching Darwinism without teaching Creationism," the superintendent said.

"I told you before that would be fine if we teach comparative religions," Paul said. "It might do our children good if they learned about Buddhism, Islam, Hinduism, etc."

"There's only one true religion," Ash said. "And young minds shouldn't hear about the others. It only confuses them. And the same goes with history."

The door opened and Charlie Tucker came in. A blunderbuss was slung over his shoulder. In his hand he carried a bible. He was followed by one of the secretaries from his office rolling a table where a laptop was connected to a projector.

"Good God, Tucker, that thing better not be loaded," Paul said.

"The gun, the bible or the projector?" Charlie asked.

"This is turning into a zoo," Ash said as the cameramen zoomed into her face.

"Step back." Paul's gavel hung in the air, but the cameraman moved back before it had to be banged against the table.

Charlie set up the computer and pointed the projector toward a blank wall. "All yours, Annie," he said. "If the chairman agrees."

Paul nodded as he'd previously agreed he would.

Annie started with a slide of the school's history books.

"Where did you get those?" Ash demanded. "If Kendra . . ."

Annie ignored the questions and started showing a text, flipping through page after page. Much of it was marked with a yellow or pink highlighter. There was much more pink, although yellow was well represented. "The yellow are inaccuracies. The pink is where the text does not go far enough."

"We don't want to burden our children too early," Ash said.

"Now on the inaccuracies . . ." For each statement she disagreed with she went to an original document. "School systems have watered-down curriculum. Kids are capable of more than they're being given. Now I'm going to show you what those that signed the petition found so offensive." She looked around. "I need a volunteer."

A man, who was with the Ash contingent, raised his hand.

She slipped in her CD and the *Mayflower* tossed about on the sea. Annie walked him through the instructions. He was given choices all the way through, what to eat, how to build his house, taking a chance on getting caught breaking the Sabbath rules. They switched over to the Indian part, discussing traditions.

King Phillip's War was presented from both points of view.

"See, see, now that's confusing," Ash said.

"That teaches kids to look at an issue from both sides." Annie asked the historian if there was one fact in either side that could be disputed.

"No," he said.

"Please tell us who you are," Paul said.

Yates listed his credentials without mentioning where he worked.

"But two different things can't be right," Ash spluttered when he had finished. "There's a right and a wrong. And worse, this CD makes the early fathers look like Taliban."

"It all depends on how you define terms and the point of view," Annie said. "If I come from a culture that believes it is impossible to own the earth and any of its possessions, it will clash with a culture that believes in property."

"We don't want our kids to believe that. How will they ever be able to function in our society?"

Annie saw a couple of school board members nodding in agreement.

"May I say something?" Dr. Yates asked.

Paul Mangone nodded.

"Although this country has produced some exceptional men—Jefferson, Adams, Franklin—many of the early settlers were reactionary religious fanatics. I've two documents here on fundamentalism, one by the World Council of Churches and the other by the Academy of Arts and Sciences."

"Does this mean the CD-ROM is eligible for an Oscar?" someone behind Yates whispered.

He turned and smiled. "The Academy researched fundamentalism. If you compare their research to some of the Pilgrims' early writing, all of which Ms. Young had access to, you'll find many were not very nice people. Their idea of freedom of religion, which has become such a wonderful component of our country, meant freedom for them. Anyone who disagreed was severely punished. I personally think Ms. Young has done a wonderful job." He sat.

Annie smiled. "Thank you, Dr. Yates. We aren't saying we should change the goal of turning our children into good citizens. We are simply recognizing the full story. In the case of our forefathers, they were a narrow group of fundamentalists who believed God was on their side. They became leaders in the New World. In England they would have remained outcasts."

The argument went on. The press thinned out. The Pilgrims and Indians drifted away, although the Youngs and Charlie Tucker stayed until the School Committee invited them to leave.

In the parking lot Annie asked Charlie, "What do you think?"

He shrugged. "Who knows? We know where Paul stands."

"I think it went well," Dave said. "Reminds me of all those American movies with the big climatic scene at the end like *Patch Adams, Beautiful Mind* and the Connery thing *Forrester* . . ."

"*Finding Forrester,*" Annie said as Des came up to the group and put his hand on her shoulder.

"You're impressive, lady."

"I just hope that Kendra is okay. She's a dedicated teacher."

Kendra walked up, zipping her coat and pulling on her gloves. "I'll be okay. I just got interviewed by Channel 5 and it gave me a chance to talk about curriculum and how we should make it harder."

"What did you say?"

"I talked about when I was teaching in the International Schools in Damascus and Bangkok my first two years of teaching and how much more in-depth the materials were."

"Will you get in more trouble?" Dave asked.

"Maybe, but I might do some good. Anyway I can always go back into the international system. For me it's a win–win."

CHAPTER 71

Thursday, January 6

The nurse pulled the covers over Melissa's belly. If her hair, held up with a large barrette, had not been dyed chestnut brown it would have been gray. As it was, the color was too dark for her skin, making her look tired. She walked tired and smiled tired as she wrapped the blood pressure cuff around Melissa's arm and stuck the thermometer in her mouth. "Probably you can't wait to get home?"

Home? Melissa couldn't go home. She wanted to. But the home she had created in her mind didn't exist. There was no happily ever after. Her yellow kitchen, her bedroom, her living room furnished in *House and Garden* perfection when she had the money would never be.

How she wanted to be in her own bed, her own bedroom. She had rescued a bed and a bureau from the trash and refinished them in her spare time. Her work had been disparaged by Jason as a waste of time. She rubbed her leg where his belt mark no longer showed. At the time she thought his anger had more to do with his frustration that they couldn't afford the furniture they'd seen at the mall.

She had half expected some story of her disappearance to make the news. Was he half out of his mind with worry? What had he told Len? Probably that she was too tired to go to work. What would Len say if he knew what had been going on? Probably would think that she had been a bad wife, although her father-in-law had only been kind to her. He never interfered in their marriage, she could say that for him.

The thermometer beeped. The nurse looked at it. "Normal like your BP."

Yesterday a woman Magda sent arrived to talk to her. She brought papers to sign that would get a court order to keep Jason away. She imagined him walking up to their house. *She would be inside with Madison. Whenever he got close the paper would provide a curtain, and he wouldn't find an opening. But then he did find an opening and came through. He grabbed the baby from her and ran. The baby dangled by its foot from his hand.*

Magda had telephoned after the woman had left to offer a safe place somewhere out of state for her and the baby. Would someone think she had kidnapped her own child?

Melissa rubbed her eyes to keep the tears inside. She couldn't be a cry baby because she had a baby to protect. If Jason hadn't kicked her in the stomach, she would still be at home working on being the best wife possible to help him change into a happier man.

Failure, that's what she was. She hadn't finished college, her marriage was a mess, but she couldn't quit. With Madison she wouldn't fail. She would protect her at all costs.

"The doctor will be in to discharge you." The nurse walked out the door.

Where would she go? Melissa swallowed her fear, but it didn't go very far down.

CHAPTER 72

Zeb and I stands in front of the Mistress in the dining room. The dishes be pushed aside. The chicken be just bones. Tonight is Sunday when no one goes to the theater where the Mistress be in a new play about three sisters and their father who worries about who loves him best. I wonders why a king don't have better things to think about, but this one don't. I watched it lots of nights from the edge, but I cain't understand all the words. People talks funny on stage.

Her parents, Evelyn and Peter, be in different plays. I never sees them. I don't call them Evelyn and Peter, but Madam and Sir Peter who teases me and says he ain't a Suh but a Sir. The Mistress says he should have heard me when she first began training me. She says I am a great maid, and I reads, writes and has decent table manners. I don't minds the teasing. Sir Peter means it fine. I can tells by his eyes. They be kind warm eyes like the sun, only they ain't yellow but bright blue like the sky.

At Two Pines everyone gets up early and goes to bed early. Here no one but the little Missy goes to bed before midnight and no one gets up before it is lunchtime. Nothing in New York be like back home.

Sunday be best. No one rushes. Sometimes people comes in and sits around and talks, talks, talks. But most Sundays they just does nothing.

Anyways after the Mistress tells me to go get Zeb from the kitchen where he be eating, I do. We stands at the table. Everyone grins with their faces stretching almost to tearing.

"Zeb, Mathilde, I have something to show you." She gets up from

the table and goes into the drawing room. I sees her rummaging around in her desk, and she brings back two pieces of paper. Along with the inkwell and pen she brings it all back to the table.

"Be carefully you don't get any grease on it, Dear," Madam Evelyn says.

The Mistress be smiling.

Sir Peter be smiling.

Zeb be unsmiling. Every muscle in his body be rigid. My back be to his stomach so I can feels the tension. If he be lightning he would crackle.

The Mistress takes out her pen and signs her name. The blotter be to one side, and she be ever so careful as she puts it on top of her writing. Then she hands me the paper. I reads it.

"Is we sold?" Zeb asks.

I throws my arms around his neck. "We be free. Free."

Zeb stares at me.

"Free!" I jumps into his arms. But instead of swinging me around, he just holds me so tight I cain't breathe right. When he lets me go, I sees tears. I starts to cry, then the Mistress, then her parents. We all be wet-faced until Sir Peter says we are going to celebrate with a bottle of champagne. So we stands around with champagne glasses just as I seen the white folks do.

"You'll leave in the morning. I've arranged a coach and you'll travel to Syracuse tomorrow with the Rev. Hiram whom you met the other night."

I looks at Zeb. I be free, but what happens when we leaves the Mistress? How would I know where to go? "What if Zeb and I be caught?"

"The worse that can happen is they write me, and if they do, I'll tell them I freed you."

"But when you go to Two Pines," I says, "if they asks about us at Two Pines the Massa will say we be runaways. And what will he do to you when you comes back without us?"

"I'm not going back," she says.

I didn't knows what to think. White folks have good marriages and bad marriages. You can tell by how they treats each other which be which. Niggahs usually be too tired to do anything but fall into bed at night. A good marriage be when there's someone to hold you and you feel safe for a few seconds.

Suddenly I be really scairt.

Zeb gots two wives back in Africa. Even though I didn't like to hear him talk about his wives, he talks about them all the same and about his babies. The older one be his brother's wife. When his brother died he had to marry her. That be the law of his tribe. I wasn't jealous of her. But the young one, well Zeb says his soul joined with hers when they be five years old. He will never love me as he loves her. What I be scairt of is now he be free, he will go back to find her.

The Mistress is talking. "Even if you have papers, you are going to follow the Underground Railroad to Canada. They won't touch you there."

"Where's Canada?" Zeb asks.

Madame Evelyn picks up the old map book with the black-leather cover. I felt Zeb get all tense again, because he sometimes gets upset that I can read much better than him.

"See Zeb, this is where Two Oaks is." The Mistress puts her finger on it.

I can finds that now anytime 'cause we always seems to start there.

"And this is New York. Now remember how long it took us to get here." She moves her finger to the small dot that says Syracuse. "This is your first stop. I don't know where you will go after that, but you will end up here. That's Canada. That's another country. You'll be somewhere near Toronto."

Zeb nods.

"It'll be colder than New York," Sir Peter says. "But Zeb will be able to set up his own business making furniture."

311

I didn't thinks about the furniture. I thinks about it being colder than New York. That be hard to imagine. And I also wondered how long it be before Zeb leaves me all alone in a cold place where I knowd no body.

That night Zeb and I holds each other real tight in bed. He makes love to me real good. He leaves his liquid inside me and stays inside me until he falls out. I don't ask him if he plans to leave me, just in case he hasn't thought of it, I ain't going to put that idea into the handsome, wooly head of his.

I barely sleeps. But when we gets up, the weather be like a demon, making us stay. Snow in New York hides the world a little bit like tons of cotton falling all over. Only cotton ain't cold.

The Mistress makes sure I has new warm wool clothes. They makes my skin itch, but itch and warm is much better than cold and no itch. Zeb too, only he don't itch. He has trouble getting used to the thick boots. He likes being barefooted. No one can be barefooted in snow and not lose their feets.

The Mistress told me the Reverend sent a message that the roads be blocked by the storm, but we'll leave as soon as they be clear.

I has another reason to be scairt. What if the Massa visits before we gets away.

CHAPTER 73

Thursday, January 6

Melissa sat on the edge of the hospital bed fully dressed waiting for the wheelchair to take her to the parking lot where she didn't have a car. Maybe she could walk back in and call a taxi, but to go where? The last time she had felt this alone was the morning after her parents died and she waited at the shelter for her aunt and uncle. When she saw their faces, severe and with a cold that had nothing to do with grief after a death in the family, she knew she was in trouble. She was in trouble again. And she still had to pay for her stay. She had to ask Annie what she had told the business office during admission.

"Hi there!" The voice was cheerful.

Melissa looked up to see Annie and Susan Young standing there, both smiling.

"We've come to take you home," Annie said.

"Ours! Not yours," Susan said.

"How did you know I was leaving?"

"Your doctor called us," Annie said. "We asked him to. Can't have you on your own." She engulfed the crying mother-to-be in her arms.

Susan handed Melissa tissues. Because Melissa was crying into Annie's chest, it was Annie who reached for them.

"I didn't know wh-where to go."

"You'll hide out with us." Annie stroked her hair. "Your husband is being served today with the restraining order. Magda will ferret you out of the area in the next couple of days."

"She's really sick, but Dad is staying with her until we get you settled," Annie said.

The sobs diminished. "I've got no clothes. Can we stop at my house?"

Annie looked at Susan who shook her head. "Too dangerous," Annie said. "We could go shopping, but it would be best if you aren't seen at all. That's what Magda said."

"I feel like a criminal, a criminal with dirty underpants."

"I've an idea, Mom, if you want to go along with it."

Susan cocked her head.

"Melissa, you've your house keys?" Annie asked.

"I grabbed them when I left. They're in my bathrobe pocket, I think."

Annie went to the closet where the bathrobe still hung. She dangled them over her head. "I'll get your stuff, just tell me where."

"My daughter will get caught breaking and entering by a man who beats women. I don't think so," Susan said.

"Nope, because we'll stop at the real estate office first. Say we're looking at a place I can stay when I come here. The house is too crowded for all of us, especially when Roger and Gaëlle are here during the summer. Keep Jason busy showing you places."

"Hmm," Susan said, the same *hmm* she used when she still wasn't convinced that Annie should be allowed to do something. It was also the *hmm* that said she could be persuaded.

"Then you can call on my cell when you leave Jason. I'll be out of the house before you can say, *allez, allez.*"

"You don't have a cell," Susan said.

"I'll borrow Dad's."

"How will you know when I'm with Jason?"

"I'll come with you. Melissa, you can call me from home

when we are in the real estate office. I'll pretend it's Charlie, and I have to go see him. Mom, you'll stay with Jason."

Susan nodded several times slowly. "It could work, but Melissa, make sure you tell Annie where everything is so it won't take a second longer than necessary."

Turning her tear-streaked face upward, Melissa nodded.

Annie looked at Melissa and imagined herself beating Jason until his face turned black and blue. She shuddered, not liking to think of herself as a violent person.

CHAPTER 74

Thursday, January 6

"Just because I agreed, doesn't mean I like you doing this." Susan touched her daughter's arm as the dollhouse in the real estate window came into view.

Annie blew her mother a kiss. Susan responded with her mock long-suffering mother look, perfected over the years.

The bell over the real estate office jingled. No one was at the front desk. No one came out.

Susan settled in one of the thickly upholstered chairs and Annie sat in the other. A coffee table had a red leather album with Haskell Realty embossed in gold letters. Susan picked it up and turned the pages of photos and listings with their descriptions. "This would work." Susan pointed to a cottage.

Annie put her finger on the address. Good, it's the opposite end of town from Jason and Melissa's. "Can you locate another? Perhaps the same area."

They looked at their watches in a movement that was as well choreographed as any ballet. Realizing what they'd done, they gave a nervous laugh.

"Maybe they went out?" Susan's voice sounded like she wasn't sure.

"Or out back. That bell isn't all that loud." Annie started down the corridor.

The door to Len's office was closed, but she heard him yell. "You're really fucking up."

"It wasn't my fault they decided on the other house."

"They might have had more faith if you didn't smell like a brewery. You're drinking too much."

Annie tiptoed back to the beginning of the corridor. "Hello. Anyone there?"

Len and Jason came out of Len's office. Len was dressed in his usually natty style with light gray wool trousers, cream shirt and blue striped tie. Annie could see a blue blazer over the back of his chair. Jason was in jeans and a blue turtleneck sweater that had some stain on it. She imagined her father saying you could pack a wardrobe in the bags under his eyes.

Len flashed his smarmy smile, at least that was how Annie thought of it. Maybe she had picked up Magda's dislike of the man, but usually she was on target identifying the good and bad guys. Dad said she was wrong. Len was a good guy, probably, Annie thought, because he was a boyhood chum. Len was the type of older man who needed arm candy, not a man that wanted a woman with a brain or a personality. Roger flashed into her mind and she was grateful that he appreciated her brain as well as the rest of her.

Some men were like Len. Some were like Roger or Des. Des liked smart women. As if the forces of the universe were at work, her dad's telephone rang. She answered it.

"I was calling your dad to see if he knew where you were," Des said.

"Standing in Len Haskell's realty office talking to you." Annie watched Len watch her.

"Wanta come with me to visit an Ipswich dentist? Old-timer willing to go through records."

She could hear the honks of another wild goose chase. "I'm busy right now, Des."

"Not asking about now. Later this afternoon?"

"Yes."

"Good, because I set up an appointment for us at 6:30 tonight."

"Why not? I'm about to look at houses and can't talk."

"Looking at houses?"

"Mom and Dad are thinking of buying a cottage for me to use when I come and for rental when I'm not here."

"Does that mean you're definitely going back to France?"

"Or Switzerland. I need to let the UBS know about a contract in the next couple of days. We can talk about that later. I gotta go. Pick me up at home." Thinking it was better he didn't know Melissa was there, she added, "Just beep, I'll come out."

"When I was growing up no well-bred girl could do that. Parents wanted me to present myself at the house before we went on a date."

"This isn't a date, it's a business meeting." She disconnected in time to see her mother pointing to the photo of the house on the other side of town from Jason's Cape.

"Dad can take you around," Jason said. His hands shook.

"Better you, son." Len's tone said, "do it" even though he didn't utter the words.

Annie's dad's cell phone rang again. After a brief exchange she said, "Now? . . . Okay . . . I need to go home and get the car, but I'll be over."

"What was that?"

"Charlie needs to see me. Jason, can you drop me off at the house then take Mom to look at that cottage?" She prayed that Melissa would obey their order to stay away from windows. If Jason were near the house, the three women decided, he would not think to look for his missing wife there—if he were looking for her. Why wasn't he raising all kinds of alarms that his pregnant wife had been AWOL for almost forty-eight hours?

"Sure." Jason grabbed two sets of keys as well as his car keys from a key board.

CHAPTER 75

Thursday, January 6

Annie parked on a street parallel to Melissa's. The side street was not visible from the main road. There were no FOR SALE or FOR RENT signs with the Haskell real estate phone number so no sales person would be coming by to show a house to discover Annie in the house. The late-afternoon sun was giving off feeble rays as Annie slipped in the back door. There was just enough light so she didn't have to snap on any lamps.

Damn. She'd forgotten a suitcase. When she opened the third kitchen closet, she found several plastic grocery bags. Within minutes she had them stuffed with underwear and four maternity dresses. Through an open door she saw a Salvation Army crib pushed to one corner. Cans of paint were lined up in front of it. Fabric with lambs cavorting matched one set of finished curtains hung over a chair.

An unfinished nursery, an unfinished marriage. Sadness overwhelmed Annie. She shoved new terry cloth suits 0–3 months in size and a pink baby dress into another bag. On the way out she passed the coat rack. My God. She had forgotten the girl didn't have a coat. She grabbed a coat and locked the door behind her as her cell phone rang.

"Get out of there quick," Susan said.

"I'm already out. Be back soon."

CHAPTER 76

Thursday, January 6

As Des and Annie walked by Haskell Realty, a man walked out the door followed by Jason screaming, "Tell me where she is!" at the back of a man. He caught up with him and spun him around.

"Look buddy, I just serve the papers." His voice carried.

Len caught up with his son. Annie saw Len's lips moving under the lamp light. His hand gripped his son's left shoulder. She couldn't hear what was said. Jason threw off his father's hand and ran behind the office building. Then Len said something to the process server. If she had to guess, knowing Len's over-the-top courtesy, Annie would have said that Len was apologizing. A few seconds later, Jason's car tore out of the alley next to the realty parking lot and disappeared.

"Some real-life drama there," Des said.

"Good thing no one was crossing the street."

"They'd be road kill. Let's go to Ipswich."

Dr. Delong's practice was in an old center chimney colonial painted a deep red, or so it seemed in the darkness of the early evening. Pine needles suggesting the recent removal of a Christmas tree were highlighted in the beam of the lamp to the left of the herringbone red brick path. The house was lit upstairs and downstairs.

Through the first-floor window they saw a waiting room. An

older man sat behind a desk talking to a woman and child. He wrote something in a book, wrote something else on a card as she pushed the child into a snowsuit.

Upstairs an older woman moved between a refrigerator and stove, pouring, stirring and putting things back.

"I'm a professional Peeping Tom," Des said. "I don't care about the sexual element. At least not in my peeping."

"I love seeing what's inside people's houses. One of the problems in France, and in fact most of Europe, people's shutters really work, and they close them."

"Wouldn't like that at all. Cuts peeping opportunities. Now, remember, we don't mention Linda Haskell."

"I don't see why not."

"Because it might eliminate other possibilities."

Annie wasn't sure she agreed, but then Des had more experience as an investigative reporter than she had as an amateur detective. And he had managed to get a list of the dental problems the skeleton had from a source at the medical examiner's. Annie didn't want to know how he had accomplished that. Well, yes, she did, but she wasn't about to ask.

Before they could ring the doorbell, the woman came out. The child was bundled in a snowsuit that left gender identification based on the pastel pink of the jacket. She held her mother's hand with her left and clutched a lollipop in her right hand.

"Making new business," Des whispered.

A small bronze plaque above the doorbell was engraved with the words Ring and Enter. Des and Annie rang and entered into a large hallway with the office to their left. The smell of onions drifting down the carpeted stairwell mixed with dentist smells. Brass runners held the maroon staircase carpet in place. The walls were covered with a maroon and white striped paper. A Victorian piece of furniture was to the left of the office. It looked like a throne with a marble seat, two arm rests and a mirrored back. However, it also had hooks for coats. On the other side of the door was a leafy green tree that stood taller than the throne. The door of the office opened and a man in a white coat came out.

"You must be Des. And is this the woman you were talking about?" Dr. Delong was one of those men whose age would be hard to guess other than over fifty. He shook her hand. When she saw the raised veins and age spots, she moved his age up a full decade. Annie tried to think of whom he reminded her with his full head of white hair and unlined skin. He was tall and thin.

"Thanks for seeing us." Des shook the dentist's hand.

"I have to admit I was intrigued by you asking for records. I wonder why the medical examiner didn't call. That happens sometimes, though they have a lot more to go on." His eyes twinkled. "Like a name. Or a date."

"Since the murder is so old, the medical examiner isn't making this case a priority," Des said.

"But we've a list of all the dental problems," Annie said.

"Assuming the damage was done before the death," Des said.

"Read about the skeleton in the paper. It's not good to laugh about a death, but it does give the phrase 'skeleton in the closet' a much more realistic meaning." His eyes sparkled. "Can I get you something to drink? My wife usually brings tea down after the last patient leaves. Herb stuff. Says the caffeine isn't good for me anymore."

They thanked him. Dr. Delong went to the bottom of the stairs. "Mildred, can we have three cups of that cinnamon stuff you insist on calling tea down here, please? Four if you want to join us."

"Hold your horses, I'll be down," the woman called back.

"When we talked on the phone you said you had all your

322

records?" Des said.

"Yup. Basement is full of them. Hate to throw that stuff out."

"How are they filed?" Annie asked.

"Alphabetically in five-year increments. Why, do you think it was my patient?"

Des and Annie exchanged a look.

"We are basing it only on the fact that you are the oldest dentist we could find," Des said.

The dentist burst out laughing. "I just found a new advantage to growing old right up there with senior citizen discounts."

"Do you remember any woman somewhere between twenty-five and thirty who lost several teeth?" Annie asked. Dick Van Dyke—that was who the dentist reminded her of.

"We've less chance in finding that than a needle in a haystack," Dr. Delong said. "I'm warning you, I never was good at remembering names of people I only saw once or twice."

Annie was tired of needles, haystacks, wild goose chases. She waited for him to say no.

"Well, why the hell not? It could be a trip down memory lane."

A woman appeared with a tray with three steaming cups. The smell of cinnamon fought with the dentist office smell. "I brought ginger snaps, fresh made, but only because of these young people," she said. "Don't let him eat more than one. I'd join you, but I'm in the middle of getting this old grouch's dinner."

"Watch out, young man," Dr. Delong said. "At twenty you marry a beautiful girl who is putty in your hands. Fifty years later she becomes your warden."

"Don't listen to him," Mildred said.

Dr. Delong told his wife what was happening.

"In that case I'll cook enough dinner for all of us. And I can help."

"Let's work upstairs. I'll bring the boxes up from the cellar," Dr. Delong said.

"Let me," Des said.

"Does that mean you think I'm too old?" Dr. Delong asked.

Annie felt she'd found the grandfather she never had. Both of hers had died before her birth.

"It means, since I'm asking you to do us a favor, I should do my part." Des winked at Annie and he went up another notch in her nice-man notebook.

The first five boxes were for records from thirty years before. Mildred bustled about with a pail of water, which she dipped a sponge into. The manila folders holding the X-rays and notes were cracked with age and the musty odor overrode the cinnamon. An olfactory day, Annie thought.

"We can eliminate men," Dr. Delong said.

"Brilliant," Mildred said. "I suggest we read out names."

"Now you see why I keep her," Dr. Delong said. "Hopefully I will remember a woman who came once or twice or someone who disappeared or . . ." He shook his head.

The banter of years of marriage, Annie thought. Her parents had it. They moved back and forth in established patterns neither was aware of. Sometimes their banter was a show for a new audience or maybe it was opening a closed circle to let a newcomer into their couple. She and Roger still had not developed that automation, but he had only been in her life three years.

"I can eliminate a lot of people that way."

"Karen Andrews," Des said.

"Dead."

"Archamps?"

"First name?"

"Dinah."

"Nope."

"Martha Archibald."

"Still a patient. Wicked overbite."

"Janice Heath."

"Moved to Tampa. I get Christmas cards."

The first five boxes were unsuccessful. "At least they're less dusty," Mildred said as Des picked them up and carried them back to the basement.

"Why don't we take a supper break," Mildred said.

"Let me call my parents," Annie said.

An hour later they were back at the boxes. Annie debated saying that this was a waste of time, but more and more she felt she owed her skeleton something more than just throwing the bones wherever old unidentified bones were thrown.

"Haskell," Des said.

"Linda?" Dr. Delong asked. "Let me see."

Des handed the file to the dentist. "We should have asked about her first on," Annie whispered to Des as the dentist pulled out the notes. "Stupid of us."

"Ladies and gentlemen, we may have a match," Dr. Delong said.

Annie looked over Dr. Delong's shoulder. "Linda was the name of Len Haskell's wife."

Des gave her a thumbs-up.

"Broken molar, cavities . . ." Dr. Delong compared the list to the X-rays. He read over his notes. "She broke her last appointment. Didn't call. Note from my receptionist that her husband said . . ."

". . . she deserted her family," Annie said.

"Can you call the medical examiner tomorrow?" Des asked.

The dentist nodded. "Sometimes needles jump out of haystacks."

Back in the car on the way to Annie's house, Des said, "I'm going to have one hell of an exclusive here. You think old Len did it?"

"Magda never liked the way he treated women. However, Melissa thinks he's wonderful."

"Always has a pretty woman at his beck and call," Des said. "That doesn't seem like a murderer. And I've never heard any of his ex-girlfriends say anything bad about him."

Annie pictured Len tilting his head with a come hither smirk and calling to a troop of Miss America wannabes all rushing to him.

She could hardly wait to tell her parents. Oh God, Melissa was there. The girl had enough to worry about without finding out her father-in-law might be a killer. They pulled up in front of her house.

Des cut the engine. "Despite the subject, I really enjoyed tonight. The Delongs are great people."

"Aren't they? Hope I'm as sharp when I reach their age," she said.

He drew Annie near and touched his lips to her.

Without thinking she responded then pulled back. "I'm not sure this is a good idea."

He kissed her again. "If you're not sure maybe we should continue until you're sure it is."

A bolt of desire shot through her, but she pulled away. "There's Roger."

"But he's there, and I'm here."

"But I'll be going back soon."

"That's not necessary. You could stay here."

Choices I don't need, Annie thought.

As she got out of the car he said, "I think that was one of the nicer brush-offs I've ever had."

"I'm a class act," Annie said.

Chapter 77

Saturday, January 8

When Annie stepped out the front door to pick up the *Globe,* the first headline she saw was about Congress and a budget battle. The second story reported that a skeleton from twenty years before had been identified. Des's byline came next. As she read that the husband, a prominent North Shore real estate broker, was being questioned, she realized she was still on the doorstep in the cold air in her pajamas. She closed the door and went into the kitchen.

She was the only one up. Even the sun had not risen. Early morning was her best time of day.

Des had e-mailed her to say the story was breaking, but she hadn't talked to him since the kiss. An aberration, she told herself. In a week or so she would be back home—her home, not her parent's. At least she would be there for a few days until she could tell Roger she was leaving again. Then she would take up her Zurich assignment. Her agent had bought her a delayed starting date and an agreement to work part time in France, but the first month it would all be in Zurich. That would give her enough money for the year and she could spend the summer in Argelès with Roger and Gaëlle. On her to-do list was booking her return flight.

Rather than use the whistling tea kettle whose piercing cry might wake the rest of the house, she took a regular pot to heat water. She shoved a leftover raisin bagel in the toaster. She would miss bagels and blueberry muffins, although she could make those, but not like here. However, she was looking forward to Les Flowers fish soup, and the fresh wood-fired oven baked bread and also the Escalvade, the roasted Catalan vegetable dish. Changing cultures meant missing certain foods.

As she waited for her water to boil and bagels to toast she read Des's story. He unfolded the tale like a good mystery, bringing up the slave diary and the pre–Civil War clothes that led the medical examiner to ignore the skeleton until she noticed the modern dentistry.

"The Haskell marriage wasn't that good. We could hear their fights. Both drank like fishes," Jonathan Mitchell, a former neighbor of the Haskells said. "Len went on the wagon after his wife left him. Concentrated on his business and did real well for himself." "Good father," another neighbor said.

Annie turned on her laptop and ran the cord from the living room for the wifi her father had installed. Her mailbox had twelve messages. She did not want to improve her sex life, nor was she interested in buying toner at the world's lowest prices. Well maybe. Toner was expensive.

Gaëlle wrote in English with only a couple of errors to tell her that Hannibal, her German shepherd, had dug up the new rosebush and scratched her nose with the thorns. They took the dog to the vet for the resulting infection. The vet sent greetings to Annie.

Roger talked about an invitation to a wedding in February. Even if she were in Zurich she could train back to Argelès.

There was an e-mail from Des. "Hey beautiful . . ." he started out, then suggested that they collaborate to find the murderer. "Or definitely prove it was Len. Which is my guess." He ended with, "but it would be nice if we could find the smoking gun, so to speak."

No word about the kiss. Good. She looked at her watch.

Only 6:30. Too early to call him to say she was game.

Her father wandered into the kitchen. His red plaid flannel pajamas were wrinkled and hung low on his skinny hips. He scratched his stubbly cheeks. "Morning, kitten." He plunked a kiss on her hair.

Without a word she pointed to the article. He searched for his reading glasses. Annie plucked them from the top of the microwave and handed them to him.

He turned a kitchen chair, straddled it, put the paper on the table and read the front page, then turned to page eight where it was continued. "Whew."

"What do you think of Len now?"

"Sorry, I still don't see Len as a murderer."

"But if alcohol were involved."

"Possible, but still . . ."

Annie poured two bowls of tea. Last week her parents had bought the bowls. Drinking morning tea out of bowls was one of their French habits. Maybe the fact they were doing this was a homesickness seed for Geneva. Maybe they would move back. Grow up, she told herself.

"I remember one summer when a bat got into this house. Auntie Helen went hysterical. We were all here, Paul, Charlie, Len, myself. I picked up my baseball bat. We played a lot of ball that summer, but Len insisted on throwing a towel over it and releasing it outside. That's not a murderer's personality."

Annie set the steaming bowls of Earl Gray on the table.

"Thanks. Is there another bagel?" he asked.

She put the last one in the toaster as Susan walked in. "Melissa is still sound asleep." She looked at the paper. "This'll upset her."

Until that moment Annie had not thought that the victim

was Melissa's mother-in-law, the most likely murderer, her father-in-law—a man she trusted.

Melissa looked at *The Globe*. The sun streamed through the window warming the kitchen to an almost uncomfortable temperature. "Oh, my God! Oh, my God!" Her bathrobe did not cover her stomach and flapped as she paced around the room. "I have to call Jason."

Annie watched, unsure of what to do. Comforting friends through divorce was nothing new, but dealing with this abused child whose father-in-law might be a murderer was more than she had ever handled or wanted to handle. However, she learned long ago that it was better to deal with rather than to run from conflict. She would never like it. Liking wasn't required. Under no circumstances could she allow Melissa to go near that family. "Are you mad?"

"He'll need me."

"Jason could have killed Madison." Annie hoped by using the baby's name, she would make the girl see sense. "Melissa?"

The girl tried to get by Annie, who blocked the girl's path. Taking the girl's hands in her own Annie looked into her eyes. "You have to protect Madison."

Melissa said nothing.

"It looks like there's a pattern of abuse with your in-laws. And a problem with alcohol."

"I've never seen Len drink."

"Maybe he's AA. Maybe he killed Linda, maybe not. But something happened. Do you want your daughter to be part of that?" Out of the corner of her eye she saw her father and mother in standby mode. The fact that they hadn't said anything made Annie more confident. Her mother would step in if needed.

Melissa cradled her stomach.

331

"Look at what you're doing. You're protecting your baby."

Melissa brushed tears from her eyes with the back of her hand much like a small child does. "What I want, I can't have."

"You want a happy family, a good husband and healthy baby," Annie said.

Melissa nodded and sniffed.

Annie handed her a napkin, the only thing handy, and waited while Melissa blew her nose. "It's normal. And maybe some day you will be able to have it, but not with Jason as he is now. Maybe never with him. Maybe with someone else."

Melissa's expression said she doubted that possibility.

"In any case you'll have a family: you and Madison. Lots of women raise children alone and have a happy life. Live for her and for yourself." Other words and phrases ran through Annie's mind, but they all sounded so trite. How could she, a woman who had never married, had never been pregnant, begin to understand what Melissa was feeling?

Susan led Melissa to a chair. "Listen dear, as one mother to another." With her finger she tipped Melissa's head so she had to look at her. "When I gave birth to Annie, I knew I would do everything I could for her. As much as I loved Dave, love Dave, if it became a choice between the two, it would have been Annie."

Behind Melissa's back Annie touched Dave's arm to stop him from saying anything.

"Today you see a happy couple, but we weren't always like that. When Annie was little, I left him for six months because our marriage had become unsupportable. It was the hardest thing I ever did, but if I hadn't I don't know what would have happened."

"I didn't know that," Annie mouthed to her father.

He nodded.

"Promise me you'll do whatever Magda arranges and

whatever is necessary, no matter how hard."

This time is was Melissa who nodded.

The telephone rang. Annie picked it up.

"Hello Darlink, how is our wounded bird?"

Annie walked into the living room with the receiver. "Flip flopping. Have you seen *The Globe?*"

"I always knew that bastard was no good, Darlink. What did Melissa say?"

"She's in shock. When is she due to go into hiding?"

"Tomorrow morning."

"You're not driving her." Annie's tone made it an order.

Magda still relied on Susan's twice-daily visits for basic needs.

"I'm as weak as a baby mouse, Darlink. No, another woman will pick her up. But I was hoping you could take her as far as the Burger King on the Mass Pike, the Ludlow exit."

"Ludlow?" From her UMass days she remembered it as being at the other end of the state.

"That's where the contact will meet her. It may not be the best route, but this woman is a nurse, in case Melissa goes into labor."

The doorbell rang. "Gotta go, Magda. And my mother will be at your place later."

"Go, Darlink, go."

Tim Doherty stood at the door, his hat under his arm. "Sorry to bother you folks, but I was hoping I could talk to you about the Haskells."

Annie saw him look over her head to the kitchen where Melissa was in full view staring at him.

"Maybe this isn't the best time," he said.

Melissa stood up and came toward him. "I'm going to take a shower."

"Call if you need help," Susan said.

After Melissa disappeared and they were seated around the kitchen table, Tim said, "I had no idea she was here. When I talked to Jason earlier, he told me she'd gone shopping." He leaned on his elbows. Doherty took a notebook out of his breast pocket and a pen.

"She's got a restraining order. You didn't know?" Annie realized that this type of lack of knowledge was exactly why Magda didn't trust the system.

"I've been concentrating on the murder and drug thingies. I need to ask you some questions, Dave," Tim said.

"I'm willing to help, but I've got trouble thinking of Len as a murderer."

"Most murderers don't plan it. It's a moment of passion or an accident. You knew Len as a teenager?"

"Even before. I started spending summers down here when I was eight. I met Paul Mangone, Len and Charlie Tucker. We became a gang."

"Gang?"

"Not in a gang in the sense we beat up on other gangs or stole stuff. We hung out, played baseball, went to the beach, rode our bikes, kid stuff. And we all shared a passion for history."

"Now that's different."

"Not really. The others had a wonderful teacher in the third grade that taught them about the Greeks and Romans. All the next summer we played Julius Cesar conquering imaginary barbarians."

"Your version of cops and robbers."

"Or cowboys and Indians. Paul's mother was mad when we cut up her best sheets to make togas." They all smiled at that image.

"The next year they studied the Middle Ages so we became Plantagenets that summer."

Tim Doherty frowned.

"A British royal family," Dave said and Tim nodded.

"Our interest in history stuck even when the teachers weren't any good. All of us ate books. We loved to read and that made us oddballs in a way."

"And you stayed friends?"

"Not in the normal sense. As we grew up we still hung around summers. We looked for girls, bragged about our conquests that existed mostly in our heads, or at least mine did."

"When did you stop coming down summers?"

"Second year of college. I worked at the Blacksmith Restaurant as a waiter for several summers, but my junior year I met Susan. My aunt hated her and made me choose between Susan and her."

"Never smart to give a young man an ultimatum like that," Tim said.

"Hormones win every time," Dave said.

"Did you keep in touch with the boys after that?"

"We didn't write each other or anything like that. Len hadn't been with us for a couple of years. He went to school in the South and he stayed there summers."

"Did you know his wife?"

"Never met her. She must have been around when we were growing up, but . . ." he shrugged.

"How did you get back in touch? With Len, that is."

"We didn't. When my aunt left me this house I wandered into the coffee shop one day and the guys were at a table talking. I wouldn't have recognized Charlie or Paul, but Len was the spitting image of his father. I asked him if he was Len Haskell, and we picked up where we left off."

"Did he ever talk about his wife?"

"No, but the others said his wife left when Jason was seven. That Len had done a great job raising the kid on his own. They teased him about the series of women he had affairs with. He said they were jealous that he was still thin and had all his hair and could get young women. Of course Paul and Charlie are happily married." Dave reached for Susan's hand.

"When you kids were so involved in history, did you concentrate on any period?" Tim asked.

"Charlie was the Revolution, I was involved in European history. I loved all the kings and queens, but I was more fascinated by what daily life was like. Len was the Civil War and . . ."

Tim scribbled in his notebook for the first time since Dave started talking.

"That doesn't make him the murderer. The Civil War was one of our games."

"And the others?" Tim bit the end of his pen.

"Paul, well he had the least interest. His thing was science. Funny that Charlie became a scientific publisher and Paul became the history teacher."

"And you became a businessman."

"Not bad for an ex-hippie," Dave said. "Annie's birth showed me that earning a living had some merit, although not at all costs."

Tim allowed a smile to play around his lips for half a second before reverting to serious policeman. "Do you know if Len collects Civil War memorabilia?"

"I've no idea. I've never been in his house since I've been back, that is. You're thinking of the diary?"

Tim nodded and looked at his watch. "One more question. How long will Melissa be with you?"

"A few more days."

"I hope she can work out her marriage. Too many divorces these days."

Susan spoke for the first time. "Sometimes a divorce is better

than a terrible marriage, especially one with violence."
Tim nodded.

CHAPTER 78

Saturday, January 8

"It's snowing again," Melissa said. She stood at the Young living room window. "I don't ever remember this much snow."

"The weather is weird everywhere," Annie said.

Lunch had been cleared away. Annie had a mystery novel in her lap while Dave was reading Bob Woodward's latest. Susan had gone to Magda's.

A fire brought coziness to the room. As flames lapped at the wood Dave got up and tossed in a pine cone. "For color." He looked at his daughter who had one leg curled under her.

"It's not good to sit on your legs like that."

"I know, but it is so comfortable," Annie said. "He's told me since I was little."

"And you still don't listen."

"Maybe some day you'll stop trying."

They heard the kitchen door open. Susan entered, brushing snow from her coat. "Seems like a wonderful afternoon for staying home. I left a casserole for Magda to nuke, so I'm in for the night."

"Let's do a puzzle," Annie said. "Like when it snows at home."

Susan went upstairs and returned with three boxes.

Dave set up a card table. "Want to join us, Melissa?"

"Doing what?"

"Jigsaw puzzles. It is something we did wherever we lived on snowy days when we were all home. Or after skiing. A family tradition."

"I never did one, but I'm willing to try."

"Well, since you're new at it, you can choose which one," Susan said. "And while everyone sets it up, I'll start a corn chowder. Perfect weather for it."

"So which picture?" Dave asked.

Melissa looked at the three boxes Dave set in front of her. One was of a Swiss chalet with three cows wearing huge bells, the second was of the covered bridge in Lucerne and the third was of the château at Chillon. "They're all so beautiful."

"Except for the chalet, we've been to Lucerne and the château," Annie said.

"Wow. I always dreamed of traveling."

"Some day you still might." Dave patted her hand.

Melissa handed him the chalet.

"We've some rules. We put out all the pieces and do the edge before anyone starts the middle. Once when I did one by myself, I didn't do it that way. Still feel guilty," Annie said.

The edge went together quickly. By the time the sky and cows were done, Susan left the table to bring in tea and the brownies she had made the day before.

Melissa concentrated on a patch of green grass with red poppies. "Look, its working."

"Good girl," Annie and Susan said together.

"Way to go," said Dave.

Without warning Melissa started to cry. The Youngs looked at each other, not sure what had caused the outburst.

"I-I'm sorry," Melissa said. "I've never did anything like this before and it's s-s-so nice."

"When you were growing up . . ." Annie started.

"My adopted parents worked a lot and when they didn't work they were really tired. My aunt and uncle watched television or read their bibles without ever really talking to each other. I saw the Huxtables doing stuff together on TV but I thought that was just television. I never really saw a real family sit together for a whole afternoon and play together like they liked each other."

"We do like each other," Annie said. Although her friends growing up had been of many different nationalities, most of them came from homes where families did a lot of things together. For no reason she remembered each fall the Youngs walking in the woods picking mushrooms, then taking them to the pharmacist to determine which were edible. Whether it was a walk in the woods, doing a jigsaw puzzle or playing gin rummy, talking together or reading, Annie had taken her family life for granted. Roger and she did the same things with Gaëlle. That was the way life should be. Poor Melissa. "When you have your baby, you can set up the same atmosphere for her."

"I could never do it with Jason."

That Annie had no doubt about. She was glad that the girl seemed to finally realize it. Maybe there was a chance for her.

Melissa insisted on clearing the table and doing the dishes. "I am not a taker," she said.

"I never argue when someone wants to clean up my kitchen," Susan said.

Banging at the door jarred the house.

Dave opened it.

"Where the fuck is my wife?" Jason filled the doorway. "I want my fucking wife. I know she's here." He tried to brush by Dave, but the older man stopped him.

"First, watch your language. Second, no one comes in my house without an invitation, and third, even if your wife were here, there's an injunction against you coming near her."

"I don't care about any fucking injunction." His words were

slurred, the smell of alcohol strong.

"Annie, call the police." Dave did not turn around to give the command.

Annie went into the kitchen and dialed 911. Melissa had disappeared. "This is the Youngs and we need a cruiser now. Jason Haskell is here, and he's threatening us."

After what seemed like hours but really was only a few minutes, a siren was heard in the background. Jason bolted out the door. A second later a rock came through the living room window. The cruiser stopped in front of the house as Jason took off down the street.

"Catch him," Dave called to one of the cops who took off on foot. The other followed.

Within minutes they were back with a handcuffed Jason who was slipping on the snow-covered brick sidewalk.

"What happened, Mr. Young?" the older one asked.

"He wanted his wife, and was using foul and threatening language," Dave said. "When he heard the siren he ran, but he stopped long enough to break our window."

"Wasn't me. I want my wife." Jason turned to the younger cop. "Brian, you said she was here."

The young cop turned red.

"If that's true, you're in a lot of trouble," Dave said. "You're dealing with a domestic violence situation here, and it certainly deserved better handling."

"Shit," said the older cop. "Do you want to press charges, Mr. Young?"

"Can you lock him up for the night? He's obviously drunk."

"We don't usually . . ."

"I will press charges in the morning. Meanwhile, I don't feel my family is safe, and you don't want a lawsuit against the department."

"I'll sue for false arrest," Jason mumbled. He thrashed out of the younger cop's hands.

"We'll deal with it in the morning," said the older cop. "You are under arrest." He gave him the legal warning.

CHAPTER 79

Saturday, January 8

"Dad, I'll go with you to Len's," Annie said.

"I'm not sure that's a good idea, kitten," Dave said. The Youngs and Melissa were in the Youngs' kitchen. Dave had his coat in his hands.

"He's less apt to get angry at you if I'm there." She went to the hall closet to get her jacket.

"Well, he's not going to attack me," Dave said.

"He could be a murderer." Annie pulled on her parka.

"And if he is, I'm not going to put my only child in danger."

Melissa shifted in her chair. "I can't imagine Len as a murderer."

"Magda would say he was," Susan said. "She thinks he's a wife beater, a womanizer and an all-around scumbag. Thought so even before the body was found."

"Fortunately, Magda's not on his jury. Len was a hot-headed kid, but he's changed," Dave said.

"I never saw his temper," Melissa said. "Although womanizer fits."

"Are you sure you want to talk to him in person?" Susan asked.

Dave reached for his wife's hand. "He's been a friend since I was a kid. If he had Annie arrested, I'd appreciate his explanation."

Annie stood in front of her father with her jacket on. "I'm going."

Dave sighed. "All right, all right, but I liked you better when you were little and I could still boss you around."

Snow filtered down, but the flakes were miniscule. The glazed streets had not been ploughed. When Annie and Dave saw a car skid slightly, they decided to walk to Len's house rather than drive. Not a word had been exchanged. Despite thick-soled boots, Annie slipped.

Her father grabbed her before she went down. "Careful, kitten."

Len lived in a pre–Civil War house painted avocado. It looked gray in the evening lamp light. Annie and Dave inched their way up the uneven brick walk and rang the bell.

Len answered the door. He had changed from his business clothes and wore well-pressed khakis and an Irish knit sweater. "What brings you folks out on a night like this?"

Annie and Dave looked at each other. If Jason used his one phone call, it wasn't to his father.

"Nothing good," Dave said.

"Come in. Can I get you a drink? I don't have anything with a kick, but there's coffee, tea. Let me take your coats."

They took off their jackets. Len put them on the coat rack. The melting snow glistened as a few drops of moisture hit the floor.

They stepped inside the living room. A fire crackled in the fireplace over which an antique rifle hung. Annie didn't know enough about guns to identify it.

A brown leather easy chair had a cup of coffee steaming on the side table next to it. *The Boston Globe* sport pages were on the chair. The real estate section was on the floor with several ads circled in red. Not showing were the stories about the skeleton.

One wall was solid bookcases. Annie read the titles, which were mostly history books. Although they covered all periods of history, she estimated half were about the Civil War and slavery.

Another wall had a collage of brown and silver photographic plates, darkening the room that was already dark with the brown braided rug and brown leather couch and wood paneling.

Annie walked over to them. They were all of Civil War scenes. "Are those Matthew Brady's?" she asked.

"One is authenticated. I wish the others were," Len said. "Sit down."

Annie and Dave chose the couch but sat on the edge.

"This is rather awkward," Dave said. "But I wanted to explain to you as an old friend what I did and why. I don't know the next step."

Len, who had been sitting back in his easy chair, changed to an upright position. He listened with growing agitation as Dave told him what happened.

"Len, I know Melissa has been abused," Annie said, and told how she had arrived at Magda's without a coat and of her time in the hospital.

If Annie had expected denials and not-my-son, she didn't get it. She watched Len shake his head. He got up and walked over to the window and looked out on the falling snow.

Dave got up and walked up behind his old friend and put his hand on his shoulder. "I know this is hard for you."

"Let's just say being suspected of murdering my wife and having my son arrested and then having you say he abused Melissa all within a few days will not be the highlights of my life." His tone bit more than the words. Len turned. "And in a way you're involved because her body was found in your basement, and your daughter helped the identification. Shit."

Annie looked at her father who shrugged. No etiquette book covered this situation.

"I do appreciate you coming by and telling me face-to-face. At least you don't cross the street to avoid me, like some have today."

No one said anything for what seemed like hours but was only a few seconds.

"Is Melissa going home?"

"I really don't think she's safe until Jason gets some counseling," Annie said. I've overstepped the bounds, she thought. Len will say I'm not a shrink. A part of her felt sorry for the man. For the first time he didn't look dapper, he looked rumpled.

Instead, he said, "That probably would be a good thing. He always was an impulsive kid."

"It's hard raising a son alone," Dave said. "You did the best you could."

"Not good enough, obviously." Len turned to Annie. "Would Melissa talk to me?"

"She has only good things to say about you."

"And does she think I'm a murderer?"

"No," she said.

"And neither do I," Dave said.

Len let out a long sigh, the kind that seemed to start from his feet. "I cannot express how much that means to me."

"I'll call her tomorrow. I don't want to be rude, but I need to call my lawyer and Tim Doherty."

Dave and Annie moved to the door. "We understand," they said in unison.

As Annie opened the door Len called, "I do appreciate your coming even if I hated what you had to tell me. Not many people would have had the balls. Excuse me, Annie."

"It's not a problem. We wish you luck." She surprised herself that she meant it.

CHAPTER 80

I never thought I'd sees the day when I sits at a table with a white woman serving me, but that be what happens when we gets to Syracuse. The wife of the Reverend feeds us this roast lamb and mint jelly. It be all ready when we walks in the door. She takes our coats and leads us to the table and makes sure we gots enough food on our plates.

At first I didn't want to sit, but she insists. "You must be so tired. And hungry." She be a little woman up and down, but she be chunky side to side. Her gray hair be pulled back tight from her face and parted in the middle. Her face falls into smiles. I never sees a woman who smiles so much.

She be right about hungry. The Reverend didn't dare stop for nothing in case someone thinks we be runaway slaves. Even with our fancy white folks clothes and our papers, the Reverend don't take no chances. We hides the whole way behind the carriage curtains.

As I eats, my bones aches from the jostling, but I don't care. I could eats a whole sheep.

There be three windows in the dining room. Mrs. Reverend draws the beige curtains with little white yarn balls along the bottom even if it is mid-day. "I don't want anyone walking by to see you. You're probably in less danger than most negroes who've come through, but . . ." she lets her words hang.

Mrs. Reverend always touches the Reverend, dropping her lips on his head or brushing his shoulder. She looks at him like there be no other man on this good earth.

347

After we eats, she says we gotta take a bath. There's a tub in the kitchen and she heats the water for me. I tries to do it, but she says, "No-no-no you've had a long trip. You go first dear, then your husband," she says.

I soaks all the soreness from my body. I wants to stay there forever, but I know Zeb be waiting. However, Mrs. Reverend makes sure he has fresh, hot, clean water instead of my dirty old water. After we be dry and in our change of clothes, she insists on washing our under-things. "I cain't lets you do that," I says, but she says, "How do you plan to stop me?" and laughs.

The Reverend leads us to the attic. "You'll sleep here."

The attic has a big bed and a little bed among trunks and piles of things. There be a rocking horse and other toys. The Reverend and his wife be too old to have children, but maybe they did once, and they be all growed now. The roof slopes on both sides and there be a window. I be glad we has a window. Otherwise the room make me feel smothered.

"Stay away from the window. I know you have papers, but the next people might not, and I don't want to draw any attention to what I do."

The Reverend sits on one bed and waves his hand for us to sits on the other. That bed has the clean sheet smell and thick blankets.

"You'll stay until the Reverend Jacobs can pick you up and take you to the next stop."

Zeb and I nods.

"This will go on until you reach Canada. Zeb, we've arranged work with a Simon Thomas. He'll give you a fair wage. As for you Mathilde, you're a rare young woman because you can read and write. Your job will be to teach other ex-slaves to do the same: and their children, of course. With education, they'll have a better chance in this world. How's your arithmetic?"

"Bad," I says.

"Well hopefully we'll find another ex-slave coming through who

knows how to figure and send them up to teach math."

I be afraid to ask how many ex-slaves be up in Canada. I be more afraid to ask Zeb if he plans to go home to his Africa. I waits until Zeb and I be in bed. We didn't pleasure each other. It seems wrong in this house.

"I be concentrating on the words ex-slave. I finds it hard to believe this nightmare is almost over," he says.

I takes a deep breath. "What you going to do?"

"What do you mean, woman?"

"When you gets to Canada?"

He looks at me like I done grown a second head. "I am going to make the most beautiful furniture in the world. I going to be a man." He lets out so much air I thinks his body going to collapse. "Again."

With that we forgets about being in the Reverend's house and he pleasures me like I never been pleasured before. He doesn't pull out, and I wills his seed to create our child. I knowd by the way he holds me he be willing the same thing.

CHAPTER 81

Sunday, January 9

"Ready, Melissa?" Annie called from the bottom of the stairs.

Dave Young's deep voice, not Melissa's light one, answered. "I'm trying to shut her suitcases. Your mother went nuts buying baby clothes."

Because she thinks I'll never give her a grandchild. Once when Annie had said she wasn't sure she wanted children, Susan had said, "My only regret is that you won't know the joy I have known in having a you in my life," then changed the subject. Perhaps a grandbaby would get them back to Geneva, a rotten reason to have a kid.

Melissa waddled down the stairs clutching the railing followed by the Youngs, each toting two large suitcases that Annie recognized as belonging to her parents.

"I've added towels, sheets, and Dave—go back up for the large duvet. These are things you won't have to buy later," Susan said.

"And this will help too." Dave tucked $400 in bills into Melissa's purse.

"I can't take this," Melissa said.

"It's not for you. It's for Madison," Susan said.

Melissa was crying.

"Stop! You'll blotch." Susan held the girl by the shoulders. "You can't start a new life blotched."

Melissa giggled then sniffed. Susan handed the girl a tissue, pulled another one from her pocket and wiped the tears from her cheeks. "Get going." She turned her toward the door.

The snow had not had time to get dirty. With the strong sunshine the world looked clean and pure. The sky was the unreal blue that Annie expected from skies in the South of France not New England in January. "Great day for a ride."

Dave packed the car. "Got your license?"

Annie nodded.

"Melissa, I know you're supposed to keep your location a secret, but if you get a chance after the baby is born, ring us and let us know you're okay. And if you need us get in touch through Magda."

"I can't believe there are people like you," Melissa said.

"I think we're the norm. You were unlucky enough to run into the deviant few."

"Let's go," Annie said. "Melissa, you navigate. I'm a stranger in these parts."

As they pulled out of the driveway, Susan and Dave waved and blew kisses before going back in the house. No one noticed the car pulling out down the street.

"It's the next left, Route 128," Melissa said.

Annie turned. "Whenever we went on rides when I was a kid we used to play games. Sometimes it was to see how many countries we found license plates from, although if it were France, Germany or Switzerland we'd try to identify regions. For example, cars from Paris proper have plates ending in 75." Maybe if she babbled enough, Melissa wouldn't think about what was happening.

"We never went anywhere when I was a kid."

Annie wished she hadn't mentioned it. What she considered as a normal childhood others would think privileged. Her life was still privileged in ways that had nothing to do with material possessions. She was much loved. She worked as she wanted. She thought nothing of jumping on a plane to change countries on a whim. She had her own flat in the South of France that left her with a sense of peace. And here was Melissa facing a birth without having access to health insurance, an abusive husband and a shaky future. Annie reminded herself never to take her life for granted. "Music?"

Melissa turned on the radio. Dave had it turned to a college station playing folk music and some woman sang about getting revenge on a lover going skiing in Switzerland. The two women giggled.

As they passed the Framingham exit, Melissa said, "I'm sorry, can we have a pee stop?"

Annie pulled into the rest stop, passed the gas pumps and stopped in front of the restaurant to let Melissa out. "I'll wait here."

"Be right back. Want something to eat?"

"Sure, tea and surprise me." Annie handed the girl a ten.

Annie looked at the map to check the distance. When she looked up she saw a car pull up. Two policemen got out and entered the restaurant. She made a mental note of the unmarked car.

After undoing her seatbelt, she stretched. She didn't own a car for she had always lived places where public transportation made it unnecessary. If she really needed a car, she rented one, but even that was less than once a year. "I don't add thirty pounds of pollutants to the air each year, and I save tons of money," she would say if anyone asked her why she didn't drive. "Besides the bus and train don't need to find parking places," or "I can't sleep or read if I'm driving," she would add in case they felt she was chiding them for their cars. Although she knew she was a good driver, if she never got behind the wheel of a car again that would be all right. As for telling one make from another, she classified cars by color and size: big blue, small green.

The back door opened as Melissa got in. Why was Melissa in the back? Did she want to stretch out on the seat? She felt a knife against her throat.

"Don't move." The voice shook.

"Jason."

"You thought I was in jail so you'd be safe to steal my wife. Where are you taking her?"

"I'm not taking her anywhere."

"Don't lie. I saw suitcases. I saw you leave the house."

The knife nicked Annie's chin. The blood trickling onto her hand felt warm and she imagined she smelled copper. In that instant she knew Jason had killed Linda Haskell. But he'd only been seven, part of her said. She should have stopped the words, "You killed your mother," but they fell from her mouth not as a statement but fact. Stupid, stupid, she thought. If she were to get out of this, if she were to prevent Melissa from coming back to the car, she couldn't afford to be stupid. Maybe she should say she needed gas. No, that wouldn't work, because he could see the gauge.

Melissa was taking her time, but she had said she was going to buy them something to eat. At this time of day it was after the breakfast crowd and before the stop-for-coffee crowd.

"Don't fight me," he said.

"You've a knife. I've nothing."

"What's keeping my wife?"

"She's pregnant. She has a close relationship with toilets." Annie saw Jason's eyes in the rearview mirror. In the mystery stories she read, writers talked about crazed expressions, but she had never taken it seriously until now. Jason belonged in a thriller or a bodice ripper. She didn't.

No matter what, she had to do something fast before Melissa

came back. "I'm turning the engine on so when your wife comes out we can start right up."

"That's being smart," he said.

The car engine caught. Annie shoved it into drive and floored the engine, driving the car through the bushes in front of the restaurant and through the plate-glass window. As she did, she prayed she wouldn't hit anyone sitting at the tables. At the same time she ducked down in the seat and screamed "Police, help!" as a searing pain ripped through her shoulder.

CHAPTER 82

Monday, January 10

"You're awake."

Annie didn't recognize the voice nor the face when she opened her eyes. She was surrounded by white walls, white ceiling, white-coated figures. A bald man with glasses and a stethoscope around his neck came into focus.

"Where am I?" Her chest felt as if elephants were beating on it.

"The hospital. You ran your car through a wall, were stabbed and passed out."

The antiseptic smell seeped into Annie's awareness.

"How long have I been here?"

"Only a day. We kept you sedated."

She tried to sit up, but the room swirled and she fell back down. A bed flanked hers, so she guessed she wasn't in intensive care. "How bad was it?"

"It could have been a lot worse. After the first thrust you rolled over and he stabbed you again in the chest. He missed your lungs thanks to your thick coat and a rib. His first hit was on your arm. From what the reports said, he was reaching over the car seat, which made it harder to hit you."

Annie realized that her arm hurt, too.

"Two staties in the restaurant pulled him off you."

Annie tried to sit, but dizziness prevented her. "I have to talk to the police."

"And they want to talk to you, but only when you're ready. Let me get your parents."

Dave and Susan went to each side of the bed and in perfect synchronization put a hand on their daughter, avoiding the drips and wires. Susan was crying. Dave sniffed a few times.

"Thank God you're all right. Whatever made you drive into the restaurant?"

"I saw the cops go in. It was the only thing I could think of. I didn't want him to get Melissa. Don't know what I would have done if she hadn't taken so much time."

Susan wiped her eyes. "That's because her water broke while she was in the toilet."

"She okay?"

"She and Madison are fine," Dave said. "Seven pounds. I think two pounds are black hair."

"Jason?"

"Under arrest."

"He killed his mother," Annie said.

"She must still be feeling the drugs," Dave said.

"No, I know he killed his mother," Annie said. "I have no proof, but I know it. Talk to Tim Doherty. And Des."

"You need to rest," Susan said. "But we'll do as you wish."

CHAPTER 83

Tuesday, January 11

The next day Des O'Flaherty walked into Annie's hospital room with a bouquet of daffodils and *The Boston Globe*. She looked pale and very vulnerable to him. His testosterone beat a message in his head that he wanted to strangle Jason Haskell. Better to play it casual. "I see you have more flowers than if this were your funeral. How are you feeling?" He shifted his weight from foot to foot. Normally, he hated hospitals because he never knew what to say. This was different. He had a lot to tell her if she had strength to listen.

"Sore. I broke two ribs in the accident, which was a good thing."

"Broken ribs don't sound like a good thing." Although he'd talked to the Youngs, they only said she was lucky and healing nicely. The hospital spokeswoman, a megabitch in his opinion for not giving him a detailed report, had said Annie was stable after sustaining injuries from the crash and stabbing. Long ago he learned medical people only gave diddly-squat information.

"'Twas a good thing because the knife hit the rib, which was at a weird angle and missed my lungs. The skin and muscles will heal. Meanwhile, they are torturing me." Annie struggled to a sitting position. Her hospital regulation gown had been replaced by a flowered flannel thing, definitely not sexy, but sweet in Des's opinion, especially the ruffled neck. Annie's mass of red curls were fastened in a braid.

"When are you getting out?"

"Tomorrow."

"Thought you would like to see this." He tossed the news-paper down.

"Man confesses to killing his mother," was the front-page headline. "Your mother gave me your message and I went to Doherty. He did the rest."

Annie mouthed the words as she read. "A twenty-seven-year-old man confessed to killing his mother when he was seven . . ." Annie read out loud. Then she scanned the article, including Len Haskell's statement that his wife often beat their son when drunk. When she had passed out on the couch, Jason had taken a fire poker and held it to her neck, choking her to death. Len, not wanting his son to be punished, took the body, dressed it in an outfit he had as part of his Civil War memorabilia and put her in a neighbor's house's hidden room that he knew about. What made Annie choke up was Len's statement, "When Linda wasn't drinking she was a wonderful mom."

"How did he know about the room?" Annie asked.

"In high school he'd done some original research about the Underground Railroad in Caleb's Landing. He found that there were three participating houses, your great aunt's house being one of them. It was mid-week so she was back in Sudbury teaching."

"Didn't he think they would notice the body was white?"

"He hoped it would be years before they found it if it ever were found. His main concern was his son." Seeing the tears run down Annie's cheeks he wanted to hug her. Instead, he handed her a tissue from the box on the nightstand. "Got a vase?"

Annie pointed to one holding tulip stalks. Petals covered the surface of the table.

"I suppose it was natural of him to want to protect Jason,"

she said. "Mathilde's diary?"

"He'd bought that at an auction two years after the murder. Figured if they found the skeleton sometime in the future they would just take it for granted they belonged together. I wonder why he thought your aunt wouldn't notice a change in the cellar. Or know about the room."

"Not according to my father. She hated the basement. Almost never went down there."

"Len knew because she sent him down there to set mouse traps." Des swept the dead petals into his hand and threw them in the wastebasket. "Anyway, Len told the police that he knew that big chest was there and he pushed it in front of the door."

"I suppose that was why he wanted my dad to sell the house. So he could get rid of the skeleton."

"By that point, he could have taken the bones and scattered them all over New England."

"So he was never an abusing husband."

"Oh yes he was. He and Linda had some knock-down fights, but she gave as good as she got." Des went into the bathroom to fill the vase with water. "I am a pretty good flower arranger for a guy," he said, not telling her that he had worked one summer while going through college for a florist. When he came back into the room he put the vase with his flowers so they stood out in front of the others. "Len admitted that he knew he was in trouble with the alcohol and his own anger. He knew it couldn't have been good for Jason, and he really loved his son. After Linda died, he gave up drinking, did a lot of therapy and did his best to make Jason an okay kid. The two women he tried living with didn't end because of violence, but because he put Jason first, his business second, and the women resented it."

"Dad said he didn't believe Len could be a murderer."

"He, Len that is, gave me an interview. He said that he didn't trust himself to marry again because he wasn't any good as a husband, and the swinging door on mother wannabes didn't help his son."

"I feel sorry for him."

"What will happen to Jason?"

"Statue of limitations doesn't count with a murderer. But he was seven. Can you try a man his age as a juvenile? I think they'll get him for domestic abuse and attempted murder."

"Attempted murder? Me?" She never thought of herself as a potential murder victim.

Des patted her hair. "Anyway, they're doing a psychiatric evaluation. There's probably a good chance he will be declared incompetent." He sat on the edge of the bed. "Your parents said they would be in to see you later. You know they have Melissa and the baby at your house."

"My parents love adopting strays."

"But Melissa is going back to her house. I'm not sure how Len's business will survive this. Small towns, etc., but he wants to help Melissa any way he can. That might help." He reached for her hand. "And you?"

"I talked to Roger last night. He says to get my butt back to France as soon as possible. Or at least the French equivalent."

"He isn't coming here?" He would have crossed the ocean if Annie were hurt in another country.

"I told him not to. I'll be there as soon as I can to travel."

Des kissed Annie on the top of her head. "I suppose I should go. Don't want to wear you out." As he got to the door he turned. "Paul Mangone. He called me to say the School Committee isn't taking any action against Kendra."

"Good. Are they taking any action to improve the textbooks?"

"No."

"Shit," Annie said.

That was how Des felt. Shit, that this woman was about to slip out of his grasp. Win some, lose some.

CHAPTER 84

Thursday, January 20

Annie stood on the escalator going to the second floor of Terminal E at Logan Airport and shifted Madison Haskell to her left shoulder where it didn't hurt as much. Susan and Melissa stood next to her. Dave tucked *Newsweek, Time* and *The Economist* into Annie's shoulder bag. She didn't say she was planning to read the diary or rather reread for the umpteenth time. She was already thinking of ways to turn it into an interactive CD-ROM for Charlie. She hadn't given up on finding out what happened to the slave after the last page. Between this project and Zurich, she wouldn't need to take any assignments for the rest of this year. Or, if Charlie continued to give her projects, maybe never.

"Take her before I decide to take her with me." Annie handed the baby to Melissa. She winced in pain. It would take time for her ribs to heal.

"Fat chance. I'll e-mail you photos. She'll be different the next time you see her."

"I'll be back in three months anyway," Annie said. "I want to see if I can find Two Pines."

"But that's in the South," Melissa said.

"I can't come to the States without seeing my favorite god-child."

"Or your parents," Dave said.

"Or my parents."

"Give our love to Roger and Gaëlle," Susan said.

Annie so preferred being the leaver rather than the leavee. She slung her laptop case over her shoulder and rode up the escalator. At the top she turned to blow each of them a kiss. They blew kisses back. Then she walked through security and looked back, but they couldn't see the tears behind her eyes.

ABOUT THE AUTHOR

D-L Nelson is a Swiss-American who divides her time between Geneva, Switzerland, and Argelès-sur-mer, France, which she loves as much as Annie. She is the author of four other Five Star books, *Chickpea Lover: Not a Cookbook, The Card,* and *Running from the Puppet Master* and *Family Value.* Visit her blog at http://theexpatwriter.blogspot.com or her day job site as the editor/publisher of a newsletter about Canadian credit unions at www.cunewswire.com.